BOOKS BY FREDERICK BUSCH

FICTION

Harry and Catherine   1990
War Babies   1989
Absent Friends   1989
Sometimes I Live in the Country   1986
Too Late American Boyhood Blues   1984
Invisible Mending   1984
Take This Man   1981
Rounds   1979
Hardwater Country   1979
The Mutual Friend   1978
Domestic Particulars   1976
Manual Labor   1974
Breathing Trouble   1973
I Wanted a Year Without Fall   1971

NONFICTION

When People Publish   1986
Hawkes   1973

Harry and Catherine

Frederick Busch

HARRY
AND
CATHERINE

Alfred A. Knopf *New York 1990*

THIS IS A BORZOI BOOK
PUBLISHED BY ALFRED A. KNOPF, INC.

It's a pleasure to acknowledge the thanks I owe to Robert Adsit, David Connell, and Lee Stiles. Their special knowledge, and their willingness to share it, are important to this book.

Readers familiar with central New York State will notice that I have made free with place-names and road designations. Nor is any person in this novel real except Catherine. F B

Library of Congress Cataloging-in-Publication Data

Busch, Frederick
   Harry and Catherine: a novel / Frederick Busch.—1st ed.
     p. cm.
   ISBN 0-394-57425-7
   I. Title.
   PS3552.U814H35   1990   89-37891
   813'.54—dc20   CIP

Manufactured in the United States of America
First Edition

This is Judy's *book*

Harry and Catherine

Chapter One

HER SON was studying Catherine as she stood at their kitchen window. She felt him. He'd been doing it more and more often, idly and with no special intensity, she thought, but with a kind of dreamy stare. She knew that sort of study, when you sit with your chin on your palms, your elbows on the kitchen table, looking at something, at the thing itself, for certain, and also looking through it. She tipped the roasting chicken and looked down, considering her son behind her, the way he must have been looking at and into and past his mother. He's looking at the rest of his life, she thought. I'm a ghost in the center of the prospect.

Before she could say that, Randy sighed, like someone waking. "That's really obscene, Ma. Fisting a bird." He snorted for his own wit and charm.

"What's fisting? Never mind. I don't want to know."

"It's what gay people do. They put—"

"I don't want to know. How come *you* know?"

"It's part of Health. You have to know how to get AIDS to graduate."

"You're such a smart-ass, you know that?"

She bent over the chicken, noting how her left hand disappeared to the wrist inside it as she inserted pignoli and cooked pasta. I'm blushing, she thought. Well, I should. What I'll say to impress him. Like a girl in the pizza parlor, making up to this big, handsome boy with his rock 'n' roll hair and his wicked eyebrows.

Bobby collided with the back porch. It sounded like more than size thirteen hightop sneakers as he banged inside. He stuffed his basketball someplace certain to be inconvenient for her later and sat behind her, facing Randy, panting.

"I guess you're out of breath," Randy said.

"You must've put a quart of oil in today," Bobby said. "I mean you're so brilliant and everything."

Catherine slammed the chicken into the roasting pan. "I will not be forced to listen to sibling rivalry, and I mean it. Everybody go someplace else, or sit here and be decent."

Which meant, she knew, that they'd scatter. She wanted to tell Randy, *Stay*. She didn't, because she knew that she'd mean not only now, at four forty-five of a June afternoon, but also, Stay past your graduation, don't go to college, and if you must go—you must—then also come home. She picked up a paring knife as if to threaten herself into not crying. She shook her head.

"Chill out, Ma," Randy said, behind her now. He put a large hand on each of her shoulders and squeezed, as if trying to compress her toward her spine. She sighed. He said, "It's an inevitable part of the family dynamic."

"Preppy asshole," Bobby said, leaving the kitchen.

She turned as if to shout him back, but Randy stood before her, over her, shaking his head and waggling his brows.

He whispered, "I promise not to kill him in front of company or while you're in the house."

She held her hand up to his face, which was slightly acne-scarred, and long, sunburned, shy of pretty but very nice. He reared back in mock horror: she held a handful of pasta-with-pine-nuts near his cheek. She knew he had to shave his mustache twice a week, or three times, but rarely his cheeks; still, the down

4

was giving way to islands of bristle, she noted. As he recoiled, a vampire shrinking from the cross, she tried to remember who had taught him how to shave.

Randy waved So long, and she waved her pasta in reply. He went upstairs, and there was a small scuffle in the hallway near the boys' rooms, and then the slam of doors, then silence. Catherine turned to the chicken.

Not Dell. He'd been long gone before Randy had to shave. And, anyway, he himself had hardly ever shaved. His skin had always gleamed, she remembered. He'd used sweet lotions with foreign names.

So it had to have been Harry. Although there had been other men to park their razors in her various bathroom cabinets over the fourteen-odd years since Dell had left and married a kid and produced some more, and had risen in the managerial hierarchy of some place small enough to overlook or maybe require his essential cruelty, only Harry had been close enough to the boys to be able to walk into a bathroom with Randy and put his hands on Randy's face. Carter could have done it, she supposed. He might have tried, anyway been in a position to try, but with Bobby. Though Bobby had simply taken one of her disposable razors, run it under hot water, and wiped off what she'd taken to calling his mousehairs from under his nose. So: Harry. She wondered if Randy thought of him. The chicken could start roasting now, while she poured herself a glass of wine and sat outside in the western light and thought about living alone all this time with two little boys and then looking up to find one of them gone, or as good as, and one of them working on six-foot-one-and-a-half at just a little past fourteen years of age, and the world becoming a possibly frightening place.

She said to the pickets of her back porch rails, the long shadows of high grass—Bobby was supposed to have been cutting it— "You're such a *mother.*"

The telephone rang. She sipped her wine. A boy caught it on

the second ring. The world was checking in. The kids were checking out. But how, she asked herself, can you have the dreaded famous empty-nest syndrome while the nest is full? And Carter isn't exactly going off to college, she told herself. It's Catherine and Carter, and of course, dear Jesus, Bobby, and the Adolescence That Ate Upstate New York.

She slugged her wine down and stood, saying to the porch, her house and land and outbuildings, her mortgage and her country road, to all of her forty-first year: "I'll trade you the whole gigful of 'em for a left-hand hitting catcher who can get me eighty RBI's." She put her hand on her mouth like any tipsy lady of a weekday afternoon. But she wasn't tipsy. And what the hell's a lady, anyway? Surely, someone more loyal than she.

She saw Randy looking at her from the other side of the screen door. He was slowly shaking his head. "Alcohol abuse," he said.

"I'm not drunk, dummy."

"Porch abuse, then."

"Self-abuse."

"Mother!" he said, his shock only partly acted.

"Oh, dear. Randy, I didn't mean *that*. I was trying to be—psychological."

"Oh, you're psychological, all right."

He came outside and held her shoulders as he had before, though this time he faced her. She later remembered how a robin in the tall spruce near the porch seemed hysterical in its scolding. Its nest must seem threatened, she later remembered she'd thought. She wanted to turn and tell her fellow sufferer not to fret on her account.

"What?" she said. Because he pushed his face in close to hers, and she smelled soap and the sweat of a day in school and the breath of an animal working on its life.

"That was Harry Miller."

"On the phone?"

"On the phone."

"Oh." She didn't go on to say, "Of course," though the words were in her mouth like a taste. Randy was beaming at her, trying to excite a beam in return, waiting for them to hug one another and cry aloud about love. His requirement that she respond made her insist on not responding. She said, "Imagine that."

Randy cocked his head to show his disappointment. She remarked again how well they knew each other's signals, how he depended on her knowing what he meant. Who else, in the terrible, vast world his years and hers condemned her to send him into, would know what he meant if he needed them to?

"He's in the neighborhood," Randy said, trying again.

"The neighborhood?" She spread her arms. "We're half a dozen miles from town, seventy from Syracuse, and two hundred and fifty from New York City. What neighborhood did he have in mind?"

"Does," Randy said. "Does have in mind. Ask him."

"He's still on the phone?" Her stomach tightened another notch.

"No," Randy said, and she relaxed, but into—she closed her eyes on it, as if it were a pain to manage—disappointment. "He's on the way."

She opened her eyes. She felt her face clench.

"Well, what the hell," Randy said. "He's our friend, right? He's our ex-friend. He asked how to get here and I told him."

For you, then, she wanted to say, thinking that a boy whose father had left, who always had to contend with notions of abandonment, whose mother had twice loved and lived with and finally, well, failed with the same man the boys had come to think of almost as *theirs*—that boy had a right to tell Harry Miller how to find their house. She wanted to say: *You* can leave, you can desert, once you get me into this. But he was smiling, so she didn't. And, anyway, she was smiling too.

"That's me old girl," he said, in his mock-English accent. "*Good* mummy-girl."

7

Without asking, he set the table for five. So he had decided on throwing Harry into the middle of them, and risking Bobby's new hobby—depraved manners indicating a retreat halfway down the evolutionary scale—as well as Carter's willingness to sit through supper with Catherine's old lover. *Former* lover, she corrected, and then she thought, What the hell, he's not so awfully young. And then, scaling stems of broccoli, she thought how easily she'd named Harry lover. And Carter? The boys had said good morning to him often enough on their way to school. He'd put the new battery into their yard mower. He'd spiked together the cracked leg of their picnic table. It was he who had wrapped the cellar pipes in heating tape this winter, and he who had worried more than she about her beloved van, which was held together, to Bobby's chagrin, with silver duct tape. How would he sit through a dinner with a man she thought of, still, as lover? How could he? Why should he?

The broccoli went into the basket of the steamer, from which she'd take it just before it was soft. Then she'd cut it into small chunks and, with some olive oil and garlic, sauté it. She'd ask Carter if he wanted wine. It wouldn't be right to put the wine glasses out unless he said so. No: he wouldn't *think* it right. Men were territorial, she thought, rinsing lettuce for a salad.

Yeah. And look who wants to be occupied, she thought. Look who goes around, some of the time, anyway, acting like territory, you treacherous bitch.

Bobby said, "How come he set the table? I'm supposed to do that."

She said, "I want no—"

"Pissant," Randy said to him. "The one day somebody does the job you usually have to be beaten into doing, you start to whine. You're such a—such a Bobby."

"—sibling rivalries," Catherine said, not turning around.

"Hope you didn't sprain your wrist lifting the plates," Bobby said, thumping out and up the stairs. She turned around to talk to

Randy, but he'd left too, in his silent way; that's what he was doing these days, Catherine told the vinaigrette she shook in an old mustard jar. While his mother talked about time, and no one listened, he left.

The plume of dust along their road signaled Carter. It was time. She turned the chicken, roasting it at high heat. She filled a wine glass with ice and poured whiskey for him. The car went by. "Servile titmouse," Catherine said. She poured out the whiskey and ice and left the glass in the sink.

Randy, back again on stealthy feet, said, "Did I get us into trouble?"

She sat where she usually sat when they ate. He sat in Bobby's chair, nearest her. She resisted the need to tell him to change his seat in case Bobby came down, spoiling for a crisis. She shrugged. "You're a person. I think I would have appreciated your talking to me first."

"But—*Harry*."

"What you're saying, sweetheart, is Harry-and-you. And I understand that. But there's also Harry-and-Bobby. Wait a minute. And Harry-and-me. And, for chrissakes, Randy: Harry-and-*Carter*."

"I blew it?"

"Absolutely. Yes. It's nothing we'll die from, but this is no fun, baby."

Randy slowly nodded. He slumped in the chair, which tilted dangerously back against its screws and brackets. He didn't look as battered by remorse as Catherine would have wished. "He taught us how to do some first things," Randy said, low, as if addressing Bobby's dinner plate.

Catherine nodded.

"He went on that killer diet to look good for you."

"Oh, I don't think he did it for me."

"No. Because you—hell, you loved him, Ma. When he was porky a little."

"Porky a little." Catherine giggled. "It sounds like he was in a cartoon."

"He was in the old house. All over it. Morning and night."

"Are you holding it against me that we—you know."

"Slept together," Randy said. They were both blushing, she noted. "No. Just that you slept together and then you stopped. It made the sleeping together *mean* less."

"To you, you mean." And Randy nodded, not looking at her still, not daring to, she figured. "You're such a moralist," she said. "Good."

"You raised me."

"I'm plenty proud."

He nodded. "I don't mean to criticize."

"But you think your mother's promiscuous."

He looked up, shocked, pale suddenly, stricken. "Ma! No! I'd never call you *that*!"

Catherine willed herself not to laugh. "Women need company. Don't guys go around boasting of—how much, you know, company they've had?"

"Guys are pigs."

"Often."

He said, "I'm getting out of line here."

Catherine said, "I respect myself for Harry, during and after. I respect myself for Carter. You may just have to trust my sense of honor for a while, kid. The way I'm trying to respect yours. Which is what has landed us in the soup."

Randy nodded. He said, "I'm sorry. I really missed him."

"All this time?"

"A lot," he said. With innocent curiosity, she thought, he looked out from under his crooked, bushy brows and his floppy piled-up hair to ask her, "You?"

Catherine, counting the dinner plates, counted them again. She didn't answer Randy. Instead, she said, "How do you know he's coming *alone*?"

She watched Randy turn wise and ancient, suddenly a white raisin, saying in some pan-Asian pidgin, "Must wait. Find out." In his own voice, he said, "One of the great scenes in *Karate Kid*. You might not remember it." Then in the raisin voice he said, "First wait. Then find out. *Hunh*!"

"Lousy kid," she said. She could hear the pleasure in her voice, and then, on behalf of Carter, she became offended.

Bobby came down again, to assert his right to eat cookies and drink milk shortly before dinner. Catherine demurred by slamming her hands on the table when Bobby opened his mouth at the open refrigerator. He still hadn't said a word when Catherine growled some sound she didn't recognize. Bobby closed the refrigerator door and, with dignity, said, "Communicate, will you?"

She was coming up from her seat at the table to communicate when Carter came home. So she turned from her son to, yes, her lover. She also turned, inside, toward the word, still bright in the front of her brain: *home*. She had thought it, she admitted. God-dam Harry Miller, she thought, turning to Carter for a kiss, and kissing automatically back. Randy was there, then, eager for the show, she figured. She was mostly dreading it. Bobby looked at Carter, impassive—aggressively impassive. Randy grinned in pure friendship, the serpent. And Catherine asked how it had gone, and Carter, nodding to Bobby the way you pet an unreliable dog and pointing a forefinger at Randy, who fired friendliness back, told her.

"I'm going to make the parking lot for the largest shopping mall outside the smallest county seat in northeastern America," he said. Letting himself drop down lankily into a chair, and accepting—titmouse!—the whiskey she poured and delivered, he rubbed his sparse blond hair and smiled. He was sunburned from construction sites, skinny enough for his hipbones to be a discussable part of his anatomy, big-ribbed and long-legged, not much more than six feet tall but larger-looking because so slender. His long arms and legs were like Dell's, and therefore Randy's;

Bobby was sturdier, like her, all shoulders, back, and buttocks. Carter had a pleasant face. People thought of him as smiling a lot. She knew him to be serious, and to care about what she tried to keep an interest in—rural and suburban sewer lines and street development. He was doing pretty well, and his former wife had remarried, so Catherine, he had told her, especially with Dell paying for the boys' educations, could one day drive a Porsche. She hadn't been trying to be clever. She truly had thought she'd heard "porch," and her puzzled expression had been the reason, he told her later—"that goddamned innocence on that goddamned sexy face," he'd said—why he had pushed her back on the sofa in her own living room and had torn the buttons of his shirt in his haste to give her his flesh. He had seen it as a compliment.

"Cath?"

"It's wonderful! Congratulations," she said. She raised her white wine and toasted him. "How do the town fathers feel about the largest mall in their smallest county seat?"

Randy said, "They probably own the land the developers are building on. I bet you they're in pig heaven."

Carter took off his sport jacket, cocking his head as he loosened his tie.

"Right?" Randy said.

Carter puffed air into his cheeks and raised his brows. Then he nodded. "They'll make a killing."

"Yeah," Bobby said, "but you will too, huh?"

"I will make a couple of bucks," Carter said.

"You'll have to subcontract earth-moving equipment," Bobby said. "And there's sewer lines, electric conduits, gravel and black-top. Curbs." They all looked at him, as if he were a surprise visitor. He went dark and then shrugged. Catherine laughed out loud and Bobby frowned a shy smile back.

Randy, getting juice from the refrigerator, jostling Bobby, who shoved him back, sidestepped much of Bobby's charge and asked, "Did you file an impact statement?"

"He doesn't have to," Bobby said.

"Environmental impact," Carter said. "I'll tell you. We're impacting on a landfill that's twenty-five years old, a disused roadway, half of a farm that's a hundred and twenty-five years old, an unlicensed front-end repair shop and six mobile homes."

"And the slave graveyard," Randy said. He turned to Catherine: "Remember? The old guy who lived there for seventy years who came to history class? He said there used to be slaves there. Then the flu wiped them out. They used to call it the plague. All the graves are supposed to be there. If I'm thinking of the right place."

"Whoo!" Bobby crooned, imitating movie music. "Poltergeists, right? Haunted sewers!" He clapped his hands. "I love it. Some guy's sitting on the toilet, and this slave ghost comes up—"

"No!" she insisted, trying not to smile. "No bathroom humor."

Carter, never as easy with their banter and battling as she wished, was looking at Randy, who seemed to be trying not to smirk.

"Chicken's done," Catherine said.

"Goose is cooked," Carter answered.

She looked at him. He shook his head and flapped his wrist: *No problem.* "So the job," she said. "When does it start?"

Bobby said, "Let's flush it. Right? Get it? Bathrooms, sewer lines, Randy's idea? I love it."

"I will not listen to bathroom humor," Catherine said. "Please wash for dinner."

"I did."

"Yesterday," she said, pointing the way for both boys to go. "This will be for today."

When she and Carter were alone in the kitchen, and he was pretending to help put food on the table in response to her last week's insistence on help, she said, "Randy got a little zealous—no. Never mind that. Listen. A man I used to know. Well, I've talked about him. Harry Miller?"

"The newspaper guy."

"Right. He called, and he's passing through, and he kind of inv—he's coming over. I guess for dinner, I'm not really sure. Do you mind a lot?" And then, because he was studying her face for *her* reaction, instead of offering his own, and because she sounded a good deal like his daughter or his dutiful wife, she said to Carter, "Anyway, that's where we are. Okay?" She smiled, missing his face with her glance, which caught the far wall and some of his long shoulder. "I didn't know if you'd want wine. Considering we're celebrating—the contract and all, I—" She looked at him. He still was studying her, and she resented his silent scrutiny—anyone's. She turned sharply and walked to the stove.

Looking out the wide kitchen window at the giant spruce and the coarse grass still lighted by a low red sun, she called for her children. They were behind her, out of sight. Looking straight ahead, she shouted the boys back into the kitchen. She tilted her head and smiled a smile of no pleasure when Carter, making corky noises, began to force open wine.

Here I come again, Harry thought. Hello, I'm driving into your life again. I'm driving out of my own. I'm a city slicker on a country road, selling the latest snake oil—put your confidence in me—and I need to know, in my forty-first year of endless boyhood, if there's one more way for us, a chance, an accident we can force to happen, almost on purpose.

He was lost on the country roads, but he knew that he'd find her place. He had found her in Schuyler, Vermont, a dozen years before. And then, when she'd sent him a postcard announcing her move to Pines, in the hills of upstate New York, he had found her again—that time driving through a killer ice storm into country he hadn't ever seen. And, he said, sounding to himself like a song on a barroom jukebox, that time I almost stayed on.

No, he decided: that time she almost let me.

14

Coming west from Albany, aiming at the northern tip of the center of the state, Harry considered telling himself not something blue and not something full of sadness, but something almost true. *That time we nearly surrendered.*

Randy had sounded so old on the telephone. He'd been a kid the last time, and Bobby had been a small solemn gentleman, looking at him from distances while Randy, ever the older brother, had dared to walk in close and check him out face to face. Of course, Randy had remembered him from Vermont, and Bobby had been just a lump of child on a sled or red wagon, he forgot which. But he did remember pulling him through Catherine's little town, Bobby all serious with his graceful progress on the only street, and Randy jealous, and too proud to admit it. And Catherine, in her blue bathrobe on cold mornings, and asleep with him in bed, and not asleep.

Harry remembered two thrills about waking up with Catherine. One was when they were young, and she lived in Vermont. He'd been visiting her for several months, flying in from New York and riding the last miles by bus to her. And on a morning in a month he couldn't remember, he woke before she did and went to the bathroom, naked, and was arrested by his body in the mirror: kind of blubbery, then, and pale, ridiculous, with his belly held in, chest puffed out (to impress only his lurking self) and the silly swaying penis like a banner about eagerness. She actually *wants* this, he remembered thinking.

For a while she had. And then her insistence on solitude, on not being nibbled at by men while her boys demanded her. And then, years later, the postcard to him at the *Daily News*, and his long ride up to accept what might have been offered—the card contained just her Pines address—and the week of his nervous stay: she, elegant in her poise because the boys were her friends as well as her labor, and her work in the museum at Cooperstown useful and hard; he, wanting to be proud of his new slenderness, but finding himself only hungry all the time, for food, or cigarettes, or her. He hadn't eaten much, or smoked at all. They had slept together, he thought as he drove—he feared this, and always shied from believing it, but now, in apprehension, he did—because she hadn't cared, because she knew he'd wanted to and didn't mind. And on his second morning there, waking first with the house in almost a bubble of frozen rain, he'd walked naked to a different bathroom in a different house, and had looked at a different but awfully familiar body—the penis, in lustless erection, had nodded as if to acknowledge him—and he had stood before the mirror, leaning on the sink, and had shaken his head, had wanted to cry like a boy. And, going back to the strange room, the well-remembered bed, he had quietly gotten under the covers, smelling her in sleep, and she had wakened, had looked at him with no surprise, and had reached for him to start a morning's long and silent wrestle with regret. When he left, he remembered the regret, bore it as a kind of trophy: at least we shared that pain. Their lovemaking had probably never been more electric with sensation, more generous or sad. He hadn't asked her what she knew or why. He had quietly agreed. They were late. Her life was blooming again, like her Christmas cactus, bright in the middle of winter, a surprise of sorts, a somehow unshocking surprise. Her clock was eccentric. Her time was hers, and her boys', and she somehow wasn't shareable. He remembered thanking her when he left, and meaning it; he remembered that she'd known his meaning, and had smiled.

He could say to her, he thought, Ask me why I never married. But people laugh at guys in their forties who never married, or nod, figuring they've learned to live with men, or they simply raise their brows and say nothing. You never expect them to say: I live alone because of love. Memory. Failure's low glow. That's as awful as *dying* of love, Harry thought. That's as unbelievable— as goddam rude, attention-getting, and ultimately infantile—as dying of love. Well, you don't. You can't. You do not die of love.

So who could believe that a man of some accomplishment, a man even said to be not without his charms, has not married on account of one big-shouldered, long-legged woman in a blue bathrobe in upstate New York?

In the aluminum booth outside a Great American market in a town called Schenevus, he had said, "Randy. Hey, kid. Before I hang up, tell me something. Have you got a father?"

"Huh? Harry, you know Dell, don't you?"

"I'm sorry, kid, I didn't mean it that way. I mean, did your mother get married again? Is there a, you know, stepfather? A *new* one. Father kind of guy. You know?"

He remembered Randy's laughter—the boy had suddenly seemed as old as he. Randy had said, "There's a main man type of relationship, if that's what you mean. We're talking intimacies, Harry."

"Jesus, Randy! Don't talk like that. I didn't mean to make you talk like that."

"Harry. The guy eats dinner here a lot. He stays over. You know what I mean?"

"Shit."

"Well."

"Yeah, what'd I expect, huh?"

"Well."

"You like him, Randy?"

"He's okay, Harry. Got me a good job for after graduation. For the summer. He builds parking lots, that kind of thing."

"That's a lot of dirt, huh?"

"It's a lot of dough."

"Good, kid, good. I'm glad for you. So you like him, huh?"

"He's a nice guy, Harry. And *she* likes him."

"Great," he'd said. "I'm glad."

"Yeah," Randy had said.

And Harry had answered, "Yeah."

"So you don't want to talk to her?"

"I'll tell you the truth, Randy. I suddenly find myself wondering. A little nervous, maybe, you know?"

"Jesus, Harry. You got to come out. Really."

"Really?"

"Really, man," Randy had said.

"How come?"

"How come?"

"Yeah. How come you really think I should come crashing into everybody's life?"

After a pause—Harry could see Randy's tight controlled face more clearly than at any time during the conversation—Randy had said, a little raggedly, "Well, I miss you, Harry."

"Give me the directions, kid. What the hell."

So the senator's press puppet, newsman turned spokesperson, advance man, depth-sounder, radar, shark lookout, and red herring, if need be, the guy the dogs could chew on while the fox slid slyly through the bush, in Albany to test several waters, was lurching westward, taking what he'd told the senator's hit woman was a dirty weekend—she might call, he knew, and he hoped she wouldn't address Catherine as Miz Bimbo—the man of words engaged to buy, sell, and sully them on behalf of the Higher Truth, ex-cityside and once a backup during his vacation for Breslin, was here in the service of the time they'd lost.

"In other words," he told the rented red Thunderbird, "snake oil. Would I lie?"

Her house was off a two-lane highway, County 29, and it sat on the crest of a rise. He imagined that in winter the trucks, shifting down, would make a racket. And the wind, he thought, looking at the land fall away from the wide hill on which the house sat, the wind would mourn. She always lived where the winds beat on her house, and where you had to drive well to survive. In the noises she accumulated about her, Catherine's houses were always silent inside. This one was painted white, was two stories

high, had a big barn nearby, a couple of cars in the gravel driveway, graceful narrow windows he appreciated—he'd bet they'd
helped to sell her on the place—and a view of long meadows, and
small farms half a mile or so away, downhill. On the galvanized
mailbox, in neat black letters, it said her name: HOLLANDER.

He turned the engine off and, as the motor cooled, as the passenger compartment heated, he sat with the windows closed and
dealt with foreboding. How can you love a woman who scares
you?

How, on the other hand, can you love one who can't?

What would she say about *him*, if she sat in his driveway, starting to sweat, waiting for a sign?

And then he gave himself instructions: HOLLANDER's the only
sign you're getting; and, as the senator from New York would
tell you, hesitation is the dance step just before death. How else
do you run—even think of running—for the presidency?

Stepping from his car, Harry decided that this was harder.
Nothing was harder than this. And an index of his folly, and the
nature of the woman in the house, was his outright wish and need
to do it. Here I am, naked in your gunsight, sweaty on your gravel
drive, looking no doubt like the last traveling salesman in America
with nothing left to sell except his dazed and rumpled self.

A screen door on the gray wood porch slammed, and Randy—
it had to be Randy, bigger than a lot of men Harry knew, and
with a plume of black moussed hair, but smiling as sweetly as
ever—came marching up. Randy didn't pause to speak or offer
gestures. He leaned in and down a little, and he wrapped his long
arms around Harry and squeezed. Harry found himself hugging
in return, and closing his eyes, and pushing his forehead, for an
instant, onto the boy's shoulder. He found himself ready to keen.

"Hey, man," Randy said, stepping back, smiling big teeth and
looking wiser than eighteen. "Hey, I'm glad you came."

Harry nodded, grinning in reply. The boy did make him glad,
though sad for the years he'd been growing, out of Harry's sight.

19

No: not so much sad as regretful. You can be happy and regretful, he thought, and hoped he might remember to say that to Catherine. "I'm glad too, kid. I thought of you."

Randy nodded, as if to say he'd assumed as much, when Bobby, it had to be Bobby, stepped from the house to the porch and stood, arms folded, like a TV bodyguard, all muscles and knotted face, almost as tall as Randy, it looked like, and broader, and much less at ease with the world in general and Harry in particular.

Harry waved. Bobby's face fell apart, into a hopeless shy smile and—he could see it from the drive to the porch—a hard blush.

"Didn't you turn into a stud," Harry said.

Bobby shrugged and said, in a voice whose depth was surprising, "What else?"

"What a Bobby," Randy said.

A man stood in the screen door behind Bobby, only a shape on the other side, but a presence to which Bobby reacted by stepping aside. The man didn't come out. His voice did. "Welcome, Mr. Miller. Catherine asked me to say hello."

Harry walked up to the porch. He paused at Bobby and patted his cheek twice. Bobby stood politely, embarrassed. Harry in his turn shrugged. "What the hell," he said to Bobby. "I don't know how to say hello to you. I used to pull you on wagons. Sleds. We were pretty good friends."

Bobby stuck his huge hand out and Harry took it. Then Harry walked a little closer to the screen door and looked in, nodding to the slender man inside. "Hello," Harry said.

The man, in a business shirt and city shoes, was looking at Harry's khakis and sneakers and dark blue T-shirt.

"Are we dressing for dinner?" Harry said.

Catherine's first word, spoken from someplace invisible, was the other man's name: "Carter."

He opened the door out for Harry, who sidled past the long arm that propped it, and then past the long man who nodded, but didn't smile or with his light blue eyes give anything like welcome away. The hallway was dark and Harry saw mostly the bright arches of other doorways, the shapes of windows; he felt as though he'd walked into a cellar or cave, and he waited for his eyes to catch up with where he was. The guy was handsome and under control and didn't give a shit for Harry Miller or his need to travel hours and miles to see the woman this guy was living with. And Harry Miller wondered, seeing how substantial and unprepared for defeat Carter was, just why he'd come.

Then Catherine came in, reminding him that sometimes you make the trip, that's all: you just, sometimes, go there. Because she stood in a doorway, tall and tough-looking in her jeans and sandals and old chambray shirt—he thought he remembered its blueness on the clothesline in her Pines house—with her hair cut shorter than he remembered, a helmet of honey that shifted about her face as her smile came and went.

Like a sign, Harry thought. You wanted a sign.

"Hi," Harry whispered. He said it louder, too loudly: "Hi!"

"Hello," she said. "It seems like Randy trapped you into pot-luck dinner. The wine'll be good. Carter buys good wine."

So the men wheeled and stuck out hands and said hello.

"Where're you staying?" Carter asked.

"You mean, sleeping? Where am I sleeping? You know, I haven't—I don't know. I'll find someplace."

Carter's face went through several expressions, then settled into tolerance. He turned to Catherine. She said, "We've got room."

Carter turned back to Harry. "She's got room," he said.

Harry nodded his thanks, looking, now that his eyes had adjusted, at the lamps and prints and photographs in the room—he recognized many of them—and the furniture he knew. That was the sofa they had sat on. No: that was the sofa on which they'd made love. Carter was watching him look. Harry took his left hand from behind his back, offering the bottle in brown paper. "Wine, I'm afraid. Château Coals-to-Newcastle, probably."

Catherine moved forward, but Carter's hand came out to take

21

it. She stopped where she was, looking at Harry. Carter opened the brown sack. "No, this is pretty good," he said. "I've tasted this. It's good. We thank you."

Harry was looking at her straight long nose, the hazel eyes that sometimes seemed nearly green, or flecked with green. He looked at her large hands, her waist grown maybe thicker, he thought, and the long neck she raised, when she was angry, until she was an angry pale bird, a hunting creature, a woman to be careful with.

"Sure," Harry said. "Yes. You're welcome."

She was looking back. Do *not*, he told himself, for chrissakes, suck your stomach in. We're past all that. Goddammit.

The boys came in, Randy to bang Harry's shoulder as he paused, then passed by Catherine and went out, Bobby to lumber in his brother's wake. Harry heard a refrigerator door, and then the sounds of squabbling.

"Well, so are you," Catherine said.

He was used to the dim light now, and he was studying her too hard for manners, and for her—friend? Come on: her boyfriend, lover, squeeze, essential action, the guy on the neighboring pillow. Carter opened his mouth and extended his arm, and whatever Carter might say, Harry knew, he'd not have a reasonable answer.

But upstairs and far away, it seemed, a giant hound made muffled barks, an explosion of them. And then it sounded like seventeen yard rakes on slate, or a brace of industrial floor sanders, or a tournament of Slinkys. What it was, was paws, four of them, belonging to what seemed to have fallen down a flight of steps, turned a corner like a cue ball banking but off painted pine instead of cushion, and roaring into the foyer, all raised hackles, wild eyes, erect tail, and yellow, battered teeth. It was a black Labrador retriever, graying about the muzzle and full of lies. His barking and teeth were supposed to tell you he was a killer. His eyes said, Don't believe what you see.

Harry didn't. He went to one knee and reached for what of

the family he'd be permitted to seize by the handful. He talked in idiot endearments to the dog, who whined at once and waved his tail like a flag, and then lay down before Harry on his side, paws extended, and tried to roll on his back.

"That's our killer dog," Catherine said.

"A little deaf," Harry suggested.

"I think it's more like delayed hearing. The noise goes in his ears all right, but then it wanders for a while inside his brain. After a while it triggers off what it's supposed to, and he comes to defend us to the death. Or to get his belly rubbed. Whichever comes first. A typical male."

Carter snorted and sat on the sofa that Harry remembered. Harry stayed down, playing with this handsome, decent, funny dog a good deal more than he'd have thought to want to; it beat standing up to face the music again.

"You don't know him, I think," Catherine said.

He shook his head. She walked a little closer. Then she came near. She put her sandaled foot out to poke and rub the tight, hairy stomach. "He's nine or ten, we can't figure it exactly."

Harry said, buzzing thoughtlessly, a fly in the soup, "I don't remember him. What was it? A few years ago, I—"

"You were passing through. I remember," she said a little hastily.

Harry did not wag his tail and howl, thinking, She didn't tell Carter everything. Or much. Not *that* much. He crouched by the dog and said, "That's right. I was around this part of the state in, was it '85? I think that's when it was." Unless you need to know to the day and minute, which I also remember.

"No," Catherine said. "We didn't have him then. He didn't have us. We saw him back at the old place—did you know there was a big lake back there?"

I stood behind you, Harry thought, and your children waded in at dusk on a very hot night, and we watched them. And I put my hand up under your shirt and unhooked your brassiere and we stood like that, you leaning back against me, and me cupping you underneath your shirt. "I think so," he said.

"We were swimming there one night, and Bobby saw this deer. He called us. It came crashing through the bushes and into the water, and it started to swim. Then old Drown—we named him Drown—came whipping through, and he jumped into the water and chased it. They were swimming and swimming, slower and slower, and Randy thought they'd both go under. The deer began to pull away. Randy decided this old amphibian, with his webbed feet and head lighter than air—how could anything that empty not keep a dog floating? But Randy figured he was going under. He went in and pulled him out by the neck and tail, and he stayed. Drown."

The sound reached home a second late, and the dog banged his tail against the floor, looking sideways with big brown longing eyes.

Harry touched him in tribute. Drown knew them better than Harry did. Better than Carter too, he figured. And now, Harry thought, if there is a God he or she will prove it by getting me up to my feet and providing me with something to say.

Catherine liked Carter (at least), so he had to have *something* fine in his soul—it was as close to an act of God as Harry needed right now—and Carter said, "It's time for another drink. I feel the need. Want to start the race a little late, Harry?"

"Gee, Carter. I hope it isn't anything with alcohol."

"Not *this* whiskey," Carter said.

We're all such wonderful friends, Harry thought. The dog got to his feet, grunting, and he walked away.

So it came to pass that, in his forty-first year, Harry Miller sat with Catherine Hollander and her boys, as he had wished to do, and with Carter Kreuss ("like rejoice," Carter told Harry), and he studied the children of the woman he'd been leaving or been left by for over a dozen years. He could see in them, like ghosts, the kids he'd walked, pushed, towed, and carried. He had read them stories, told them nifty tales, and had walked with them in silence, one heatwave-staggered July night, down the middle of the shallow Sangerfield River, Bobby on his back, Randy by his side and hanging to his belt, Catherine behind them, hooting with relief from the temperature and maybe even for love. Harry remembered the feel of the rocks on the silty bottom, and the drag of the current on his legs, the sound of the water as it gulped at the bank. Catherine's splashing had grown louder, and then she'd shrieked, and Bobby had shrieked in turn, and then Harry had too, for she'd launched herself at them, sweeping Randy along with an arm, and they'd all gone rolling in the river, Randy protesting for the danger his mother had plunged them into. She had worn just shorts and a halter, and Harry was remembering how she'd stood, legs apart against the current, hair streaming, silt on her thighs and Bobby in her arms, as the water ran hard between her knees.

"What, exactly, do you do?" Carter asked.

"He writes for the papers. You know, the *Daily News*?" Randy was proud, Harry suspected, because the *News* sold well upstate; it carried word of the state's best teams, even though its weekend sports, Harry believed, was as substantial as a president's word of honor.

"No," Harry said. "Not anymore, kid. I never got a chance to tell you. No, I'm—they call me an aide, now. I'm a communications guy for your favorite Democratic senator and mine. He hasn't announced, of course. They never do. That would be like truth. But he's running, it looks like. He's going to make a run. Or position himself for a draft, or hard bargaining, anyway."

Carter was interested. Power clearly interested him. His face lost its incipient sneer, and he permitted himself to look at Harry's eyes. "What's an aide do?"

"Everything," Harry said. "I do not fetch the coffee and doughnuts. Or type the thank-you notes. I do the rest. I make a lot of his language for him."

Catherine said, "I never knew you cared about politics. You were always writing pieces about kids getting bitten by rats, and the statues in Central Park getting cleaned, and, I don't know, cabdrivers. Subways."

Harry said, "You mind if I pick the rest of this up with my fingers? It's delicious. Great wine, Carter. Incredible."

Carter nodded—Harry had never known a man who could help doing so—as if he had blended and bottled and labeled it himself.

"Well," Harry told Catherine, "I just thought it might be fun to get on the other side of what I was doing. You know. Make the events instead of talk about them. Help to make the events."

"But what do you write, then? Do you write anymore?"

He nodded.

"Speeches," Bobby said, almost mourning his mother's dumbness.

Harry smiled in agreement.

Bobby went on, "You don't think senators write their own *speeches*, do you?"

Harry said, "Some of them can't even *read* their own speeches."

"You wrote a movie," Catherine said.

Harry labored at nonchalance. "Two, really," he said. "One of them for NBC, about a nursing nun in a hospice who fell in love, didn't get made."

"Barfo," Randy said.

"*You* go write something," Bobby said.

"I will not listen—"

"—to sibling rivalries," Bobby finished for her.

"What was the other one?" Carter asked. It apparently seemed like power to him. "Maybe we saw it."

"We did," Catherine said. "The thing on public broadcasting about Peress, the dentist McCarthy went after?"

Carter nodded. "I remember it," he said. "I saw the first half. To tell you the truth, I wasn't all that, I don't know, grabbed by it. Catherine didn't tell me you wrote it."

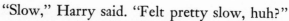

"Slow," Harry said. "Felt pretty slow, huh?"

She shook her head. She still had the awesome ability to not blink for long moments of conversation. He still had the woeful tendency to notice her eyes. "I thought it was wonderful. He really didn't matter that much, in his life. I mean, in *his* life, he mattered. In the national life, he didn't. But you showed how they all lost sight of him, but used him. Publicly. The good guys and the Communist witch-hunt guys. No. I thought it was very moving. I remember it." Carter swung an arm and a wine bottle out in front of her, and he poured. But she said, anyway, "I saw your name under the titles."

"Credits," Harry said.

"Far out," Bobby said, and he smiled. He relaxed in the smile, and there was Bobby, two years old, glistening with food from chin to forehead, and happy to be happy in full view. He'll be all right, Harry thought. She's given him that smile, and a reason to learn how to use it again.

"I don't do it anymore," Harry said. "I needed the money, back then."

Catherine looked out from under a few more ridges of forehead wrinkle, and laugh lines folded her skin a little harder, when she asked, unlaughing, "For alimony? Or are you still married?"

Thank you, Harry thought. Thank you. He didn't grin. He looked at Carter. Carter dropped his glance and looked at pine nuts on his plate. A man who doesn't eat pine nuts from pasta stuffed into chicken by a woman who looks like that and who has a lot more useful things to do with her time than the laying of hands on roasters is a man you should not trust. He'll sell you good cement, and he will not molest orphans. But he cannot deal with flavors. This is a woman of flavors. Harry said, "No, not for alimony. I never did get married."

She couldn't help it this time, Harry saw. She did go crimson. Randy watched with delight. Bobby wasn't listening, again. Carter was watching Harry. But Harry watched her flush.

"It's unusual," Carter said, "for a man to never marry, these days."

"How many times did you do it?" Harry asked.

"Just once."

"Well, that's only one time more than me. What the hell, right? We're both unusual guys."

Carter said, in an even, unhappy voice, "Can I offer anyone wine?"

Harry held his glass out, and then he held it up. "I wonder, having presumed on your hospitality so far, if I can intrude upon your patience somewhat further."

"Oh, you *have* been on the ham-with-raisin-sauce circuit, Harry," Catherine said.

But Harry was standing up, and he wasn't drunk, he thought. He felt a little dangerous, though. He felt a little endangered. Carter looked at Harry the way most people watch their dentists as they line the drill bits up. Catherine touched her glass but didn't raise it. Carter folded his hands. Randy raised a tumbler of celebration soda.

Harry said, "Hello." He sat down. They waited. He smiled.

"Well," Carter said.

"One thing I've learned about words," Harry said, "is how little to trust them. Do what you need to do, and shut up."

Catherine snorted.

"Really," Harry said. "I have come to believe that."

"Then you've changed," she said.

"Of course. And you?"

She shrugged.

"But I've also stayed the same," Harry said, "in some respects."

Catherine nodded to Randy, who began to clear. She turned back to Harry. "Pardon me," she said, "I wasn't listening."

Harry couldn't help the grin he grinned.

Her lips worked, and she nearly grinned back, but then she didn't.

"Nothing," Harry said. "Idle chitchat. Dinner talk. About now, if the chicken had been horrible and if there'd been peas, out of a can, boiled until they were the color of an old canoe, then the president of the local Rotary would be up and belching into the mike about now, and people would be talking to each other about taxes and sports and the Negro crime rate or the Hispanic birthrate, and the senator would begin to look at the speech I'd written for him to give. That's how I've been eating, except for hot dogs in airports and sterilized beef on the planes, and I thought it might be fun, one time, to stand up at a table after dinner and, instead of saluting the famous defunct tannery or the almost-convicted mayor, to say what I meant. It felt great. Jesus. Really. You know? *Hello*."

Carter said, "It sounds to me like you could use a better job."

Catherine smiled, passing behind Carter's chair. She patted Carter's shoulder, dragged her hand from his left shoulder over behind his neck and along to the end of his right. Carter smirked.

"I didn't think it would be easy," Harry said.

Bobby, waking to them, said, "Think what would be easy?"

Drown, who had lain beneath the table in some prone attitude of prayer for the fall of what was edible, now shifted and groaned.

In what seemed to be instant motion, Bobby was away, in another room, having leaped into a television set's car-chase noises and toneless tenor leading-man sounds: "Turn here!" "Drop it!" Randy had excused himself too, and he reappeared in a Columbia T-shirt and wrinkled cargo pants. Catherine, who seemed to know her part in the pantomime, held up a metal ring choked with many shapes of key, and Randy swiped it, grinning like a dolphin who had snatched the fish but not his feeder's hand. Harry would have held him by the shoulders if he dared. He would have said to him, "Aren't you the voice out of my past that got me into this?" On Randy's behalf, he told himself he would have answered for him, "No. I'm the one who gave you the permission you wanted me to give and didn't need to ask me for." Or, Harry thought, he would hug him hard, if he could, and ask him not to disappear.

He realized that Randy was standing beside his chair, a little behind him. In the voice of Robert Duvall in *Apocalypse Now*, crazed Air Cav commander surveying the dead, Randy said, "Jesus, I love it."

Catherine said, "Randy."

Harry turned in his chair and patted Randy's hard stomach. Randy bent like a boy at bedtime and kissed him on the cheek. Then he flushed and, straightening, shrugged. Harry said, "What the hell, kid."

Which, after the car sounds outside, left Carter and Catherine. Carter carried plates from the table and Harry turned to place his elbows on the cloth, lean on them, and finally—it felt like lying down on cool sheets, beneath a soft comforter, in a bare, clean room—look at what had drawn him. She sat back, so he did too, as if she were a nervous cat or dog and needed reassuring. She smiled tentatively, and then confidently. You're what I threw my youth away on, he thought. And I did it in your absence. He shook his head.

"What?" she asked.

"Are you marrying him?"

Catherine looked at him hard, maybe angrily, he thought. She lifted her chin a little, and he remembered the gesture. It had always made her look like one of those ducks in Vermont they'd seen that wandered from farms and stood in the road, lifting their heads against oncoming milk-tank trucks, too brave or stupid for something like perspective, or retreat.

"Did you come all the way here to ask that?"

"No. I don't know, really, why I came here. You. You."

"Well, I thought of you," she said.

"Good."

"Yes?"

30

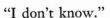

"I don't know."

"I don't, either," she said. Carter came in and looked at them casually—tried to look casually, Harry would have said—as he took a pile of dishes away. Harry saw that her hands were knotted, hard, and that her face was red. He couldn't help the smile.

She saw it, and she stood at once. He raised a hand—he'd no idea what to say, and neither did the hand; it dropped to the tabletop, and Catherine said, "To answer your question." She didn't, at first. She loaded dishes along her arm like a waitress. "What I'm doing with him right now," she said, and then Carter came in for the salad bowl and serving pots, "is going fishing."

Carter nodded as if he'd been consulted.

"We often do," she said.

Carter went back to the kitchen, and she followed.

Harry waited for Catherine to reappear. Maybe, he thought, I can strike every question from the record, every comment, every echo of each syllable, and the sounds of my breathing. I'll give the food back, and we'll start the meal again. He looked at the large oval platter of chicken remains and stood with it, his pass to their kitchen. And Catherine, as if she'd been timing it, reentered the dining room with a graphite fishing rod and a perforated carton.

"Worms," she said.

He lifted the platter. "Bones."

She had to grin, and Harry briefly thought to kneel with the carcass as an offering.

She told him, "Make yourself at home," and then she went to the kitchen, leaving him with a reamed-out formerly stuffed chicken, and the doorway, formerly filled with her, now excessively empty. As the back door slammed, he entered the kitchen and inspected it. They had scraped and stacked the dishes. They had worked as a team—as a family, you could say. Don't say it, he told himself, thinking of Carter, the man of the house.

Harry sat down at the old pine kitchen table. Drown crawled

out to shake himself, then push at Harry's thigh with a paw. Harry gave him a pat on the head. Drown moved his head as if to take the hand away. "You don't want friendship," Harry said. "You want food, right? A tale of our times." But Drown apparently wanted neither. He went to the screen door that opened off the kitchen to the back of the house. He lay his head on the door and butted it, then, with an elegant sidle, he was out and on the trail of something that mattered. Harry, in the kitchen alone, wondering whether to stay for the night or turn and drive to Albany, retraced the Labrador's steps. "Not nourishment, either," he said to the vanished dog. "Not sustenance, and not affection. Adventure? Some kind of risk."

He walked through the downstairs rooms and saw little he might describe as having been added by Carter. He said to Catherine's house, "Some kind of risk."

The river they fished was really an extension of the last century's canal system. It eddied and gurgled, but didn't race. It was a spur, an offshoot, probably the result of a factory owner's bribe. They fished near old piles on the wide water, where the dock had probably been, and the private wharf. "We're fishing in corruption," Catherine said.

In his day's cotton button-down shirt, still looking as if he wore a tie, though he'd taken it off, sleeves rolled up and tails tucked into dress pants, Carter stood at the bank and dropped his line in, again and again. He seemed to take no pleasure in the ritual of waiting. After a few seconds of watching his cheap red-and-white bobber, he reeled in and cast again, the impaled worm flopping in the air before the splash. She hated what the worm looked like, that soft stiffness. What could care enough about eating that to take a terrible hook in the roof of the mouth? You'd think by now that evolution or instinct or something useful in nature would have taught the small bass and sunfish and carp to stay away. She was convinced that Carter caught nothing because of his impatience. He looked up blankly and saw her watching him. "What did you say?"

She shook her head and checked her rod. It was propped on a flat rock, weighted down by another flat rock, and there wasn't any life on the line. She didn't use a bobber and she didn't use bait. Carter didn't know that. When he baited up and cast, he became absorbed in the surface of the water, in the endless back-and-forth of his casting and reeling-in. He was hypnotized, and she fished with him because she was convinced that his Friday evenings here convinced him that he'd relaxed. She thought he possibly never did. If he did, though, it was here, and sometimes in bed with her, and maybe, once in a while, on the site, when he looked at the plans and talked to the men, and drank a swallow of beer with one of them late in the day, and became assured that they were going to finish, or start, or cover, or unearth—whatever it was they really wanted to do—on time, at cost.

Carter's forearms shifted and the long muscles in them moved. She'd never told him that when they made love, just as when they didn't, the aspect of his body that she liked the most lay in his arms, the strength of which you'd never guess from seeing their length and slenderness. He'd want to hear—and he'd never admit it—that his low-hanging scrotum or his short, thick penis, his bony shanks, were what thrilled her. If she had to confess—and apparently she did, because she was looking at the man whose body her body restricted itself to these days, she was thinking these thoughts—then she'd admit that the body she most considered when they made love, which was far from every night and all the time and into the dawn's ecstatic light, was her own. That was what got her over: the slow descent by her mind down the length of her nerves and into, well, *her*. But what the hell. Sex was in the brain, she had come to believe. And she was falling through her forties, and there was plenty else to worry about. Like Randy. And, actually, not like Randy. He was growing, he was nearly grown.

Was Harry? How old had *he* become? He had always had balls—he would take a breath and bathe his body in burning kerosene, in the old days, if she had asked him to. And he had risked his life, years back, driving in an awful ice storm to see her on the strength of a postcard with no message, just her address. Of course, the fact that she'd sent it had been the message. And he'd received it. And had slid through six or seven hours of risk to stay with her and the boys and all but marry her. If he had said to her, "Catherine, goddammit, we have to get married," she'd maybe have done it. Maybe. Maybe. But, anyway, that wasn't Harry's way. Just as it wasn't his way to tell her that he lusted after her. He'd sit in a chair and read, looking at her over the book, shifting when she shifted, waiting for a sign that it was safe for him to give a sign that she'd respond to. He was the most hesitant brave man she had known.

Because he's scared of you.

Yes, but I'm with *him*. I'm fishing with *him*. I'm part-time living with *him*. That's why I'm sitting here on a fishing line that is programmed never to catch a fish—for this man's sake—and being eaten by blackflies and Christ knows what-all else, and sweating in the river's mist, because Carter and I are in—

Say love.

Love.

Say it and mean it.

Love.

Liar.

Not quite, bitch.

Say love.

"Love," she said, as if her throat were sore.

Carter looked up. His long, sad face smiled the sweetest smile.

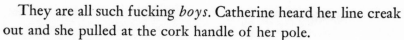

They are all such fucking *boys*. Catherine heard her line creak out and she pulled at the cork handle of her pole.

"Brake it," Carter instructed. "Use your finger and—yeah. Now, slowly. Slowly," he said.

But Catherine didn't hear him. She was watching the surface of the water as she alternately tugged, reeled, tugged and reeled, with what she knew was finesse, real touch, until she saw the dusk-dazzled silver of the river's skin break into foam, and a little bass come free and into the air. Carter crossed on stones, slipping, almost falling in, but reaching the fish and seizing it.

"Small," he said. "Let's throw him back?"

What she threw was the pole, as she strode off the bank and splashed to where he stood, the baitless hook in one hand and the fish in the other. Midges were at her nose and eyes as she grabbed his forearm and wrested the slippery fish from his hand. She ended up grasping it in both hands as she walked back to the bank and, breathing as if she'd fought a salmon for an hour, stood at a willow, then leaned against it, then straightened and took a deep breath. She held the fish in both hands as she swung it hard against a branch of the willow. It went stiff.

"You don't even like fish," he said. "You don't like fishing."

"I didn't know you knew that."

"Yeah," he said, "I know you didn't know."

"You have any other surprises?"

He shook his head. Then he said, "You?"

She had intended her body to stand still while her head shook *No* once or twice. Instead, her mouth gave a terrible, insincere smile. Her shoulders went up into a deep shrug that made her neck descend like a turtle's, and they held the posture for too long. Seeing herself in that instant as he must have, she thought she was signaling; watching herself on behalf of them both, she couldn't imagine the message. But she left the pole and little carton of worms for Carter to gather, and she walked sideways

35

up the bank, knowing that she was going to walk ahead of him down their two-lane road for half a mile from the site of the old grain mill toward home.

Drown came limping on to meet her. He wagged and panted.

"Yeah," Catherine said, holding the fish for him to inspect, "me too."

She made herself go slower. Carter all but plodded toward her, dragging his step a little, now that he saw her pause. She nodded at the justice of his pace. She stopped in the road to wait for him, knowing with certainty that she would find the kitchen surfaces scrubbed, the dishes washed, and Harry Miller gone.

Chapter Two

So Harry—who had supped on the slick sweating small of
Catherine's back, who had bitten at the side of her neck
stretched in love, who had grazed on her from eyelid to nipple
to crooked small toe, without her but somehow strong enough, as
if, tomorrow, she might pull her red wagon full of sons into the
office, demanding a lover who was lean (leanish) and cured of
cigarettes—Harry had kept to his diet, year after year. He had
stayed, first of all, off Catherine: hadn't written or called, though
he once had contrived to accompany the senator on a New York
trip to a Columbia ceremony, and had looked for Randy, but
hadn't seen him, had forborne from phoning the kid to say hello.
And of course the boys would be harnessed to pull the wagon,
wouldn't they? Catherine would be their cargo. But she hadn't
come, and he hadn't gone, and, though the red-wagon days were
over, Harry had stuck to his diet.

That's what he had thought. But was he not, this morning,
sitting on the bed of his grim white apartment about to slide his
legs into the size of khakis he had *used* to wear, during the dieting-
down period, which were a size larger than the ones he couldn't
zip without threatening his flesh as well as his zipper?

Still in his undershorts and maroon-striped English linen shirt, Harry strolled his floors. They were little different, he thought, from the surfaces of his tables, his desk, the other side of the double bed; they were littered, with single socks and souvenir T-shirts, underpants and books and magazines, postcards from friends en route (the resort of choice among the congressional-aide set), courtesy ballpoint pens, a rose a woman had given him at the start of a terribly promising, ultimately saddening, two-day date; and they were connected, one pile to another, by parking-garage and airplane tickets, fund-raising letters and bills, courtesy notes, invitations, birth announcements, concert programs, and movie stubs—all that paper which, if you added in the words he'd written for the senator on the torn sheets and twisted fragments that lay like clues to a vastly unimportant crime near every mound of what had been heaped by Harry Miller over several months (he would have sworn he could see the several layers of D.C. dust and homegrown cobwebs), *nearly* told the story.

The food clues were missing. No Mars bar wrapper hung on the frame of his Matisse poster, nor did his Pueblo bowl contain the Big Mac box he could still remember opening. Among the soiled shirts and crumpled speeches was no paper from frozen burritos or half-gallon boxes of chocolate marshmallow ice cream. His litter was dishonest. Its leaver was too. Here I am, he thought, waddling around like a white mole, congratulating myself on abstinence. All I've been doing well is *hiding*.

Harry, in his underwear and shirt, began to segregate his dirty clothing, his tax receipts, his unanswered personal mail, his unfinished senatorial fragments. It took him under an hour. He rented only a bedroom, living room, and bath; the dinette was an exaggeration of closet without door, and the kitchen was a four-burner stove beside a sink beneath a cupboard. And though he was sweating, he was also smiling. Finally, in fact, he was laughing. For though the cobwebs were rearranged and the dust mostly up in the air or inside his sinus cavities, what he had achieved, he saw, was a rebuilding of Harry Miller's mounds of dishonesty: everything looked intentional, not accidental, and surely he had sorted well and hard. But nothing was cured. The shirts still lay in one another's empty embrace, the boxers in another pile were only a rebuke for sloppy peeing and a joke about size.

"I am going to start running," he announced to his apartment. It sounded like something the senator had said. If he had, Harry had written it for him. Anyway, the chances of a presidential run were slipping for the usual reasons (his man wasn't qualified, popular, well-enough known, maybe not hard-enough driven); and the senator *did* jog, which was what Harry wished to do and—he knew it as he said his prayer—would not.

"I am going to start dieting hard," he said, thinking of pizza with anchovies and a glass of Czechoslovakian pilsener, thinking of too much pizza and too many bottles of beer, eaten alone, at night, here, in the apartment, while he read the sports section and heard the almost hysterical suction, swallowing, *sighing* of a person who, for whatever reasons he eats in such a virtual daze of solitary feeding, does not do it out of hunger. He was blushing for himself, he knew. He took big plastic garbage bags from the two-thousand-dollar-per-month cupboard and he loaded bottles of pickles, butterscotch sauce—*butterscotch?*—and the heart-shaped candies given him by the woman whose congressman made his money in candy; he would print your slogan on his hearts for five bucks a hundred. Harry threw in unmatched socks and typed or printed fragments of political fealty, social concern, and personal commitment. In went shirts, a rep tie he couldn't remember wearing ever in his life (he had found it pinned to the parquet by a sofa leg), and in went his noisome shorts. "Buy new," he said. "Buy American. No little Japanese shorts with those four-cylinder crotches."

It took him under half a minute, far from the record for snuffling in trash by guys with softening bellies, to find the congressman's assistant's bag of candy hearts. Each one said, in different colors, YOUR MESSAGE HERE. He crunched a mouthful, thrust the bag back into one of the garbage bags and, with food-dye juice at the corners of his mouth, chewing loudly, Harry sat at his clean desk, surrounded by bags of his recent history as if he had piled sandbags against a rising tide, and he swallowed hard, dialed the number, sputtered a little candy-heart juice, but got through to Mrs. Talliaferro—you said it "Tolliver," and she could tell you how many Talliaferros had been in Washington, associated with government, "since the War," she would say. By which she meant the War her side had lost. She was from Columbia, South Carolina, and so far as Harry could tell, her long legs and strong long face, her shadowy eyes and busy brain, were animated by only two causes: the senator's ease, and vengeance on General Grant for burning her city 130 years ago. The senator had never told him why she served an Irishman from Manhattan's West Side. In her fifties, she looked younger; there were rumors about bubble baths with the senator, who, in his fifties, could look like seventy-five. Harry swore she wore a .25 pistol strapped to the inside of her left thigh. He called her ma'am, and she accepted the tribute.

"Ma'am," he said, "I've been burgled. I've been robbed. Stripped clean. I have to go out and buy clothes and things."

"They took your clothes, Harry?"

"Yes, ma'am."

"Then they couldn't have been Nigra junkies. They only take TV sets and VCRs and jewels. Only jewels you got, you can't take off," she said, in her level soft voice. "And as I recall your TV is one of those imitation Korean things. But who would take your clothes? I mean: *your* clothes?"

"Yes, ma'am. You'll need to see to his statement on the pollution bill; it's done, and in my word processor. Ratner can run it off and fix it up. And I'll try and get in this afternoon. Tomorrow. Pretty soon."

"A crime of major proportions, then, Harry," she said.

"Ma'am: a one-apartment crime wave."

"Then I wish you luck with whatever it is. And if you do buy clothing, you might look into the ties at Garfinckel's."

"Garfinckel's?"

"See if they can pick you out a Dior."

"Dior," he said. "Thank you."

He went to the bedroom and put on the next-size-up khaki trousers. Wearing chukka boots and no socks, he carried his past few months down to the basement; it took him a couple of trips. And then he was alone in his clean apartment, sweating in the stillness of a hazy sour day in October in D.C. He remembered the cold winds at night in Schuyler, and the winter in upstate New York.

Tuna fish, he thought, with a lot of mayo, and chopped red onions and hamburger relish mixed in. On hard French country loaf, sliced a little thick, and a cream soda.

He said, "I hope you're learning your lesson, Cath."

He carried the empty canvas duffel bag to Dash's Designer, where he charged shirts and underwear and socks, a cotton sweater, and some dungarees. He looked the salesman in the eye when he measured Harry's waist, and he repeated the number: "Forty-four," he said, as loudly as the lean and elegant salesman had said it—as if he had discovered fours in that combination for the first time at this latitude during the early fall. Harry bought a lined lightweight parka, and a very expensive pair of walking shoes that looked like thick sneakers. Then he went to a sporting goods store, where he bought an enormous black leather baseball glove that looked like the one Tommy John had worn while pitching at advanced old age. That would do for Bobby, but he needed something to leave off for Randy. He settled on a Rugby shirt with wide stripes and a white collar. Finally, a wine merchant convinced him to buy a bottle of 1979 Vosne-Romanée for $190 for Carter. On his way out, he loaded up on small bottles of Perrier and little low-calorie rice cakes, and some apples. Then, outside, on the way to the rental agency, he stopped and ate two extremely long, thick hot dogs, with mustard and sauerkraut.

"You don't drive all that distance on goddamned *rice*," he told the man in sunglasses who sold the hot dogs.

"Fuckin right," the man said, with no expression in his voice or on his face.

So Harry, in a Mustang that made terrific noises when he shifted up, but that seemed barely able to hold both him and the bag, began to drive north. He made three blocks before he was hungry again. Sitting at a long red light, at Corcoran, he decided he'd been right not to buy a present for Catherine. He would wait until he was on Route 81, say in Pennsylvania, or even New York. He would pick wild autumn flowers. He would plait them in his hair and curl them around his ears and loop them through his belt and buttonholes, goddammit. He would assure her that his arrival had nothing to do with the slave graveyard and the senator's run and Harry's own career. That would be true. He would offer his big self, autumn's desperate seedpod, take it or leave it.

That would be true and false, to be precise, Harry thought, seeing his long-nosed white car crawling up a road map like something albino out of an underground nest, seeing himself in similar light behind the wheel, shifting down unnecessarily just to make the engine growl: bugs within bugs, the ultimate government life form. The senator had been interested and had written beside his initials on Harry's memo about his summer's upstate trip—how else to haunt a lover's life and get expenses reimbursed?—*Follow up, pls.* Mrs. Talliaferro, to whom privacy, in matters vaguely touching upon the senator, was an insult, had scribbled in red felt-tip pen, *Possibility!* In parentheses she'd added (*Northerners and Negroes*). So Harry would telephone panting, and Mrs. Talliaferro would keep him on the payroll in exchange for his hot pursuit of a possible vehicle for the senator's ethical outrage and thirst for true democracy. Harry figured to steal two weeks. He'd settle for one. If after all their years together—most of them apart—they could not resolve in several days what Catherine hadn't lately invited him to help resolve, then there wasn't any hope, and Harry would go back to Oreo-flavored ice cream in malt whiskey sauce, and to hell with Perrier and Golden Delicious apples that looked greener than gold and tasted like soft, sweet wood.

He stopped in Pennsylvania near a long curving bridge above a wooded valley. Eighteen-wheel trucks moaned and thundered, and cars made the sounds of giant mosquitoes, whining by at seventy, while he drank warm Perrier and walked on the tar-smelling gravel at the end of the concrete bridge. He would not look down for condoms and Coke cans, he demanded of himself, nor would he chance upon scraps of newspaper and the plastic remains of a roadside picnic. He would stroll over gravel and grass, and he would drink French seltzer, think French thoughts. In French movies they got in their car and they drove. Yes, but only if you were Trintignant and she was Anouk Aimée did she fall into your arms. And, twenty years later, you do not look like Trintignant; neither did you twenty years earlier. And there's the other one about twenty years or so later, with Depardieu and Ardant, oh dear—he stopped as traffic sang cruelly past—when they loved each other again after all that time and it couldn't happen again, and they made love so hopelessly on the floor of her former house and then, as he came, she reached for her purse and took out her little pistol, and she killed him. And you wept, Harry. You reporter of the news. You political realist. Just as you wept for Trintignant and Aimée. Sitting alone in the dark, in the black mouth of fantasy, you wept.

The slipstream of passing traffic made the high brown milkweed on its woody stalks whip back and forth. When the first frost came, the milkweed would burst. Harry went farther into the brush near the road, and he found a little dirty stream, a rainbow sheen of gasoline on its surface. He was going to fill the

43

Perrier bottle with autumn weeds and hand it all to Catherine
when she opened her door. It was the sort of self-conscious, self-
denigrating gift a boy would bear, he thought. She'd have little
patience with such an effort to purchase her mildness. He left the
bottle in the stream, recalling the language he'd written for the
senator's wilderness preservation bill. That was just words, Harry
thought. This is—he parted them as he returned to the road, a little
beyond his car—milkweed pods exploding, goddammit.

He remembered how, after four or five years of living in New
York and writing for the *Daily News* and hearing nothing from
her, he'd received a card from Catherine. On it, her address had
been the message he had waited for: it said *Here I am. What will
you do with that information?* And he had driven through a winter's hell to reach her house. He had sat in her driveway, he
remembered, appalled by the weather, impressed with the need
that had pushed him through it, looking up at the lightless windows
of her second floor, and wondering how to tell her he was there.
He had thought of throwing pebbles, he remembered, recalling
then, no doubt, the films of thirty years before, when lovers intro-
duced themselves with little scratching sounds. Of course, he was
up to his axles in snow and freezing rain, no pebbles in sight. He
remembered considering snowballs, lumps of ice. He remembered
asking himself, then, what you did throw to tell your lover you
had traveled over space to travel back through time. And now, in
his car again and passing trucks that had passed him at the bridge,
hitting eighty and leaning into his acceleration, Harry knew the
answer: you throw yourself.

It was the sweetest time of the year, she thought. Coming home
from the gallery, over the hills through Edmeston and New Ber-
lin, she had watched the sallow final green of the fields go ocher;
she had seen the brush, under a silky darkening sky, turn sere.

The sumac was brilliant with its final burn. The wind, though still warm with late September, had a touch to it of October's chilled-wine autumn taste. And here she was in a bulky sweater and jeans and her boat shoes, walking behind the house and sipping at the wind. There were late tomatoes in the little garden she should harvest while Bobby did homework or napped or lay in a coma from drugs. She was always knocking wood when she thought of Bobby and his sudden growth, his moods like jokes about wretched adolescence, and his all-but-spoken yearning to be secret from her, invisible to Carter, beloved of his always distant, suddenly absent, adored older brother. He listened to rap music—morons chanting doggerel to electric ticktocks, she'd told him—and he lay in, on, or under his bed, and he grew. She knocked on the slim strong trunk of a locust tree. Please no, she begged about the drugs.

The garden behind the house, a hundred by a hundred feet or so, still held the heat of day. She kneeled in the friable soil that she'd worked, manured, nourished, rotary-tilled, and weeded for years, and she stayed that way, on hands and knees, looking into the low sun. The green mulching plastic she hated but used because it kept down weeds now caught the sunlight, and the garden looked striped into rows of rich earth and rows of shiny green liquid. The dark tomato vines on their green bamboo stakes were drooping with the weight of plum tomatoes she hadn't yet plucked. Most of the vines, in spite of their crutches, lay along the plastic mulch. Some were blackened, where slugs had crawled in and eaten from the inside back out. Others were still green. Most were dark red, and even going soft. There were hundreds to take, and though she hadn't planned to harvest tonight, the low orange sun, the sky that looked like a dark—an African—skin, and the smell of the vines (not the acid tomatoes themselves), that luxuriance of greenness, made her take off her sweater and, with goose bumps pricking the flesh of her arms and her neck, tie its

45

sleeves together and fill it with all the dry, firm tomatoes she could fit inside its upside-down torso.

She carried the tomatoes over Drown, who, in a patch of late sun at the kitchen door, looked up and away, wagged as if to make up for his immobility, and went on being immobile. Inside, the metallic repetitive voice on Bobby's tape player droned something about fever or lever or *geev*-er, probably the latter. Catherine thought: I'm outside being both Bobbsey Twins, and he's upstairs with one hand down his pants listening to songs about doing some underage delinquent the greatest favor of all time. You are *old*, Miss Priss.

At the sink, she tumbled all the tomatoes under running water, untied and shook out her sweater, and put it back on. There were days when the light and temperature made you want a sweater on not so much because you were chilly as because the day or evening looked like chill, suggested that being a little cold would be appropriate, and you wore something heavy, to acknowledge the world: Canada geese overhead, out of sight but hooting the shrill, sad cries; the sky going one tone darker of blue; the roadside milkweed bobbing in a wind that would bring enough cold within the week, she thought, to burst them into white silk hairs and crusty brown shell.

"What?" Carter had come in behind her; she had heard the distant geese, but not his car.

Without looking back, washing tomatoes and stacking them in colanders to drain, Catherine said, "Paying dues."

Carter wasn't staying for dinner. He was going on to a meeting at the Sherburne Inn—roast beef and civic protest—to discuss ("Defend, with my Swiss army knife and my teeth, if I have to," he said) his need, his company's need, his creditors' need, to make a vast parking area for a country shopping mall. Various ecologists and church groups and students and hunters had been registering protests. "Now," he told her, setting down a newspaper and repacking a thin leather folder with legal pad and felt-tip pens and a booklet of specifications, folded, frayed drawings, a thin calculator, "*now*, there's some kind of black action group made up of *white* people. Something like that."

"The graveyard," she said, turning at last and wondering if they usually kissed when he came home.

"The fucking graveyard. I am going to hand-carry every corpse to someplace wonderful and new," he said. "At my expense. I'm going to be so respectful, the dead will turn over and sigh and sleep again. And these *liberals* have to come out and paint me up as Mr. Posse Comitatus of the Year. You don't hear it from the *blacks*."

Catherine said, "That's ugly, Carter. What you're saying is ugly. I would like you to sit down, and have a cup of coffee with me, or a glass of wine, and get yourself calm. You sound ugly now."

He didn't look ugly. He was hard and thin and strong-looking, and he looked competent, and able to take on those liberals she was rooting for to win enough of an edge to delay his new project or break it up entirely.

"Anyway," Carter said, letting himself smile and losing the coarse flush of his anger—he grew angry by mottling—"it's harvesttime." He gestured at the tomatoes behind her, or maybe at her and them both. "All I'm proposing is a little *picking*."

Catherine said, turning back to face the sink before she knew she would, "Is it true I used to let you touch me?"

She looked at the tomatoes, and her fingers sorted out a bunch she would use for making a fresh tomato sauce for dinner. She heard his chair scrape, and then his footsteps—away, into the rap music, then returning to pause. He said, "You know who said loyalty is the most precious commodity?"

"Who?"

"Me."

He went, and there was only the music, and then—she heard them this time, and she heard no geese—the noises of his car. Catherine said, "It's not a commodity."

She sliced onions into olive oil in a heavy skillet, and she chopped some tomatoes in, and garlic and basil from her door-yard herb garden. She put water on for cooking up spaghetti, and then she opened a jug of red wine and poured some into one of the thin, dimpled green glass tumblers she'd found in the house. The wine looked purple in the green glass, and Catherine smiled for the color. At the counter, near the phone, she left herself a note for tomorrow, about a print they were selling unmatted: a dark red, even richly purple matting might sell it to someone susceptible, she thought. And then she picked up the phone and did not dial Randy's number at school and hung it up. You do not call your boy in college when you're feeling middle-aged and a touch discouraged by life among the grave robbers. You beg for him to call you. And you never tell him you're begging.

Bobby's music shut off, and she braced herself for his descent, but he was only changing tapes—doing homework, he would tell her, if she was unwise enough (and she would be) to ask what he'd been doing upstairs. Now she heard a man singing a vaguely Oriental-sounding tune about "selling England by the pound." She smiled for the pun.

The sauce was simmering, and she turned the spaghetti water up. Bobby would be pleased, for he hated all foods containing fat or gristle, any meats that weren't hamburger, which of course was *all* fat and gristle, but in disguise, and he was appalled by poultry and fish. Any form of noodle or long spaghetti, with any form of tomato sauce—he could not, naturally, eat tomatoes in their natural state—was acceptable. Every other night she cooked chicken or fish or turkey or a stew, and she forced herself to sit through his agonies of protest and sorting. And she had descended, over the recent months of his adolescent fever—he was burning with *self*—from saying, like a joke about mothers, "Because it's *good* for you," to "Eat it or there's no more food tonight, not even a banana," to "You eat the damned bluefish or I'm going to have Carter hire a man to come here tonight and kill you."

She called upstairs to Bobby that dinner was ready. The music played, but nothing stirred. He had finally found the right rhythm for sleep, she thought. Or he's not going to answer me so he can be free, independent of grown-up requirements. Somebody hand me my cattle prod. "Fine." She said it to the staircase up which she had called. She said it to the tomato sauce which she poured over the drained and rinsed spaghetti. She said it to Carter in his absence and Randy in his silence. She said it to the tumbler of coarse Sicilian wine. "Fine."

She was reading *Art in America* and shaking her head at the prices fetched by inept watercolors of boats moored off Maine when she heard neither the tape from upstairs (it had shut itself off) nor Carter's tires on the gravel of the drive (it was too early). Whoever it was shut the car door quietly, for she had barely pushed herself back from the table when this fast-moving person had knocked at the front door. She pushed away to slide her feet back into her boat shoes when Drown, true to form and running late though loud, came chugging around the house, barking. She heard the man—she sensed the low vibrations of a male voice; she heard no words—say friendly, happy sounds. Drown yipped his repulsively sycophantic greetings, which meant that it was any-one not shooting at him. Then the door opened in as she was coming through the living room and almost there.

In the most saddeningly hesitant voice—everybody, she thought, ought to feel more welcome in a place they had come so far, unannounced or not, to be—Harry said, "Hello?"

She reminded herself again, as he was deftly rolling spaghetti with his fork and soup spoon, and dipping bread into her sauce, and drinking the wine that Carter had brought home the night before, that it was not fair. It wasn't fair to let him break what he said was his diet, though he surely looked like a man who'd been doing everything but diet: he was puffy, uncomfortable with his body. He's been sad, Catherine thought. And it wasn't fair—to whom? Carter? Harry? Both of them? *All* of them?—to be so pleased to see him that her hands and arms actually wanted to tremble as if with cold. It wasn't fair not to wake Bobby, who would sleep through the night, most likely, and wake up not having had a chance to rush sloppily through his homework. And it wasn't fair to her, she thought, for him to keep on coming back. When is over *over*? And no messages from the coach, please: operas are so often over before the fat lady sings; and it is over before the last inning is played, the last down run, the last basket shot. There is a time—she looked toward the kitchen window, the mounds of tomatoes on the sill above the withering grasses out-side—when things are simply done. And it wasn't fair, of course, she knew, for her to be happy enough not to be standing on the table, one foot in his crimsoned pasta, announcing, for once and for all, that they were at the instant of closure, eat your food and drink your wine and turn your car, go home. She looked at the disorder of his hair and the wrinkles of his shirt. She looked at his arms beneath his rolled-up sleeves. She looked at his face—longer than she'd remembered it, and more set about the mouth, the top lip coming slightly further down on the lower one than she'd recalled. The fur of his chest was all but growing from his collar, as usual, and the stubble of his whiskers needed its second shave. She still remembered when he'd worn a beard. It was conceivable that he ought to have kept it, she thought. He was watching her watch him. He was setting down his fork and spoon, reaching for his wine, then letting his hand bang gently down to the tabletop, and he was staring hard.

"Don't even begin to say it," she said.

"You want to say it for me?"

She shook her head.

"You could, though," he said.

"I'm settled, Harry. I'm not living like that. I'm with my children in this house. Child, mostly, but Randy also, still." He nodded. "And there's Carter." He nodded again. "My job." Another nod. She said, "So."

"So it's what you said, what you acted out, like the north country's longest-running pantomime show, when I was here last time. I am not deterred."

"You were," she said.

"Let's say delayed."

"What was stopping you?"

"What difference does it make, Cath?"

"None. No: lots. I'd like to know, if you don't mind my being frank in my own kitchen on my own time, both of which you opened my front door and walked into."

He shook his head.

"So, what kept you?"

He said, "Would fear make any sense?"

"Fear of what?"

"Later," he said. "If the conversation develops, sometime we can talk about fear of what."

She sat back and wrapped both hands around her tumbler. "That sounds like a phobia. Fear-of-what. It sounds like the biggest phobia of them all."

He nodded. "Speaking for me, in this personal case, I would say that's exactly what it is. Have you got someplace I can sleep?" She watched him grin at the expression she'd apparently just showed him. "And have you got a pretext I can use for sleeping there? Because I really came here, Cath, to see if I—"

"*Don't*," she said. "I don't want to hear that talk, talk that talk, be *part* of that kind of talk. I'll be me, and you be you. Between now and half an hour or an hour from now, you come up with whatever lie feels best to you. Just don't tell me."

Behind her, Bobby's daily-deepening voice asked, "Why would

he have to *lie*?" And the sudden brightness of Harry's smile as he looked over her shoulder, the ease that smoothed the forehead furrows she had wrapped her hands around the glass in order not to touch, made her place the edge of the glass against her lips and sip so that she wouldn't echo Bobby and ask herself, out loud and truthfully, "Why?"

Bobby slid into his seat at the table and helped himself to dinner with a smooth silence that told her he knew he shouldn't be fed on account of lateness, but was going to sneak as large a feed as he could while his mother was distracted by Harry's return. She sensed her son considered Harry's arrival interruptive, dangerous, but linked to his boyhood past and therefore somehow legitimate. He strove for his manners, she saw, and didn't pour his milk into his mouth as if it were the oil line of a pickup truck.

Harry said, "Bobby, why did the Yankees die this year?"

"Pitching," Bobby answered, from around a half a pound of number nine spaghetti.

"Yeah, but how about that Tommy John?"

"He was good. He pitched good—"

Catherine had to: "Well."

Bobby shrugged, then finished: "For an old guy."

"He's older than I am, thank God," Harry said. "I'm so grateful for senile presidents and middle-aged pitchers."

"You need the news to make you feel young?" Catherine asked.

Harry nodded. He said, "Excuse me," and he left. Bobby said, "Is he mad?"

Catherine shook her head, watching the kitchen doorway, in which Harry then appeared. She turned toward Bobby and said, "Nah."

"Nah, what?" Harry asked.

Bobby was looking shyly and with greed at the shopping bag Harry deposited on the table. "You answered the question, I think," Catherine told him.

"Well, good. Good." Harry looked at Bobby and told him, "This is for you if you want it."

Like a mongoose striking, and yet with an air of decorousness, Bobby was inside the bag and then wearing the long black mitt. "Cool," he said. "TJ."

"Tommy John," Harry said to Catherine.

"I keep up," she said.

"Maybe we could all drive down to New York and catch a game some time," Harry said.

Catherine asked, "Didn't the Yankees finish the season already?"

He nodded, blushing. "I forgot I kept up," he said. "I got excited. I started making plans before I thought."

"That can be a real mistake," she said. Bobby looked away— because he's really listening, she thought. Because he knows. Knows *what*?

Harry asked, "What?"

"Nothing," she said. "Thinking."

"I'll clean up the dishes when I'm done, Mom."

"You will?"

Harry said, "I owe you for that."

Bobby shook his head and held the glove up. He smiled and sucked noodles simultaneously.

Outside, in cooling breezes that weren't yet cold, under a dusk with some light left in it—orange, segmented by tomorrow's gathering rain clouds—Catherine walked toward the fence of the back field that ran up their hill and away from the road. Drown followed her, and Harry followed Drown. She waited at the slack single strand of barbed wire, and when Harry came up, panting a little, she said, "The poor kid couldn't wait to get us out of there so he could slurp away in peace. He feels the tension. The way dogs are supposed to." Drown was on his side, with his spade-shaped head twisted almost straight up at the sky; he was watching the rising of a fat moon, and soon, she knew, he'd growl at it, preparing to defend her. Drown always raged at the sky when he felt protective.

"What tension?"

She looked at him. He grinned stupidly and shrugged. She could shrug in response, but couldn't grin, because nothing, she felt, was funny then. Weren't they in *trouble*?

Harry—he was good at it once—almost read her mind. "You see this—"

She bit at it: "There is no *this*. You came up. You'll go back."

"—as a threat to your, let's call it order. Okay? Something like that?"

"I don't want to get into a discussion, Harry."

"Then just, I don't know: strike your hoof against the ground if you think I'm describing it right."

She turned so as not to smile.

"But what if you didn't think of it like that? What if my being around you isn't a threat, because it isn't disorderly?"

"Since when haven't you been disorderly?"

"Since when have you been so in love with being a hive queen and not much more?"

"Is that what you see here, you son of a bitch? Li'l Miz Home-maker?"

"I'm talking about order, Cath."

"I'm talking about out of order, Harry. Who asked you to be here? Could we discuss *that*? Who invited you? Who says I'm stuck up to my knees in boredom and I needed you to be here like a brisk shot of cologne on the inside of the elbow—"

"In hot weather. I remember," he said. He picked her arm up, and pulled back the cuff of her sweater, then unbuttoned the cuff of her shirt and, holding her hand beneath his right arm, he used both hands to push her clothing back gently until her arm was bare and turned so that the softer, whiter underside faced up. He bent and kissed the crook of her arm, where the tendon showed, where the blood pulsed. "I remember how you did that in the hot weather. One night, you put cologne behind my knee. You said—"

"No." She pulled her arm away and rubbed where he had kissed. She drew down the sleeve of her shirt and then of her sweater, and she fastened herself in. "It's getting buggy," she said. "We should go."

"The wind's keeping them off, Cath."

"Then think of another reason."

"No."

"Carter."

"He's not a reason. He's not your order. *You're* the order here. You and the boys."

"I have to call Randy."

"I'd love to talk to him, if I could."

"You get a night's hospitality," Catherine said, conscious of the snap in her voice, the underlying sulk of her tone, and the way, for all her language of withdrawal, she had not withdrawn: they were almost toe-against-toe, like fighters on the verge of a clinch or an exchange. "You stay here tonight, because you're a friend. You're an old friend." She said, "I think of you, Harry." She said, suddenly meaning it, "Aren't we too old?"

"Not for anything I can think of, Cath, except maybe getting ready for the giant slalom at the Olympics."

She moved, then, walking around him—Drown stirred, cocked a suspicious white eye at the moon, which was then behind clouds, and settled for a low groan, then a swoon back onto the grass— and their positions, then, were reversed: he stood on the higher ground, and she stood below. She knew, after she had done it, what she'd had in mind. She wanted to be considerably smaller than he. She wanted to feel little. She was acting like a goddamned woman, and she didn't want to.

But Harry knew her. He knew, she thought, enough to understand how when she loved him there had been a need sometimes to be engulfed, to be protected and invaded at the same time. She said—because, she knew, they'd traded thoughts—"I changed my mind."

"You just got scared."

She smelled the rough sourness of the wine, and the richness, almost the earth smell, of the tomatoes she had picked a few hours ago: his mouth was open, he was leaning toward her, and his hands were at her neck, light and tremulous. "I'm right to be," she said.

"Aren't we both."

She turned, because she'd been following the sound of the lone car on their road as it came east toward them over the darkening two-lane road. Harry's hands slid down her neck to her shoulders and then, because he'd misread her, he slid them forward and down to her breasts. She leaned into his hands, then back, and then she stepped away from him, shaking her head, walking toward the house. She stopped. "I'm sorry," she said.

"God, I am too. I shouldn't have—"

"No," she said.

"No what? That I shouldn't have touched you, or I should have?"

"Carter's here," she said. "He had a meeting. It's all right."

"What is?"

What your hands, like a scared boy's, did on my breasts, you idiot. What your fear of me means. What I want from this, whatever that is. "I couldn't tell you," she said.

Carter's lights, flooding the far side of the house and throwing a nimbus around the building, went off, and a deeper darkness came on. But the clouds continued to blow, and the diminished moon threw a little light. It was enough for Drown. Catherine, turning to see Harry looking down the hill toward her, watched him jump as a stiff and bristling, high-tailed, ruff-maned Drown, all teeth and eyes, lurched forward a couple of lock-kneed steps, staring up as if he watched an enemy approach, and then began to warn off everything above. She expected poor Harry, confused as she, she figured, but already gathering himself—she watched him smooth his shirt over his belly and pull his belt—to lean his long pale face back and start to howl. If he does, she thought, so will I.

He did not stay outside with a watchdog who fended off the moon, or a retriever who sought to bring it back, because he was sulking. She had always chided him for sulking, as he had teased her for lifting her chin like a tough duck and trying to take on whole townships or weather fronts. He wouldn't dare sulk now, because he had no rights here: you pout only when you can get away with it. He stayed, of course, for physiological reasons. When she had faced away from him, he'd thought of times together when she'd back toward him, naked or not, and slowly revolve her buttocks against him, and of course he'd made the wrong assumption and every wrong move. She'd been turning to greet her—whatever he was: greet Carter. Wrong as Harry's brain had been, his penis had been wronger, rising to greet her like a deaf, dumb welcoming committee of the flesh. So he was waiting for his body to subside. And he was, while on the topic of his loins, girding them. For he would have to walk into Catherine's house which now was also Carter's, or which, more likely, was occupied by him with her sufferance and at her invitation, and he would have to exchange glances with the man and take what he dished out.

When he and Catherine had been together, or when he and Merri were together in D.C., or Sarah at Public Broadcasting in Boston, he had always been as jealous as he thought he could get away with being. And he remembered hating the interlopers not just in bars and at parties and in offices, people who threatened his order, but interlopers in movies and books and on TV: the slick, sly border-crossers on whose side the Technicolor world always was. So here he was, now, at this very barbed-wire fence, and whoever was directing this show was clearly changing the rules. Carter's car arrived on time, as if scheduled. "The trouble, dear Drown," he said, "lies not in the stars but in our meat loaf." He pulled at his belt and jiggled, tucked, and then walked.

In the kitchen, minimally clean, Bobby sat with a textbook. Drown hurled himself at the back door. Bobby went to admit him. Harry stopped and put his hands out to Bobby, who took them before Harry remembered how old the boy was—the hands were hard, from sports, probably, and very broad and strong. "You're a moose, aren't you?" Harry said. "I used to pull you in a wagon, you know that? Don't you hate it when we talk to you like that? I'm happy as hell to see you, Bobby. Whatever happens."

Bobby blushed. He said, "Mom's always right, she always says. Ask her."

"I appreciate that advice. And I'm going to. I'll catch you later. Hey—you miss Randy?"

"No. Yes. Kind of. He *never* calls home, almost."

"Maybe we could call him up or something."

Bobby nodded, looked at Harry, then dropped back into his chair and hid behind what looked like graphs.

"See you," Harry said. No one rescued him, so he continued to the living room, where Carter, with his shoes off and his stocking feet on the coffee table Harry remembered putting his stocking feet on, sipped a dark drink at the sofa. Carter raised the glass as Harry entered. But Harry put a hand—*Right back*—into the air, flashed what he thought of as his winning political grin, and went out to the car. When he was there, feeling the cold now, and wishing to pause for a sweater but afraid—he couldn't tell why—to be gone from the house he so feared to be in, he realized that he hadn't seen Catherine in the living room. He found his gift for Carter and went back.

"Listen," he said, standing before the pinch-faced man who pretended, he saw, to relax, "I got this for you because I remembered how much you like wine, and you were very hospitable to me. I mean, I all but broke in and demanded a meal, last time I was here."

Carter put his drink down on the table. Harry put his hands in his pockets so he wouldn't take a straw coaster from the pine end table and put it under the glass before a ring formed on the cherry wood. Carter looked at him, and then at the bottle of wine.

"What would you call it this time?"

Harry said, "The burgundy? Oh. No, you mean the coming back."

"The Return of Harry," Carter said. "It's a beautiful bottle of wine. I never tasted it. I've heard of it. I'd love to drink it. Maybe I will. Maybe we'll be civilized, and some time I'll open it an hour or so ahead of time and wash and dry some good wineglasses and pour us a little and we'll sit and talk. Thank you."

"But you don't think so," Harry said.

Carter stood. He shook his head. He stooped to bang the bottle onto the coffee table and retrieve his drink. He took a long sip, gave a theatrical sigh, pursed his thin lips into something between a smile and a frown, and said, "No."

"No," Harry said. "How could you?"

"How could you have thought I would?"

"There's a kind of innocence you sometimes fake," Harry said. "You know what I mean? It's like, I don't know. It's—"

"Begging for mercy," Carter said. He raised his chin as Catherine did, and Harry found the echo devastating.

"Fair enough," Harry said. "Though I don't know if I'd say begging."

"You needn't," Carter said. "I did. Listen: begging."

"You sure said it," Harry said. "Now you got me pegged. I apologize. It was a churlish gift."

"Presumptuous," Carter said. "Did you think for the price of a bottle of wine, I would let—"

Harry put his hand up. It did not say *Right back*. It said *Stop*, and Carter did. Harry found himself imitating Carter's imitation of Catherine's chin. He didn't know whether to weep for what the man had appropriated—that he had been with her, and so intimately, to be able to—or to laugh for all three of them waddling around in various poses of scared or furious duck. Harry said, "I don't have much right to say too much too harshly, but I can't imagine that you think of Catherine as someone you can *let* do anything. Nor that anyone in *this* room was granted the right by her to even halfway think so. *Nor*, damn it, that I am dumb enough, or frightened enough, to try and buy her. Off of you. And for a couple of hundred bucks."

Harry sat down where he was. His knees gave out, and he sat on Catherine's coffee table, spilling Carter's drink. "I'm sorry," he said. "I just caved in."

"Not so's I would know it," Carter said.

Harry was remembering Dell, her ex-husband, who had come to the house in Vermont to punch as much of Harry's body as he'd been able to reach. He was a dean at a college someplace, Harry thought, probably still punching people out: the fighting dean. And here was Harry, still at it, too, the quailing lover.

Harry leaned his arms on his knees. Carter picked up ice, tossed it into his glass, and went out to the kitchen. He came back with two small shot glasses. "Bourbon," he said, handing one to Harry. "I do not think of her like that, and you probably suspect that. But I did sound a little like your father back there, talking about the wine. A little patronizing, I mean."

"My fault," Harry said. "I brought it to you."

Carter held his glass up and almost toasted Harry, who did his best to return the gesture in precise duplication, though his hand still shook. Harry knew a man in Washington who called these little glasses shooters, and for the first time the word felt right; the oaky bourbon went down his throat without touching, but it landed with a cold explosive impact that made him move where he sat. "It's twelve years old," Carter said. "It's a killer. One of the guys I use for asphalt gave it to me."

Harry nodded speechlessly to show his appreciation. He worked at breathing.

Carter said, "You're fucking up my life, you know."

"And mine," Harry said.

"And Catherine's?"

Harry said, "Probably not as much as I had thought to."

"You're making the move, though. You're coming in here under cover of—shit: you do it in full day, don't you? And you're saying, here I am, a dozen years out of your past, and I'm taking you away from all this."

"It's nothing against you, Carter."

"Sure it is. It's everything against me."

Harry nodded. "Yes."

"What is your estimate of what I'll do?"

"Have me cemented under one of your projects?"

Carter didn't return Harry's smile. He put his finger into his shot glass, ran it over the surface, and then licked at his finger. Harry looked away. Carter said, "I could. Some of the people I deal with are connected. Some of them would do it for decent money."

Harry said, "Jesus, Carter, I wish you wouldn't do that."

"You don't think she's worth dying for, Harry?"

"I meant lick your finger like that."

Carter looked at him, and then he smiled, all coldness, tooth, and crinkled eyes. He tossed his shot glass into the air and caught it. Harry tossed his at him, and Carter used the other hand to snatch it from the air. "You find it unsanitary?"

"It's intimate, isn't it? I was hoping we could be respectful and a little, I don't know, distant. Does that make sense?"

Carter said to him, "Who'm I to make sense, when I'm talking to my woman's ex-lover who wants to steal her away, or back, or whatever, and I'm standing here with a shot glass in each hand?"

"I swear that I apologize," Harry said. "As far as your own discomfort goes."

Carter nodded.

"And mine and Catherine's," Harry said, "for that matter. I doubt I'm doing anyone any good."

Catherine came in. "What?" she asked.

"We're being civilized," Carter said.

"I just talked to Randy," she said, smiling with the real pleasure of it.

"You couldn't wait, huh?" Carter asked.

"I did," she said. "He called me."

"I didn't hear it ring," Carter said.

"What's the difference?"

He said to her, "The difference is, you swore you wouldn't call him because you wanted him to feel like he was off the leash, and then you *did* call him. Because I would have heard it. Which means you're so screwed up over this guy's arrival, you're lying to me. That is what strikes me as the difference."

Catherine's chin rose. Carter's was already up. Harry was about to quack out loud when he saw how Carter's eyes had misted.

"I'll leave," Harry said.

"You will?" Catherine asked.

Harry closed his eyes, but forced them open again. "No." He wanted to see what Catherine thought, but he was afraid to. He looked at the coffee table, with its faint ghost of a ring. That was when he knew that he was standing.

Carter said, "I will, then. I'll take a couple of days. I'll deal with the entire resurrected African-American populace." He cupped Catherine's chin. "I'll call you. I really can't handle this unless I go a while."

"It isn't necessary," she said.

Harry thought: Say it is.

"Good," Carter said. "Good. You're throwing him out."

Catherine said, "Harry's my friend from a long time ago. We were good friends."

"This makes me want to puke," Carter said. "All this civilized fucking *talk*. When do people get rights, goddammit?"

She looked at Carter. Harry breathed shallowly, as if he were hiding to spy on them, and didn't want even the rise and fall of his chest to betray the need and greed behind his observation. She said, "I don't control you."

"You could."

"Thank you. But I couldn't. My whole life with the boys taught me that."

"I don't want you for a mother, thanks." He slapped each shot glass onto the table. He shook his head wildly. "I can't do this, all this talk, this pretty arguing. I know facts. I know what facts act like. Feel like. I asked you for—I'm going to be home or near the site. This is *me*, Catherine. And I'll be back, I'll probably be back. Of course I'll be back. But I can't stay here now." He turned and seized his folder and suit jacket from the wing chair, and he went to the door. Catherine walked quickly to where he paused, and she kissed him on the side of the cheek. Harry watched Carter's large hand reach around her waist, and he watched her step back out.

"Don't go far away," she said.

"Truly?" Carter asked.

Catherine shrugged, but sweetly, Harry thought, not dismissively. He also knew the shrug, and he knew it had never been enough for him; he was with Carter: he wanted guarantees. This time, seeing her shoulders drop like that, he wanted to applaud. Carter went out, and though he didn't slam the door, it made a loud enough noise to summon Drown, scratching his claws on the floorboards and snarling as he entered the living room to fend things off.

"Okay," she said to the dog. "Okay."

"Is it?"

Catherine said, "Is what? For who?"

Harry said, "Right. Right. Is, uhm, Randy all right?"

Catherine looked as though she were trying to solve the riddle of what species Harry belonged to. He looked at a piece of ice Carter had left on the carpet, and he thought of kneeling to pick it up. He thought that if he did he would never rise—would roll over onto his side or back and just snuffle there on Catherine's floor, waiting for guidance and mercy.

Catherine said, "Randy sends you his love. He says—" She paused, but Harry didn't look. He was studying the ice. "He says hooray."

Catherine had changed into baggy cotton drawstring trousers that were off-white and stained, along one knee and below it, with what looked like grass; she wore a Black Watch plaid flannel shirt tucked into the pants, and her feet were in boat shoes. She looked competent, and she looked annoyed. Harry couldn't imagine who had annoyed her more, and he hated not knowing her well enough. He said, "Look, he'll come back. He's pissed off with me, not you. He'll be back." He watched her stoop to rub at the ring on the table. "Won't he?"

Her face was pale, and her eyes looked pouchy. Even in the dim light of the living room she looked less taut than before, less composed. She has so much more to hold together, all of a sudden, he thought. She stood up, and then was standing up before him— *to* him, he realized—her body almost touching his, her head tilted back, Quack Quack, and her eyes baggier-looking because she squinted. He smelled her breath as she scolded him. He would have known it in the dark and in a crowded elevator, its rich mulch of a day's spent energies, and flooding adrenaline, the staleness of wine and ripeness of tomato, the sense it gave him of crumbling earth. "Don't be innocent, Harry. Don't *fake* innocence with me. You know why you came here. You think Carter doesn't? Randy did. Over the *phone*, he could tell. I didn't ask you to come. I *never* asked you to come. I don't want you here."

She winced. "I didn't know I felt that way," she said.

Harry said, "It isn't true."

She stepped back. He was going to follow her, seize her. But she'd stepped back tactically: she swung her hand behind her and, elbow straight, wrist only somewhat cocked, she brought the heel of it around and clouted him along the ear and cheek and neck.

Tears flooded his eyes. The pain along his mastoid bone was enormous. He found his hands cocked, left in front, right alongside his unsmacked jaw, and he thought he was going to slam her back. So did she. "Go ahead," she said, leading with the famous chin.

He shook his head, but it hurt to move. He held the motion, dropped his hands, blinked at the tears, and said, "A major blow, Catherine. You beat the hell out of me in one shot. I can't move anything from the shoulder up."

She came closer again. Now she was crying, of course, and he found that he had begun again. "Carter deserves better."

"Anyone you love, Catherine. Anyone you love."

"What about them?"

"I have to honor them."

"You really feel that?"

"No."

"Good. I hate it when you make speeches. Don't sound like a goddam political speech writer with me, Harry."

"I will sound like the old H. Miller, cityside ace of the *News*."

"Harry, just fucking *talk straight*!"

"Do you love him? Do you still love me? Do you want me to stay here? Could we make love on the floor? Coffee table? Sofa? On what's left of his ice cube down there? Can we get married? Can I adopt your sons?"

She backed away from him until she was at the wing chair across the room. She fell back into it.

"Cath, come back here. Let me touch you. Can I come there?"

"You did enough traveling, Harry. Stay where you are."

He did. He sat on the coffee table. He rubbed at his ear and neck. "You really belted me."

"Poor Carter," she said.

"Carter! I'm the—"

"You know what I mean. You know damned good and well what I mean. What if you were Carter?"

He said, "I'd have tossed fucking Harry out of here the first time around. Last summer. Are you kidding?"

"That's what I mean. He thinks too much of me to do that."

"Oh," Harry said, "I know what you mean—he doesn't want to own you. No: he doesn't want to let himself say out loud he *wants* to own you. He's being deferential to your feelings. That's very political, Cath, do you know that? We're talking domestic politics here. Well, here's one for you. I want to completely own every inch of your body and your life. I want all the cells inside the most completely secret parts of the darkest places in your body. I want the goddam pancreas, Cath. I want your digestive juices. Understand?" He found that he wasn't weeping, but that he'd come to his feet and was walking toward her, that he was shaking as he walked. "I didn't know you could shake while you walked."

"And rattle," she said, "and roll."

"Now, I'm not saying I *demand* that stuff," he said. "I'm not saying it's my right, or I expect it, or it'll happen, or I'll die if it doesn't, though who knows for sure? I'm telling—you said talk straight. Okay. That's it. Straight. That straight enough for you?"

He was in front of her chair. She leaned back into it. He reached down and took hold of the front of her shirt. He knew his face must be red because he could feel blood every place else in his body—his skin felt so tight, he thought he might faint, or have a stroke, blow gouts of blood out his mouth and nose and ears and lie down and drain before her.

He pulled her up. She pushed back on the arms of the chair and leaned away.

"Don't," she said.

"*You* don't."

"I'm *trying*."

"When did I ever kiss you against your will?"

He pulled her forward and up by her bunched shirtfront. Her chin was up and he kissed her, or she let him kiss her, or she suffered his kiss, or he forced himself upon her. But they kissed. Her lips were as soft as anything he'd touched, he thought. It was like his first kiss, when he was fourteen, the soft pursed lips going back, as he pressed on, against her teeth. He kept his lips together too. And when he did leave her gathered at the front edge of the chair, her shirt still bunched in his hand, they were panting.

"Damn it," she said.

"You're in trouble, Catherine."

She closed her eyes. "I know it. So are you, big boy."

"I'm used to it. I have been, for a long time."

She opened her eyes. "You really mean it. You've been—"

"Whatever that is, uh-huh. Yeah. I've been, for all those years without you. I don't want to know about you."

"Yes, you do. You always want everything. You want to know everything and have everything."

"I want to have you," he said.

She gently opened his hand and pulled her shirt out of his fingers. She kept hold of the hand, and he turned it over, as a child falls into a grown-up's lap, as a puppy rolls over for stroking. She held his hand in both of hers. She touched his fingers, the nails and knuckles, the calluses and etched lines. He looked down at the helmet of honey of her hair; she was staring into his cupped right hand. "How did you do this, Harry?" Her finger traced the several scars at the base of his thumb—the short, raised, three-part vertical one that ran from the thumb's second joint on the underside, and the wider, longer one, parallel to his lifeline, raised too, and white, reminding him, as he looked down past her hair at it to see what she saw, of a mountain range on a photographic survey such as the senator received with intelligence reports. The Urals, he thought to say to her, the Apennines. But her voice was too sad. "Harry?"

He said, "It was a fund raiser. We were doing his reelection rounds, and kissing ass someplace on Long Island Sound, and I was getting tired of smiling. You know? When your face begins to hurt? I was inside—it was all too salty and healthy and everyone in blue blazers and white twill outside, so I had come inside to see how much whiskey I could get into a glass. Something. I don't remember. And there was this couple there. Nothing special. He was nothing special. He was a kind of short, stocky little guy with a belly and hips. You know, doing the gravity shift into middle age. He was all sunburned and he had a bushy gray beard. Nothing else distinctive. Bald, chunky, shrimp sauce on his checked shirt. And he was there with his wife. She looked like you. She reminded me of you. They didn't know I was in there. See, the senator and all the other touchies and feelies were outside. And they were backed into the farthest corner of the room, the darkest place they could find. She was leaning against the wall, and I could see her face. He was about at a three-quarter view. And he was holding her hand, and he was kissing her fingers, one at a time. And she looked into his eyes and she took his hand and, one at a time, she slid each of his fingers all the way into her mouth and then out. Very slowly. And I turned around and slammed the damned patio door open with my hand."

"It broke?"

"It wasn't supposed to swing. It slid. Which could be somebody's epitaph, couldn't it? There was a really unbelievable amount of blood, and thirty-seven stitches, and I think I killed their Iranian carpet, and the senator thought seriously about firing me because Mrs. Talliaferro told him to. She's the power behind the whatsit."

She looked at him, and then down toward his hand. She bent

to it, and she kissed the larger scar. He felt as if someone were gently touching, with one finger, the naked bottom of his foot, pulling the nail across it from the toe down to the heel.

"So I can feel it now," she said.

"What, Cath?"

"Some of what I missed. I can touch it when I want to."

"Do you want to?"

"Yes."

"Do you want to do anything more?"

"Yes."

But he knew her. "And will you?"

"No."

"Because of Carter," he said.

"Harry, isn't that *right*?"

He was afraid to lose her touch, but he stepped back.

"What?" she said.

"We have to do the dishes, right?"

"Bobby did them. Most of them."

"So we have to do the rest."

"No," she said. "I think we have to talk."

"Yeah," he said, "except I think I already told you everything I know. And I think I'm afraid of what you might say."

She folded her hands. Her legs were parallel, and her feet were flat on the floor. "I'm sorry I hit you," she said. "It's how frightened *I* was."

He nodded.

"You sleep in Randy's room," she said. "If you would like to."

"I'm going to work while I'm here. Senator work. Whore work. I know you'd like it better if I had stayed with the *News*, moved up to the *Times*, say, or one of the news magazines. TV."

"I don't think they're necessarily, at all, less whorey. Anyway, who am I to judge like that? And I'm glad you like your work, and that there's stuff for you to do. I go to work every day. We can cook together, if you like. Eat dinner. You know. You'll be a houseguest. A houseguest who's an old-time friend."

"Is that what I get to be?"

"Harry. Let's see."

"*You* talk straight, Cath. Let's see *what?*"

"Oh, God," she said. "I have no idea."

"So now—"

"So now," she said, "we're going to sleep. I'm going. I'm leaving the chair, this room, and the first floor. Lock the doors, please, and turn off the light, and maybe you want to tell Bobby you'll be sleeping next door to him. We won't kiss good night. We won't shake hands or hug. Understand? No more talking and no more touching. I'll wake you up from outside your door in the morning. I'll call you in time for coffee and toast. I'm going, Harry. Good night. Good—" She walked so quickly, he thought of ducks, and he snorted his laughter. She waved her hand without turning.

"Good night," he said after her. "Good night in the same house."

He heard her pause on the stairs. She said, "You're very close to too damned sentimental to live, Harry."

"And patient," he said.

The stairs creaked beneath her. "More like hungry," she said.

Harry nodded as she went up. He nodded so happily, his neck ached harder where Catherine had slapped him into breathing.

In his station wagon, driving in the dark, Carter was in a fever. He thought that his cheeks would never cool, and that his breathing would not stop clawing at his chest from inside, that he would not be able to stop repeating, in his highest cruel whine, what she had said, then what he had said.

"Don't go too far away," he said in Catherine's low voice, always husky but now, in his imitation, a joke about seduction.

And then he drove the blade home by sniveling what he had said—had *begged*—in reply: "Truly?"

He leaned on the horn, he jammed the gas pedal down and swiveled through cutbacks on a steep dirt road he'd taken at random, blowing invisible dust behind him, but knowing it was there in the darkness, and thinking, as he drove from nowhere to nowhere inside his headlights, that it spumed up and back like an artery cut and pumping. It was a big, soft-cushioned, lolloping Ford Crown Victoria station wagon, and its rear end felt thirty seconds behind the front end as he steered. But it was the front end that betrayed him, finally, as he flashed past dark farmhouses and dense evergreen forests, driving deeper into the Chenango valley on roads that, in two months, would be sealed by snow to all but four-wheel-drive trucks. The front tires seemed to chatter. Carter thought: Shale. The nose got away from him. The instant his control lapsed, his rage died, and he knew how fast he was going—not the actual speed in miles per hour, but in relation to the darkness, and the size of the long, wide car, the narrowness of the road, and its slithery surface. And then, like the duck or rabbit in the kids' cartoon who takes a walk on a cliff and then off it, but doesn't fall because he doesn't know the ground is gone, Carter felt the front end take over, and he held onto the wheel, bracing his elbows against the collision, and then in the darkness he shut his eyes.

But he was driven by the Ford and by chance between stripped maples and hard lean birch. He hit brush, he drove directly over a stump and didn't blow the tire—he felt the wagon tilt up and to the right before it settled—and he ran over dead leaves and big rocks, burst through rotted fallen trees and came out a hundred yards, it must have been, downhill from the road, to stand still in a brightly moonlit meadow in a stalled-out car, shaking and gobbling for his breath, still holding onto the steering wheel as if he'd any vestige of control over anything at all. He smelled the ammo-

71

nia of his urine on his pants. He smelled the dark foulness of the
sweat he'd poured up and that lay on his skin now like oil. As he
sat and listened to his chest working, something on the car and
underneath—an exhaust pipe, maybe, or the whole muffler—
dropped with a soft metal plopping to the ground. He shoved at
the key and pressed on the gas, and the wagon started. It growled
what must have been an indecent noise in this meadow in the
middle of nowhere. Muffler, he thought. No more than ten or
fifteen yards away was the remnant of a farm road, now no more
than a track. He steered for it, and the car went, although its
motion was hard; Carter figured that he'd blown out the shock
absorbers. He couldn't steer straight, but he could more or less go
in a general direction. That was all the specificity he needed, he
thought, so he went in several general directions—along the track,
and past a collapsed small hops barn, and up the hill, far more
gradually than he'd descended it, and toward his house.

He didn't know where it was yet, lost as he was, but he would
find it. His sense of direction had always eventually been adequate. He leaned forward to check his watch against the car clock
in the glow of his dashboard instruments. It was not eleven yet.
He'd done a lot of damage in a little time. His wrists ached from
the impact of the hits he'd taken from stumps and stones and
Christ knows what. But something had blessed his dark descent.
It must be the luck of the very stupid, he thought.

He wondered if they'd gone to bed. *"Truly?"* Oh, you sucker,
he thought. That's what comes of trafficking with older women.
They had joked, when they went fishing and she stood in water
she didn't want to be in so his pulse rate could come down, that
they should have been doing something for *her*: she was the forty-
one-year-old, and he was the kid who wouldn't turn forty for
months. Nothing older about that bitch, he thought. See her
crack the whip, and usher you out the fucking door because her
girlhood bang came back with his little pot beginning to sneak up

at his pants, and that soft dead skin around the chest. He probably bought oversized sport coats, and the little salesmen diddled him and cooed about his big strong chest. But Carter worked out in gyms and spent his summer days on job sites with shirtless men, often shirtless himself, burning on the job and drinking beer, and he knew what a muscle was, and what was pods of fat. Maybe she could buy him a training bra.

Yes. And who was driving a half ton of dents held together with luck and dead leaves? And who was playing pajama party at Catherine's house? Sleazy politician gofer to a sleazy politician—liberal, of course—who always looked like someone had stolen his bottle while he slept. Except, he thought, you're the one who peed himself, huh? You're the one, not Harry. *You* get to go back to a house that has for its major claim to fame no sheets on any bed on any day of the year. He groaned for the bareness he was driving toward, if he had chosen the right county road, because he knew every sheet that Harry might be sleeping on tonight.

He had bought the house because a man should live in a house, he'd thought, and because his alimony payments had all but made it impossible for him to afford one. I will rise, he had thought, when her second-rate country lawyer set on his cheap round maple conference table her list of what the lawyer called "requirements." She had permitted him to keep the white wood toilet seat, but not the one of dark stained oak. He had read her list and had told himself, as if he were a battered army or an ousted king or someone nailed on a cross of creosoted four-by-fours, I will rise. And he had borrowed money, hoisted prices, worked on too many jobs at once—he'd even pushed on a backhoe for a rival in Oneida, driving the dark roads through Bear Pass in the late afternoons to collect on time-and-a-half contracts for nightwork under lights. He'd sold her his rights in their house, and he'd taken the money to her lawyer and had given him $2600 for convincing his client, Carter's ex-wife, to take a lump cash payment in lieu of support. Carter had suspected he'd skimmed some more before passing along the money, but he'd only enjoyed the prospect of her being cheated, she, with her bright hair, who had cheated with a number of men, some of them in his employ, and—she'd made a point of telling him this at the end—who had never once dreamed of him in their three married years.

He had met Catherine when she'd furnished the art for a local motel that HarJoe had built. Carter had gone to the opening because his firm, the firm of a man who had risen, was the principal contractor for all the parking and delivery areas, and HarJoe was rewarding him for coming in on time. He was pulling into his dirt-and-gravel drive, which he'd never had time to blacktop, in front of his house. It was lightless, and it looked squat and mean and scary under the maples that broke up the night's bright moonlight. He sat in his car in his urine-soaked trousers and he thought of standing with a drink and trying to make sense of a painting over a sofa in the motel lobby. The woman in a tan linen suit said, "*Mutter mit drei Kindern*, Kokoschka. It's a lithograph. I thought all the white would work here, with so much snow outside, so much of the time, and the dark leather furniture. You think? And it keeps a softness, even though he's made so many verticals in the top half."

" 'Mother with Three Children'?" Carter asked.

"You know the picture?"

"German grandmother. She was always counting the cost of stuff, and she was always talking about mothers and kids."

"I'm Catherine Hollander. I sold them the art. You know, picked it out and framed it."

"The art contractor."

She'd laughed, a big laugh with clean, tall teeth and lips that tried to cover them. He'd liked the contradiction of such opposite motions. "Yes," she'd said, "exactly—the art contractor. And you?"

"The blacktop contractor."

"Oh," she'd said. "Oh. You mean"—and she'd pointed as if toward what was outside—"the parking lot?"

He had nodded.

"Well, I parked in it tonight. Good. You know, it's—good: smooth, that lovely new smooth blackness. Good."

He'd told her, "This is the first time I got a critic's review of a job I did."

"I didn't mean—"

"No, I appreciate it. Keep it up."

"Mr.—I'm sorry."

"Carter."

"Mr. Carter."

"No: Carter Kreuss, but would you call me Carter."

"Catherine," she'd said, holding out a large hand that, when he shook it, was strong and met the pressure of his grip. She looked him in the eye the way women in business did, refusing to be other than malelike on meeting men in professional circumstances.

He was at his door, somehow hoping that he'd lost the key, but of course it was on the ring with his car keys. Something called from the woods around the house, and then it rustled and flapped—maybe an owl, he thought, and maybe a vampire. He pointed at his own long neck with a forefinger, and he called, in the direction of the forest as he pointed, "Here. Sink 'em in right here. Drink all you want. We're serving *everyone* tonight." He let himself in, refusing to turn a light on, refusing to see what he knew he would find: bare floors, a single sofa from the HarJoe office lounge, discarded, and a black-and-white television set with a screen too small to see. Upstairs there were two bedrooms, with old mattresses on the floor. The one downstairs had a Sears, Roebuck bed made of so-called Tiger Maple, which he knew to be a painted veneer—he liked being tricked by Sears, and he liked his knowing it. In the bathroom downstairs there were two towels; one he used as a mat outside the narrow metal shower stall, and

75

one he used for drying off, and every once in a while he swapped their functions, and when their grayness bothered him, he'd sworn for months, he would wash them. He'd told Catherine that the house wasn't furnished because he'd never had time. And that was why, when they made love, and at first they'd done that a lot, they rocked on Catherine's bed and never on his.

So in his kitchen, between the stove and the washing machine, Carter set water on to boil—he'd found the kettle by feel—and then stripped to throw his pants and suit coat, white shirt, rayon tie, his underwear and socks, into the washer. He fumbled in the cupboard over the washing machine and knocked down tuna fish and tinned soup until he found the high glass jar of instant coffee. He remembered that it was nearly empty, and shaking the jar confirmed his memory. Standing naked, smelling the hot hard water, the swampy earth cellar underneath the kitchen, its stale breath leaking up through the old pine floorboards, he poured the barely boiling water into the coffee jar—he sprinkled water on his stomach and penis, and he bellowed, "Of fucking *course*!"—and he sloshed the water in the jar and tilted it back and sipped. "Dagwood comes home," he told the dark, still house. "Hey," he called, "Blondie! It's me!"

The bedroom he used was off the kitchen; these, along with the small parlor and the bathroom grown mossy and dank, made up the whole downstairs. Except for the kitchen, the floors all had linoleum rugs of a uniform and murky brown. Even in the dark, he thought, he could see them, islands surrounded by wood gone pulpy and the color of old people's skin. Old white people, he reminded himself, you racist. For old *brown* people, you would have to check out the HarJoe job site, of course. Although the tap was off, he thought he could still smell the water, rank, sulfurous, pumped from the shallow well in his earthen cellar, reeking and possibly poisonous and, like the house, exactly what he had sought. It was a place for penance and imprisonment. He knew he'd wanted it, and even now, unsure why, he was as satisfied as if he stood in the gentle light of a clean room inside a sound building.

Moonlight found its way to his brain, and he could see, now, in the darkness of his house. On the table, where he set his instant-coffee jar, lukewarm and bitter and not that bad really, he thought, he saw the cereal bowl and the box he didn't remember leaving there after some breakfast of days before. He was sure that creatures of uncertain species did backfloats in what milk he'd left in the dish, and that in the box itself there were by now high-rise creature apartments from which they commuted each morning to the bowl. In the morning he would sweep them all inside a plastic garbage bag. "You guys enjoy your night, now," he said. He reached out to the dish drainer and took the big aluminum stock pot he'd used, apparently, some days before, and he slammed it down on top of the box and bowl, crushing the box a little, but imprisoning all within. "Remember," he said pleasantly, "this is a hard-hat job."

Naked, but in his shoes again, he waved good night to the room, as if he were drunk. And, a white long shape in the general dimness, he walked through the short hall, then through the little parlor with its linoleum oval, and into the bedroom he would use. It was small, with only one window and a little closet in which Carter had packed all sorts of suits and work gear, most of it clean, all of it neat, though dusty now, he suspected, and possibly inhabited by large organisms. In the bureau were clean socks and underthings, and shirts from the laundry, starched and folded. He did not fail to bathe or shampoo, and he shaved with care and wore clean clothes. If he chose to live in a way that reminded him of certain elements of his life, he did so in such a manner as to give no offense, he thought, considering what he did and how, as though he were in the room beside Carter Kreuss, watching him, naked in his shoes, walk with stiff knees and braced shoulders, as

77

if he were drunk but all too sober, to stand beside the imitation Tiger Maple bed, and then fall face down upon it, on damp blankets which, in daylight, would be the color of old bologna drying in an uncleaned refrigerator. He saw, as he lay there, his white round legs with calf muscles thick from standing on sites, and his fairly well-muscled back, his long arms spread out as if he dreamed of flight.

Looking down on Carter Kreuss, he thought of the first words spoken to him by his mother: "No, I'm just amazed that you managed to *find* me." He thought of Catherine in her house, introducing Randy and Bobby: "There are my boys." He remembered how her hand, hanging in the air, indicated her sons and then moved to sweep their attention to him; he remembered their manners—the step forward, the shake of the hand, the nod and smile—how all of it, which seemed to him to be about her connection to them, choked his throat solid and nearly drove him out. But he had stayed, as much because of them-and-her as because of Catherine alone. And then he had stayed for her. And, at last, he'd stayed there *with* her, feeling the lurch and panic and pleasure as he hadn't since early in his college days, at the State University College of New York at Oneonta, when the first girl with big breasts and a beige smile who'd been kind to him in class won his puppy allegiance for a month. He couldn't remember her name. He knew he always thought it was Jean, but he suspected it might have been Jane. Her last name had been Rimers, though his roommate had called her—what else?—Reamers. He had actually carried her books to class from the dormitory on the heights over town. He had said to himself, and often, "I'm in *love*." He had wrapped her in the gauze of his devotion, she'd told him in the poem she sent by way of breaking it off. *The gauze of your devotion.* At first, he'd assumed *gauze* was a typo for *gaze*. Eventually, he consulted his roommate's paperback dictionary, and gauze had been what he'd come to fear it really was. The poem had gone on for several stanzas about mummies and breathing, suffocation and an overall thank-you-but-no-thanks, good-bye. He had waited, over the past few weeks, for Catherine to say something about gauze. He had to wonder, Carter saw the prone Carter Kreuss thinking, whether Harry's arrival in June for that crazy hit-and-run dinner visit hadn't actually prolonged Carter's life in her life. He wondered whether she'd wanted him around to show Harry she wasn't alone. There were all kinds of spite and anger and overall *demonstration* going on between them, he thought. And that was not fair to Carter Kreuss, Carter thought as he studied himself.

His arms ached from bracing himself. He was sore, as if beaten. He *was* beaten, he thought. He giggled for the pun, and pushed his face into the flat pillow. In the morning, he would have to do a wash. He would have to buy a bath towel or two, and scrub down the kitchen. The Carter Kreuss who watched him walked on stiff legs to the bed and lay down on Carter Kreuss as if he made love to him. Carter moved his pelvis with its thick limp cock on the bed. Carter was on him now, thigh to thigh and chest to back and groin to ass. Carter moved as if stimulated by the return of himself. But he wasn't, he knew. Though, on the other hand, he just might have to suffice.

She loved her bedroom. Its floor was of wide old softwood planks, frayed and gaping so that at one point she looked down past the joists and through the seam of downstairs ceiling sheet-rock to see the kitchen lights. Over her head, the ceiling curved softly so that the plaster tucked neatly over the headboard. When she lay beneath that ceiling arch, on cold sheets and underneath her comforter, she felt as though she were in a tent. She felt as she had first felt in one of Harry's flannel shirts, and as she'd felt in one of Carter's pima cotton business shirts with the sleeves rolled up and the tails hanging to her knees: insulated, cozy, surrounded. And the best difference between these bedclothes and the clothing of those men was that this particular hiding place was all hers. Even when Carter stayed over—and how long ago was that? how long would it be?—she thought of it as *her* bed, *her* comforter, *her* room.

She was too excited, or too exhausted, or too much some of each, to sleep. She lay in the dark, wanting explicitly not to read, wanting no one else's thoughts or needs. She heard Drown rock himself into position on the lowest step, then pitch himself up, and then along the hallway corridor to Bobby's room. She heard him lay his big hard head against the door a few times, and then she heard the click of the latch, and then its closing, and silence. She loved to listen to her house at night, especially when Randy was home: the deep soughing; Bobby's more typical snore; Carter, when he was over, buzzing and humming like one of his huge yellow leveling machines at idle. And then, beneath them, she would hear Drown's nails on the wall as he turned on his back in his sleep with his goofy head hanging off the smelly cedar chip bed they'd bought him. She knew which windows rattled in which wind, and what shutter needed tin screws to affix it to their old aluminum siding. She could tell by which floorboard's creaking who had wakened to pee.

But tonight she heard her own voice, shrieking—what a harridan she must have become!—to tell the man to go home who had come so far, and for so long, to steal her from Carter, for certain, and maybe herself. And she heard his deep rumble of a chastened voice, a combination of bewildered boy and angry man at once, as he waited—the tension in his tones kept speaking to her of the wait—to discover from her and himself what to do. She couldn't imagine that his job would wait forever, although he seemed to have more leeway with it than employment she'd heard of. And that Mrs. Toll-whatever, who'd wanted him fired for bleeding on contributors: she wouldn't help. She thought of him watching the woman place her lover's fingers, one at a time, deep in her mouth. She saw him jam his palm ferociously to swing the door that didn't swing. At the start of their knowing one another, he'd have written to tell her about it. He'd have sent her a note in blood instead of ink, or would have pressed his bloody stitches to the bottom of the page below his signature. She wrinkled her face against the sight of his hand. So would he really stay here? And for how long? And what would he achieve? She was not about to be carried off in a rented car.

She turned onto her back. She never slept for long on her back. So she was setting herself for a long night's waking, she thought. But here she was accepting the given: *Given that Harry will stay*. When you accept the given, the argument has a chance to persuade you. Here she was, surrendering to the son of a bitch in a different room down the hall—except he wasn't. She heard the kitchen light, and the soft board near the sink which she had personally cut and fitted and nailed into place, and which always sounded like branches over a pane of glass in a horror movie. He was downstairs—feeding, probably. He'd grown puffier, a little, since he'd crashed and stumbled in last June. He was unhappy, therefore eating; she knew his habits, and she knew—it wasn't flattery: he'd all but told her so—why he saddened and ate. Lovers are supposed to starve and fade away, Harry; you grow round with despair. I grow round with mere *inconvenience*, he'd tell her, she thought, and she hated the smile that went all across her face.

And there was poor Carter, in a trailer at the site, probably drinking with the security man. Maybe drinking at some shabby bar. Screwing a local hooker in revenge. Damn it, woman, that's in movies, she scolded. And who has to think about screwing right away. You sound like some man.

She heard a sound that startled her. It wasn't the refrigerator's sticky door gasket, or its click or thump. It was the pantry light. So he was about ten feet south of her now, not directly beneath her, in the old narrow pantry with its cupboards and its zinc counter. What was there? Tuna fish for midnight snacks? Instant coffee? Was he looking for something stronger to drink? He'd seen where she kept it, in the kitchen, under the far counter, near the phone. And then she heard a lighter sound, a zipper being pulled. Was he stripping down in the pantry, she wondered. Did he need clean clothes? She identified the zipper, then: hers, on the pocket in her purse.

Harry was in her purse. She envisioned the bare bulb in the ceiling of the pantry, and the shadow it made of his thick arm in the mouth of her worn, beloved Coach bag. She heard objects tumbling to the zinc. He was searching her. He was seeing who she was. He was looking for clues. It had nothing to do with theft, at least in the usual way: Harry was honest, and he'd never take from her—not, anyway, something so unimportant as cash or coin. Surely—he had said so tonight—he would plunder her of all the Catherine he could gather against his body with his big hands. She rolled her head back and wiped at her neck. Why sweat, dammit? She thought of him pondering on the half-used pack of Life Savers; had he known that she ate them as others chewed gum? And there were allergy pills in their scratched, cloudy brown plastic vial; he would wonder at the medicine, and at the secrets in her cells. And the ring of keys, she thought— wouldn't Harry want to know where each one slid? Her night-gown was tucked above her knees, and she pulled its hem down as far as she could reach and turned on her side. It was like having someone's hand on you, she thought, seeing his arm in the mouth of the purse. Or *in* you, if you were pornographic. She turned onto her stomach, and she pressed her legs together. She put her arms on either side of the pillow and spread them wide to reach each side of her big bed. She spread her legs a little, and then she swung them shut. You're so easy, she thought. First guy comes back into your life after twelve years, swearing pillage, loot, and rape, and you go weak for him. Her forehead was against the pillow, and she felt like a medieval criminal, tied between young trees, their branches pegged to the ground by ropes that, once cut, would let them spring in opposite directions. Talk about being torn, she thought, and she started to giggle. She tried to think of Randy at school, being a little man, but that didn't help; he wasn't little, he nearly was a man, and he'd be fairly good at it. She thought of Carter in his suit, of how *excised* he must feel, and she shook her head. The giggling got worse. Harry came to mind—surprise!—and she laughed out loud into the pillow. The ones who make you laugh are dangerous, she thought.

She fell asleep to the gentle sounds of a man investigating how to love her—whom to love—illicitly at night inside her house, and welcomed in, she admitted, by her. And she woke to noises, too, surprised that she remembered no bad dreams, no frightened wakings. Downstairs, Bobby was making coffee for Harry, and cooking eggs. The best Bobby could do, with a tail wind and good visibility, was open Drown's kibble sack. But here he was, pouring something thick and sandy and coffee-colored for Harry to drink. And here was Harry, in the shirt and slacks he'd clearly slept in, smiling for Bobby and sipping and talking, without once sighing for the pain that what he swallowed must have given him. Bobby was wearing an old shirt that said GEORGETOWN inside a basketball. She wondered if Harry suspected that a Washington team's logo was as close as Bobby could come to wearing Harry's uniform. Poor Carter, she thought as she walked barefoot into the kitchen and sat without words after kissing Bobby's cheek.

Bobby said, "Harry, can I get you anything else?"

"I love the eggs, and I love the ketchup. I'm coffee'd up, and I'm happy. Thank you, Bobby."

"Would you excuse Mom and me for a minute?"

Harry raised his brows and nodded his head. He still hadn't looked at Catherine.

She said, "How'd you sleep? All right?"

"Happily," he said, looking at her. He blushed. She thought maybe she did too.

"Where?"

"I ended up on the sofa. It was more—I don't know—"

"Like an overnight guest," she said. "You're not indecent."

He inclined his head. "You're all right, too," he said.

"Excuse us, then? Bobby wants me."

And what he wanted, in the living room, his breath fresh with toothpaste and his face gleaming, which meant that he'd been up early and worrying, was to ask her a question. He put his big hands down to reach her shoulders, and he leaned over and into her face. "Mom," he said. "Look. How's this gonna be with, you know, Carter?"

"Baby," she said, "are things feeling shaky?"

His face closed down. He shook his head. "I just wondered what you were doing."

"It must be strange, this man coming in all of a sudden."

"It's *Harry*, Mom. And it isn't strange. Half of my friends' mothers have different boyfriends moving in and out all the time."

"Bobby!"

He stood back and put his hands in his pockets. His mouth was puckered, petulant. She needed to get her arms around his broad back and hold him *in* for a minute, but as she stepped toward him, he retreated. She raised a hand in surrender.

"I thought I'd ask," he said. "That's all."

I am not a snapper bringing men home every night from Legion halls, she wanted to holler at him. I am your mother with her *life* going on, and I'm trying my goddam best to get you in it and keep you safe there. *Dammit.* He was watching her carefully, she knew, and wondered if he could read those thoughts. "As you should, baby. As you should. I don't know what's happening with Carter. He's unhappy, right now."

"Because Harry came."

"Yes."

"And Harry's staying?"

"He's a houseguest, Bobby. You know what I mean?"

"He isn't your boyfriend. Like Carter."

"If that's what Carter is. Bobby: I am making no moves without talking to you, understand? It's you and me and Randy first and in the middle and last. Understand?"

"Randy doesn't even call," Bobby said.

"Oh, baby, you are feeling all of it, aren't you? Let me hug you, Bobby. Please?" And before he could answer she had rushed him, had gotten her arms over his shoulders and onto his head and had tugged him down into a kiss. She kept him surrounded that way, and he let her.

"I have to get more coffee for him," he said.

"I'll do it, sweetie."

"Mom, I'm trying to make him feel *welcome*!"

"God, I love you. You know how much I love you, Bobby?"

He said, "Of course," preceding her into the kitchen.

So she watched Harry slide undercooked scrambled eggs and ketchup onto overdone toast—at least his second, and maybe his third, helping. He sipped at the coffee and kept his grimacing in check. Catherine drank gritty coffee—the filter must have burst under Bobby's hard hands—and wished, as she hadn't wished in years and years, for the first bite at the lungs of a morning's unfiltered cigarette. Bobby slammed Harry casually on the back, nearly undoing him, as he left the room to dress for school after what would be a twenty-minute shower. He chewed, and she sipped, and then he sipped—he moaned aloud at the coffee—and then she sipped some more.

Finally, Harry looked up. He put his coffee mug on the table. He looked into her eyes as people did when they made meaningful statements. He said, "Catherine. It was good for me. Was it good for you?"

And she spurted coffee onto the table and down the front of her blue robe. She tried to set the coffee mug down on the table and missed it. She heard it break as she lay back in her seat, helpless, all but choking to death on his joke.

Harry was behind her, and, it seemed, on his knees. He was

locking his arms around the chair and her belly and was pulling back in short, painful compressions—the Heimlich maneuver. She swatted, flailing behind her, until she caught the side of his head. She hoped it wasn't the ear she'd slammed the night before. She heard herself cry through her hooting laughter to the man behind her—suddenly she remembered them up on the hill, his hands so desperate at her breasts—"It's pleasure, Harry. *Fun!*"

She lay back in her seat, the laughter mostly gone, then. He stood slowly, grunting. "Is that all," he said. "Damn. I always wanted to save somebody's life."

Catherine bent to retrieve the handle of the mug and what fragments she could find in the puddle of grounds and tepid water. She said, "You never do know."

He was back down, now, using his hands as shovels, and recovering shards. She wanted to warn him not to cut himself, but she was years late, she thought. And she grew sad, as someone in a hot sun grows cold when clouds cut off the sky.

The telephone rang. It would be Carter. Harry seemed to know it too. He said, "I won't offer to get that for you."

When she drove to work later, after waving to Bobby and Harry at the Mustang in which Bobby was getting a maximum-prestige lift to school, she thought of herself face down on her bed, forehead in the pillow, arms to each side, her legs beginning to separate. I slammed them back together, she thought. As if that was all this all's about. She shook her head, violently, and not because of her mind's-eye sight of herself in bed, in the dark, while Harry Miller rummaged. She was thinking, she realized, not about that, now, or about wherever it was that Carter woke to tear up trees and move small mountains of earth. She was remembering the last time Harry had sailed full speed at their lives, and she had left the house: when she'd come home, he had been gone. And she'd expected it, then, and even had welcomed the absence, she'd decided. Here she went again . . .

"I'm sorry," Carter had said on the phone.

"I am too."

"We have to talk about this."

"Whatever *this* is."

"I think that's something you're going to have to tell me."

"If I *knew*."

"*I* sure as hell don't. Is he there?"

"In the house?"

"Yes, dammit. Of course."

"Yes."

"And—"

"And *what*, Carter?"

"Nothing."

"You bet."

"Wait," he'd said. "I don't have a right to know?"

"Know what?"

"Christ, you're working me over, Catherine."

"I shouldn't. I don't mean to be."

"But you don't mean to make it easy."

She'd shrugged and said, "Meet me for lunch at the Otesego. Can you get over? We can talk a while."

"Thank you," he'd said.

"Have *mercy*," she'd said, "you're making me feel like Raquel Welch."

. . . and this time, she thought, riding the back roads through West Edmeston, over the old wooden bridge, I would like it, three and a half hours before lunch with Carter, if Harry would be there when, after that lunch, and after work, I come home.

Chapter Three

BOBBY CAME out to the car, walking stiff-kneed, as if injured. Harry remembered that big kids walked that way when watched. Worrying about so much body on display must bind their muscles, he thought. Bobby pointed the way to the central high school, and Harry drove them, downshifting unnecessarily, every now and again, to give Bobby a little of the low murmur that seemed to be part of the fun of the car. The sun lay full on the windshield, and the sky was cloudless. Harry gathered himself inside his sweater against the cold, but Bobby sat with his jean jacket undone, T-shirt bared to the world, and he stared out the right-hand window. It took Harry several miles of dew-gleaming tan and gold landscape to understand that Bobby was staring into the off-side mirror on its outside mount. When he drew out a hairbrush and began to stroke, over and over, the mane that hung outside his collar, Harry looked away. When he was a kid, you didn't pick your nose or comb your hair in public, he remembered. On the other hand, you wore a tie to school every day, and your hair was so stiff with Wildroot that it didn't need to be combed.

"You hear much from Randy?"

"Not a lot."

"Miss him?"

"No. Sometimes a little."

"Talk much?"

Bobby shrugged, blushing, and Harry winced for the embarrassment he'd caused him. He remembered how he'd burned with a fever of *self* on the way to all the public exposure of his freshman year in high school. Everything, he thought he remembered, had been dangerous: walking in full view, standing up in class to get the room pass, navigating halls.

"I didn't mean to be a smart-ass," he said. "I was realizing how long ago I saw you. I really missed you, you know."

Looking into the mirror as they crested and then began the descent to the school in the valley, surrounded by yellow buses and the pickup trucks and long old cars of the students—faculty, more likely, Harry thought—Bobby said, "You were gone a long time. I didn't know you, did I?"

"I was gone a hell of a long time. A lot too long. And we did know each other. You just don't remember it. I wasn't all that important in your life."

"In Mom's."

"Yeah. We were friends when you were little. We were friends off and on."

Bobby nodded into the mirror.

"You want to ask me anything, kid?"

Bobby turned to him. He had little-boy's eyes in a man's face. His skin was smooth enough nearly to bring Harry's hand up, like a father's, he thought, to stroke with the back of his knuckles. "What's gonna happen?" Bobby asked. "Do you know?"

Looking at the road, at the wide, long, low cement school in its blacktop lot, looking at all the children, little and big, whose lives depended on the answers to such questions, Harry, slowing for the approach, said, "I'm sorry, kid. I don't."

Harry turned, then, but Bobby merely nodded as he let

89

door close and strode into the other world of the school. He waved without looking and stalked up the hillside walk that went to one of the doors. He was digested by the crowd of others. Harry felt as if the morning were bruised when he drove away. They aren't your kids, he reminded himself: you're not responsible for all of their life. But I would have been, he answered. I volunteered to be. And as far as they can tell, I deserted the only lives, their own, that make sense. You were meant to be a father, he told himself disgustedly. Don't you love the pain.

That goes double for any husband of hers. And look how hard you're volunteering for *that*.

Bobby had mumbled and pointed, suggesting how he get there, and Harry opened his window, brought in the calling of the crows and the cold steam of ground fog and dew going up into a hot-enough sun, and he drove to where he thought the shopping mall site would be. He went to a few wrong towns, and he ended up on a dirt road, once, that took him past a farmhouse inside a picket fence where a tall woman in white painter's overalls was standing in a side yard, her face to the sun, a cup of coffee in both hands, smiling up and listening to the day begin. He thought very seriously of stopping. Maybe she'd be unmarried and available. Maybe she loved politics and middle-aged men. Maybe they could raise sheep and sunflowers and send a sneering Christmas card each year to Catherine and Carter, or Catherine alone. He thought: Catherine alone. Then: Catherine and Harry. Why not? He sighed, raising dust behind him as he left the woman in her sun. And he did find his way, drifting south, finally finding the two-lane roads, picking his way through a town called Norwich, heading out toward Binghamton, though not that far.

It was hard to see the whole site because it was on the same level as the road, called U.S. 12. What he could see were mounds of stone and earth, tarpaulins covering equipment, porta-toilets of brightly colored plastic, row on row of trucks, two trailers near the road, and stacks of pipe, some stone and some metal. The dirt here was clay, red and hard, and its dust hung over the site in the sun like smoke reflecting its fire. Thirty acres of fire, he thought, looking at the little clipping from the *Times*, which reported on impact studies and a hearing and the protests of some historical society; the item had been dropped in the second edition, and all that Harry knew was in it: Carter, not named in the piece, was doing the parking lot for this mall, and somewhere beneath it were said to be the souls of the dead, wrapped in their soft bones, threatened by impending commerce. The protesters had no chance, he knew. By the time the papers were filed and a preliminary hearing held, the shop interiors would be almost completed. And too many people would have too much at stake—through honest investment, favors asked and done, bad money siphoned into bad and good men's hands—for any local officer of any law that any *pro bono* naif could argue about to reverse the construction of fifteen temples of fiscal citizenship and the all-important space for country shoppers to park their cars.

He could imagine the senator saying the words he might write: Our darker brothers and sisters lie here. They lie beneath the ground they wept and bled and died, yes, to reach. They were brought here by the ancestors of the strong, industrious men and women of Chenango County, a hundred and thirty years before. For this was the Underground Railroad, the freedom trail! Will we permit mere profit, which is not always our most admirable motive, as the history of this administration's cabinet officers will remind you—will we let profit motives disturb the rest, in freedom and peace, of those we fought a war to try to *save*? I think that you will not. I pray that you will not. I pledge you that I will do everything to let our brothers and our sisters rest in peace. It is the least this nation owes them. And we are an honorable nation. We always pay our debts.

Oddly enough, no one here would buy it, he thought. Or not that many. Up here, according to the studies, Harry knew, there were many millions who wondered about the propriety of giving the vote to women, Hispanics, and blacks. But it would play a little in Syracuse, and in Utica and Binghamton, and surely downstate. It would play in New York City. It would not win an election, if he did decide to run. But it would be a part of the picture. It would bite off nicely for television. And TV was most of the picture. Do you hear me, Catherine? How much do you hate me for it?

He found a packed earth road that ran along the northern edge of the site, up to a ridge where telephone trucks and huge spools of wire were parked. He looked down, through the burning dust, at giant vehicles that rolled jerkily back and forth. Men in bright yellow or tin-colored hard hats stood and waved at the drivers of enormous insect-shaped machines. He noticed for the first time the small scuttling vans and pickup trucks that beetled between sections of the site over roads laid out in raw earth. The red haze caught the light and made it look dirty. He rolled his window up.

In the file folder on the seat beside him, along with the little article about protesting locals, was a longer piece about Seneca Rocks, West Virginia. The federal government prohibited the violation of grave sites in its forest lands. He had thought to suggest to local lawyers that they call the feds in; now he thought that the senator should, but in either case it would do no good, and the cheesy bones beneath those machines were going to be ground into soft meal. The workmen would think they were walking on rotten wood, he thought. Even on this high ridge, even with his windows closed, the sound of the motors and of tree stumps groaning free, of half-ton blades moving mounds of earth from someplace to someplace else, was painful. He couldn't find the graveyard, and he didn't want to ask the men in hard hats for directions to the source of nothing but trouble for them. Nor did he want to consider any further what proportion of his visit—he would have to invent the perfect word for what he'd done, what he was doing—had to do with fled slaves' graves, and what was solely hers. *All*, he could tell her, and not lie.

What she mustn't do, though, in order that he keep on telling the truth that his trip was a fabrication for the office, an excuse to come not quite begging to her, was to ask him whether Carter was a part of it. For, according to what he'd heard in June, and the scrap of a phrase ("the contractor in question") that he'd seen in the *Times*, it was Carter who had to choose, not the owners of the land or renters of the stores. It was Carter who could go around the graves, or move them, or crush and cover what was left of buried headstones and crumbled coffins. And had Mr. Harry Miller, speechwriter and aide-de-camp (second to camp followers, he liked to not quite joke, in frequencies of senatorial penetration), dogged once-was and would-be lover, doggy rambler of Catherine's life, come here with hackles raised and tail erect, teeth starting to show, in order that he piss on Carter's post? Was he here to do what harm to Carter he could? And would Catherine see such motive as insult not merely to the man—you have got to say this, Harry—she probably loved (trouble enough), but doubly insulting to *her*, with its assumption that she'd be so easily parted from him.

Far too complicated, he thought, and it's best not to ask.

Don't ask me, Catherine.

He replaced the woman's letter in the folder with his clippings, and after looking at a map that offered no help at all, he put the car in gear and went in search of Mrs. Olivia Stoddard, Rural Delivery Route 2, Box AA, White Store Road, White Store, New York. It took him six stops at markets and gas stations—at four he ate: three hot dogs (flabby, undercooked, tasting vaguely of kerosene and what he thought might be mouse), two large pretzels (stale), what they called submarines (feeble heros with too little onion, barely any oil, luncheon meat of human foot), and a diet soda. At two o'clock in the afternoon, having driven a hundred miles, he estimated, and having peed three times in the woods, on a country road that left Route 8 near—sure enough—an old white store called White Store, in a hamlet called White Store, on a dirt

road named—what else?—the White Store Road, down a shallow
hill past an open red barn that seemed to hold only lawn mowers
and a long maroon car, he found a square low farmhouse shingled
over with dark-stained shakes.

Mrs. Stoddard was so lovely, he thought, in a driven way. Her
heavy hair lay down her back in a thick braid. It was reddish-
brown, and its color reminded him of sun through the earth over
the work site. She was short, and not quite chubby, so that beneath
her olive-drab cargo pants and white hightop sneakers and the
dark blue oversized Cub Scout shirt she wore, there was a lush-
ness that disturbed him. Her anger, so apparent on her compressed
lips and behind her wire-rimmed glasses in her dark eyes, seemed
somehow to be at odds with the generosity of her hips and breasts.
She was small but large, pinched but generous; she was confusing.

She said, "That's a rude inspection, Mr. Miller. I don't know
if I'm letting you into the house, now. Do you have some credentials you can show me? People do anything, these days. And you
just *looked* at me like that!"

"Mrs. Stoddard, I apologize. I think it was the Cub Scout shirt.
Excuse me. And here"—he pushed his wallet forward—"my pass
to the Office Building, and the Senate. Here. I'm really sorry.
Wait a minute, I have your letter in the car—"

She was shaking her head. "No," she said, "I should apologize
to you. Dressing like this—well, I didn't know you were coming,
did I? Not today. Not this week. I thought nobody would come
after the letter I wrote. I lose my temper a lot."

"Are you a den mother?" Harry asked. "I was a Cub Scout."

"No." She shook her head. She moved back so that he could
enter. "No, we don't have children, and I didn't want to take care
of other people's scouts. I mean, that's just baby-sitting."

He nodded, walking past her and standing in the little foyer
with its marble-pattern black-and-white squares of linoleum.

"The sitting room, I think," she said, and walked springily, on
the balls of her feet, to the left, where, in a tiny living room, on

94

dreadful furniture, they sat. She kept her knees together, slightly sideways, perching on a deacon's bench. He sat in a Windsor chair where he all but held his breath, fearing to shatter it with motion, much less his weight. The rugs were rag, the paintings dark and ugly primitives, the walls an apple green with maroon stencils, and the television set clearly hidden inside a large dry sink with modern hinges, oversized doors, and a coaxial cable snaking from its rear to the leaded window behind it.

"A beautiful room," he said. "You're a collector?"

"I just like authenticity," she said. "I check credentials on everybody and everything."

"Are you D.A.R., Mrs. Stoddard?"

She smiled. "Are you Jewish, Mr. Miller?"

"I'm the senator's aide."

"Then I'm your woman," she said. When she smiled, she looked desperate. When she frowned, she looked pleased to be disapproving. He noticed the downiness of her little cheeks. "My husband always says that: 'I'm your man.' Somebody offers to buy him a drink at the country club, or one of our functions, and he laughs and tells them, 'I'm your man.' I always wanted to say that. He's going to be president of the bank. It has eleven branches, ten of them very, very rural."

"Money's money," Harry said, a little quickly. "Town or country, upstate or down." He nodded, as if he'd said something coherent.

So did Mrs. Stoddard.

"So can we prove it, Mrs. Stoddard? That there are fifty-seven graves from the time of the influenza epidemic of—when was it?"

"Eighteen sixty-four, the winter. But we aren't *sure* it was flu. The locals who heard it from their great-grandparents *think* they called it the plague. I have two still alive who heard about it, and there are three mentions in local histories—you know, those awful manuscripts people place in local libraries in towns like these? Everybody called it the plague. So it could have been smallpox. It

could have been *measles*. We always specialized in killing aborigi-
nal peoples with measles, after all. If I were black, I think I'd call
it the honky disease."

"No," he said, smelling her for the first time. "I'd call that, with
apologies to your husband, ma'am, I'd call Western civilization
by that particular name." She wore a heavy larding of deodorant,
he realized, something he remembered from locker rooms in lesser
places, gyms in small-town schools where he and the senator had
shot baskets in lieu of running in bad weather. It was a cheap,
highly perfumed drugstore deodorant, and she'd laid it on so
heavily that its sweet synthetic scent mixed with her sweat came
up each time she moved. He imagined the Cub Scout shirt was
laden with the musk of thickly haired armpits and unwashed
breasts and four-dollar cologne named something like Dawn to
Dusk. He had an astonishingly hard erection, he discovered, and
his mind returned to the sweat of her breasts, the hair beneath
her short arms. I'll be fucking wounded deer on highways, he
thought, stray cats; dear Lord, protect me from this thing between
my legs.

"—local registries, of course, so it's mostly traditional wisdom
we're working with. Are you all right, Mr. Miller?"

"Harry," he said, despising himself. "Yes. I flashed back to my
Cub Scout days. It must be the shirt."

She actually sat up straighter. "I'm glad you like it," she said,
smiling her angry tight smile. "My husband disapproves. He isn't
such a"—she hesitated—"square, do you know, disliking the shirt
because of his position in the community and so forth. It rather
turns him on, if you don't mind my saying so. Men seem drawn
to women who dress up. Have you noticed that? No. It's—Harry.
My grandfather *and* the head of the color guard in high school
were both named Harry. It's such a straightforward name. Harry.
Actually, though, I think Perry, that's my husband's name, Perry
gets jealous. He wants me more demure in front of strangers.
What do you think?"

He sneered at himself as he said, "I'm grateful that you held out for your point of view, Mrs. Stoddard."

"Olivia. And thank you."

He nodded and smiled. He thought he *probably* wouldn't think of it as simpering, later, when he drove away remembering this dark, juicy plum of a woman with her angry face and the smell of secrets.

"Would you like something to drink, Harry?"

"No," he said, "thanks, but I'm really fine."

"A martini," she said. "I've some Boodles gin." And she was up and on her way to mix their drinks, swaying her ass while she walked on her toes. Harry studied rotations.

"Olivia," he called, as she was nearly out the door.

She stopped and turned. For an instant, her face was a girl's.

"Do you always wear your hair in a braid?"

"What a sweet question," she said, turning to walk more slowly away.

And at five o'clock, they sat side by side on the highly polished deacon's bench, drinking martinis she had set on a tray on top of the lacquered wooden trunk with iron stays that was her coffee table. The top three buttons of her Cub Scout shirt were undone, and her shoes were off. Harry's shirt was sweaty, but he kept his buttons done. His cotton sweater lay across his lap. Beside the gin and ice was a sheaf of scribbled-on newsprint, photocopies of old books, smudgy light carbon copies and memos on Olivia Stoddard's pale blue personal stationery. The small, furious woman believed in what she spoke of, Harry knew by then, and she was a compost of odors. He kept sniffing to be sure he was right about the sharp, acrid richness of her. He had given up moving away on the bench from the pressure of her short, warm, rounded thigh.

"Men and women and children," she said. "What children weren't suffocated on the way by people desperate only to keep them quiet. They were trying to save their lives, not take them. Peterboro, Norwich, East Hamilton. Arriving singly and in pairs, almost never as whole families. Waiting to learn if husbands and wives had made it. Mates. Whatever you want to call it. It doesn't *matter* what you want to call it, or what I want to call it, or what the disgusting, arrogant Salaparuta Construction Company wants to call it, or what the HarJoe Management Associates want to call it. Those people fled here looking for new lives. People distantly associated with my family drove the wagons, some of them, that brought those men and women and two dead babies. We *know* about them! I've *read* about them! They came under the floorboards of wagons and in provision barrels. Here. They came for refuge. Men and women were burned with hot pitch and raped and castrated and buried alive. The lucky ones were shot and even sometimes brought to trial. Just to get those human beings here. It doesn't matter whether they were legally married or not." He shook his head, bewildered by her caring. "No. That's right. I keep thinking of their hands. They must have been hard hands, how could they help but be? Settling onto the babies' faces to keep them quiet so the bountymen would pass them by where they hid. What terror. What they must have found, afterward. What they must have *felt*."

He turned to her, as if they were going to embrace—he thought they were—and he said, "The children matter most, Olivia?"

As if he'd violated something more than flesh, she moved away and back, to lean against the seat of the bench, her hands in a knot in her lap. "Are you a psychoanalyst, Harry?"

"I'm sorry."

"Do you need to . . . I don't know. Do you need to measure my concern? To analyze it for its purity?"

He shook his head. "Absolutely not. Never. I was curious, that's all."

"Perry and I will have to live with what concerns me most about children, won't we?"

"Yes, ma'am."

"And what concerns me, Harry, is whether Salaparuta or Har-

98

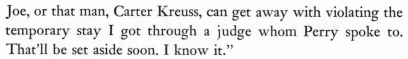

Joe, or that man, Carter Kreuss, can get away with violating the temporary stay I got through a judge whom Perry spoke to. That'll be set aside soon. I know it."

"He's into them for money?"

"It's all legal. His wife's a Salaparuta, though, and her mustache is bigger than his. He did us a little favor. To buy me some time and get Perry owing *him*. There are millions in local money—jobs, prospective sales, rentals, you name it. No pudgy white woman with her black corpses is going to turn that money off."

"You're not pudgy, Olivia."

"Harry, neither are you."

They looked at each other, and they laughed. He watched her relax, and he felt his own breath easing out. He slumped, unerected, on the bench. "Are there black action groups I should see?"

"There are almost no blacks *here*, Harry. This is the Chenango valley. White man's country, mostly. Why would black people leave Syracuse or Binghamton to move here? It's just wacky housewives like me, with their little hobbies. Saving the dead."

"Look," he said. "The senator knows about this. He's interested. His staff is on it. I may have a personal lever into this. Which could mess it up for us, or ruin my life. But don't worry about *that*."

"Details," she said, waving them away. "Your life. My life. I mean, you can't imagine a banker in Perry's position is *happy* about this? He's just more scared of making me unhappy than he is of making the local colleagues mad."

"He's a good man, Olivia. And he's right."

She patted his leg. Then she squeezed it. She leaned in closer, and her redolence settled about him. She kissed him on the cheek. "You and I," she said, "we'd have busted the bed."

He flushed and hardened. She looked only at his face, and then laughed.

"Let's stay in touch," she said. "All right?"

99

"I may be here for just a day or two more. I've got some fires to put out."

She gave a mock growl. "Me, too." Then she laughed again. "But I mean this. Those people have their rights. And what scorn, what disrespect we want to show them! The honkies are the disease, Harry."

He held the sheaf of papers below his belt as he stood.

"Should I call you, Harry?"

"Some of the fire's where I'm staying, maybe."

"Well, you had better call *me*, then."

"Yes, ma'am."

"Yes, sir."

As he turned to leave, she patted him on the ass. He almost fell, and she laughed a high, hearty, happy woman's laugh.

Neither of them wanted food, so they drove to the lake and parked near the aqua-painted motel and restaurant, soon to be shut for the winter. The lake was choppy, the gulls wheeled low.

Carter shivered, as if he were cold. He said, "Want to rent a boat? We could go out and drown in each other's arms, or something. Except you, I guess you don't feel like dying right now."

"Don't you, either," Catherine said. She had taken the emergency blanket, dirty and tattered, from her van. She wore it over her shoulders like a shawl as they walked in the little park, under Natty Bumppo's statue, by the edge of the lake. "You want to get a coat from your car?"

He shook his head. "It isn't fair," he said. "This guy coming in—"

"Harry?"

"Harry coming in from so far away. From so far *back*. Isn't anybody on the guy already there's side?"

"All his family and friends, no doubt. But you're not my husband. I'm not your wife."

"Catherine's terms."

"You've been gracious about that."

"Bullshit. I've been scared I'd scare you off."

"Carter, maybe people who love each other shouldn't worry like that."

"I wouldn't know. One marriage, a couple of girlfriends, and then you—I haven't learned a fucking thing, Catherine. All I know is I do what I'm told."

She clutched her stomach and gagged as if ill.

"Who was that guy in the movie who was always so humble?"

"Yes," she said, "that's exactly what you sounded like. Heep."

"Heep," he said, looking up at Fenimore Cooper's Indian. "Heap horror show. Like the Indians on the site."

"I thought they were slaves. Black people."

"I doubt it. Wouldn't Jesse Jackson, the NAACP, and Louis Farrakhan's black army have descended on us by now? I doubt it. I think it's Indians if anything at all. I suspect there's skunk cabbage, shale, and maybe an old garbage dump down there. I suspect old Perry Stoddard's got his eye on financing somebody else's deal to use the land or something. I imagine that it's dollars we're talking about, not dead slaves, for Christ's sake."

"It's dollars we're talking *now*," she said. "I can't take more than a half an hour for lunch. Nobody else came in. I'm alone in the gallery, we've got people coming through looking for primitive paintings here in our unspoiled antique bonanza, and I have to get back and you have to get back, and we're talking about money."

They sat on a bench and looked at the lake. Catherine heard how harsh her voice had been as her words echoed. Listen to the last realist on the face of the earth, she thought.

She asked, "Do you know yet why you walked out like that last night?"

"Because you wanted me to."

"Wouldn't I have said so if I wanted you to?"

"You didn't ask me not to."

"No," she said, "I never would. I never did. You know that."

"Well, I thought it'd be a little appropriate last night for you to come outside with me and, you know—"

"Cling," she said.

"Maybe."

"I don't do that too awfully well. Are you sure I'm the one you want?"

"Oh, don't put it off onto *me*, now. Damn, I hate it when you do that."

"Whatever that is."

"Women, I mean. People arguing. I don't know. Do you love me, Catherine?"

"What shall I say? You're dear to me, of course."

"How?"

"You mean, is it easy? Or do you mean, how much?"

"Anything," he said.

"Oh, Carter, don't sound so unhappy. You and I, we went *fishing* together. That should tell you something."

He pawed in the air as if to push something aside. "Nah. You did that as a present. You did it for me. You hate fishing."

"So it should mean more. Especially that I never told you."

"Thank you," he said.

She felt herself shrug. She felt herself shrug inside as well. But he knew, she knew. He was sometimes obtuse, and they were very different, but he was the man she'd made love with, and whose toothbrush she'd used one time, and alongside whom she'd worked in a kitchen. "Several months, right?" she asked. "Have we been together for a year?"

"Almost. Nine, ten months, a tiny bit longer, I think."

"That's a long run in a grown-up's life these days."

He said, sounding, she realized, like a sullen, sore boy, "I was hoping for years, not months. Permanency."

She nodded, but mostly to herself. For she had not once, since she'd driven Harry from her house in Schuyler when they had been on the edge of renouncing separate lives, wanted anything permanent except her children at home. And she'd been required to give that up for Randy. She thought: How to talk about our maybe owing one another separateness?

"Well," he said.

She said, "What?"

His face looked shiny, she thought. Maybe he was sweating, and in this cold wind. If you love someone, do you have to run with sweat? She wasn't about to ask.

"I'm willing to do what I have to do. That includes letting go, some."

"Which is why you left last night."

"I hated that. Yes. But I hated doing it. Walking off like that and leaving him with you."

"I'm not an undefended virgin, you know. I don't need defending."

"I didn't think you did," he said. "And I don't. It was me needed defending. That's why I wanted to stay. That's why I left. To show you what I could yield."

"My fair white body," she said. "Is the world made of cunt?"

He stood. "That's such an ugly word, Catherine."

"You go grow one," she said, "then try and tell your father and your husband and the ramrods on the block that it is *not* the reason for the last argument, present tension, and the failure of the Treaty of Versailles. I have to leave, Carter. Come to supper tonight, all right?"

His smile, the change in his carriage, and easy access that she gained through his eyes to his woundedness: she wanted to apologize to him on behalf of the world. They walked up from the lake toward the car. Some tourists in white cotton outfits standing near a camper bus watched them walk, as if they were part of the scenery. She felt Carter's stride change, and she knew what he was thinking as he said it. "Now I feel like a stranger being welcomed. Supper," he said. He snorted disbelief or anger. "What time do you eat?"

"Now," she said. "Come on." And to the mom and dad—same size, same pale coloring and straw-colored hair—and to their sullen fat daughter and lean sullen son, she said, "You think we're something, you should see the bird life there. Terns and gulls, even cormorants." At Carter's station wagon, she said, "I'm going to walk up, all right? You go on, I'll walk." She patted his arm, knowing that she should kiss him, and she strode up the street past the giant old houses and their hundred-year-old shade trees, knowing too that Carter watched her walk. She was careful not to strut.

Chenango had a huge medical complex, and rich retired people, and small-town men in coveralls who bought coffee at the Chenango House every morning from the women who had waitressed there for twenty years, and there were overpriced clothes and overpriced art—didn't she know?—and you could buy good fresh bread and decent herbs and eat quite well. There was a lovely small collection of early art at the historical society, and of course Cooperstown was twenty miles away. People in matching white cotton outfits with matching white children drove hundreds of miles to look at statues of baseball players and small, hard gloves and pieces of Ebbets Field and the Polo Grounds from New York. She couldn't imagine going to a baseball game, and she had *gone* to baseball games. For her boys, she had sat through the Utica Blue Sox minor league games, watching the kids eat hot dogs while she sipped at Genesee beer. It hadn't been that different, she thought, from watching the men drink coffee at the Chenango House: everyone knew who was coming in and when, and the women set down cups of coffee as they walked through the door. In Utica, and at a game in Oneonta she had suffered through for the boys, everyone knew that this one would swing, and this one would catch, and they would move on the pretty bright grass like clockwork men who spat tobacco juice, and

104

nothing happened faster than very, very slow. That, in fact, was like her life in this town, she thought, approaching the gallery, in what had been the lobby of an old savings-and-loan. Come to work, and open the door, and in the winter goose the thermostat up, and in the summer slap it down. Turn on the lights and grind the espresso beans—is it art without espresso?—and set up for brewing. And sell the mostly second-rate to the mostly unin-formed or impaired of taste, and then drive home in the low sun, and *then*, wearing jeans or khakis, in boat shoes or moccasins, often without a bra under an old flannel shirt or tatty sweater, get your hands into dirt and plant things or pick them, tend them, water and weed and nourish (as you do with the boys), and be tired early, and sit outside with Drown and sometimes a kid who has time for it, and worry about being alone so much and not worrying. She set her bag on what she thought might be, just possibly, a rush-seat straight-back chair designed and even stained by Dante Gabriel Rossetti and built by Morris. She'd refused to sell it a dozen times. She loved its round seat against the slightly unparallel legs and frame of the back, its wonderful red stripes against its blue—the tones of paint were Morris wallpaper tones. She promised herself not to sell it until Randy married someone so poor, she'd have to pay for their wedding. Maybe she could convince them to elope. So she stood in her Victorian bank lobby, with tears in her eyes, paying for the marriage of a boy in the start of his freshman college year. She must look like the clowns she'd seen standing in Cooperstown in front of Ted Williams' bat, or whatever it was they worshiped at the Hall. She thought: Men are striving to get to *this*?

She plucked her bag from the chair and slapped the OUT FOR LUNCH notice back into the door, which she slammed behind her. This time she marched up the business street, past the pharmacy and deli, and the wonderful sort-of-bookstore that sold old-fashioned stuff like broad green desk blotters, and she came to the purposely old-fashioned hardware store. She knew what she wanted, and she refused the advice that she buy one smaller, more manageable, more in keeping with her sex and her size. She said to Mavis, Murchison's wife and chief salesperson, "That's nonsense, Mavis. I'm taller than your husband and stronger than him too. Give me *this*, please."

Which was how she came to arrive at the house at five that afternoon, greeted only by Drown (Bobby was sleeping or doing homework, and she didn't know if his body knew the difference), with a sack of veal she couldn't afford and a heavy-headed, long-handled ax.

Bobby made no noise as she put the food away and looked at the mail. And only Drown, as ever, was there to accompany her when she came out in jeans and flannel shirt and boat shoes to march to the back door of the barn, where the man had dumped the wood. She started to split the oversized pieces, working too fast at first, and winding herself badly, but then recovering, and finding a rhythm, and impressing herself with how she went through red oak, birch, cherry, and maple, getting through knots, and not missing the log or the splitting block too many times. When she did, and the handle of the ax slammed the block, she could feel the vibration run up her forearm and into her shoulder. As if she were being watched, she wiped her forehead and shook her head—it doesn't hurt at all: I barely noticed it—and set up and swung.

She felt an hour pass (when she checked in the kitchen it was thirty-seven minutes), and she washed her face and hands at the sink with a bubbly noise. She was singing, and it made her happy to hear.

So when Bobby came down in grotty-looking sweatpants and a T-shirt she'd seen an awful lot that week, but not in the laundry hamper, she only waggled her brows at him. He gave her a stone-faced stare and she shrugged and went on to rub the veal chops with rosemary and start to slice up frying peppers and zucchini and onions. "Legumes," she said to Bobby, who sprawled and drank milk with loud suction. "Jesus," she said. "It sounds like you're trying to get it back inside the *cow*."

Her hands hurt where there weren't calluses yet. But she knew that they would come. And she knew how she'd enjoy showing Randy what she'd split and how she'd stacked it. And maybe, she thought, Bobby would see what she'd done and be shamed into helping.

She said, without turning, "You have any shame, sweetheart?"

"Why should I?" he said, as if challenged to a duel.

Dell, she thought, I think this one is mostly yours. Poor baby.

She looked through what she still thought of as Carter's wines until she found a bottle of burgundy with a lovely label dated 1979. She shrugged and uncorked it.

Bobby watched her, as kids his age watched television, she thought: unattentively and with a slackness at the jaw. We're motion, hence watched. I'm *your* motion, you little pisser, she thought. And before he could defend himself she strode to him and seized his head by his much-brushed hair, and she kissed him hard on the nose.

"Ouch, man!"

"Man," she said, holding his face by his cheeks. His big, hard hands rose to seize her wrists and pull them apart. It was like not having muscles, she thought, to be escaped from like that. Another one is on his way.

"Exactly eighty-nine percent of all major human drama takes place in the kitchen," she told him.

"You're becoming a very crazy old lady," he said. "I can't figure out why these guys come around."

"Your mother is a femme fatale who throws a cruel enchambrer. They have no choice. We're using candles tonight. Will you get the candle holders you made in pottery shop?"

"Ma. No."

"You gave them to me for my birthday. They're mine. I love them. So fetch them, please."

She didn't find matching candles in the old living room hutch, so she had low, bulbous, off-orange ceramic candle holders with one six-inch purple candle and a lime-green stub about two inches high. She set the table with cloth napkins, some green and some nearly purple, and she put out the blue-green goblets for wine. Bobby was in the bathroom, no doubt brushing at his hair, or just leaning with one long arm on either side of the old framed mirror, watching his face, studying his hair, trying to catch his life by surprise so he'd know how he was doing. Drown outside began to bellow.

"Someone's here," she called.

Bobby said, "Big deal."

But when Harry came in, she noticed, Bobby was in the kitchen with her, waiting, shy and lovely, a boy inside a man. Harry was a grown-up man, of course, but she noticed that he seemed hesitant, too, and she found herself annoyed. Some afternoons, after splitting and stacking the goddam wood, you're in the mood to be with another adult, goddammit, she thought.

But like a man who had rehearsed, Harry in his marigold-colored sweater, with a piece of his shirt hanging down below its hem, came marching to Bobby, paused to reach for his hand and pump it twice, then marched along, around the table, to Catherine, who stood with her back to the sink. He reached for her hand, which she raised in response. He shook it, hard. She met his grip and pumped his hand. He looked a little wide-eyed, a little hysterical, maybe drunk, very happy. "I spent the afternoon among the committed," Harry said. "I nearly jumped all over an undersized, provocative woman."

"Harry!" she said.

"I'll tell you about it." He put his hand on his mouth. "Whoops. I wasn't going to do that."

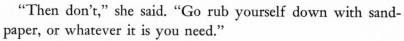

"Then don't," she said. "Go rub yourself down with sand-paper, or whatever it is you need."

"You," he said.

"Oh, I am not in the mood for this, Harry. Is it woo, or just barn bottom you're pitching here? Stop."

"Yes," he said.

"Carter's coming for supper soon," she said.

Harry stood at something like attention. He looked her in the eye and declaimed, "He will always be a welcome guest." He turned around and left the room.

Bobby said, "Is he all right?"

"As I remember," Catherine said, and she hated the smugness she heard, "this is more or less par for it."

"For what?"

She said, to the broiler pan she jerked from the oven, "Never mind." She scorned the smile she gave the veal.

Harry had showered in the upstairs bathroom by the time Carter arrived, and he'd put on a dark T-shirt and jeans. In sneakers and no socks, in clean clothes, he felt tall and almost lanky. Which is what happens, he thought, when you give a guy a pair of pants that don't require pulleys and levers to get into. For all his satisfaction, though, with how he felt and what he'd done (and not done), he carried an unhappiness in the back of his mind, like a mild headache, or a small sore. And it wasn't until Drown was leading him down the stairs that he understood, because it clearly was Drown's house, and he was acting the host, how in the bathroom there had been a soap-on-a-rope from Grey Flannel hanging over the shower head (he hadn't used it), and two deodorants in the medicine chest, and an electric razor for men, and a man's sponge bag hanging behind the door next to a man's striped bathrobe unsuitable for Catherine except in circumstances he didn't care to imagine. It was still Carter's house as well, maybe; surely it was his more than Harry's. A sore *and* a headache, he decided, entering the kitchen to find Bobby standing with his arms across his chest and his lips sealed tight in anger, his sweet face pale with it, Catherine's almost grim.

"Hi," Harry said. "Want me to take a walk, or something?"

Bobby refused to look at him. Catherine flashed him a parent-sharing-the-madness semi-smile. Harry wasn't sure what to do with it, if that's what it had been. Catherine, turning to Bobby, said, "Now please mow the lawn."

Between his teeth were the words, "It's too short to cut till the weekend."

"Since when does the *grass* call the tune?" Catherine said. "I want it cut now."

"I'm not cutting it," Bobby said. "I'm waiting for the weekend. It's almost hard frost, anyway. If it's alive this weekend, I'll cut it."

Catherine turned to Harry again. "You're in politics," she said.

"The art of the possible," Harry said.

"So negotiate this."

"Where's the mower, Bobby? I'll cut the grass," he said. Bobby smiled uncertainly. Catherine looked up from under her brows to the ceiling.

"I was hoping," she said, "that out of this exchange might come a sharing of chores, a mutuality, a respect for the household's needs."

"I have all those," Bobby said.

"You're just not doing what I want until *you* want to do it," she said.

He shrugged. Harry said, "I'd be wil—"

"Shut up, Harry?" Catherine said. He nodded that he would. Bobby held up a hand, as people do in restaurants when seizing checks: I'll get this one, his gesture said. He left by the back door.

"Sorry," Harry said.

"You're not in practice," she said. "Of course, neither am I. I'm still waiting to know what to do."

Harry said nothing about their learning it together.

Catherine asked, "What should we have for a starch? We're having grilled veal chops, a vegetable fry, and—what? Noodles with butter and parsley, hold the butter, maybe a little marg? Sautéed potatoes?"

"You never used to like to cook that much. In Schuyler, I remember, I did most of the cooking when we were together. Then, in the other house, when you moved to Pines and I came up, you did a little more. But this."

"It started to happen when Randy all of a sudden was grown. When I was the last to find out he was grown. Growing, anyway. I was filled with this need to feed him. The last taking-care-of, you know?"

"He's a beautiful boy," Harry said. "So's Bobby. He looks like a movie star. And he strikes me as a world-class brooder. Tough adolescence."

She nodded. "When I go crazy and run around the house looking for guns so I can shoot us both, I tell him, usually just before I give in and cry and win that way. I don't plan it. I hate it. He hates it worse, though. He feels terrible. I shouldn't do it, and I can't help it, and it happens sometimes." She paused for a long breath. "I tell him, we're going to be happy when I'm old and he's a middle-aged bachelor who can't leave me for *anyone*. We're going to laugh a lot, I tell him."

"What does he say?"

"He takes naps."

"Catherine," Harry said.

"Oh, Harry, of *course*."

"Of course what?"

She turned from him and addressed the washed, cut vegetables and unheated olive oil. "Of course everything. Yes, I remember. Yes, I *did* remember. Yes, I thought of you. All kinds of ways. Too many times."

He straightened his cutaway and adjusted his black tie, but did not yet begin to dance. "Too many for what?" he asked her.

She said, "Guess. Here's Carter. I hear his car. He's a decent, nice man." Harry saw her turning to Carter, in a dark room, her light eyes darkening with speculation—admit it, fat boy: with passion for that long, scrawny frame—and he saw her lips, soft, softening further, as Carter's head came between Harry and Catherine and Carter kissed her. She was wearing Carter's bathrobe, he saw. She was naked beneath it, and her chest was blushing as the robe fell open. Catherine was saying, "For us all."

"Excuse me?"

"Be *nice*," she hissed, and he loved the warning: it was what the hostess says to the host, and not the interloper. He and Drown, extending the courtesies.

Carter didn't knock or pause, from what Harry could tell. He came marching through the front door with what Harry guessed was supposed to be nonchalance. Carter said, "I'll need to get a few things, I think. You think so, Harry?"

"I'm just a houseguest," Harry said.

Carter said, "Heep."

Harry asked, "Of what?" but Carter was past him and in the kitchen. Harry followed. Carter was leaning over Catherine and kissing the top of her head. Drown was leaning his own head against Carter's calf. Harry figured that he was supposed to complete the chain by sniffing Drown's tail, but he held off. Outside, a motor started up. "*Now* he does it," Catherine said.

"That's because he knows it's time to come to the table," Harry said.

Carter, turning, looked at the Vosne-Romanée on the table and then at Harry. He said, "You any good with kids?"

Harry shrugged. "The only ones I know belong to my friends."

"That's right," Carter said, going to the cupboard and taking out liquor bottles, "you never married, did you?"

Harry said nothing. Catherine said, "Noodles and parsley all right?"

"I shouldn't," Harry said, wondering why he gave that to Carter, who stared at his belly and hips.

"Mostly it's for Bobby," Catherine said. "He needs about ten thousand calories a day to have enough energy to take his exams and sleep afterward."

"Did you?" Carter asked.

Harry remembered a night twelve years ago, almost, when Catherine's husband, ex-husband, separated husband, Dell, gone from the house in Schuyler for some time, had gotten himself liquored up for reunion or rebuke, and had come back to find that Harry was at his table with Catherine and the boys. Catherine had later described it for him. What he remembered was loudness and motion, fear, then anger at his fear, then a lust to be the man in the world with a claim to Catherine, and Dell beating on his body and face. It occurred to Harry that if he were going to be forced by this woman to leave periodically, and then insist on every now and then coming back, he might have to be slugged a few times for falling into the pattern. It also occurred to him that he might deserve the beating, for acquiring one more bad habit, and for being obdurate, and—especially—for letting her force him to go.

Catherine had stood outside and screamed to Bobby, who was taking his time in responding (the politics of the lawn), and Carter had managed to seat himself first, then point out to Harry where he too might sit. Harry had decided only to nod his thanks, and he did. Then they both stood up to help Catherine carry broiled chops and sautéed vegetables and noodles in parsley to the table. Catherine sat. She told them not to wait for Bobby. Harry watched her eye the wine as they waited to see whether Carter or he would pour for the guest. Harry smiled as she skipped the definition and seized the wine and poured it for them all.

Bobby entered the kitchen with a studied casualness that might match his own, Harry thought. Personally, he wouldn't believe either of them, and he imagined he was speaking for Carter, too. He drank the wine, which was rich and rusty-tasting, soft and very dark, and he wished that he and Catherine could finish the bottle together, outside, with Drown grunting at stars or the moon, and with Bobby inside, chatting happily on the phone with his big brother at college. He was toasting the dream of a happy family, he knew. He kept his face closed and his eyes on his plate. He forced himself to eat only the veal and the vegetables, while Catherine chatted with Bobby about his classes. He answered sullenly or shyly, Harry didn't know which, didn't know how you were supposed to tell, wondered if you were supposed to take it personally that your own kid treated you like an annoying stranger, warned himself that Bobby was Catherine's own kid and not Harry's, and found himself, at last, imagining what it might be like to somehow, in a novel and convincing fashion, win this boy's attention and allegiance—maybe *love?*—and what the muscled, almost Mediterranean lines of that face would look like in pleasure, or repose. He would win over and then present to her the family's baby boy, he thought, as a gift, commemoration. But of what? You know, and never mind.

Carter said, finally, as Harry watched Catherine glare her son's elbows from the edge of the table, "So you're interested in dead people, Harry."

"It beats collecting stamps," Harry said.

Carter said to Catherine, "The Stoddard woman, the goddam do-good socialite with nothing better to do. You know she takes dance lessons, Harry? Interpretive dancing? At the Chenango School of Dance? I mean, we're talking about someone who is such a joke, she gets up in public in *tights*. Not that she doesn't look like a, like an hors d'oeuvre in them. Jesus." He said to Catherine, "She calls up HarJoe and warbles something about how *now* she's got their ass. Excuse me, Bobby. Because the very important assistant of the Democratic senator from New York is in town. He's on the case. He's going to save the bones of our Native American brethren from having to wander."

"They're African-American," Harry said. "They really are. It's a fact, I think. I don't know if that matters to anybody except black people and Indians."

"Oh, it does," Carter said, offering the wine bottle. "Have some more, Harry. It's a great bottle of wine."

Harry said, "No thanks. I brought it for you."

"I think maybe you're watching your weight a little?"

Bobby looked up. He understood *those* tones.

Harry said, "Couldn't hurt, eh?"

Carter smiled, but also flushed unhappily. He made do with bending to the wine and the glass as Catherine's eyes swung up at him.

Catherine said, "Is this something you're, I don't know, working on in a major way, Harry?"

"It might be interesting. We could leave it at that."

"It might be interesting," Carter said, "if HarJoe lost a mall and Salaparuta lost a contract, and I lost out on a bid I already won for a—for a lot of cash money. Some of which I owe, already."

Harry said, "A constituent wrote to the senator's office, and he thought it might be of interest. That's all."

"If he runs for the White House," Carter said. "The big liberal, huh? Walking on water and turning Indians into blacks and blacks into votes? Oh, yes. And Harry, wouldn't you hate it if something bad happened to my business interests?"

Catherine said, "Carter."

"Not accusing," he said, "just describing."

Bobby said, "I have to study, Mom. Can I help with the dishes?"

"Good man," Harry said.

"What a lovely surprise," Catherine said. "I'm sorry, that was inflammatory and not true. No, sweetheart, you mowed the lawn. Go study. We'll clean up the mess."

"I hope we can," Carter said, waving to Bobby, who waved to them all. He did seem almost at peace. Maybe conflict brought out the best in him. Maybe seeing adults act like children did. He learned that he wasn't alone, Harry thought.

Catherine said, "We can."

"Good," Carter said. He leaned at Harry, across the table, and he said, "Stay out of my business, please." To Catherine, he said, "I'm going to pick up some things of mine, all right?"

"If that's what you want to do," she said.

"I don't know but that it's what I *have* to do." Walking around the table, he paused beside Harry and leaned down and breathed some wine at him. "Business *and* pleasure, if I had my druthers."

Harry impressed himself by gaining the presence of mind to say, "*Ha.*"

As Carter left, Catherine leaned over to say, "Good one, Harry."

"Miller doesn't mess," he said. And because she was closer to him, because he fancied he could smell the warmth of her skin, he said, "Do you know what we're doing?"

"No."

"He loves you, right?"

"He would like to. He would like to stake his claim."

"Is he entitled? Never mind. Nobody's entitled."

Instead of beaming approval or radiating something of a clue, that Harry Miller, believe it, Ripley, or not, *could* be entitled, Catherine abruptly stood up and tore dishes from the table and slammed them to the counter next to the sink.

"Cath?"

He heard Carter walking upstairs. He wished, and he wondered why, that he would not go to Bobby's room.

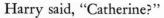

Harry said, "Catherine?"

"Never mind," she said. "I'm sorry. I'm just tense, or something. I mean, it's like running a bull semen warehouse here."

"No," he said. "Please. Tell me."

She bent to scrape dishes. Drown, his head almost in the garbage pail, awaited his chop bone. Me too, Harry thought. "You were doing me a favor, you thought, when you put the thought in my head, the words in my mouth, whichever—and we have sometimes nearly shared thoughts, I know that. About nobody, according to me, being entitled to a claim to me."

"That was wrong?"

She threw the oval white dish into the garbage pail and reached for a dinner plate to scrape next. Harry went to the pail, retrieved a bone for Drown, and gave it to him. The soft gentle jaws accepted both the bone and Harry's fingers, separated the bone, and went away. Then he took the oval plate from the garbage pail and ran it under hot water in the sink. When he looked up, Catherine, beside him, was looking at his hands.

"What, Cath?"

"I haven't seen that," she said, nodding toward his hands. "Them, doing that. It's been a long time."

They stood side by side. He could feel the heat of her arm, he thought, and he began to let himself lean toward it. He stood with his hands under the water, afraid to remove them from the sink. "I won't try to talk for you? Is that what you mean? Or am I doing it again?"

It was she who leaned in against his right arm with her left, and his body took her weight along that narrow line of cloth and muscle. He felt himself harden the bicep, and forced it to relax; he would want, later, to feel that he hadn't been quite adolescent.

"Shit, Harry," she whispered, and her voice was almost lost in the water's hot hush. "You're in the soup. Like a fly, caught in the soup. Everybody worries about the diner, nobody thinks about the fly, hot and swimming so hard. Well, listen," she said, still leaning on him, "when you're in it, and you think the soup's all right, what the hell. Dine."

He turned, but she pushed off and left the kitchen. Don't go upstairs, Harry wished. He turned the water off. I am not wishing, he thought. I think that this will qualify as prayer. He turned the water back on and studied the opalescence of the white English serving dish. He couldn't see his features, or anything else, underneath the soapy surface. What you must learn to control, and what you thought you'd renounced, was the *wish* to control. Because you did think, with sickness in your stomach, of Catherine with other men, in every way. You have not learned the lessons of the revolution. That wanting anything is selfishness, a callowness, unless it's her idea. Well, listen: it *is* her life.

He turned off the water so hard, he thought he might have unthreaded the faucet washer. Wrong: it is also—it has also always been, simultaneously—mine.

He stood at the sink and looked over the kitchen cabinets he hadn't known, the Hoosier cupboard he had, its dark pine glow shined by hands for seventy years, the photographs she'd hung in Schuyler and in Pines—orphans sliding down the snowy hill in Cooperstown below the orphanage, their faces cruelly stretched by their efforts at expressing what they must have thought should be fun; the Walker Evans photo of a clapboard house, open to the kitchen, its bare wood boards and plain plank table—and he felt at home. He saw Carter's shadow, and then Carter himself, descending the stairs. He carried a sponge bag and the fucking oversized bathrobe. Carter came into the kitchen, and Catherine followed.

He stuck his long arm out to Harry, and Harry shook his hand. Neither squeezed hard. "I expect I'll be seeing you, Harry. You're leaving soon?"

Harry looked into Carter's eyes and squinted against the humor in them. Carter, he realized, was laughing at him, or was trying to. Skinny men never fear fat men at love. Harry turned on his Washington-conference savvy look. "Well, they're expecting me, Carter."

"And you won't let them down."

"You'll be back, you said?"

"Harry," he said, "I will."

Harry, before he knew his lips were going to move, asked, "Can I lay a question on you, Carter?"

The laughing eyes widened, then narrowed, and Carter all but patted him on the head. "Go right ahead."

"How come you're marching up and down with the fourteen-trombone marching band and making such a spectacle of leaving?"

Catherine, behind Carter still, said, "I'll be back," and she walked upstairs again. Smart move, Harry thought. Carter leaned in at Harry. "Because, cocksucker, that's what you did right here three months ago," Carter whispered. His big white teeth were bright when his lips drew back to sneer.

Harry whispered in return, "You're imitating me and you're making faces at me while you do it? You're taking me that seriously but you're talking with disrespect, Carter. You're telling me we're enemies, here. You should admit your respect for your enemy."

"You should have a tumor, cocksucker. *I'm* not taking you seriously. *She* is." Harry didn't know what his face did, but Carter apparently read something new on it. "Shit," he said, turning away, then back to Harry. "You didn't know it, did you?"

"I've had suspicions."

"No," Carter said, "you didn't know it. You might have gone home if I'd have stayed here."

"I don't know what I know. What I knew. But I wouldn't have gone home. I did that already. I did it a number of times. Next time I go is the last one. Guaranteed. No. I'd have stayed a while, no matter what."

"Son of a bitch," Carter said. "Wanna fight?" He put his hands, one laden, one not, out and up like a nineteenth-century boxer.

Harry shook his head.

Carter said, "If you tell me you're a lover, not a fighter, I'm gonna slug you. I could hurt you, Harry."

Harry held his open hands out straight away from his shoulders. He said, "You think a man like me can steal a woman like that? And you've known her for a year? Who ever told her what to do?"

Carter pretended to smile. He whispered, "Stay away from my business, Harry. And go home soon. I'll be back."

Harry said, "Maybe we can compare notes on graveyards and stuff when you get back."

"You challenging me?" Carter said.

Harry looked at him for the space of a few rapid eyeblinks. "Damned if I'm not, I think. What's *your* best guess?"

"Lardass."

"Yeah. You think so too."

After Carter slammed the door, and after his station wagon spun out in a spray of gravel, Harry went back to the kitchen. Like a good bourgeois, he finished cleaning up the dishes, wiping the surfaces of table and counters and cutting boards, and turning out all but a single light with its parchment-colored shade. We've stepped around war, he thought. All that's left now is everything else.

They wore sweaters and old, cracked yellow slickers that Catherine took down from hooks in the pantry. Most of the lights in the house were out, except for those in Bobby's room, which was brilliantly lighted and which flooded the far side of the yard as Bobby panicked for his history paper. Drown came with them, sensing mission and bounding crookedly for a few yards ahead of them, seizing a giant fallen piece of limb from the basswood tree, and dragging it. "He won't go anyplace unless he picks a stick up and carries it," Catherine said. "All his play is work."

The moon was brilliant, and Drown noticed it. He dropped his stick, looked up at the moon, down at them and their shadows, then at the moon again. He raced away from them, hardly hobbling, and was across the road, on the gentle rise of hill, jerking and barking as he ran. What few clouds had drifted near the moon blew off in a freshening wind, and the moon lighted the far hillside, and the sloping stony land around the house. It was a blue-white light, and almost sunny in its intensity. Catherine shivered in her coat. Harry put his arm around her, hesitantly at first, and then more firmly when she didn't resist. "Just like in the movies," she said. "Remember? You casually drop your arm on the seat behind her, taking only the first forty-five minutes of the picture? And then you go for shoulder bone and clavicle? And you spend the rest of the movie wondering how far down you can drop the first joints of two fingers onto the top of the slope of her breast?"

"You've been talking to Randy."

"It was *my* slope, Harry."

"I'm not trying to feel you up." He took his hand away.

"I am counting on you not to sulk," she said.

Drown, his body recoiling as he barked, reached the top of the far hill. He crooned a long, slow, thin wailing howl at the moon. He sounded as though the news could not have been worse. As if cued, the wind increased. "This is cold," Harry said. "I mean *cold*. How come you always live where it's cold like this?"

"In country like this," she said, "you get to feel the seasons. It's always changing."

"I noticed. Do you ever, ah, get in the mood for *not* changing?"

"Is that a metaphorical question?"

"No. I didn't mean it that way. You want to answer any metaphorical questions?"

"No. You want to help me pick tomatoes?"

"Huh?"

"Full moon. No clouds. Wind coming up. It'll be a frost tonight. A real one. Hard frost. Let's get the last of the garden in, all right?"

She sounded so happy, he thought, to be running down beyond the house, dragging bright blue plastic tarpaulins and moldy liquor cartons and a couple of dark plastic garbage bags. Drown alternated, across the road and away, between yipping at the sky and howling as if wounded by it. The big rectangle of the garden, bounded by leaning, barkless gray posts with rusted barbed wire drooping from them, shone in the moonlight. The plastic sheets of mulch caught the light and threw it up as if they walked on the surface of a midnight sea. Catherine spread the tarpaulin in the middle of the garden, over a giant rutabaga plant, and she began to pluck things and throw them. Harry did too. He hated the feel of cold mud and yard dirt and the chilly slime of slug-infested tomato, but he reached and pulled and tossed whatever he thought was vaguely ripe and apparently healthy. Catherine told him to leave the leeks and onions, they'd survive the frost. Everything else was to come with them when they left. So under a moon, and in winds that grew higher, his hands growing painful and soon almost numb, Harry harvested.

The smell of growing vegetables, a green kind of deep richness from the vines of tomatoes and the rot that surrounded them, lay on his hands and on his clothes, where he couldn't help wiping them over and over. Bright yellow leaves that were beginning to blow off trembled as the winds picked up. Catherine called them quaking aspen. The sound of the soughing wind grew louder, and soon it hissed like heavy rain, like sleet, and Harry burrowed into his borrowed slicker that, when he buttoned it, he thought, must make him look like a giant banana. He heard her breathing under the wind, and his own, and he realized they were working at a rhythm governed by one another's breaths. They stooped and sorted, plucked and tossed. Catherine wandered away, toward the herbs, with a garbage bag; Harry thought he could still hear her breathe. And over it all, even over the wind, and especially when the wind let up and the trees stopped hissing and rattling, he heard the howls that Drown repeated crazily across the road.

Soon enough he was not only out of breath, but gasping for it. He turned to see—he prayed to see—if Catherine might be resting. But she was on her hands and knees in the almost freezing soil, studying the round dark bell peppers, the long lighter frying peppers, and when she found them, no matter her haste, she turned the vegetables gently while she pulled, as if she were unscrewing them. The garden was nearly as bright as day, and Harry had nowhere to hide. He finally didn't care. He tossed a last tomato at the mound on the tarpaulin, and he then tossed himself, flopping onto his back, so that he landed on the icy ground much harder than he'd expected to, and let out more of a sound—you could call it a moan, he admitted—than he'd planned. He looked up through fringes of aspen at a cloudless sky so silver that he saw far fewer stars than he expected.

She was standing over him, concern already leaving her face and pleasure replacing it. "You have to work back into shape for this," she said.

He raised his head and shoulders from the ground. "An invitation?"

"Observation," she said.

He lay back. "Agreed," he said.

Without any hesitation that he could see, she straddled him and sat, not hard, on his belly and his chest. "Tell me why you came," she said.

She looked down at him, so she couldn't raise her jaw like a furious duck. But she looked plenty insistent, he thought. Her chin creased more than it used to when she looked at him that way. And he remembered that the only time he'd seen it crease, had seen her looking down like that, was when she'd lain on top of him naked, and had seized his shoulders and, biting her lip, had slid down the length of him and onto his penis and, adjusting them together with a hand she then left on his belly, had risen so that they were perpendicular, and in unison.

"Harry," she said. "Why?"

He said, "You."

"And the grave site? The protesters? All of the local politics?"

"It's probably national politics," he said. "If the senator gets involved, it is. Catherine, *this* is politics."

"Don't give me smart-mouth Washington answers," she said, bouncing on him so that his legs splayed and his arms flopped, and he fought to find his breath.

"I told you," he said.

"Again."

"You."

"And the graves?"

"Aw, there's always time for dead folks, Catherine."

"Harry," she said, "this is no joke."

"God, I know it," he said. "I came here for the same reason I came here last June. Same reason as whenever it was before that. And before that, every week, nearly, right? By plane? By bus? You think a man makes trips like that because it's fun? Well, it *was* fun. Being with you and the boys, I mean, that was the fun. The trips were like dying."

"And this one?"

She lay along him now, matching her shoulders to his, her legs and arms to his, her face above his in the bright moonlight and cold wind. Her eyes weren't older, he thought; some of the skin around them, maybe, but not the eyes, not the goddamned bullying girl inside of them.

"This one?" she reminded him.

She let her face drop lower so that the tips of their icy noses touched. She let her lips barely touch Harry's lips. Her tongue slid out and stirred at his mouth and he opened it to take her in. She drew back and kissed him primly, but then leaned to bathe his mouth with her tongue.

"You're torturing me," he said. "Is that it? You're punishing me?"

"Why did you leave last summer, you bastard?"

He put his arms clumsily around her in her slicker, and moved his buttocks on the cold garden bed. He held her as well as he could, providing what he best could give beneath her: bulk.

Carter stopped outside on the packed earth and strayed gravel of her drive. He knew that they would not be looking at him, that he could strip to the buff and prance in circles, but he held himself straight and stared at her van as though it were a glance he had to meet and hold. Its color was rich mud, and its finish was nearly matte, it was so corroded and scraped. In the dim yellow light that fell across the porch and lawn and drive, the van looked immobile, a rusted mass that had been deposited by junkmen in the night. The tires were the only saving grace, and those he had nagged her into buying. They were worth more than the truck, in net trade or measured by the pound. On the holed, corroded quarter panels which were streaked by stone strikes and rusted as if painted to simulate splashing mud, she had used two-inch silver duct tape, a boast about negligence, an ostentation, as far as Carter was concerned. The bright silver tape was on the rusted seams and was wound around the trimwork that had sprung its bolts and clamps to wobble in the wind as she drove. He thought that if he pulled the tape off now and let the car's natural elements, rust, rot, eleven years' accumulated road dirt and grease, be its sole structural support, it would fall apart one day in transit, bumpers rolling off and fenders, rain gutters, and door handles. How could a woman such as she was drive a car like this?

And wasn't that the sort of man she'd welcomed to her life? Back to her life? As if he were a habit of hers? A fellow held together with all sorts of synthetic gadgets? He was pudgy and podgy, afraid of the countryside, you could tell that, and worried to death about making Catherine dislike him again. Though it wasn't quite that easy, was it? Carter put his things into the back of his station wagon. Because she had been struck dumb and red and shaky when he'd returned last summer, and then it had been *he* who had left, and *she* who had wondered (Carter knew right away) why he'd done it, and where she fitted in his life. Harry was the only man, and the unlikeliest man, who could make her wonder like that, Carter thought. Christ knows, *he* had tried. She had counted on him. The tires on the van were an example. And she'd liked him, and in the darkness of her bedroom she had loved him, in a way, he thought. But she had never, ever, wondered because of Carter Kreuss.

And that fact, that stone-hard, stone-heavy fact, was what caused him, as he sat behind the wheel and started his engine and lighted up her drive and drove away on busted shocks, to want to bite very slowly down through the skin just behind his lower lip, and then the very meat itself, until his teeth protruded from the other side, and into his own twisted mouth. He had to stop, of course. You always have to stop, he thought. You can think of dying, and Carter had, more and more, as he had come to his thirty-ninth birthday and now was edging toward his fortieth, you can think of doing it yourself. Ramming head-on into an eighteen-wheeler doing seventy in the opposite direction on 81 or 12; eating the front of a shotgun with deershot; taking every pill they let you buy at the counter in the Rite Aid drugstore. But then you don't. It isn't living, Carter thought. It's praying. You keep on hoping it gets better, and you believe it can happen. She can change. You can change. The world can change. And you could find her, some night, in her stupid flannel old ladies' nightgown that she wears instead of the see-through white lace that you bought her for her birthday, staring at you from the other side of her bedroom, biting *her* lip, and wondering about you. So do you stay alive because of Catherine? Would you die, if not for her? And shouldn't you do that now, then?

126

He was driving so quickly, and slipping on the curves as he made the long dark trip to another meeting at the Inn. He started to smile. He didn't know this grin, and, craning in the darkness, he couldn't see it in his rearview mirror, but he knew he hadn't grinned it before. It frightened him, wearing it, or being worn by it, and he lifted his foot from the accelerator. He flashed past a deer crossing sign, and then a T-junction, and a bright blue barn that Catherine had commented on as a new level of ugliness. He knew where he was, and fixing his location slowed him further and made him see the road through his lights and made him watch the speedometer and think about the wheel and his hands around it, hard. "You're such a dangerous guy," he said.

He parked behind the Inn and used the back door because he then had to walk through the bar to reach the meeting. He bared his teeth and slid a double down before he continued. He knew the barmaid, and he left her a dollar. Because you are always hoping that women will help you, he thought. He saw Olivia Stoddard in the lobby, waiting near the Adams Room with Truscott John, the conservationists' local historian and all-round yeoman, and several other country people of rectitude and pro- bity and other characteristics adding up to an enormous pain in the ass. Except her, he thought, looking at her wonderful small body, and thinking how he would happily fuck her upside down if only she would promise not to talk about Negroes in the ground for one solid month. He might fuck her as a favor, he thought, without the promise. You see what I mean, he thought, about relying on women. You should convert and go Catholic and live on your knees and pray to Mary. He nodded and waved, and flashed what he knew to be a winning, shy smile. He tightened his good-luck tie, purple and white stripes on a navy blue back- ground, pulled at the collar of his hard white shirt, buttoned his navy blazer, and walked into the room. Olivia, never looking at his face, he knew, followed him, and Truscott John followed her.

Inside the Adams Room, overheated so that condensation hung

on the windows as if the room were sweating on their behalf, the rows of folding chairs were full. Olivia and Truscott sat side by side on a giant library table in the left-hand corner at the back. He watched her legs dangle, and he thought about her thighs. She and Catherine disliked one another, and he thought about that as well. He knew some of the faces, bored shopkeeper princes of the tiny realm who were there to be seen or because they felt they owed the town their presence at every meeting, but most of them were strangers to him. Some were men in good suits, and there were women with intelligent faces in casual clothes. The ones who frightened him the most—of fucking course, he thought—were the lean, unpretty women in jeans and boots or sneakers who wore glasses and no makeup and who looked committed.

A man named Serge, whom Carter had long suspected of really being Sergio, and whose complexion was so greasy, he thought, you could scrape it in a pinch for tallow, called the meeting to order, referred to the last informational meeting, on a different subject, and named the topic of the night: Preserving the Rural Landscape. Carter hadn't known the topic. It made him want to moan. There would be long speeches by old people who would talk about the days of their grandparents, and how the Chenango Canal spurs had nearly brought ruin, and not the business boom they'd been promised. College professors, panting with eagerness to star in the world outside their campuses, would talk about toxins and impurities, ecology, indigenous this and the impact of that. Fat ladies from the International Congress of Distaff Bingo Unions would talk about moral values. And then they would turn to—no: they then would turn *on*—Carter Kreuss. And Olivia Stoddard, fueled by what madness or need or rage he'd never know, would deliver her lecture to him, would pour it upon him like radioactive slag, and he would stand before them, clothes still smoking from her heat, and he would have to defend a rural shopping mall that, so far as he could tell, had one overriding and singularly justifying reason to exist: he had the parking lot contract.

As a weatherman from a Binghamton station testified about acid rain and holes in the ozone layer, Carter stood in the corner across from the sliding white-painted doors and looked down the back wall at Olivia's legs. They had almost been friends, once, until they had made the mistake of going to bed together. And then they had come to have expectations of one another, and to trade confidences—he about his loneliness and she about her husband— and though attracted by their flesh and by the excesses each, for reasons he'd never understood, had felt free, even happy, to demand of one another, they had not trusted each other out of bed. Maybe that's what guilt is, Carter thought, remembering how she had propped herself on her knees and forearms, folded to support her head, and had opened herself, had *directed* him (you are always being ordered by women, he thought), and he had made a love to her that had made her grunt with pain and pleasure at once, and had made him groan his fear. He looked at her legs, swinging. He knew she knew he looked at her. The Adams Room was paneled with heavy plywood stained dark and waxed to simulate hardwood. It didn't work, but at night, under the two crystal chandeliers with their small pointed bulbs, and against the dark maroon carpeting, the walls looked better than they were. The high windows were the leaded originals, and the drapes, maroon and heavy, lent a gravity that echoed on the walls. He imagined that the Adams after whom the room was named might be a Colonial American. And it thrilled him, he was forced to admit, that he stood there in the corner, looking up Olivia Stoddard's legs and thinking of her offered ass in the midst of the room's effortful decorum while good citizens spoke of local health.

When, after they had shared a good part of a liter-sized jug of white wine, and after Bobby had gone to bed because it was a school night, they'd fallen to bed together naked, he had tried to interest Catherine. He had turned her over and had prodded at her, and she had whispered, "No."

He'd been desperate to be in her anus. He hadn't known why. Perhaps the darkest of his lusts were for Olivia, he thought. It was a thought he hated. But he remembered how he'd wanted Catherine like that, and had pried at her thighs and lifted her waist, had lain on her ass with an erection so hard and painful, he thought he might bleed from his prick.

"Please," she'd said calmly, "Carter: no. Let me turn over, and we'll—"

But he had lain on her and nuzzled her neck, and had shifted his thighs and pushed at her buttocks, until she had whipped herself around, had thrown him back and away, and was sitting, unembarrassed, legs crossed on the bed and her nipples hard, and had asked him, "Why? I've only—I don't enjoy that, Carter. All right?"

He'd rolled away.

With his face in the pillow, he had thought, to his shame and distress, of Olivia. Catherine's hand had pressed down on his own buttocks, and she'd patted him, then had leaned so he felt her breasts on his back and then her lips on his ass. She kissed, she nipped with her teeth, and then she'd sat up. "You're too big for me, big fella. Okay? Now get back on here, will you?" And she had lain back and had pulled him to her.

He had always wondered whether she'd played him that night, by saluting his size, by thinking, and correctly, he admitted, he'd be flattered, like a boy. He wondered if there were other reasons she'd refused. They were ones he wanted to know, yet he'd never had the nerve to ask her. He wanted to ask if she and Harry— Olivia caught his eye, and she raised her brow, and he thought of her in bed. He met her glance, and he smiled, shrugged, gave a well-here-we-are with his curled lips and moving hands, and she nodded. He nodded back. He wondered what they were saying to one another. He wondered what the speaker was saying, and he turned to listen.

Economic impact seemed to be the topic. The speaker was a man in a corduroy suit the color of goldenrod. He wore a blue workshirt and a dark tie. He spoke of jobs the mall would create. He mentioned "trickle-down," and several members of the audience groaned aggressively. "Oh, of course," the speaker said. "You're Democrats, and the president says trickle-down, you *have* to fight it. But let me remind you of a few things." He smiled. "You're in such a minority as Democrats in this county, you might as well be Chinamen. And second, trickle-down works. It's exactly what FDR used. He was a whatchamacallit, a—oh, yes, Democrat."

Several people applauded. One man, a farmer and smelling like it across the sweaty room, stood up and said, "FDR didn't use trickle-down. He used honesty and hard work. He didn't build a runoff storm water system that's guaranteed to flood across the highway and lay my oats under eight inches of water." When he sat down, there was more applause.

Olivia called out, "Let's ask someone on the job. Ask Carter Kreuss." She looked at him with her hungry, angry eyes that made him want to rape her and suck on her toes at the same time. "He's building the parking area. He knows all about civil engineering. He can tell us. Will it flood, Carter? Will it make us rich and wet, or can we stay dry and count our money and still have countryside that looks like that?" She pointed across the room at a giant painting of a valley, seen from a small meadow that was crossed by a brook. A cow, looking toward the viewer, seemed to be smiling about it all. Carter thought of Olivia's smile, and then he thought of her buttocks. He looked at her and walked to the front of the room, where the man in the goldenrod suit seemed annoyed to have to move from the lectern.

Carter realized that, standing before them with his hands in the pockets of his trench coat, he looked like an uncommitted observer, someone on the run. Someone put to *flight*, he thought.

He took off his trench coat and then his suit coat. He undid his tie a little and rolled his sleeves to the elbow: the workingman speaks.

A middle-aged man in the front row fingered his ear furtively, as though he were brushing back hair. Since he had none, the ploy was mildly distracting to Carter, who saw a round-headed fat man in his fifties jamming a finger into his large, furry ear, and then waving at the air behind it as if bothered by insects. He did this repeatedly. Beside him, one of those lanky dangerous women in jeans and a flannel shirt who could cross her legs at the knee and wind the calves around each other twice sat absolutely still and stared at him through her rimless glasses. Her short dark hair probably was a haven for moths and crawling things, maybe grubs, he thought. He thought of her as the professor. In the back of the room, his old lover and never friend, his sexual better, his longtime antagonist, Olivia Stoddard, waved her legs and smiled a knowing, unfriendly smile. Truscott John, in a wool-lined dungaree jacket that looked ironed and in old stiff work boots on legs that didn't move where they hung, as if nailed, from the table edge next to Olivia, smoked his cigarettes to the filter and watched.

"I'm not part of the HarJoe Company," Carter said. "They bought the land, and they're developing it. They subcontracted with me on a fixed-cost contract to put the parking area down— that means bays, the place where you park your car. Where the white lines'll be painted. Curbs and bays. That's my business. A lot of you know me." Some of them nodded, and Carter found himself pleased to be known by the people who sat in the Adams Room of the Inn. "Now, I've contracted for stone, asphalt, and concrete. I don't know if you write contracts like these in *your* business. But what it means is, I pay. Whether or not the mall goes in. If I lose my shirt on the deal, and it looks like I could, I have to do two more, say, malls real quick, I have to work nights, in other words—and I've done that. I've done that." He made the mistake of watching them watch him, and he became lost in their stare.

Harry Miller talks to people on behalf of that liberal faker every day, he thought. He sticks a hand in his pocket, and he smiles, and like Catherine they just smile back and he owns them.

"Well, not quite," he said.

The shift in their focus as they realized what he'd said, the sound of seashells held to the ears as *he* realized what he'd said, gave Carter the sense of seeing things as if his head were cocked. It wasn't. This is where "cock-eyed" comes from, he thought, unless it's about having just one eye, like a prick, and seeing things from below the belt.

"But you didn't ask about that, did you?" Olivia, her eyes wet and wide, a big smile scratched across her face, slowly shook her head and lippily mouthed the word *No*. "Okay. Flooding to the farm across the road. Won't happen. E and S Controls—Erosion and Sedimentation Controls. HarJoe's required to make sure silt and mud from the work, the construction, can't run into any streams nearby, any running water. And of course, if they do their job right, and they do, they have good people, pros. It's safe. There's stream water management controls in place. No more water's going to run off the site than before the mall and the parking bays went in. What they did, and I consulted on this with them. Let me tell you, I know what I'm doing." The fat man waved at his ear. Olivia nodded. "What we did there was, we figured out what would come off, flow off the ground, if we didn't have the job there. Then we figured out what difference the job would make, and we dropped in the right size pipe to let the equivalent amount of water run off, but into the pipe, so that we weren't *adding* any to the runoff onto the ground or into the streams. Does that make sense?"

The professor half-shrugged, as if to say, *So?* The fat man dug

133

at his ear. Olivia had turned to Truscott and was talking, and the man in the goldenrod corduroy suit stared expressionlessly.

"We bermed up an area," Carter said. He looked at them, and only a couple understood, he thought. "Made a dike? A pond, kind of, that'll hold the excess runoff that our catch basins and storm pipes won't manage. Nothing gets out that's not supposed to."

"Tell it to Three Mile Island," the professor called out. There was laughter, and a patter of hesitant applause.

Olivia, in her rich deep voice, with her mouth he couldn't stop looking at while he thought of Catherine and Harry in positions Olivia had taught him two years before, said, "I think, to be fair, that Mr. Kreuss *has* answered our question. Sir, do you agree?"

The farmer nodded. He paused, and then he said, "If it's true. Not to say you're a liar. If it was done, if it was done right. And if it works. I been hearing all my life about what protects me, from cars and tractors and bailers through to life insurance. All I know's how I end up dishing out the money. Nobody who *made* the goddamned things, if you'll excuse me."

"Pretty damned near foolproof," Carter said.

"I hope you know the quality of your fools," the farmer said.

"Yes," Olivia called, swinging her slender pale legs. "You mentioned storm water pipes, Mr. Kreuss. When I was getting deeply into things," she said, and he knew she was telling him to remember her fingers, slippery with lubricant jelly, inching in, "I seem to remember that, oh, say five feet down—would that be right? Five to six or seven feet down?—you have already laid in sanitary pipes to the septic system, inlets for storm water pipes, gas and electric thingies—I don't know what you call those."

"Facilities," Carter said. "We call them all facilities."

"Well," she said, "how very—facile."

Carter nodded and closed his eyes an instant. Because he could not think of holes in the earth or pipes without thinking about Harry and Catherine, which sent him back to Catherine and him, which sent him like an archaeologist down to him and Olivia, sliding greased across her sheets.

"When you were down there," she said, and Carter knew what was coming and actually looked at the door as if he might run. He had, while lost in flaps and folds and sphincters, actually failed to remember why they'd summoned him to climb on their little cross. "When you were down there, you kind of bumped into some bones, didn't you? And then you covered them back up?"

"I wonder if we could avoid using any form of *cover* and *up* in the same sentence?" He thought his smile was charming, and he made his eyes go wide. Boyish innocence, he thought.

"Bones, Carter," she said, harsh and hard and stinging.

"Yes. It's not uncommon on a construction site, at that depth, to find remains."

"Human bones," she said.

Their faces were a little embarrassed, he thought. They might care about the unburied dead, but they heard in her voice something personal, a secret she had kept. He wondered if they resented her, or were only intrigued, surprised. "They might be," . he said.

"You think they're not?"

He sighed. "I know they are."

"Whose?"

"Local Indians, I'd guess," he said. "Maybe Oneidas, but I don't really know. I'm not an expert. This was Indian country, once."

"And two or three hundred yards up the grade from where you found the bones and shoveled back the dirt and tried very hard to keep it quiet, it was African-American country, too. Wasn't it?"

He nodded.

"Where black families lived and had a church and then a graveyard?"

"Niggertown," he said, checking that no black had come.

"That's what they called it. Quaint and charming as the name is, it is also true. Many black people lived there. And died there. And were buried there. And then were dug up, when the turnpike was laid in. And the dead were dumped on your site."

"Well, it wasn't my site, exactly, when they—"

"You know what I mean, Carter. We shouldn't be buying underwear and reclining chairs by walking on the bones of the dead. Whatever their color. Or especially *that* color. Given this country's history of walking on them while they lived."

The farmer said, "Lady, I load that stuff on a spreader every day."

The professor told the farmer, "Mind your fucking manners, you racist."

Carter shouted across the room at Olivia, "So what am I supposed to do? Tell HarJoe to eat the interest on their bank loans? Tell my asphalt man to shut down, what the hell, he's got my money? Send the crew home? They've got my money too, it's promised. Sit at the table with HarJoe and eat the loss and take a job at night cleaning up your husband's *bank*? For who? Who says it's black people? Who says a black person living really *cares*? You notice all the black people sitting around you?" He gestured at the pink-white audience.

"We care," Olivia said. "Some of their history's ours. Some of ours is theirs. All of us are *Americans*."

Carter said, "Maybe I've just been overexposed, recently. To all you fine folks in and out of government."

"In," Olivia said. "In. We are all of us in. We are all of us *it. We're* the government."

The farmer got up, put on his down vest, turned to Olivia, and said, "You could grow corn on the moon with a few loads of that." He leaned over the shoulder of the professor, who winced from either his boots or the tobacco he chewed, and he patted her shoulder gently, saying, "Only women ever talked to me about fucking was women who knew how it went. We'd have to lay a can of 3-in-One upside your zipper just to even think of it." He

walked across the others in his row, then down the aisle and out
of the Adams Room of the Inn.

"We have an injunction," Olivia said to the audience, milling
by now, in the process of dismissing itself. "We have to call our
so-called town fathers, local government. We have to be at the
courthouse to let the judge know how we feel. Cable your congressman. *Do* something. We have lists of people for you to call."
The professor was up and handing out mimeographed slips, and
so was Olivia. Truscott John smoked his cigarette and speculated
on Carter, who looked away from him. The fat man picked at his
ear. Olivia's voice came up again: "We're in touch with the Senate. A man is here from the Senate, and we're on the verge of
federal intervention. Really. I promise." It was her final words
that made him know he wanted her again. They reminded him of
a girl among girls, a kid who was desperately lying to keep her
circle of friends from drifting away. He knew that she almost
wasn't lying—for he knew, now, why Harry had come back. He
knew as well that he would rescue Catherine from Harry. That
he could try to. He had right on his side. It wasn't only that
Carter had been there first, this time around—he was *protecting*
her. And as he thought so, as he told himself how sure he was,
while wondering what his motives actually were, he was disturbed by sympathy for Olivia his tormentor, and by visions of
her thighs and ankles, of her high, presented buttocks, of her
hiding face that peeped out, underneath, all appetite and mischief
and, despite her posed availability, control.

Bobby was asleep in a room shattered by history panic. Socks
in dirty balls, and underwear, notebook pages covered with a
hasty rounded hand, books scattered from his easy chair to his
bed, and coins—when he grew insecure, he counted his money or
his baseball cards—made the room look like an aftermath. Every
room is, she thought. Rooms are either waiting for what's going

to make them matter, or they become the scene of the crime. No
neutral rooms except in museums, she thought. And this was no
museum. This was her baby's catastrophe. He was face down, in
his clothes, with his covers around his waist. She pulled them up
and decided not to turn off the tape player connected to the ear-
phones he wore. She was reluctant to disturb whatever gave him
rest. And she was pleased that he was enveloped in noise, she
admitted.

She turned off all his lights and went downstairs to call in
Drown. He limped in, exhausted after harrying the moon, and
headed for the living room sofa. "Don't," she warned him. He
turned those guilty white eyeballs on her and dropped on the
carpet where he stood. "You think I think you'll stay there?" He
banged his tail against the floor. "Well, try, will you?"

She turned out lights in her house, and hung the slickers on
their hooks in the dark. She found the decanter of Calvados that
HarJoe had given to Carter, what the hell, and she pulled two
glasses from the shelf above the phone. I seem to work without
lights these days, she thought. The last one she turned off was in
the hall outside her bedroom. Harry, she knew, was inside.

He said, as she entered, "I found where you keep the sheets."

"Yes?"

"I changed them. On the bed. I changed the sheets."

"Did they smell funny?"

"You know why I did."

"Shouldn't *I* have done that? If I wanted to?"

"I decided I was going to take some chances, Cath. All the time
I haven't—we haven't been together, I've been scared of losing
you."

"Good."

"Yeah. But you can't lose what you don't have. And, you get
scared of too much too often, you lose the habit of, I don't know,
acting. Doing stuff. I don't think I could stand being any more
crippled than I am."

"How do you mean, crippled?" She poured Calvados and pulled her sweater over her head. She heard his breath catch as she did, and she hoped that he would take his clothes off too, but she was going to be naked even if it *did* look like a middle-aged strip show. She said, "Strip 'em, will you?" Don't giggle, she instructed herself, and she heard herself snort a sort of giggle.

"God, what a pleasure," he said breathily. "I mean, I'm afraid to say boo sometimes, because it'll offend you. Because you've been off with yourself, or Carter, whoever. You know. For so *long*. I'm afraid maybe you'll be someone else, and we won't *work* together. I feel like I've been waiting most of my life so that we will."

Naked and lighted, she knew, by the full frosting moon, she walked closer to where he stood, by the bed. "You want to change the sheets," she said, "you change them. Here." He held onto his glass and stared at her. He was bare-chested, and the top of his jeans was open. She was going to reach for his pants, where the belly that he'd fought so long was trying, and not unsuccessfully, to return, when she stopped. He was staring at her, and she fought the impulse to look down, to where her own flesh rounded and mounded and hung. "Oh, dear," she said. He was looking at her as though—dammit, woman, he's *said* it: as though he'd been waiting all his life to see her here like this.

She watched his eyes as she dipped a finger in her Calvados and touched it to her nipples. He dove to her, holding her waist, dropping his glass, causing her to drop hers, and he sucked the brandy, licked it, and the breast around it, and she almost fell to her knees. She caught herself with one hand on the brass bedpost. "Have a drink," she said, and then she *did* giggle, and—she was thankful that they weren't grim, theatrical—so did Harry. But he wouldn't let her go. One arm around her waist, still, he wrested her sideways, and they fell onto the bed, and all her brandy-applying ingenuity fell with the brandy itself. She hadn't a thought, she thought. Neither, apparently, did he. For they had made love, before, with some invention, with an artful delaying, with cruel and delicate stallings, and with all sorts of noise. Now they were silent, and they didn't laugh any more. She lay on her back beneath him, her legs almost around him and up in the air, the calves and feet flopping as if disconnected, as Harry, with no cunning foreplay, his fingers touching only her arms and her neck, her face, and then at last her back, plunged deep into what, she was interested and grateful to know, was like a liquid core. There was little rearing and watching, no out-to-the-tip-and-slowly-back-in, as there used to be between them. It was, she thought, as if they didn't choose to separate by even that much space. Their pelvises were together, and he was deep inside her, and they rocked together not all that slowly because she couldn't wait, she didn't care if he came right now. He didn't, and neither did she, and she didn't care if they never came. Yes, she did. Yes, she did. Yes, she did.

She said his name. He panted harshly, as if he'd been running, or weeping, or both. She held him hard and moved at him selfishly, relishing the selfishness, and came—a string of firecrackers going off was what she saw, like something in the Saturday cartoons the boys had used to watch. He tightened his thighs around hers now, and squeezed her thighs together around his penis, and he groaned a deep startled sound, and Catherine came again, so hard she yelped, but she heard him. He said, "*Cath.*"

Then they lay together on their sides, still locked, and then apart on their sides, him still panting, and then Harry turned toward the bright-as-daylight windows, falling into sleep as if his body knew that this would be his best night's sleep in years.

Catherine lay on her back. She touched her gluey crotch and was tempted to linger, or to wake him. And then she turned onto her side, so that her arm lay over Harry's soft chest—hard enough a couple of minutes ago, you bitch.

Now I lay me down to sleep, she thought. Thanks for the tomatoes in the pantry waiting to be washed, and the peppers and zucchini, the oregano and thyme. But I have to ask, she thought, pressing her nose and mouth into the side of his neck, its salty taste, what's supposed to happen next? To remind us for sure that we are *not* supposed to wait a long time and love long-distance and finally hop in the sack to find truth, justice, contentment, *and* measured form while living sweetly, stupidly, happily forever after?

And what happened was that she woke. Nothing saddened or disturbed her, and the falling temperatures and rising wind, the gentle, expected music of windowpanes shaken, were soothing, not unsettling. But she'd been asleep, in deep, exhausted, grateful sleep, and then she lay with her eyes open, a light sweat on her skin, and her breathing just a little fast. As if he sensed her unsettlement, Harry pulled at her. Did he know she needed comforting, or wish she did? Or was he just a great, greedy boy? He was a comforting and greedy man, she thought. But she felt that what she needed more than his needful generosity was air. She heard it outside, and she thirsted for it. And he had her pinned.

She had forgotten how Harry slept, at least how Harry slept with her. She would return to how he might sleep with whomever else, she knew. She had visited the question before. Now, though, he had reached, when she'd wakened and stirred, and had curved around her. He lay at her back and embraced her. Even in his deepest sated sleep, he reached. He lay, now, with his arm stretched over her hip and his hand cupping her abdomen, just brushing the top of her pubic hair, tickling her and stimulating her at once. She thought to wake him up, reward and punish him for turning her on, like a bright bulb in a small lamp, all heat and strange shadows thrown into corners she hadn't thought to peer at. And, on the other hand, even sexy, even languid and damp, she didn't mind being alone with Harry. The best way of being with a man, she thought sadly: alone. True? Catherine: *true?*

Okay, she thought, sliding from under him, out of the bed, tiptoeing for her old blue robe and a trip through the house. Okay. And *now* what?

The floors were cold, and she was certain that hard frost had struck. Downstairs, she put on wellingtons—clammy, cold on her calves, smelling of mud and sweat—and then a slicker over her robe. She took a six-volt lantern, but she thought she wouldn't need it. She was right. It was bright blue-white outside, the sumac waved like—how could she help it?—giant phalluses. They hadn't blown up, although the milkweed pods along the road surely had. Now they were an explosion suspended, the fluffy interior of the pods clinging to them on top of the thick stems. The moonlight gleamed on them, and she felt mournful, though she didn't know what she mourned. Maybe one more year. An increasingly worthy object of sadness, she thought. She wandered around her house near the empty road. She was looking, she realized, at scrubby strong weeds, some past their brilliance. She loved them as much as she liked prettier flowers like columbine and monkshood, the purple crowns of chive. Her body felt heavy, rich, as if her blood were a syrup. Her breasts were sore, her thigh muscles jumpy. She unsnapped the slicker to let in the wind that rattled the aspens and made the Norway spruce moan. But it was too cold, and she wasn't about to lie down and stuff herself with daisies like Lady What's Her Name, just to celebrate the return of D. H. Lawrence and the end of the growing season. God. Those women in town with their seed catalogs that sounded as if you were window-shopping the Wadsworth Athenaeum and not a company! What she was after was a garden and what grew and—

She'd been about to tell herself Harry's name. She kicked a soda can on the road and turned back to the house, stumbling over Drown, who of course had sneaked away with her. Midnight missions and hikes at high noon, all were the same to him. He was only along for fun, she thought, for a good pee on the boundaries—she watched him lift his leg and squirt a stand of brown brush—and a survey of the general surrounding life. Me, too, she wanted to say. Me, too: adventure, and a walk in the moonlight, and what the hell else.

She was around at the other side of the house, now, and flopping in the wellies down to the garden, her coat closed against the rising winds, her hands in her pockets, and everything, she saw as she rounded the gatepost, gone black. The light patina of ice crystals lay on the post and on the vegetables, the big sweeping ugly leaves of horseradish and broccoli, the high, waving—goddam the phallus, anyway!—stalks of asparagus. The garden glinted at her, and she could see the season to come. Tomatoes were blackening, almost as she watched, it seemed.

She contemplated frost, and fall, then pumpkins in October. Pumpkins reminded her of the boys, of carving pumpkins every year for them. First she and Dell had done it, and then she and Harry, then she alone; by the time Carter came, they were through with separate pumpkins, and the ritual cutting-in on newspaper folds in the kitchen, the rich rotting smell of the white-orange pulp, and how she read into what they carved: sad Bobby always made smiles; Randy, who'd invented well-adjusted behavior, made sneering satanic faces. She always read wrong, she realized. "All that makes me is a parent," she said. Drown was asleep, on a sheet of plastic mulch that flapped around him. This year, she decided, she would carve a pumpkin for herself. Carter had hated doing it; the odor offended him—reminded him, he said, of his stepfather's compost heap. She stood beside hers, in its cage of chicken wire and metal posts, and she inhaled it: leaves, fruit and vegetable rinds, juices of what had rotted into the soil she kept covered with peat moss and lime. It was a good house-smell, and necessary, she thought. This year, there will be a pumpkin. I will not read into what Harry thinks to carve, or suggests I carve, or does or doesn't do about the carving. And who told you Harry would *be* here in two weeks?

"I'll carve it alone and wear the bastard on my head if I have to."

A forty-one-year-old woman in a robe and slicker, naked

underneath, in wellington boots and probably out of her mind, standing in a frost-blighted garden at who knows what hour of the night, talking to herself about Halloween.

Talking to herself about a man.

Trick or treat.

She sighed, then sighed again, to see whether her breath condensed on the cold air. It didn't, or she didn't see it, and she turned to climb to the house. Tomorrow was Saturday, and she and Bobby would have to find the chore-of-the-weekend to fight about. Poor little bastard, she thought, seeing him, taller than Carter, taller than Harry, gorgeous to girls (and his mommy), and slugging it out with his own body. It might grow too quickly for the soul inside it, she thought. It was the life his life was asking him to wear. She wondered how it might be different for him if Harry was around. Randy would probably quit Columbia, come home to work at the I. L. Richer carrying sacks of feed, and take a course a term at night at Mohawk Community College. There are worse fates, she thought. You could be around Harry Miller and not excite my sadness, she thought.

And are we making plans, she asked herself in as cruel a psychic voice as she knew, pausing at the Canadian hemlocks outside the back porch. She tore a piece of branch off and crushed it, rolling her palms, and smelled her hands. It was the floors of forests in summer she smelled; she thought of New England, not New York, and of being younger in Maine, tenting and being scared at night by the prospect of bears that never came.

She thought of Harry in the dark, bulky as a bear, and furry on his chest and back and arms, growling into her neck and breasts and groin. Harry was a bear who came. And though she'd solved nothing, outside of learning that something had to be solved, and though she knew nothing more about her children and her pumpkins and her—what? longtime friend? newfound lover?—*Harry*, dammit, upstairs, asleep, she dropped her slicker in the pantry and, reaching the stairs, began to loosen the belt of her robe as she climbed to wake him now, and tell him that the frost was on the pumpkin, that the year was on its way.

The stairs creaked, now that she'd torn off them the old striped runner that had come with the house. She knew that she was the sort of householder who is always archaeologizing. On a whim, without knowing that she'd do it, she had slashed a putty knife through six layers of old wallpaper in the kitchen, forcing herself to repaper the room. She had cut through the runner with a filleting knife on a late Friday night last summer, when she'd thought to sit on the porch and look for shooting stars going across her sky. She and Carter were going to sit on the porch, and stop sweating from a long summer day's pursuit of other people's needs, and drink cold beer and look at the sky and think of their own needs. What Carter had meant, she'd thought then and thought tonight, had been a long rolling screw on the chaise longue. What she had meant, she realized, had been sitting back and bearing no one's weight or presence in, on, or about her person.

He'd been courteous enough about his disappointment, holding her bottle of beer and sipping from his own as, veering from their kitchen cleanup, she had taken the long filleting knife and begun to cut through the hemp runner with its nice-enough stripes. After that, she worked with a thin screwdriver to pry up the big staples that held the runner down. And then, just to see how the stairs would look when she rented a small sander and really went to work, she'd scratched away with sandpaper to cut through the years of paint and plain dirt to expose the wood which now, under her feet, was sanded and polyurethaned to a high, dark gloss.

The steps creaked under her feet. They'd creaked like tree limbs cracking since the padding of the runner was removed. And Carter, she thought, decent enough about the removal, had never been as comfortable about walking upstairs to her room. He'd been able to do it in silence; now, just-before-now, he'd been unable to. The stairs announced to her children that Mommy's

lay was on his way. She wondered what they did say and think
about Carter and her, now Harry and her, or any man at all.
Randy had been uncomfortable, she remembered, fearing that his
mother was promiscuous. She loved him for his wonderful young
propriety, that moment, her big boy who would probably try to
screw the knothole of a sapling that waved in the wind. Oh, he
wouldn't! And stop thinking this way. It's incestuous and immoral
and unseemly.

Carter had been strong in bed, and in emergencies, and on
shopping trips. He had gone away so easily. She thought he'd
meant his departure as a rebuke to her inconstancy. She wondered
if he'd meant to invite it. Men leave me, she thought. Or is it that
I drive them out the door? Ask Harry. She was going to, at the
top of the stairs, when she saw the light in Bobby's room, down
the hall to her right, come harshly on. She went there. The bulb
was too bright, and the reading lamp near the bed was close to the
wall and aimed mostly at it, so the light was reflected from his
light wallpaper, and it cast great shadows. His room was like a
cave, she thought. His light was like a sun, setting. He lay face
down under his comforter, his arms at his sides, his legs straight
and together.

"Hi, sweetie," she said. "You look like you're floating. What
are you doing up?"

He shrugged.

She sat on his bed and touched his shoulder. He didn't shrink
from her, but his back surely didn't relax to welcome his mother's
hand. She kept it there, though, on the comforter, pressing at his
bony shoulder blade. "Are you all right?"

He shrugged again.

"Want to talk about stuff? About anything?"

He shook his head.

"Want *me* to talk?"

He didn't move.

She said, "This is a little like being alone, Bobby."

His voice, muffled by the pillow, said, "What happened with Carter?"

"I think he's angry that Harry came back. Came over. Whatever Harry did. I think he resents it. I think he sees Harry as trespassing. Maybe he's jealous. Well, he is. He ought to be. What I mean by that is, you like someone a lot, you should want to—no, I don't know about jealousy. It's not as if Carter and I were married or anything. We didn't talk about getting married, you know. I'd have talked to *you* about it before I'd have talked with Carter. You and Randy. You miss your brother?"

He shrugged.

"You do."

He nodded, reluctantly, pressing his face into the pillow.

"It doesn't feel quite that we're whole, does it? With Randy in New York and everything."

Bobby turned his lean face sideways, and Catherine saw how long his lashes were, and how dark his face was from the heat of the pillow. He kept his eyes closed, as if retaining darkness or the pillow's protection. He said, "Randy, and Daddy—our father—went away. Harry went away. Carter went away. Then Harry'll go again. Who's *staying*?"

"I am," she said at once, putting her hand, open, palm down, so that it lay along the side of his face. She would have lain alongside him in the bed and held him if she thought he'd let her. The hand was on behalf of all her body, and it covered his jaw, the half he let her see. "I am. And you didn't know Dell, your father, not really. Did you?" Under her hand, his face shook, No, not much more than a tremor. "Or Harry? Way back in Vermont?" Again, the No. "But you feel these departures." He lay absolutely still. "Sometimes I think most of a person's life consists of saying good-bye to people. It's a bitch, Bobby, isn't it? Listen. You and I had to say good-bye to Randy, but he'll be back. We'll be stuck with him for holidays and all of the summer, I guess, and we'll all get sick of each other. You and I get sick of each other right *now*. But we'll be getting sick of ourselves together, and you and I and a lot of Randy and this house and Drown, we're steady. We're here. We're the scenery here, we're not going away. I swear to you, I promise you: we're one—what is it? Did you recite it in school? Do they still do that? *One nation . . . indivisible?* Very important idea. We're indivisible. You and Randy and me. One family indivisible, a single thing that will not, I guarantee it, come apart."

She'd shut her eyes as she'd prayed. She knew it when she opened them, to see her fingers spreading on his face as if it were a flat, hot rock she must pry from the earth. She turned her hand over to stroke his cheek with its drier back, to comfort and not only clutch. Then she did bend down to him and kiss his cheek, and smell the day's dried sweat in his hair—it once had smelled like apples in autumn, that lovely head—and she found herself rubbing her forehead along his temple, as if by pressing and breathing on him she could make him feel that not all their life was dangerous change.

"And Carter?" Bobby asked. "And Harry?"

"What, baby?"

"Are they part of us? Indivisible?"

"Are you inviting them? Both of them?"

"That wouldn't work," he said.

"No. Then one?"

He shrugged.

She lay almost on his shoulder and embraced him. She kissed his cheek again. "Go to sleep. In the morning, you and I will be here. Saturday morning. We can fight about chores. And Randy will wake up in Manhattan, and he'll miss us. We'll miss him. Isn't life an amazing bitch, Bobby?" She sniffed as silently as she could and pulled the comforter unnecessarily around him and kissed the back of his head. She turned the light out. She whispered, "Thank you," and she left before he could ask her what she meant.

In the hallway, along the wall outside of Bobby's room, she walked into Harry in the darkness, his body naked except for shorts, his hands already stroking her upper arms to assure her that what startled her was only the bear from her bedroom. She could see his eyes gleam; in the darkness, their light looked enormous. She walked behind him to her room, touching him on the small of his back with her fingertips. She felt muscle rolling, not just lard, and she pressed at it, enjoying its resilience. And in her room, lighted by a bedside table, she watched him turn from her. So she walked around to find his face. It was wet.

"You were outside there, listening?"

"I heard sounds. I thought there might be a problem. Then I figured I couldn't go charging in in my boxer shorts. I wouldn't have, anyway. That was for you guys, not me."

"So why are you—you were crying, Harry."

He nodded. And she could tell from the contortions of his face that he fought right now, prodded by his own reaction to his saying that he'd wept, not to weep.

"Harry, why?"

"I wanted to be in there with you."

She nodded. Her throat was constricted. We could go around crying at strangers' funerals for fees, she thought.

He said, "You know. Indivisible."

She reached for his waist, his ribs, and she held him—away, but in her grasp, within her reach—and hard.

She said, "I was in the garden before."

"I heard you leave."

"I thought you were sleeping."

"Ah, yes. The hasty screw and quick sleep, eh?" He smiled and shook his head. "I was lying there replaying it. And you went, and I figured you needed the time alone. Wanted it. Whatever-it. So I kept my eyes shut and thought about you."

"I thought about you. I was in the garden and everything started to freeze. The whole cycle clicked along another notch.

Like a huge wooden wheel. Like something. I don't know. It was beautiful. It was scary."

"That sounds like what happened here *before* you left."

She dropped her hands to his waistband and tugged.

"In wellingtons, Cath?"

She looked down at her feet and saw boots.

"It's just one more garden to you, is it?"

She sat on the floor and stuck her legs out, like a girl in school. Like a girl, she thought, in a rucked robe and boots. And Harry, with his shorts supporting a penis that bobbed above the waistband that she'd pulled at, bent to take her boots off, one at a time, and to remain on his knees, to kiss her left big toe, left instep, then arch, the stubbly left shin and then the knee and then thigh. She was going to lie back on the floor of her bedroom and pull his head down into her when he reared above her, still on his knees, and took her hands and kissed them, then let her fall, supported by him, backward onto the rug. She lay there with her hands on her groin, held there by him, as through her own fingers he kissed and licked. The bear is in the garden, she thought.

Chapter Four

Harry's face still smarted because he'd had to shave twice—once on account of his whiskers, and once because he was the only man over twenty with shaving tackle in Catherine Hollander's upstairs medicine chest. He'd scraped himself to say how glad he was, and now his face ached as he drove over blown bright leaves on a narrow country road in the hills above a county route that was locally called the King's Settlement Road. He was searching for the man Olivia had arranged an appointment with, Truscott John, called Trus by Olivia, who had known the graveyard when he was small.

Truscott John waited for him between two enormous trees with leaves that glowed gold-red. Their bark was thick and deeply scoured with lines, and so was Trus's face. He sat in a soldier's squat, a kind of knee bend, with one foot slightly ahead of the other, and he didn't shift or bounce as he smoked a cigarette and watched Harry come. Dust had followed the Mustang up the sparsely settled road, and he'd slowed so as to keep from fanning it into the small old-fashioned trailers and occasional four-room shacks, their sides more often than not lined with tar paper held down with furring strips instead of shakes or clapboard. He had drifted in under the branches of wide old trees on a road hemmed by dense brush that was tan with October and venous with dark limbs as the leaves lightened or fell, and that occasionally glowed with the long, sore, scarlet centers of sumac. The light dust, more brown than the red of the site, dyed the air.

Truscott John slowly stood and threw his cigarette down. He was very tall, and terribly thin, his waist as narrow as a stylish girl's. He was dressed in dungarees and flannel shirt and work boots and a light, cheap-looking windbreaker. He opened the passenger's door to ask, "Harry Miller?"

"Truscott John?"

They nodded at each other and, when John was in the car, shook hands. John's handshake was light and unmuscular; his hands were the size of two of Harry's, it seemed, and as coarse as raw wood, with calluses and scars. "I know the woman you're visiting," John said. "Olivia Stoddard said you was staying with Catherine Hollander."

"That's right," Harry said. "We're longtime friends."

"Well, good," John said, smiling all his lovely, large false teeth. His nose was beaked, and it sprouted hairs, as did his ears. His hair lay under a long-brimmed light-green baseball cap that said JOHN DEERE. "Yes, I've did her plumbing and electric for a good number of years. Good person. I like her boys."

"Me, too," Harry said. Then an idea struck: "Is she involved with you and Mrs. Stoddard in the graveyard thing?"

"I don't know who's involved," John said, pointing at the fork he wanted Harry to take. "Don't know, really, about involved in *what*." He lit a cigarette and Harry had to fight to keep from seizing it and inhaling all of it at once, it smelled so good. I am the man, he thought, who's never lost an appetite, for long, in sadness or joy. "All *I* know's they know, Olivia and her friends—"

"Not Catherine?"

"Never did see her at one a them meetings they hold."

"Uh-huh."

"They ask me questions," John said. "I go back a ways. I've lived here more than sixty years, and kept my health more or less, and my memory. And it turns out I do work for a lot of them. Olivia and them. We get along. So they pour me some coffee and make me some cake. I have a terrible sweet tooth. They ask me about the town, and I tell them what I can. You see, I used to cut the grass at the colored cemetery." He turned to look at Harry for a reaction. "That's what they used to call it. I sapect they didn't mean any insult. In them days, 'colored' was acceptable, you see. I mean to the colored people, too."

Harry nodded. "Sure," he said, in the voice he'd used at the *News* when soliciting stories, the voice that would have with pleasure labeled Adolf Hitler "sweet" and murder "fun," if he could have what they knew. "That's the way it was all over," he didn't quite shout. "And Negro was polite."

"I know some people would call it an insult, nowadays. Whereas," John said, tossing his cigarette from the window, "it was *black* could have been the insult, depending on who said it to who."

"So it was black people, then. Colored people."

"Sure. Leastwise, that's what they told me when they give me a scythe and said to go there and cut the grass down near the road. I worked for the town some summers. That was one of my jobs. Nowadays, of course, they'd drop a boy off with a can of gas and a mower. Then, I walked out with a scythe and a jar of well water."

They drove past Catherine's house. There was no station wagon in the drive, he saw, cursing himself, as he looked, for how hard he had looked. Then they swooped down the hill and up the next rise, passing few other cars. Truscott John lit another cigarette. "Where are you from, Mr. Miller?"

"Harry."

"All right. I'm called Trus. Like what you wear for a hernia." He didn't laugh at his name, though he smiled around the cigarette.

"I'm from New York City, originally," Harry said. "But I live in Washington, D.C."

"You work for that senator, the Irishman."

"I do," Harry said. "Olivia told you?"

"She did, yes. But now you mention it, when I come to think about it, I remembered something Catherine told me, it must have been years ago."

Harry did not whinny. "No kidding," he said.

"Yes, it was something about—" John tapped a large tooth with a long, wide finger. "Taxes, I recollect. I sapect I was bitchin about taxes, which is something a man will do. And our friend Catherine said, 'I know a man works for that senator, I ought to write and ask him.' She said something about she was meaning to, for some time. I guess she gets behind in her correspondence."

"I guess I do too. I didn't know she knew I'd changed jobs."

"Well," John said, "she's what you'd call a perceptive woman, if I use the word right."

"You sure do."

John laughed and nodded toward the cigarette in his fingers. "Well, good," he said, happily, while he inhaled the smoke.

Harry remembered the tax bill fight the senator had lost, and he remembered when they'd fought it, when Catherine might have read his name from reports on a briefing he'd run. She had been telling Truscott John, over a clogged water pipe or blown-out circuit, about Harry in Washington when Harry, in trouble, had been seeing Lauren Lamb. Seeing her, and rolling in the ground behind her, like a marlin towed, still almost fighting, in the wake of a sleek cruiser. Lauren was the tallest beautiful woman he had known. She was six feet three, and she worked the Nautilus gear in the Georgetown gym three times a week. Her second marriage, to a poet at George Mason, had just foundered. She had caught him *in flagrante*, in her car in their garage, with his graduate assistant, of whom Lauren kept asking, "How could he kiss a man with a beard? They were *kissing*. With a *beard*." Lauren taught political science at Georgetown, and when the Soviets rolled into Afghanistan, she'd been sixth on the CIA's call list: wakened before the day grew light (that dawn demarcation became the academic border for career definition), she had prospered. And Harry, whose senator chaired the intelligence subcommittee before which Lauren testified, had grown fond of giving briefings, and drinking iced vodka with people who received briefings. Harry had prepared her to testify, and they'd stayed friends.

But Lauren was a busy woman, busier even than Harry, and more worried about staying busy. What had begun as frantic, if unimaginative, lovemaking in the Senate Office Building, had declined to what they did if Harry pestered and when there was time. While at first he had climbed her, a cub up a tree, he latterly had sniffed around her legs, he thought. "Don't be so *needy*!" he figured she'd been telling him, about the time that Catherine told Truscott John where he worked.

"We can stop," John told him, on a ridge that, Harry guessed, was across from the ridge where he'd parked to watch the blood-red dust hang over the building site. Now he saw earth levelers and giant bulldozers and trucks on wheels higher than he'd ever seen, all still. And so was the dust.

"Looks like a great big hole to dump trucks in, don't it?" John asked. "My grandson digs pits like that and puts them scale-model yellow trucks, I forget what they're called, inside like that. Looks *just* like it. I can show you now."

They climbed out and walked along the ridge, to where the single-lane road petered out and became a path which disappeared into a birch forest above the site. There were other trees too, though Harry wasn't certain of their names: maple he thought he knew, and the ash that Catherine had shown him near the garden, and aspen with its trembling leaves. Their colors were a shining maroon, a yellow-gold, deep red. He thought to ask John what the names of the others were, but he was thinking of Lauren and how, when they'd ended as less than friends, she had asked him, "What kind of a man who isn't gay stays single all this time? You aren't, are you?" He remembered saying, "Not as far as I know," and hating himself for months because he hadn't slugged her—he'd have needed a footstool, he reminded himself—not for the content of the question, but because she hadn't the imagination to consider someone like Catherine in the life of someone like Harry.

Daylight broke through long bare branches. There were bright blue weeds that looked like eyelashes, and a rustling ahead in the quiet grove, as if something fled before them. Truscott John looked up and around, though most often he looked at the ground, and when they were at a huge stump, cut low to the floor of the grove, and rotted, above which a fat, errant bee weakly stumbled through the air, John said, "Here, I sapect, is where you'd like to look."

Harry could tell that the ground had once been cleared, while around them, in a rude square about the size of Catherine's garden, there had grown up dense brush, slender trees, and a kind of bush that whipped in the wind, looked almost metallic, and had thorns all over it.

John saw what he was looking at. "That's hawthorn," he said. "Nobody has much use for it. When I was a boy, I used to chop it down for my father. I hacked enough of it away right here. Three summers after high school let out, I come up here regular, and I cut the grass, pulled out or chopped down the seedlings, sawed away the brush, and this here." He pointed at the low, slanted stump, its top worn smooth, yellow-white, pulpy, dissolving into thick, soft splinters. "I cut this down my last summer on the job. Took me a day. I had to make sure it didn't fall on any of the graves. By then, no colored people come here to supervise me or nothin. It was the white preacher who inherited the church

156

they used to run that the coloreds belonged to. It died out. Nobody went. And I don't blame them. Bunch of white sissies and weepers run it, prayed in it, and organized the picnic for it once a year. They hired me to cart them up on a haywagon hitched to a pokey tractor somebody donated to the church. Then I had to clean up behind them. They drank Kool-Aid and they ate potato salad that give me the runs for two days. Anyway, they made sure I didn't let the tree strike any stones. Not that I necessarily would have."

Harry had his pen and notebook out, but he didn't write a thing. He looked at this tall, handsome man with a cigarette bobbing in his lips, his pale eyes looking back almost the length of Harry's life. "Did you read the stones?" Harry asked.

"Sure."

Harry waited, but Truscott John said nothing more.

"Can you remember what they said, Trus?"

"They all give the same year, pretty much. I'd say every second one had the same year on it. They had a plague. That's what they called it around here."

"So most of them died at the same time?"

"A goodly percentage, I would say. Yes."

"Do you—I guess you wouldn't. I was thinking you might remember some names, though."

"A lot of them never got a second name. Most of them died with first names. John. Rebecca. Bill. A lot of them was children, I think. They didn't have a lot of years on the stone: 1860–1864. There was a good deal of that. They didn't have too much more room anyway, you know. They give them very small stones to begin with."

Harry looked down from the little ring of slightly younger forest in the midst of all the wild tangle of the ridge. He could see the two trailers, side by side, in which he thought the bosses of the site must meet. "Wait a minute," he said. "The site's down *there*."

Trus was smiling and lighting another cigarette. "I wondered how long you'd take. Olivia said you're a sharp fella."

"So why're we here? Or: why the fuss down *there*?"

"You seen how the road petered out we come on?" Harry nodded. "Didn't always," Trus said. "Once, it was a brand-new road. Started out as a farm right-of-way from the Flanagan sisters' farm. Then the town widened it, pushed it all the way through to come out down below a mile or two and meet up with the highway. Of course, it's all forgotten now. It kept washing out, on account of the drainage and the shale here. They let it go. Used it just long enough to need to move the colored people's bones."

"Wait a minute," Harry said.

"No, that's right," Trus said. "Thirty years ago, easy, they come up here with tractors and wagons and mules and men from the jail in Leonardsville. Dug up every body, so they told the church people. Carried 'em down there, and gave 'em a home."

"You think they did?"

"I thought at the time," Trus said, dropping into his soldier's squat, "that it was peculiar"—he said *pakooler*—"how they never did move the gravestones down at the time."

"Why not?"

"Ever hear of a saying goes how the road to hell is paved with good intentions?"

Harry looked down at Trus, then dropped himself into a similar squat, except that his belt pushed into his belly and his knees were instantly sore. But he stayed that way. He said, "And? I mean, yeah. Sure. Of course I've heard of it."

There was the low, steady sound of the wind as it pawed the dense brush around them and ranged over what Harry now would have sworn he could make out: the barest depression that went through what he guessed was the old black cemetery, the road the town had built, the road that forced the town fathers— gave them an excuse?—to condemn the graveyard and move the fled slaves and their children away. "But I'll be fucking god-damned, Trus, if I can find any good intentions here. Excuse me."

Harry felt his eyes watering, and remembered, again, why he had finally failed at the hardest parts of cityside reporting: he'd believed what middle-class children are told at birth and grow up confirming, because they're rarely allowed to believe otherwise, eventually refuse to believe otherwise: that you're born with a right to be happy.

Trus said, "All right. The intentions'd be hard enough to locate. But how about the paving part?"

Harry looked at this man with his long legs and short torso, sprouting ears and nose, amused, inured intelligence. Trus looked back at him and smoked. And then Harry dropped onto his hands and knees. He swept his palm over the grass. "No," he said.

Trus said, "I've found 'em."

Harry pawed at fallen leaves and twigs and dead or dying grass and stems of weeds. Like a dog, he set himself on spread legs and tore in a paddling motion with both hands into the earth before him. He found a thick piece of fallen limb and he used it as a rude shovel. When he looked up, Trus was sitting with his back against a tree, his legs crossed at the ankle, his arms folded across his chest, and a cigarette between his lips. Harry dug and set aside, sifted, set aside, scrabbled, set aside. And then he sat on his haunches, panting, and studied each piece of rock he'd dug up. As he worked, he noted how a thin film of ooze, even on this dry autumn day, lay an inch or two under the crust.

"Was this the worst spot for drainage, Trus?"

"I think they must of thought so."

"Because it's wet."

"Isn't it."

He chose another site, and he dug again, and set aside and sifted, and Trus sat back and watched. Finally, like the dog who'd dug, he went panting to Truscott John with four frag-ments. "Yes?" he asked him. "These? Yes?"

They rubbed at the pieces of stone. Trus spat on one and rubbed the saliva in, like a polish: *64* came up, in rounded shallow carving. "I'd say so," Trus told him, depositing the stone on his dungareed thigh, which was stretched out before him. Another had a fragment of a letter, *N* or *M* or *W*, they guessed. Another said *RN*.

"They paved the county road with the headstones," Harry said.

"I believe that's what we're saying."

"Are you the only one who knows it?"

"Lord, no. Not that many's left, but the ones are, know."

"Shit," Harry said. "And the bodies are down there?"

"See that gray pickup with the alumeyum chair in back? It belongs to one of the foremen. That's how they take their ease while the crews work. They call it supervision. It pays better than work. Right about where that truck is parked, I'd say, you'd find what's left of the colored bodies. Inside them bright-colored tapes they strung."

"Unless they came back at night and took the bodies out for making, I don't know, *soup*, huh?"

"You have a powerful imagination," John said. "Olivia said you was a writer."

"No. I work for government," Harry said. "Well, I write speeches. That kind of thing. Believe me, making soup out of dead people's bones isn't imaginative, in Washington. *I'm* always surprised when they wait until the bodies are dead."

"If you stay up here," John said, "and you buy yourself a house or rent from anybody local, you know, I'd be pleased if you'd call and tell me if you have a problem. Of course, there's plenty of people can thread a pipe or miter an angle on a piece of cove. But if you need my help, I'd be happy to give it to you."

"I'd be honored to have it, Trus. I hope I stay here long enough to need it."

"Meanwhile," John said, "you keep them pieces off of the colored people's stones. Does that sort of thing constitute proof in Washington, D.C.?"

"If I can tell my boss what you told me today. Would you let me quote you?"

"Using my name?"

"Yes."

"My middle name my mother give me is Wendell. I never, ever told people hereabouts since high school that she called me Wendell. Would I have to use it for Washington?"

"Never. I guarantee it. My word of honor."

"You give me yours, so I'll give you mine, then. Word of honor back." Truscott John stood up and reached out and shook Harry's hand, loosely, and then let go. He said, "I always thought you could judge a person by what made them the maddest."

Harry waited to be praised more roundly. Truscott John only nodded, though, and turned to walk ahead of him, out of the ghost of the graveyard, along the ghost of the road. Harry watched him, then he followed, carrying his notebook open to a page still bare, and the little pieces of stone.

Catherine was at the barn, splitting wood. She wore what she called Saturday clothes—frayed jeans, old canoe shoes, a chambray shirt with its sleeves rolled to her elbows. She was puffing and perspiring and having fun, setting up a half of log, or a whole piece of limbwood, eyeing it, then seeing the ax descend a second before it came down, seeing it go through, which it usually did. This time she'd hit a knot, and her hands stung. She lifted the ax and the roundwood it was stuck in, and she slammed them at the floor of the barn, slammed again, and the blade went through. She almost fell, and she was panting, feeling quite content, when Bobby came in, wearing a bathrobe and white athletic socks.

"Nice," she said. "Didn't I buy you slippers?"

"Can't find them."

"And good morning to you."

"*I'm* not the one who started shouting about slippers first thing."

"I didn't shout!" she shouted.

"Is that new?" He gestured toward the ax. She nodded. He said, "You should have bought a splitting maul. Or a sledgehammer and wedges. That little thing—"

"It's not so little that you've gone around *lifting* it all week."

"You never asked me."

"That's all right. I can use the exercise. I like the feeling."

"Of being in charge."

"No," she said.

"Being alone, and in charge of things, and you can do anything that you need done, and you won't ask."

"I've asked you to cut the grass."

"You haven't asked me to cut the wood."

"Does that matter?"

"Nope."

She held the ax across her thighs and she looked at him, not much more than his ass covered by the kimono robe that, when she'd bought it for him, had come down at least to his knees. His legs were hairy, the feet in the socks impossibly long. "You'll be bigger than Randy when he comes home," she said.

"Do you think that'll make him treat me with some respect?"

"Doesn't he treat you with respect?"

"Not a lot. No."

"Baby," she said. Holding the ax in one hand now, she spread her arms out for him. She stepped toward him, and he stepped back. "Come on," she said.

"Well, look out for the ax."

He stepped into her embrace and leaned down on her. Motherhood will give you a strong spine, she thought, as if advising a younger woman. You'll become a load-bearing mammal.

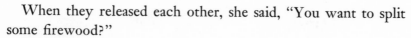

When they released each other, she said, "You want to split some firewood?"

He shrugged.

"Then you won't mind if I keep on with it, and you jump in later on, if you feel like it."

"I'm making French toast," he said. "I need it for studying."

"You need it for the maple syrup."

He went back across the side yard, bouncing on the balls of his toes, and she watched him a second, then returned to setting up firewood, eyeing it, then leaning into the overhead swing from the hips up through the small of the back and then shoulders—like a whip, she reminded herself—then leaning back even as the ax came down to see the wood divide as if it had grown into two separate pieces. Huffing after a while, she laid the ax down and toed the pieces into a heap. Then she went back to splitting, feeling the cool wind on her face, feeling the sweat on her sides and feeling her body swing and settle as she swung the ax.

Drown came in, his tail a little limp. She watched him as he gave his imitation of a slink. "You're a stick thief," she said. At *stick*, his ears jumped, but then he dissembled, and they flattened. He sniffed at the wood behind her, then he looked up, wagging. "Yes," she said. "What the hell." He lay his nose on a piece of limb that was small enough for his mouth. She said, "Go ahead." He tensed. "Stick thief!" she called, and advanced as if to stop him. That was the signal, and he seized the piece of limb and, bearing it in a grin, took off. "Stick thief!" she called after him. His tail rode high, and he settled in the thick grass a few yards away from the barn mouth to work at the stick as if it were a bone, and occasionally thump his tail on the ground.

Looking past him, she saw Carter's long station wagon pull slowly into their drive. She didn't know why, but she wondered if Bobby would use the baseball glove that Harry had brought. She set up a slab of what looked like maple, and she split it in two.

She had what seemed to be cherry set up and was about to begin her swing when Carter, advancing, called out, "Catherine. Can I talk to you?"

She swung. She skinned down the side of the cherry unforgivably, barely taking bark and a splinter, and almost dislocating her elbow when the head of the ax hit the concrete floor. Before she could properly set her legs and back, and reorganize her breathing, she swung again, and connected, and split the log, though her feet seemed to her to slap at the floor, and she couldn't help but stumble. Goddam show-off sow, she thought.

Carter wore what looked like suit pants, and which appeared to have been slept in. His business shirt was wrinkled, and he wore no tie. He was shaved and clean-looking, and she smelled the Chanel she had given him.

"Good morning," he said.

She said, "Hi."

Carter asked, "Is Harry here?"

"You mean, is he still staying here? Or is he here right now?"

"I assume he's staying here. He didn't come from Washington just to take off when he's got the—"

"Are you planning on a figure of speech that has to do with me being some kind of prize or something like that?"

He looked at her and smiled his tight, tense smile. "Not now," he said.

"No," she said. "Good. He's here as a guest, he is out on some kind of business, and he's going to be back. You're welcome in for coffee, or anything that'd feel comfortable, Carter."

"You're speaking of food and drink, I take it."

"Jesus. Has my house suddenly been mistaken for Boys' Town?"

"Catherine, I'm doing my fucking-all best. This isn't easy."

She swung the ax and it dug into the side of a log in the mound of wood still to be split. It, and the log it sat in, slid over. She hoped the gesture would feel to him like an answer; she had nothing better to offer him, or anyone else with questions, she realized. She sat down gingerly halfway up the pile, and she leaned back. The logs stirred, then held her. "No," she said.

"I need to ask you something about Harry. Would you mind?"

"I don't know. Probably." She barked a laugh that *she* wouldn't trust.

"Yes. Well, it's important to me, and we've been—what?"

"Friends? We've been friends, we've been lovers. Lovers are friends, aren't they?"

"I haven't had enough to know. I know my ex-wife's no friend."

She said, barking the same unreliable laughter, "Are you suggesting that I'm the more experienced at having lovers and all of that? Sort of the scarlet soulmate around here?"

He shook his head. He was very pale, she realized. He'd been prodding himself into coming, or holding himself away; in either case, he'd been struggling. She hooked her thumbs in the pockets of her jeans, and she said, "Lay it on me, Carter. We can talk. Of course."

Instead of looking down at her, he looked over her shoulder, at nothing else, she reasoned, but logs, lichenous logs, logs bereft of bark, logs with bark so scaly it looked like reptile skin, and logs that were green with sap next to logs that were gray and checked and ready to burn. He studied them, and she studied him. Finally he let his eyes drift down to meet hers. They bounced away, and then returned. "Catherine," he said, "were you waiting all this time for Harry?"

She knew what he meant. She said, "Pardon me? How do you mean, waiting? After all, I knew him a long time ago. What— twelve years?"

He shook his head.

She said, "Waiting."

He said, "Waiting."

She said, "All those *years?*"

165

He lifted his shoulders and when he let them down again, she had the impression that they were a heavy burden today.

"Why, Carter? Why do you want to know?"

He'd been waiting for that, she could tell. He said, at once, "Because I need to know if during this time of our being together, this year—it's been nearly a year, Catherine." She smiled and nodded, to show him that she appreciated the fact, and the nature of their time together. "Was it *me* you were with, or was it somebody filling in for Harry, is what I need to know."

"Oh, that's ridiculous, Carter," she said. "You're *you*. That's all."

"It isn't. I don't like to be insistent."

"There isn't any need to be. I answered that."

"Answer yes or no, would you?"

She climbed off the woodpile and stuck her hands all the way down the front pockets of her jeans. She felt her chin rise, and she saw how his own chin came up, in unconscious imitation.

"I don't *know* if I have a right to demand," he said. "That's how much you've got me whipped."

"Pussy-whipped? Isn't that what the fellows say at the American Legion bar? She's got him pussy-whipped? I make you crawl before I let you get any?"

"No," he said. "Come on, Catherine. You know I don't talk that way."

"So what'd that mean, *whipped*?"

"Let me say it differently."

"Do, please."

"Devoted?"

"Are you asking me, Carter?"

"Devoted," he said more flatly. "You know, it's like you're in charge here, and I'm just one of the serfs."

She caught herself nodding, as if in agreement, and she held still. Then she said, "I'm sorry that's the feeling you have. Obvi-

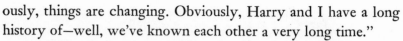

ously, things are changing. Obviously, Harry and I have a long history of—well, we've known each other a very long time."

"Maybe, if you add all the days together, maybe not as long as we go back, you and I."

"I hadn't thought of that."

"I hope you *will* think of that," he said, turning to leave.

She called, "I never had any intention of insulting you. I hope you'll stay in touch."

He turned, faced her, folded his arms across his chest, and asked, "Why?"

She felt her eyes widen and her brows rise, as if her face were asking the same question he'd just asked. She raised her hand and like a little child she waved. Carter waved back, and then he left. Catherine returned to setting up logs and swinging the ax and splitting them. Then Carter came back. His usually even complexion, yellow-tan from a lot of sun in small batches, was florid. He was rolling his shirtsleeves back, and he looked angry. She went ahead and brought the ax down twice, through the burl of maple she'd been working on, and she was breathing hard by the time he reached the woodpile. His forehead was sweaty. Carter rarely got all wet over anything, except maybe a bass, deep in a lake, fighting hard. He stared at her, chewing on his lip, and she, letting the ax on its head lean against her leg, stared back. She at last said, "*What?*"

"Do you know what that son of a bitch is trying to do to me?"

"This is about *you?* I mean, I can see your interest. I thank you for it. I mean, I'm touched by it, and flattered. Pleased. But you are not the only person involved, Carter. Come *on.*"

She turned to the pile and pulled out a nasty-looking chunk of oak. It was chipped with ax marks, where her wood supplier had tried to break it down; it had two splitting-maul strokes chopped into it, but still it hung together by shaggy tentacles of a vast knot that large men hadn't broken. It felt wet, as if it had lain on a forest floor for six months in the snow, which it probably had. And it was so heavy, she had to use both hands to haul it and settle it between Carter and her.

He stepped back as she raised her ax. "I'm talking about the site," he said, "not about sex."

She stopped in mid-stroke, and her back, she knew, would pay for that kind of awkward, unwise control. But no ax was going to fly off her shoulder, now, unless she told it to. "I didn't mean to say, before, when I thought you were talking about human affection, that sex was the subject, thank you."

"Oh, Jesus," Carter said. "I'm not—there's no way I'm getting out of this discussion alive, is there?"

"It doesn't look promising as hell," Catherine said.

Carter sat like a boy. One minute, he was up on his long legs, flailing his arms about and looking silly and red, then next he was sitting before her with his knees drawn up and his long forearms dangling over them. "Let me try again," he said, surrendering by sitting, and looking up. She couldn't swing the ax when he sat this close, in the cool, damp darkness of the barn. It smelled of wet bark, cut wood, fungus, and Carter's aftershave. The combination was rotten, high, and sexy, and she breathed at it consciously.

He said, "Your old friend Harry has gone to see Olivia Stoddard, who is, as they say, my arch foe. Apparently she sent him to Truscott John."

"Well, he's not your arch foe, is he? He fixes things."

"Olivia and her comrades use him. Mostly for information. He used to cut the grass at this famous cemetery, if he's right, if they're right, if the graveyard ever existed out there, which I considerably doubt. At least in the terms they talk about it."

"Why don't you find out, Carter?"

"Because I'd have to take them seriously, and they're ridiculous, and because they refuse to take me seriously."

"No, it sounds like they take you, and the other companies, very seriously."

"I mean in terms of dough. They don't understand how much serious money is involved. You just don't stop a job like this. Too much money's been invested already. HarJoe is breathing interest instead of air. It's October, and they have to be in business for Christmas shopping, so they're late already. There's guys putting in partitions, Catherine, and shelving, the signage is up."

"Signage?"

"Signage. Damned right. I'm supposed to be providing the bays where people put their cars and get out of them and go inside and *spend*. It's October, for Christ's sake! My blacktop people gave me notice: they're closing down for the winter. For me, big deal favor, because we're talking so much money is why. For me, they're staying open one more week. How's that for a deadline? To lay down my stone, my binder course, wearing course, all of it. And these liberals are telling a judge to tell me and HarJoe they need some kind of *pause*? We're talking big pause here, let me tell you."

She thought of Drown's enormous paws. She put her hand on her mouth and turned away.

Carter said, "You ever look at a million dollars?"

She turned back and shook her head.

"We're talking so much more, all around."

"And if the graves are there? If they belonged to black people who escaped from the South on the Freedom Train?"

"Jesus," he said, "now you sound like them. What if they are? What if they do? What if they did?"

"Wouldn't that make a difference to you?"

"Sure," he said. "Yes. But the project would have to—Catherine, millions of dollars, when they're invested, when all those people are in *motion*, they don't stop. They can't."

"And you wouldn't want them to."

"You see?" he said. She thought of giant paws, walking, not stopping, connected to no body and in motion with heavy crunching steps. "See, I don't think that son of a bitch *gives* a shit about black corpses rottin in de cole cole groun'. What it's about for him, is it's two things. His big-deal Washington job, and you. And both ways, he gets what he wants by going over *me*."

"Big paws," she said. "And who told you I'm available for getting? By anybody? And who said he wanted me that way? And who said we should talk about me like a bone two dogs are snarling over? And who said Harry's the kind of man who *uses* people, dead or alive, for whatever it is he's after, if he's after anything?"

Carter stood. He stepped back just in time, because Catherine swung her ax with her eyes fixed on the end of log a couple of men had previously labored at. She thanked them when the blade of the ax went through and struck on the floor, spiking up a chip of the old concrete. Catherine thought of blazing eyes. She wanted her eyes to be huge and fiery, full of conviction, raging and inviolate, all at once. Blazing, she thought, turning them from the split log Carter stared at with what she thought of as admiration. She lay those eyes on him, and she blazed. It worked. He took a casual step backward.

"I don't know exactly what it is I've said that offends you so much," he said.

She could only think: Good.

"But I apologize, if I've—"

"No," she said. "No need."

"I hope you'll think about what I said."

Blazing, she thought again.

"I'll keep in touch."

She thought it possible her chin was so high, she was squinting down over her cheekbones to look at him.

He waved, a resigned kind of sad little wave, and he walked over the side yard back to his car.

Catherine walked farther back inside the barn, as if she were searching for one particular chunk of wood. It was dark inside, and she should have turned the light switches on, but she was not looking for logs to split. She sought, and found, the old rubber raft the boys had inflated to float in on ponds and over fishing creeks. She'd wanted something soft to sit on. The raft was flat, but she sat down heavily, as if it took her weight, buoying her on slow water. Catherine hid out.

By the time Harry came back, presumably from ruining Carter forever, slowing American commerce to a crawl, and rescuing the souls of black folk, she had stomped her way to the front of the barn and had started in splitting again, and she'd stacked half a cord of split hardwood. And now she was in the kitchen, a blue tin basin of cool salted water on the table before her, and her hands plunged inside it. The opened blisters were terribly painful. You had to be a special kind of fool, she thought, a variety of masochist, to be soaking opened blisters in salt solution. On the other hand, although both of hers were throbbing and terrible, there was still the other hand.

Harry found her, came to kiss the top of her head, and when he saw the state of the hands she curled and uncurled in the cloudy water, he pulled at her wrists. She resisted, and he let go.

"What'd you do to 'em, Cath?"

"I split some wood."

"And got some blisters. And opened them. Is that cloudy stuff pus?"

"It's salt."

She watched him place his hands in his trouser pockets. His fists in his pockets were lumpy-looking. He said, "Do you have to do that, or do you want to?"

"It toughens them," she said.

"I read about that, too," he said. "In *Sports Illustrated*, right? Boxers doing that to toughen up the skin. Sure. You fighting anyone I know? What weight class?"

"Don't even *try* and guess," she said. "I'm splitting wood."

"And?"

"It's a long autumn. A long winter. A cold spring."

"And?"

"I want to be sure there's enough wood, that's all."

He sat where he did when he ate, sliding low in his chair so that his hands could remain in his pockets. He stared at her, and she thought again that she'd known him all his life. She could, if she worked at it, see the younger man inside the thickening older man; but what she saw, and who she thought of, was the amalgam, the way she saw her boys. His face was a little red, and his dark eyes were wide, and she knew that he'd come in with an excitement running through him. And what did he find? A lightweight boxer. Well, maybe close to welterweight.

"How much do welterweights weigh, Harry?"

"One forty-seven, I think. It's a good class, welterweight. They can do a lot of damage. What color trunks are you wearing, do you know?"

She said, as coldly as she could, "I don't believe I'd make the weight, thank you."

"No," he said. "So you're soaking those busted-up hands in salty water to toughen them." She nodded. Her hands were fists, and she couldn't make them open because of the pain. "Because you have to chop wood." She nodded again. She didn't want to open her eyes.

So she felt him before she saw him as he stood, and tore her hands from the water, but still with a kind of gentleness, and then pulled her by her forearms and walked her out of her chair to the sink. She looked only at her chopped hands. He ran cool water and held her hands beneath it, and then with a dish towel he softly patted them dry. He blew on them, then, as if she were a child who'd burned herself. She closed her eyes, as he did that, because it hurt, and because he was almost intolerably kind. And she knew that he was thinking only of a way to make her all right. I know you, she thought.

Then, cradling her hands in his, the towel over her palms again, he said, "And you won't ask anyone to help because you are on your own. And not weak. And not about to be weakened by asking."

She felt her lids blink. I'm a goddam fluttering belle, she thought. I'm going to fucking swoon, next thing. And her knees did in fact feel wobbly, and she leaned her shoulder on his chest.

"So you cut too much wood too fast. You don't wear work gloves. You don't give your big, strong son a chance to demonstrate how honorable and responsible he could be. You don't ask me—think how much *force* all this tonnage could generate, swinging an ax! You could ask Carter, I'm sure he'd want to help out. Or you could do fifteen minutes at a time every hour or two, if you had to go and cut it alone to prove to the world just how solitary you need to be."

She had turned and, her hands still in his, she looked him in the eye.

Blazing, she thought.

But he said, "Where's Bobby?"

She shrugged. "In his room?"

He shifted his hold, so that the towel remained over her palms. He held her by the wrists, both of them, with one of his hands. He pulled.

"Oh, no," she said. "I'm busy."

Tugging her, he nodded. They went that way, through the kitchen and to the stairwell, and up the stairs, and through the short corridor to her bedroom. Harry shut the door and, red now, and breathing hard, he very gently unbuttoned her shirt. It wasn't difficult for him, she thought, because if she stood any stiller, birds could have nested on her. He stripped it from her shoulders and then very carefully pulled it over each arm and each hand. The dish towel fell to the floor with her shirt. He held her and reached around from the front to unhook her brassiere. He unbuckled her belt, undid the button, unzipped the fly of her jeans. He pulled down her panties. And she stood still.

He walked her backward to the bed, holding only her shoulders, and then he tugged and tore, with a lot less grace, she was pleased to see, at his own clothes. He sat her down on the edge, and then laid her down, and then with great care, kneeling astride her, and hugely erected, and possibly shivering, she thought, he took each arm by its wrist and placed it at the edge of the bed. As if I were tied to the bed, she thought, interested at how she did not fight to move her hands to hold, or fend, or in any way control. Is that the idea? she wondered. Or is it tender care?

Harry said, "First aid."

"Who for?"

He held her arms and again, with no play or preparation, as if they knew what their bodies did, pinning her as she volunteered to be pinned, he entered her. She rose to meet him, and he moved back so that he was barely in her.

"Bastard," she said.

He moved farther in. She rose. He retreated. So did she. So he moved in again. She lay as still as she could, and he came farther in, and then she had to rise, to move her legs around his back, and he pulled almost out, and then rose up on her, though not leaving, and straddled her thighs with his so that she was closed around him but not able in any way to seize him. He slowly, gently, moved back and forth, in and out. The angle was changed. This was too good. He didn't need to move very far until she was fighting to have more of him, and he was refusing to allow her. And yet he was kissing her neck and her eyelids and ears, and moving in her, moving in her, and she knew that her head was back on an arched neck, that her face and chest must be rosy and sweating, and that Harry must be over her and looking down, looking in. She moved, moved, and then opened her eyes to see his face, smiling in almost a kind of sadness, his eyes closed hard. She shut her own. She felt him start to come. With her body softly pinned, she wrapped herself around him, somehow, anyway, and she felt the uncontrol pour up through her, wondering whether he had meant it to, and whether he had meant her to know.

He did not tilt himself off her. He lay above her, resting on his forearms and on her thighs and groin. He opened his mouth—she was watching him now—and she said, before he could speak, "No."

"No what?"

"You aren't too heavy on me. You always ask that, if you don't roll off. You're embarrassed about your weight."

"I always do that?"

"Yup."

"We've slept together twice in how many years, Cath?"

"Always *did* it."

"You remembered it."

She was feeling it again, rolling through her, and she tightened on him and disappeared inside her sensations, grinding on him selfishly, wondering if apologies were in order, and knowing at once that this grave, courteous man would bow, if you could bow in bed while you were jammed halfway up the lady underneath you, and he would say, unsmiling, *I insist*. All she finally said was, "Oh."

And after another silence, he said, "I think it's actually their faces."

"What? Whose?"

"I think the fighters soak their *faces* in salt water. To toughen them, if they cut easily. To keep their eyebrows from splitting and bleeding into their eyes. That's how fights get stopped."

Catherine saw herself on the floor, face down in a blue tin pan of salt water. "Not now," she said.

Because it was Saturday no one was at the office, so Carter went there. He had to drive to the little town along the Chenango

River between Earlville and Hamilton where, in a former body shop that was really a small pole barn, he received his mail. He'd hired men to paint the aquamarine building barn-red, and had himself built the room into the right-hand corner. He had spent his weekends, long before Olivia and longer before Catherine, studding up ten feet, sheetrocking, insulating, laying a floor on two-by-sixes of unfinished hemlock, wiring in 220 so he could run electric space heaters, and rounding up used furniture at tag sales and the lower echelon of auctions. In the rest of the barn, unlighted and unheated now, and empty, were stripped and cannibalized yellow machines, and a tractor he had bought and never used, a Post Office Jeep with right-hand steering he had bid for and not used either, and the bays where he parked and serviced his dozers and backhoes and scraper and trucks. Coming in from the main street of the crossroads hamlet, with its fast wide river and abandoned stone mill, its several white houses and the long fields behind them ocher and bright on a clean October morning, he panicked in the damp, cold darkness of the pole barn: all that emptiness meant machines on the site, committed, along with money committed to pay the men who operated them, and six days until all of it was over, and he was broke again, or nearly, and driving a backhoe over the Bear Pass, if he could find the work, to dig holes for strangers at an hourly rate.

He went through the old thick wooden door he'd bought from salvagers in Whitesboro, and he turned on his overhead fluorescent lights. They buzzed, and the heater, set on low all season, whispered as its fan cut in, as if to prove how faithfully it served. His desk was a wide six-footer he had bought from a realtor going out of business. Its soft surface was scarred and dusty and neat— the woman who came in to answer the telephone and type and keep the books liked to tidy. Her name was Mignonette Laurie, she weighed about two hundred pounds, and she moved, in her elegant blouses and handmade skirts, on pointy high heels as if she were light, and as if his office were someplace pretty. It was

176

Mignonette, whose husband was in the Rome, New York, hospital for the criminally insane, who had papered his walls with the dark paper with its maroon-and-clay-colored fleur-de-lis, and it was Mignonette who had persuaded him to buy a decent rug with a weave in it that almost picked up the paper's maroon. She, herself, wore only shades of apricot and peach and raspberry, and she dyed her shoes to match. She'd left his mail in stacks, with notes about the disposition of certain letters. She had left the books open for him, the week's pages marked with a big stone she'd brought him from Maine when she went on vacation with her Weight Watchers group. Carter sighed and threw his coat on the visitor's chair. He sighed again, thinking of Mignonette, and he retrieved it to hang it on the wood-and-brass rack.

Mignonette wanted to divorce her husband, he knew. She wanted to stop visiting him, which she did by peering, she told Carter, through glass that was reinforced by wires, while he sat at a card table and shook from the drugs they kept in his system. She cried while she drove home, she told him. He suspected that she wanted to marry Carter Kreuss, and keep his books, decorate his house, and love him to an early grave, their mutual skid in that direction lubricated by Reddi Wip and semi-sweet chocolate. He thought of Mignonette in the majesty of her nakedness, and he found the imagined hugeness of her breasts, the conjured rolls and ripples of her belly, surprisingly comforting. He thought of burying his face in her, and then, even though interestingly roused, he thought of her delicate, small, precise handwriting, as accurate and graceful as her steps around the office during the occasional days when they were there together, he at his desk, and she at her desk, which was, she had told him as he'd written the check in response to her request, a harvest table and in good condition and a good antique. Her notes said *I answered & signed for you,* and *Do, pls?* He was comforted, even as he thought of Catherine's spiky handwriting, and Olivia's unreadable scrawl, by her instructions. But instead of doing what he was told, he pulled the ledger book over, rolled the stone away, and stared at what other men in other businesses, he thought, could manage to call cash flow. Carter Kreuss had cash paralysis. Cash constipation. He giggled. Cash freeze. Carter rubbed his hands as if he were cold.

"Cash *death*," he told the humming lights, the whispering heater, the cold stone, the gray-and-cranberry carpet. He leaned back in the captain's chair he had carried with him from his foster parents' house (against his social worker's instructions), and he thought again of someday buying himself a swivel chair such as other men with offices used. "Except, they have money," he reminded himself. You, he thought, have foster parents who are dead, and of course your mother, someplace.

You know where to reach her.

Yes, but "someplace" will do, thank you.

He leaned, hard, at the back of the captain's chair, and he thought of the couple who, some years after he and a hundred other children had gone through their house in Buffalo, had moved to a condominium retirement village outside Tallahassee, and had smoked cigarettes and eaten fish and sent out birthday cards to every abandoned, abused, orphaned, and neglected child who had lived for a while in their two spare bedrooms packed with two beds each, on washed and ironed, much-repaired harsh cotton sheets that Carter still missed. At night, when he put his face down, he could smell in them the wind and sunlight of the backyard where they'd waved on the line like the children's own banners, he remembered. He could smell them now. He closed his eyes, and when he opened them, he was holding the stone that Mignonette had brought him. He put its coolness against his cheek.

The coolness spread over his body, in spite of the whisper of heat and buzz of light. His feet, up on the desk now, felt numb. When he swung them down to the floor, the return of circulation didn't seem to help, and he pounded on his legs, though that didn't help, either. He felt his face, and it seemed cold too, and he said, in the office he knew to be warm, "The corpse is cooling." Mignonette would have laughed. Catherine would have frowned at such self-pity. Olivia would have sat back in her small muskiness, watching him with large eyes.

Carter's hand reached out for the telephone, and he saw it dial. It lifted the receiver to his ear and so he knew that he would speak. He didn't know what he would say if a banker answered. But one didn't. A banker's wife did, and Carter said to Olivia, "This is the enemy of the people."

"Which people, Carter," she said, and he couldn't tell if she was pleased.

"The people who love old bones."

"I don't love old bones," she said, snapping her voice as if she were angry, but far from it, he could tell. "I respect them. What bones do you respect?"

He leaned back. He cupped his groin and pushed against his hand, then made his hand go away. "Yours," he said.

"Oh. Oh, my. And what about Miss Artistima, the middle-aged vampette with her perfect ass?"

Carter felt as though he'd eaten too much ice cream and still wanted more. He said, "I'm not comfortable, talking like that about Catherine."

"How'd you know I meant Catherine?"

"Come on, Olivia. Don't. I moved out."

"I know."

"How!"

"Trus."

"Are you banging his old bones, Olivia?"

"Men and women can talk without having sex. It's called civilization. Trus just heard it from someone, and he mentioned it. Did you call to fight with me, Carter?"

He knew she knew he hadn't. He managed to say, "No."

"Then did you call to tell me you're not going to dig up the site?"

"A compromise," he said. "What if—didn't Truscott say one time they'd been buried on the ridge above?"

"He thinks so, yes."

"Well, what if we take them up there? I'll move them up onto the ridge, and they can be buried where they used to be. How's that for a compromise?" He hadn't known he was going to suggest it. He hadn't known he was thinking of it. And as his words disappeared into the static of a rural telephone line, he felt his queasiness ease, a kind of pleasure replacing the sourness in his gut. It had been his loins behind the call, and now, he thought, his brain was involved. Something like a conscience, he speculated. As he did, his resentment, like a headache, began at the back of his neck.

Olivia sighed. It was so deep, he thought, it must be theatrical, flashy, and cruel. "No," she said, and he thought he could see her head shaking. "No, I don't think so. It's got down to where it's about the site," she said, and her voice sounded true, now, "not about the bones."

"Wait a minute," he said.

"Well, we're in court, darling, and we're talking to the Corps. It's gotten beyond what started it."

"You're calling in the Marines?"

"You know I mean the Corps of Engineers. The judge gossiped to me, and he gossiped to you. We all know it can happen. Everybody knows. And why are you giggling?"

"Because it's crazy, Liv, it's—*beyond what started it*? Is that what you said?"

"Yes. You know it. And you know what I mean."

"No."

"Yes, you do. Come over here."

"What?"

"He's at a Rotary goddam chicken fucking barbecue, Carter. Come over here and talk," she said. "Would you?"

"You think so," he said.

"Yes."

"You think I'll—"

"Yes."

"Why?"

She'd hung up. He saw himself sitting in his office, horny and ignorant and powerless and sick again, saying "Why" a half a dozen times to a dead phone. But he thought, You've got too much pride. Standing, he added—But only for that. He shut the lights off and he closed the office door. He locked the barn behind him. He'd expected it to be night. Women made him think of night. It was clear early afternoon, opening beneath a bright, high chilly sun, although, as he started the car and began the drive toward the White Store Road, he felt that it soon would shut down.

Olivia wore a very short black miniskirt over black tights and pink bedroom slippers with the faces of puppies on them. Her top was a black leotard, long-sleeved, and he wondered if it was connected to the tights. She wore no brassiere. He knew she'd seen him looking for her husband's Buick. Her small face was scrubbed, he thought, shiny and not made up. She wore an actual ribbon in her hair, pink, to match her slippers. She'd dressed up, Carter thought, and he became wary and excited at once.

"Are you going to rape me or talk to me?" Olivia asked at the door.

Carter thought, he later boasted to himself, of seven replies. He looked down at the pink puppy faces with protruding tongues and he blushed. She slapped him gently on the side of his face, then touched his sternum and gestured him in. It was like something she bathed with, he thought, more than a sign of neglect; he always found himself sniffing for it, and liking it. She sat on the deacon's bench, and her skirt rode up. She saw him look, and she raised her brows.

"What?"

He shook his head.

"Nothing," she said, "you're not looking at anything?"

"That isn't what I mean."

"You want to sit over there, or stand, or what, darling?"

"Liv, when did you start calling me darling?"

"I saw some film, to tell you the truth, and the woman in it, I think it was Moira Shearer, managed to say darling without sounding like everybody else in the movies. So I thought I'd try. You don't like it?"

"I don't know who in hell you're talking to when you do it."

"Let's use your name," she said, "so you don't get confused."

He sat, and he gathered his trench coat about him, like skirts. "I thought my idea for a compromise was good, Liv. I don't know about that thing, that beyond-what-started-it stuff. Let's settle it, Liv! I'll go broke, HarJoe's getting crazy with me, Catherine— never mind her."

"She threw you out, I hear."

"From who? Don't tell me. The Blue Ox oil-delivery guy."

"She didn't throw you out?"

"I left."

"Because of Harry."

"Him too?"

"You know, imputations of promiscuity are offensive to every-one with any sense of dignity. You've got me screwing every-thing male except raccoons."

"I'm sorry."

"I thought you and I had an *affaire*."

"It wasn't foreign and it wasn't movies, Liv. We went to bed a couple of times."

"And you got scared."

"It just didn't work for us."

"Prove it," she said. "You called up with a voice full of hormones, you looked up my dress all night at the town forum, you're doing it now. Tell me how it didn't work. Or are you just, as they say, looking for a whatchamacallit, *port*, now that Catherine—sorry: now that Catherine didn't throw you out."

"I really left on my own."

"Why?"

"I'll tell you. We were friends. We *are* friends, maybe. Because Harry came in and she—"

"She didn't mind."

"They know each other from a long time ago. You can't compete with a person's history. Let their life happen, and then you see what's what. Anyway, I don't compete."

"You're one of the stubbornest, most competitive men I know, Carter."

"No, I mean, I won't compete for friendship. Love. Whatever it is. I won't beg. I won't ask for anything. Nothing. Nothing. Nothing." He was afraid he was going to get wet-eyed and choke up. Fag, he thought. He clamped his jaw.

"You're afraid," she said.

"Of what? Like hell, I am. Of *what*."

"Of losing. Of somebody saying no. If you don't ask, they can't turn you down."

"No," he said. "Nah."

"Carter," she said, "you want a martini?"

"I want to go to bed with you," he said, looking at his unshined loafers, and thinking, suddenly, of his unwashed floors, his devastated bed.

She said, "I know," and when he looked up he saw that her smile was courteous, graceful, mild, and that she wouldn't sleep with him again. "I know." She crossed her legs, and she clasped her hands in her lap. "We had fun," she said. "I'm a little desperate, sometimes, I think. I had an analyst once, in Cooperstown, who said I thought I was dead. You never thought I was dead, did you?"

He said, "No. I'm sorry."

"I'm a confusing person," she said. "I send mixed signals. I feel mixed feelings. I could sit here like this, and clamp my little thighs together just the way I'm doing, and be thinking of sticking my tongue down like a honey bee to lick your lips. I apologize, but what the hell, Carter. Life isn't only sex, and if signals are mixed, they're mixed. Right? They're calling in the Corps of Engineers, I'm positive."

As Olivia spoke, he thought of Catherine's sad, slow descent onto his body. He saw Olivia and then Catherine, as if watching an unfocused television screen, when the figures in the picture have a ghost that moves in unison with them. He saw Catherine, then he saw Olivia. He was trying to see who was lying in the bed when he realized what he'd heard. He had intended to tell her how he marveled at his lack of disappointment, as when he'd been a boy, and hot to bring himself to climax, and was disturbed by someone at the bathroom door—how, after replying, and seeing that he'd shrunk a bit, and grown softer, he was not sad or angry, and less than absorbed in his perfunctory, almost automatic fantasizing, and the diligent friction with which he came. He would have said that, because he felt, again, as he had before they'd made love, like Olivia's friend.

You're so easy, he told himself.

But he knew she'd told him Army Corps of Engineers, and what he had feared was coming true. He stood, so suddenly that she shrank. "I'm sorry," he said, sitting again. "I was thinking. I was thinking about you. What you said. It's definite?"

"The senator's deciding, I think. He can call in the Corps. And they can shut down HarJoe. And you. The whole thing. They can do a wetlands investigation that'll last all winter, I'll bet. And Harry would sit down and type up a few speeches, and the senator would copter in and give them, maybe on the site, surrounded by imported blacks. We'll know tomorrow. I think we could have an announcement of intention to run for the presidency made in Chenango County. It would be a first, wouldn't it?"

"But we could stop the whole thing," Carter said.

"No," she said, and her voice was so sweet, her smell so exciting to him, he wondered if he could go on his knees and rest his head on hers. He would lick at her thighs, he thought, thinking too that he was very close to not knowing what to do. "It's all going on, now. And it's also about Harry, and what he wants."

"To stick a tomcat up my exhaust pipe."

"And the senator. His staff. And what Catherine wants Harry to do. I imagine she has some influence with him?"

"Only whether he should breathe or not."

"Maybe she could stop him, then."

"Olivia, what are *you* after?"

She looked at him with wide, surprised eyes. And then she shrugged, slowly, genuinely. She said, "Carter, I'm goddamned if I know for sure, you know? I want—I do know, I want to breathe. No: I want proof of it."

"Even if it ends up so I'm out of business, Liv? Broke, and working for somebody else?"

"Oh, Carter. Darling—sorry. Carter, I didn't want to hurt you. Remember me in bed? Did I ever want to hurt you? Think of me."

"That's dangerous. You're dangerous. I don't know."

"A lot of women are, you'll find. And no small quantity of men. I'm sorry. I got you into trouble, and I don't *think* I meant to. And I can't get you out. But you're going to find, darling—I *meant* that!—you're going to find all women are dangerous to *you*, Carter. You don't think so, but you need them too much. You might need everything too much."

He pulled at the tails of his trench coat and stared again at his shoes. "I need this to stop. I need to get organized here. I need it to stop, Liv."

She shook her head. "We're dealing with government. Nothing ever stops. Everything keeps going. I'm sorry. I believe in it, what I've told you—about the black people here, about what we owe their dead. I do. I did. I do. But I regret what's happening to you, Carter. To me. It's rolling over me, too."

He thought that Mignonette would be in Rome, talking to a distracted nurse about what the doctor had said about psychopathology. And Catherine in her kitchen would be getting ready for winter, wouldn't she? She would not be in bed with Harry Miller on a Saturday afternoon. She would be chopping basil—no, she had done that already, and he had sat at the kitchen table and watched. She would be hanging bunches of tarragon and dill to dry on wrought-iron hooks on the wall above the counter. She would be pestering Bobby about caulking the windows in the north upstairs hall. He remembered the cornices below the roof, near the chimney. She had climbed her aluminum ladder, wincing as it shook but refusing to come down when, as she was three rungs from the top, out on the extension, she'd begun to bounce in the wind. He had watched her hanging on by one hand, a paintbrush in her hip pocket and a can of outdoor semi-gloss oil-based white in her other hand. At one point, the ladder, slanted in too close to the base of the house, had threatened to come down. He had jumped onto the bottom rung to weight it. She hadn't cried out, he remembered. He had looked up the ladder as, at the same instant, they both leaned in and the ladder stayed in place. He had seen her foreshortened, made bulkier, stronger-looking, all solid thigh and buttock, and he had admired her as you admire a sturdy field dog or a tall horse. He'd been ready to enlist in any war with her. And he had called up the ladder, begging to be allowed to paint the cornices before winter. This had happened between Harry in summer and Harry in fall, and Carter was thinking that his had been the shortest season of all. He looked up, in a banker's wife's living room, surrounded by frail old furniture and a woman with huge eyes, a provocative outfit, an essence of sex in the air about her, and a distance between them that lengthened each time she looked at him, as he found her doing now, with sympathy.

He said, "I really need it to stop."

Olivia said, "You expect too much of women, you know. *Do you know?* Have you been told?"

"Oh, yes," he said. "I've been told."

"And?"

Carter said, "I really never knew what else to do, Olivia."

In the garden, in the late October afternoon, with steady winds carrying the crazy flocked calling of crows from hedgerows half a mile away, in sweaters and jeans—they wore no socks, as if they'd decided to wear a badge of their earlier nakedness—Harry helped Catherine put the garden to bed. She made no jokes about this putting-to-bed. He understood that she never used words about sex except directly. Harry helped her roll the plastic sheets of mulch and stuff them into plastic garbage bags. They were heavy with moisture and dried mud and small stones she'd used to hold them against the wind between the vegetable rows. His fingers grew cold, and then numb. He blew on them, chafed them, held them in his pockets for warmth, while Catherine in canvas work gloves went on steadily, rhythmically, tearing and rolling, seizing and wadding, cleaning away, making ready. Her gloves proved she was at home, he thought, prepared; his numb hands were a sign of separateness from what she knew. Being naked wasn't always natural, he thought.

When they had lifted dozens of sheets of plastic, some of it in tatters, some in long strips, and had stuffed it into shiny brown sacks, Catherine handed him a heavy rake. She held a long, narrow hoe with a V on the back, like a claw hammer's.

"What am I raking?"

"Tomato vines. Zucchini. Pepper stalks. Everything except the asparagus—that's over there. Those long—" He made a grotesque face. "Okay. I didn't know if you knew. Just leave the rutabaga and the big sage plant and the asparagus. Everything else, we move down to this end of the garden, and we jam it into the compost bins." She pointed at the cages made of chicken wire and corrugated metal posts.

"Randy made those, I bet," he said.

"He was going to. Bobby got jealous, because I always ask Randy to build my stuff. So he came out and hammered the posts into the ground, and he hung the chicken fencing with picture-hanging wire."

"Smart kid."

"I raise 'em big and smart," she said. But she shook her head a little. "I raise 'em by mistake, I think. Bobby— You know, I still, after one whole one and most of another, I still don't know what I'm doing?"

"You love them so hard, Cath. They love you. Whatever it is, it works."

"You think so?"

"I admire the hell out of you for it. You know I always did. I love them." He said it again, into the wind, the crows, the rustling of the yellow and red leaves, the giant sky under which her house sat, looming over the garden they slowly stripped. "I love your sons."

She stopped tugging at tomato plants with the broad end of her hoe. She was ten or fifteen feet from him, too far to stride to gracefully and hold, though he wanted to. She looked broad-shouldered, capable, and strong. He could see her eyes. He could see her throat gone just a little soft. The skin above her wrists looked deep where the skin folded just before her gloves began. She was small and large, strong and needful, and he was filled with the same lust he'd felt some hours before, too strong to be called tender and gentle enough to make him despair of ever saying it precisely and therefore with usefulness for Catherine.

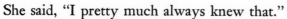

She said, "I pretty much always knew that."

"You think they ever did?"

"Randy," she said. "I'm confident about him."

"There'd be time yet with Bobby," he said. And after the daring of that statement, he had to lean above his rake, and pull the frost-killed vines along the rows she'd planted last spring. He couldn't look up.

After the rest of the row and the start of another, she spoke into the strengthening wind. He had to walk closer, to ask that she say it again. She said, "Carter was here this morning. Harry, my hands are killing me."

"Let's stop. Let's finish later."

She nodded, leaning her hoe against the fence, flexing her hands in the gloves. "Promise, though," she said. "It has to get done."

"I promise." He stood near the fence beside her hoe.

She said, "He was, you know, talking about me and him. About you. The graveyard at the site."

"I showed you the stones," Harry said. "You know it's true. You know I'm not lying."

"Why would you lie?"

"Oh, shit, Catherine, there's rewards for lying. I'm in politics, don't forget. I got a man in Washington, he could have a double-frappe with cashews over this. I'm thinking about that. And there is a certain virtue in stopping a project like that just in *case* there are people buried under the parking lot. Those are two reasons to lie. And there's you. Wouldn't I love to shame his name and stop up his nostrils because of you?"

She said, "That's what Carter said."

"But you saw the stones. They knocked over the markers and paved the road with them. Truscott says they moved the corpses down where the mall's going. I believe him. Olivia Stoddard believes him."

"She's probably trying to get a piece of ass off one of the bodies," Catherine said.

"Is that her reputation?"

"Yes. And also, unfortunately for Carter, it's for knowing what she's talking about, being organized, being smart. She make a pass at you?"

"There was a certain tumescence in the air."

"*That* would have been worth seeing. So you're telling the truth, and Olivia's telling the truth, and Truscott's telling the truth. Now, what?"

"I bet, from what I've heard, the restraining order falls apart on Monday."

She nodded.

"And the curbings are already up."

"The shops are being worked on, Carter said."

"Which leaves us with whatever they have to do for the parking, right?"

"To make it pay this year, Carter says, they have to be in for Christmas shopping. And his blacktop man says he's closing down for the winter. Apparently, below a certain temperature, the stuff doesn't jell, or whatever asphalt does. The plants close, which means no asphalt, which means no parking lot, which means no business, which means no money for anyone, especially the developers and Carter." She said, "He has a week, he says, before it's all over. The calendar's against him."

"Fall is a bitch of a time," Harry said.

"You do sound happy about it."

"I'm doing what I do, Cath. I'm calling some people today, and if I can reach them it could get interesting. That's often what happens. In this case, it wouldn't be fun for Carter, though."

Then she did step closer, and then he did think she was going to lean against him. But she stopped short. Near him, however, and a potent force—her nose and cheeks red from the wind and working, her light eyes intent—she said, "Do you have to make your calls? Do you have to do this job?"

He had to admit, but only to himself, that he wondered, too.

And then he wondered about offering to trade his silence. And then he wondered why, if she were tempted, she *would* be tempted. How much, he wanted to ask her, does the comfort of the man in asphalt really mean to you?

"Let me call," he said, "and find out what's going on. It's possible I've been fired for just taking off."

"And if you haven't been?"

"Maybe I do the job."

"Because—"

"Exactly," he said.

Catherine said, "You know, I hate it when you're cryptic. I want you to tell me everything. Now. *Tell* me. Why you're here. What you'll do. Why you'll do it."

"In short sentences," he said, playing to her smile that was partly a frown. It was exciting because he often didn't know whether a moment would end with her mouth turned up or down.

"Short *syllables*," she said.

"Yeah," he said, reaching for her with his short arms—he thought of Carter's, slender and long—and holding her by the biceps, but not pulling her in. He didn't feel resistance in her, but he wanted Catherine to fall in onto him. He wanted to make love to her in the freezing garden.

Her eyes were merry, and her smile stayed wicked. "Much too cold," she said. "Will you tell me?"

"There wouldn't be much reason for the rest of the visit, then, would there?"

She said, "It's a visit?"

"Would you like it to be more?"

"Would you?"

He was squeezing her, and hard, in a way he hadn't meant to. It had been like a spasm. He waited for a word he might use to describe this intensity. She was looking at him from an inch away, now, as he searched. He wanted to shout at his inability, scold it,

191

anyway confess it. She leaned all the way and kissed him with her cold lips alongside his nose, then she pushed off on him and took up her hoe, and went back to work with her blistered hands. He watched her and then he worked, too.

Catherine went to her knees at the broccoli, and she groped with her gloves among the sea-green stalks, swearing and pinching and hurling. She showed him the insect-infested plants. "My damned broccoli always does this," she said. "I don't want the bug egg bastards in my compost, waiting for the growing season. So we stuff these into the bags with the mulching sheets." And, dutifully, with cold hands that didn't want to be plunged into a bag filled with bugs and slugs and dead things, he plunged nevertheless. He was on his knees beside her, panting a little, he was ashamed to note, and he could smell the cold earth of the garden, a sort of fungus smell, a cellar-in-the-summertime smell. It reminded him of wine, a little: something expensive at Windows, in Roslyn, among the mauve walls and brass-trimmed tables, something the senator would order and name and then not quite complain about, reminding Harry that a St. Estèphe can be fragile. He smelled a strong bath soap and her skin and her shampoo, and he thought of bed a few hours ago, and of moving in her. Short sentences, he thought. Syllables.

And she was wonderful because when you were about to burst into fully orchestrated song, complete with harp and maybe a revolving stage under colored lights, she tossed the tools toward the side of the yard, strode to the bright blue tarpaulin near the compost, pulled it from under the bricks that weighed its edges down, and revealed the red rototiller and its cans of gas and oil. "My toy," she said.

He knew that Carter had given it to her. He would know what machines to buy. And clearly he had known that it would please her; he was formidable, Harry thought again, and you have to watch him hard. She poured in gas and checked the oil, added some, pulled the choke out, pushed the throttle ahead, and pulled

the rope of the starter. It turned, but didn't start. On the fifth or
sixth pull, it sputtered, and on the next try it roared. She pushed
the choke in, throttled back, pushed the machine on its rear
rubber wheels until the turning horizontal screw on its front was
poised above the farthest edge of the garden, near the fence
between the garden and the field that sloped away from the
house. She let the machine down, engaged the digger by seizing
the dead man's switch and squeezing it, and the screw began to
turn up dirt.

Small sticks she'd used for labeling were thrown into the air,
rocks surfaced, little and big, and what seemed to be a heavy
black piece of rubber. The sun was low, now, on the other side
of the house, and Harry had a sense of brightness and dimness at
once. He stood in the center of the garden and watched her turn
its soil. She was sweating by the end of the first row, and dripping
by the time she reached the space between it and the second.
Clearly, she was going to turn over every inch, for whatever
horticultural reason, and he could see that her blistered hand on
the wide-mouthed dead man's grip was hurting already. So he
went to her and put his hand on the switch over hers as she paused
for breath. Then he reached in front of her with his right hand
and took hold of the handle near the throttle. She raised her eyebrows, shrugged, made a face of resignation and sat down on the
cold, darkening autumn ground, her legs sprawled before her,
while Harry pushed the surprisingly heavy machine, pausing as
he'd seen her do, to let the screw work fairly deep, then pushing
on, working as hard to hold the self-propelled tiller back as to
guide it forward.

He worked the length of the garden, then returned in a parallel
and slightly overlapping row, so that he missed nothing. The
fumes of the engine took away the smell of wine and Catherine's
skin. The dropping darkness, and the darkness that seemed to rise
from the soil to meet it, took away the colors of the trees. He
heard nothing but the bellow of the motor as he pulled back while

193

driving on. And Catherine sat and watched him, her legs crossed and tucked, now, her hands resting on her thighs. He knew she watched. He wanted her to watch. He was a kid playing ball in the New York schoolyards, whacking the pink Spaulding with a trimmed broomstick, or driving the softball hard on the summer grass at the Caton Avenue Parade Grounds in the fast-pitch league: lean and shirtless and studied by a girl he was going to cup and probe that night with romantic carelessness and memorized clinical tactics that he laughed at and mourned even as he forgot the simultaneous pain and freedom of being that young, that fleet, that invited, and that dumb.

He was up to the center of the garden soon enough, sweating and achy at the shoulders and arms, wanting to stop and take off clothes and feel the wind on him, but eager, also, to work as hard as he could for her. The ground opened before him, the machine took its interior and spilled it up and out, the soil a darker black than its surface, and rich with shale and fragments of vegetables planted years before—haired roots that writhed like worms, the bulbs of shallots and garlic, thick old leeks that had shrunk upon themselves and turned sore red—and then he was before her where she sat. She looked at him as he came to, himself surfaced, realized where he was and before whom. She looked at him as though it had occurred to her that he might harm her with the machine, be unalert enough to injure her in her own garden that she was making ready for the long harsh winter of upstate New York, and then the early planting—of peas, she'd told him—in April, with snow maybe still on the ground, and surely in the air. (I can live in a climate like this, goddammit, he noticed he thought; looking at her, vulnerable, a part of the sprawled soil before him, he thought of living on this land.) Her shoulders sloped. Her eyes were wide. Her hands were unclenched. She was open before him in the roar and stench of the digging machine. He let the dead man's switch go, and the blade stopped turning. Then he pulled the throttle back, and the machine was off. The silence seemed vast, though soon enough the calling of crows and the honking of geese, the rush of wind through the aspens about them, ebbed in. His arms felt sore, and his hands tingled. The small of his back hurt from tugging against the engine's heavy pull. And Catherine sat before him, the woman he had traveled a dozen years to see—to *see?*—with a girl's huge eyes, open to him in a garden not over, really, and not yet begun again, but simply in its autumn, aimed at return.

He nodded at the uselessness of any language here. He pulled at the choke, started the engine, and braced himself against its drive. He looked at Catherine. He couldn't look away. The machine kept sinking deeper, digging, while he looked at her.

She mouthed, "What?" over the engine's noise, but Harry didn't know. He shrugged, and the rotor dug deeper; he let go of the dead man's switch, but the turning metal screw had already found it and tossed it up: he knew from her eyes, not yet from sight of the thing itself. Her eyes grew enormous, and her face went pale, then almost a yellow-white. She lay back, then pushed away with her heels. He let the machine go and strode around it. The snake he'd dug up, in a rocky part of the row, had been maybe a foot and a half below ground, stupid with cold but not in hibernation yet, he figured, because it writhed in a slow stunned sideways roll. It was two feet long, and a muddy blurred black. It had no business on top of the surface of the garden, and no way, now, of getting back down. He took a breath and reached for it, but he couldn't force his fingers down. It looked oily, and he thought he smelled fish. "I've got it," he said, not moving. Catherine climbed to her feet. She was there first. She lifted it by its tail and she tossed it toward the garden fence. She sniffed her fingers and made a face.

Drown, at the entrance to the garden, studied them. His tail was up, and so were his hackles. He raised his head, and worked his nose. "Timely as ever," Catherine said. "Snake hound." Drown circled the garden, looking watchful, and missing the spot where the snake had landed. "I hate them," she said. "But they keep the insects away. It's funny, finding just one. They're usually together when they hibernate."

Harry went back to the tiller and started it up and finished the row. Catherine walked beside him, as if they were talking, but they both stayed under the cover of the engine's noise. Harry couldn't see the snake.

And when they had finished turning the garden over, had stowed the tiller and put away their tools and were in the kitchen, Harry's arms felt as though they were shaking. His left hand was cramped from the dead man's switch, and his forearms tingled nearly to throbbing. He smelled, to himself, like snake and gasoline. Catherine was scrubbing her hands while Harry made the call.

On the fifth ring, when it was answered, he said to Mrs. Talliaferro, "How did I know you'd be in the office?"

"Are you under the illusion, Harry, that you're still on the payroll?"

"I wondered."

"He thinks you're an interesting man," she said. She sounded as though she were smoking and reading a letter while talking to him. "I told him you were *only* interesting, and he said that was a very Jamesian distinction. Do you think he meant Henry James or William James?"

"I'd guess *Harry* James."

"Betty Grable's fellow. Cheeri-beeri bim."

"I am working for you, then? You wouldn't be making conversation, otherwise. Would you?"

"Oh, no," she said, "I'd be polite no matter what. I'm a *southern* woman, Harry."

"Conversation as castration," he said.

"Thank you, dear. Yes. He'd like to see you. We had to let Mr. Ratner write some impromptu remarks for the American Library

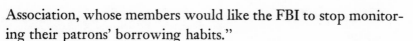

Association, whose members would like the FBI to stop monitoring their patrons' borrowing habits."

"He doesn't need anyone to write for him, and he knows it. And he can talk about any kind of freedom in his sleep."

"He did. It sounded that way. Mr. Ratner writes, as you know, like a rabbi in a bull session. When will you be coming home to us, he'd like to know. *I'm* dying to hear, as well."

Harry looked at Catherine, who was pouring white wine into tumblers. He lowered his voice. "The graveyard thing," Harry said.

"Are you alone, dear?"

"No."

"Well, why not call from someplace more private, then?"

"There isn't any need," he said more loudly. "I'm not hiding anything."

"Right," she said, still sounding preoccupied. "An honesty gambit. All right."

"No," he said. "It's—look. The graveyard exists. I verified it. As far as I can tell, it's where the parking lot of this little country mall's going in." At *little country*, Catherine turned a blank face on him, then quickly looked back at the wine jug. "They dug up the graveyard once—it was an Underground Railroad stop. They dug it up, moved the bodies, but used the stones to pave the road. I don't know why. Some town supervisor couldn't resist it, I guess. And the people who wrote to us got a restraining order. But people here who know figure it's gone come Monday: vacated first thing in the morning. The asphalt's due to go in as soon as the order's vacated. I figure they won't get the asphalt out, transported, laid down, all of that, until Tuesday, earliest. The guy's under a lot of pressure from his asphalt people, I hear. And the land developer is a heavy-duty guy around here, with a lot of dough and lot of pull, and the order *will* get tossed. Tuesday, then, all right?"

"We act on Monday?"

"If we do it. If the order does get vacated. If the guy dumps the blacktop."

"Why let him do that? You *like* your Nigras in amber?"

"Maybe he'll change his mind." Harry was looking at Catherine and she, hand holding out his tumbler, looked back hard. "Maybe he'll decide it's *wrong*. Maybe—look, I don't want to ruin this guy."

"Then you shouldn't have told me, Harry. I ruin guys. That's the work. And you *surely* shouldn't have told the senator."

"I think maybe I should look down at the bones and tell you I saw them. On-site verification, to use the Russian phrase."

"All right. But you sound hesitant to me. If we need to pull the trigger, let's just pull."

"Yes," he said. "It's a right thing to do."

"Well, that too," she said. "You telephone me on Monday, latest, hear?"

"Yes."

"I'm doing a little research for the senator. Wetlands, Harry."

"Jesus, Mrs. Talliaferro."

"Isn't it a *lovely* idea?"

She hung up, leaving him with a dead phone in one hand, a quarter of a tumbler of wine in the other, and an unhappy Catherine standing before him. She said, "Are you as frightened of that woman as you sound?"

"*Any*one who makes Jamesian distinctions," Harry said.

"What are those?"

"They're marked by a preference for Betty Grable's legs."

She shook her head. Bored with his banter, he knew, she opened the refrigerator and looked in. She shut it and shrugged. "You want to cook something? There's a breast of turkey. Otherwise, I'm stumped. I didn't think about it this morning. You threw me off stride."

"Good," he said, and was reaching for her when Bobby came in. Harry pulled his hand back, saw Bobby watching his hand retreat, and did what he did when in trouble—chattered stupidly. "Bobby!" he sang. "You should have seen the snake we dug up."

"On purpose?" Bobby asked, slapping a textbook and papers onto the kitchen table.

"Good question," Catherine said.

"Accident," Harry said. "I think he was trying to hibernate. Would they do that in a garden? Bobby," Harry said, "good to *see* you."

Instead of softening, Bobby's face went deadpan. Because you *must* talk, Harry thought. Because you can't just *live* it. Make the kid take hold of some emotional live wire, why don't you.

Harry said, "How about some kind of eggs? I can make home-made french fries. The real thing." He said, to Bobby, "As good as McDonald's. Really."

"Well, I guess that would take care of our daily minimum adult cholesterol requirement," Catherine said.

Hearing her disapproval, Bobby said, "Great."

"Okay, Cath?"

"Sure," she said, looking at Bobby's papers. She read, " 'Cleopatra was, in my humble opinion, more than just a lusty temptress.' God," she said. "That's wonderful. You wrote that, right?" The deadpan nodded.

Harry said, "And a salad. To fight the fun of the potatoes. It's a gorgeous sentence, Bobby."

Bobby sat down, folding his paper into very small squares. Catherine pulled out the wine jug. Harry asked, as casually as he knew how, "I'm wondering how many potatoes to cut up. Carter be here tonight?"

Bobby looked up from his essay. Catherine leaned her head sideways. Harry let his face look innocent. As a baby, he instructed it: as a newborn babe.

"I don't believe he'll be here," Catherine said.

Bobby bent to fold his paper one more time.

Harry thought: Babe.

Chapter Five

O N S UNDAY MORNING Catherine drove Bobby to town for
touch football and wandering with friends from the pizza
parlor to the NFL games at someone's house. Part of Bobby's
revolution this year was, with his height and weight and, Catherine had heard, more than adequate skills, to refuse to play football for the local coaches. Instead, he played touch ball with kids
and fathers and uncles in a cinder lot near the town barns, where
snowplows and sand for the roads were stored. The coaches telephoned, and Bobby said, "No, thank you," or grunted something
like it; they telephoned Catherine, who was so relieved that he
wasn't risking knees and skull that she was sharp with the men,
biting and hurried and smug. On the way back, she drove with
her window open to the suddenly icy autumn air, listening over
the engine for the crying of geese.

Harry was in the barn, splitting wood, grunting *"Ugh!"* each
time he swung. When he saw her watching, he stopped, and a big,
happy smile hung on his face. Pausing not far from him at the
mouth of the cold, dark barn, she said, over his gasping, "Where'd
you get the T-shirt?"

200

"I think it used to be mine," he said. "Jesus, it isn't Carter's, is it?"

"No. It did use to be yours. I suppose it *is* yours. But where did you get it?"

He said, "Oh. Or maybe whoops. In your drawer, Cath. In the bottom of the bureau drawer where you keep knee socks and work shirts and corduroy pants. All wadded into a corner."

"You really had to go exploring," she said, as tonelessly as she could, thinking of his large hands pushing between the edges of folded shirts.

"I'm sorry."

"No, that's all right," she said. "It was yours. You've been halfway up inside of *me*. You can surely investigate my clothes."

He said, "I wasn't investigating. I just remembered—"

"You remembered your navy blue T-shirt?"

"I remembered you wearing it, yes. A long time ago. One summer in Vermont? Remember? It was horribly muggy, and you wore a pair of my boxer shorts and this shirt." He rubbed his hand against his belly through the shirt. "You didn't wear anything else. All day. No brassiere, because of the heat. And I kept *stalking* you. We made love sitting on a chair on that little back porch, when it was dark out. The neighbors were on *their* back porch. Remember?"

He looked into her, as if through a window. He was waiting to see who was home, she thought. She wondered if she were the person he sought. "I couldn't do that now," she said. "My breasts would fall to my waist."

"Not hardly," he said. "All middle-aged women say that."

"You've been in bra-less-under-T-shirt situations with a number of middle-aged women? Middle-aged. God. Have you?"

He shrugged and smiled, and she *was* a little resentful. She said, "*Your* breasts don't fall to your waist."

"Thank you," he said. "I think they just miss. Do you mind it

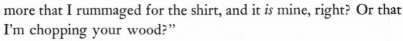

more that I rummaged for the shirt, and it *is* mine, right? Or that I'm chopping your wood?"

"It's yours," she said. "And my blisters hurt."

So they compromised. Catherine handed the wood down, set it up for the splitting, and Harry swung the ax. Catherine then tossed the split chunks onto the pile for stacking. She regulated the pace so that after a while Harry moved more slowly, more regularly, and panted a good deal less, and they split a lot of wood. She smelled the bath soap from his shower, and the sweat of his work, and the sachet scent that the T-shirt had acquired in the corner of her drawer. She'd worn it sometimes to paint in, and once, on a warm day, she had in fact worn it bra-less, and had thought of their afternoon in Schuyler, their lovemaking that night on the small back porch within earshot of her neighbors. He had sat on the chair, and she had sat on his lap, and he'd pulled aside the wide leg of his boxer shorts that she wore and had slid himself up and into her, and they'd played with one another, moving only a little, making love—she had always thought of it this way—from *within*. Painting, and thinking of that, her body had tried two activities at once—a sentimental teariness, and a trip to the suburbs of excitement. She remembered standing in the corner, her paint roller up and dripping, her wall two colors, her body sensitive to the soft, worn cotton of the shirt, her legs crossed while standing, and her eyes slowly shutting, though she didn't know whether with sadness or pleasure.

She sniffed him and studied him. The way his eyes looked tired—the smallest, shallowest of darkened pouch beneath them, instead of the concentric, etched lines that scored Carter's harder face. The way his skin reddened so easily when he bent or laughed or was frightened. The thick heavy muscles of his biceps and his bunchy forearms—different from the long leanness of Carter. She remembered when there had been no pouches at all beneath Harry's eyes. No gray in the hair above his ears or on his furry arms, the dark hair of which she'd loved to tug. His throat was

fuller now, though neither fat nor jowly; it was a large man's
heavily muscled neck, and she had bit at it last night, and she had
bit at it so many years ago. It was hers. It could be. Its rings and
folds, its veins beneath the surface and the muscle cords, were like
a map of countryside she'd known all her life but could study
now, looking for landmarks and for new terrain. She felt at home
with how he excited her and easy with how he didn't—how he
simply, sometimes, felt like some of herself.

Of course, she thought, placing a log of birch and taking away
two chunks, still barely connected—she tore them apart—so much
had gone on when they weren't together: when he was in Manhattan and then Washington, when she was in her Pines house and
then this one, and alone, then with Bryce Wolff from the Historical Association, and with Carter, whose absence, acquiescence,
worried her. Because he didn't give up. Did I want him to fight
for me? Did I want to see a duel? Do I want it proved that two
decent men ought to live their lives exclusively in terms of *me*?

I'm going to walk up to him and say, I love you.

God. You should patent your insights. I'll bet old Harry stands
on his hands.

"What would you do," she started to ask him. He was leaning
into the downward stroke of the ax, and half a log went flying.

He said, "What?"

"What's wetlands?"

"A terrible policy," he said. "According to the Army Corps of
Engineers, and their little brothers at Environmental Resources
and U.S. Fish and Wildlife, wetlands have a certain kind of soil—
saturated, not much oxygen. I don't know why. Well, it's under
water a lot is why, I figure. Did you ever see over at the mall site
how they built up the ground to make a dike? And all the storm
water pipes they put in? It's wet country, for sure. Okay." He
sat down and stuck his legs out. Catherine sat too, not minding
that he took a break and breathed more evenly: love in the middle
ages, she thought. "They want, these plant and land cops, they

want to know if there's roots growing above the surface, as I
understand, swollen tree trunks—again, water, all right? And if
there's enough water in the soil long enough to change what kinds
of plants grow there, I really don't know what you call it, but I
know that's the sort of thing they look for. Those are the criteria.
I don't know how they measure them. But if they suspect wetlands, which can be affected by construction of anything at all,
the Corps can issue a cease-and-desist. Just in case. They can
suspend all the work on the site. They can, at their pace, very
leisurely, conduct an on-site inspection and gradually make a
determination.

"Now. You think the senator can't pull a string to the Corps
that gets a colonel or general in Buffalo, or wherever the Corps is
located in New York State, to come down in a long black car and
lay an order to cease and desist on the developers and—for certain,
Cath—on Carter? It'd take a day. Maybe two. And it's all noble.
It's all in the name of protecting the environment. Talliaferro's
talking to conservation people and politicians, and she's going to
be ready, come Monday, to move. Whatever happens to the local
court order, Carter and his people are probably going to have to
deal with the feds."

Catherine said, "He'll lose his shirt."

"I lost mine for a dozen years."

She didn't smile, though she wanted to. She didn't argue. She
thought of Carter talking to soldiers about the sorts of regulations
he despised—the red tape and detailed, annoying codes he gave
cases of good whiskey to bad local officials to acquire help in
navigating through.

Harry said, and she was surprised to hear a soreness in his voice,
"You deal with art. Preserving art. That was the program you
took in Cooperstown, right? You can understand conservation."

"Of course. Is that what this is about?"

"You could say that."

"But would it be true?"

"Partly."

She said, "What would the other part be about?"

"Making a fuss over buried black people."

"Because your man wants to be president."

"That, too, maybe."

"And Carter," she said.

She was so relieved by the way Harry looked straight at her and said, "And Carter. Absolutely. Everything comes to light."

He stood, and he reached for the ax. She positioned a log for him, and then stepped back, and he swung.

She asked, "How long could the Engineers make everybody wait?"

"As long as they wanted to. As long as the senator needed them to."

"Or you?"

He shrugged.

"Carter has a week," she said. "Four or five days. After that, the asphalt plant shuts down. The parking lot isn't done. The HarJoe people can finish the stores but they won't be able to get anybody into them. They'll lose a fortune."

"They're losing it now, I figure," Harry said. "They borrowed money to build the place. They're paying interest they could have recouped by being open early for Christmas shopping. I hear that's the only decent time for malls, anyway."

"They're ugly people, Carter said. Would they do anything to fight this?"

Harry said, "Let them fight the army all they want."

"No, I mean, what if they decide to fight *you*? I know Carter isn't a pushover, either. I know he might try and fight you."

Harry made a Bogart noise that reminded Catherine of Randy doing imitations. "They can try," he growled as if they were in a film.

She said, as sweetly as she knew how, "We can turn Olivia loose on them." And then, very quickly, she asked, "Is much of this about me?"

Harry breathed as though he had just been chopping wood, instead of talking about the government machine. He said, his hands on his hips and actual steam still coming off his shoulders, "Catherine, it's all at least a little about you." He turned his face away. Sitting where she was, on a pile of split wood, she wanted to rise and embrace him. She hugged her drawn-up knees instead, and sank her face to her legs, where she hid.

Harry split wood, this bulky, ungraceful city man, developing a rhythm and staying in it, hiding within it from Catherine, who worked like an apprentice, carrying oversized logs and lugging off what he made of them. The barn seemed to grow colder as they worked, though neither of them commented on the temperature, or on anything else. Catherine watched him rise and fall with the ax she had bought for herself, for the long winter to come, and she listened to the clatter of split wood tumbling, the puffing noises Harry made as he heaved the ax and slammed through dense wood, then recovered to await her delivery of the next piece. Her hands felt raw, even where the blisters no longer hurt much. She kept them in her pockets while he swung the ax. The pile of split wood grew, and she knew that she should be feeling a resentment of his taking over. She had not requested service, or any kind of help. She had wanted to prepare her house for the year. Now Harry was doing it. She wondered if he thought to get her ready for, along with deep cold and deeper snow, his absence. What he was doing was pleasing her, she admitted to herself. She liked the work. She liked doing it with him. She was filled with householder's joy—the cupboards are full!—as she watched the mound of wood grow.

She thought of what he'd said about wetlands, a fuzzy notion still, but clearly a political lever. She thought how much she detested politics—little men using various kinds of noncontact judo to throw you all over. And yet hadn't he tugged her to bed and held her down, imprisoning her, no matter how tenderly? And wasn't that politics? She would not ask him.

"You used to write poetry," she said, interrupting his swing so that he missed the log, and the ax blade bit cement and sent small pieces flying. "Sorry," she said. "I don't know where that came from. I didn't know I was thinking about it. Did you hurt your back?"

He shook his head. He let the ax sit on the floor of the barn. "When?"

"When you were coming to Schuyler to see me. You brought me poems."

He reddened. She loved to see him blush. She loved to make it happen. "I've changed," he said.

"Yes. You lost weight. You stopped smoking. You went from writing stuff about New York life for the *News* to writing lies for politicians."

"Well, we all grow up."

"You out*grew* poetry? Mind you, I'm not saying you're obligated to write it."

"I hope not," he said. "Usually, people write poems and send them out and everybody sends them back. Please don't *write* poems, the magazines and publishers and the other poets say. We've got enough for the next two centuries, but do you have anything about dogs, in prose, with color photos?"

"You stopped because they wouldn't publish you?"

"No."

"You're saying that as if there's something else to say that you want me to extract, inch by inch. I'm willing to do it. I'm the one who asked in the first place. But I don't know anything about it. I don't know what to say. I just—I used to like to read your poems, that's all."

"You did?"

"I told you that. All the *time*, Harry."

"Yes," he said, "I used to love to hear you say it. I stopped writing them, Cath, because I didn't know who I was writing them to."

"You mean it's *my* fault you stopped?"

"No. I wish it was that simple. I could have blamed it all on you—backsliding on my diet, missing deadlines, getting mugged on Central Park West and 90th—"

"What were you doing up there? A story?"

"A woman, actually."

"Who? Do I know her?"

"Not even her husband knew her."

"Harry!"

"She was looking for some easy excitement, Catherine. I am the easiest she or I happened to know."

"Did you write poems for *her*?"

He sat on a heap of wood, shaking his head, smiling shyly. "I only wrote poems for you. I only showed them to you, except, for a while, when I was sending them out. Then, I showed them to college kids and graduate students who were editing quarterlies, literary magazines. They sent them back. No. I never showed her much more than, well, me."

"Did she like it?"

"Like what, Cath?"

"What you showed her."

"I thought this was a literary chat."

"So did I. All right. You stopped writing poems because—"

"Because, after a while, I wondered who in hell I was talking to that way. Turning sentences on their head. Cutting the ends off of them. Okay. It was a way of speaking. But who to? I started asking that."

"And?"

"I never answered."

"Yourself?" she suggested.

"Maybe. But I don't hear like that. So why talk like that, as if the talk's directed at me?"

"When you were writing the poems, were you writing them to me?"

"I wondered when you'd get around to that," he said. "Maybe. Probably. I don't know."

"That would make me a muse, wouldn't it?"

"A very conventional role. I couldn't imagine your accepting the job."

"No," she said. "Maybe you were somebody else when you wrote the poems. Maybe you stopped being that person for a while because the you you were used to stopped listening to him. Or something else."

"Who I stopped being, if I follow the sequence of events," he said, "was your—may I use the word?—lover."

"Both times?"

"No," he said. "After Schuyler, I stopped."

"I didn't know."

"What the hell," he said, standing and taking the ax. "What the world doesn't need, for sure, is more poems."

"I was wondering," she said, "so I asked. I hope you don't mind. And I'm sorry you stopped. That was an okay person writing the poems. I feel like I *killed* someone, Harry!"

"Nah," he said. "I'd have stopped anyway. I wasn't very good."

"Says you."

He held the ax across his chest diagonally, and he declaimed, his breath smoking in the dark barn, his dark eyes large and round, his face very happy: "I think that I shall never flog/An object harder than a log/A log whose dum-da-dee-da-doe—"

She jumped up and threw her arms toward him. "A log whose bark is ringed and white/So Harry chops both day and night."

He winced. He put his hand to his chest, dropped the ax, and fell backward onto the log pile. He said, "Cath."

"What?" she cried. "Harry!"

She was on her knees, the edges of split wood biting at her legs, her hands on the heaving T-shirt, pulling at him. And then she saw him grin. "You son of a bitch," she said. "I thought—"

"That the woodsman's bark was worse than his bite?"

"You *son* of a bitch."

"I'm sorry," he said. "I didn't mean to frighten you. I'm sorry. It's doggerel. It always gets me that way. I may not be able to write it, but I do know poison-baloney when I hear it. The son of a bitch hears *dog*gerel—that has to be a cue for Drown." And there he was, wagging, wriggling, leaning over Harry to lick his face, pausing to smooch at Catherine too, and grinning around his long pink tongue. "The family that brays together stays together, Cath. Forgive me."

She sat with him in the cold barn, thinking of the man who'd disappeared, and wondering how much of Harry had gone with him, how much she'd helped dispatch, and assuring herself that no fault was involved. Men make decisions, women make decisions, poets come and journalists go, and you keep on living your life.

"Cath?"

"What?"

"Do you forgive me?"

"I don't want to ask you that, Harry."

"But I'm asking *you*."

"Well, just stop, all right?"

Drown peed on the woodpile while they began what would be a neat row of split wood. Catherine told Harry how they'd build several alleys-worth of wood, and she showed him how to make a corner turret by laying thick, flat pieces two-by-two: first set at right angles to your toes, then, at right angles to the laid logs, the next set on top, and then the third set perpendicular to your feet again, until there was a solid, heavy tower of wood next to which you could stack the split wood, and which would keep it all from rolling out into the barn and on top of you. They stacked what they'd split, Harry delivering the wood to Catherine, who laid it down the way she wanted it. They didn't speak until after their second break, when Harry, breathing deeply and stretching his back, said, "You do this every year? Alone?"

She told him, "Every year."

"But not alone."

"Randy and I used to do it. Sometimes other people helped. Hey: you got your uptown ladies, all right?"

"Yes," he said. "Yes." And she was enraged by his calm acceptance of the other men, and she infuriated herself because her teenager's mind in her middle-aged body was taking over again. He said, "You miss Randy a lot?"

Her throat filled at once; she couldn't speak, and she was afraid that her eyes looked wet. Just park that Freud over there, fellas. "Yes," she finally said.

"I would," he said. "All that time with him. And he was a great kid. I mean, great at *being* a kid. He's what a kid ought to be. And then he's gone."

"Boy. Gone and gone again."

"It must feel like everything's going, all of a sudden, when they go to school. I mean, *I* miss him."

"I'm glad Bobby's here. He's a different boy, though. And Randy: anything after this, I figure, any coming home, you know—temporary. He's away, from now on. It's right. It's the way it should be. I'm almost ready. But I also hate it." And she hated, too, how her voice closed off before she was ready, and how, now, her eyes *were* full of tears, and how he approached her, and opened his arms, and she leaned onto the big sweaty chest beneath his shirt, or hers, or theirs.

Inside, they made sandwiches of sardines, mustard, and red onion on toasted rye. Harry insisted on diet soda to counteract the bread since he had made them five sandwiches, and they carried it all to the back room with its wide pine boards and high

windows and old sofas covered with a faint black shiny patina of
Drown. There, they turned on the Redskins-Giants game, and
Harry rooted for both sides. He cheered for the Redskins because
he lived in Washington, and he cheered for the Giants because
he came from New York and had loved them all his life. While
she paid little attention to what he said, Harry filled his head
with sandwiches and football, and Catherine alternated between
watching Harry and watching herself. She was filling up with
Harry Miller, and no amount of diet soda, she thought, was going
to do her any good.

"So do you love him, or what?" Harry said.

She watched someone in a bright blue uniform slam the man
in white to the ground and then stand above him, as if to warn
him never to come that way again.

Harry said, "Cath?"

"Yes. What?"

"Where were you?"

She said, "Harry, if you have to know: in you."

"Oh."

"What was it? Did you ask me something?"

"No," he said, "never mind. Go directly back where you
were."

He watched the game, she watched him, and she felt the con-
tented relief she'd always figured only parents are entitled to. It
was composed of fatigue—the hours most recently spent with the
children—and evasion—they were away, and for a long while, and
she knew pretty much where, and that they were as safe as she
could expect, and that she wasn't, at least directly, responsible.
And for a time she could pretend that there wasn't such a thing as
laundry, or next week's meals, or plants to water, a checkbook to
balance and some bills to be paid; there was only the self and its
soft cry. So before she was aware that she was doing it, before she
could remember that Harry might be gone again, and soon, that
she was wasting time, she had stood, had patted his shoulder in

passing behind him where he sat on the sofa, had stopped to kiss the top of his head—he was beginning, with a perfect small white circle, to go bald, she saw—and she had left the room and gone up.

She ran the tub hot, with very little cold water mixed in, and she tossed in the secret vice—not a man she had known, not a man who had known her, no matter their intimacies, had heard about it—the crystals shaken from a box decorated in pastel colors with cartoon characters. She stirred the powder, dropped her clothes on the floor, and slid—she thought the word *swooned*—into her afternoon bubble bath. She stirred until the bubbles had foamed around her wincing skin. She leaned back until her neck and head were on the cold rim of the long tub, and she stretched, and then let go: arms, legs, the midsection tired of control, all floated like her breasts and back, and she was away, with only herself, wasting moments with a man who had mattered for almost a third of her life, but away because she needed to be.

She'd done this since her childhood, stealing to the water. Some-times it was swimming pools, as in college, where she'd swum laps while debating boyfriends or memorizing formulae; she remem-bered the damp spiral notebooks on the tiles at the edge of the water and how she'd sprinkle them as she hoisted herself to read some notes, then slip away and back into the green-blue water and swim on her back for a length, reciting to herself the way mosses propagated, or key incitements to German nationalism. In her one year of graduate school, she had cheated on her husband, Dell, with a professor who kept a sauna in a shed behind his house. It was paneled in birch and nearly too hot to bear. The professor was lean and pale, and he, as well, was too hot to bear. He'd liked a woman to whimper. He'd clawed and pinched, he'd bitten her thigh so hard she'd bled. Once was enough with him, and her conscience had been as sore as the body she withheld from Dell, although she'd known, at the time, that he masturbated often every day in preference to sleeping with her. But she'd liked the steam, and she had wished, she remembered, that she could have tried it alone. So in southern New Jersey and in central Illinois, she fled to the water. And from every man she'd known, and from her children thereafter, and from cleaning women, houseguests, casual friends, and everyone in between, she had sneaked to the farthest place, more and more recently tubs and heat, where she could violate friendship, suspend obligation, and slump in her baby bubble bath to surrender her weight while giving nothing more.

But she was a mother. For eighteen years, she had listened for scary noises while not always wanting to. So she heard the footsteps outside the bathroom door. It had to be Harry or Drown, and since there was no sound of claws against the floorboards, and since no shovel-shaped head was laid hard against the door, it had to be Harry. She made a little splashing noise. It was all she was willing to tell. The pause was small. The floor took weight and released it, and he went, knowing that she was inside. Having come for her, he went away without her, and his unsatisfaction was his gift. She lay against the water as if she were embraced. She felt sexy and private, absolutely safe, grateful against her will.

Carter checked his watch and wondered why. He stood on the site, and it was a dead Sunday morning. It was like a graveyard, he thought, then winced at the thought. He worried about what came next, and he had worried enough to telephone Seymour at seven in the morning, before Seymour left for church, before Carter walked through his dark house with a bucket and hot water and a sponge mop, cutting trails through dust and pushing dirt into dampness. He had worked in his underwear and socks, with goose bumps on his legs. The sight of his pale legs in the dark rooms had reminded him of walking bare-legged in Catherine's house, and he had quit, after a while, and had sat with his back against a hallway wall, telling himself that it wasn't any use, he would have to have a cleaning woman in. He remembered Olivia, telling him about his expectations of women. He'd almost wailed, and surely had shouted it, "You can expect 'em to *clean* for the money you pay!"

Tomorrow they would be told, as helpless as little men like Seymour in their churches, what was going to happen next. That's what they get, he thought, for believing in reasons. He looked at the mountains of stone he wanted to lay before the binder asphalt course went down. He looked at the immense yellow pan, sitting like a dead monster insect. Everything about it, the articulated body, the scraper, the dumper, looked dead. *Dead* is a very fine word, he thought. I like it more than *because*. *Because* is a lie. The work site, the grave site, was littered with dozers and rollers and eighteen-wheel trucks. His Barber-Greene, parked near the office trailers, wasn't built to sit, he thought. It's dead if it sits. It's supposed to be paving. And you don't pave without asphalt, and the plant stays open until Friday, no longer. And why not, with the temperature dropping? That's a *because*, he thought. Because under forty degrees, and you don't pave. But that's a *because* that means dead. He checked his watch and looked at the back of the site: the aluminum shells of the Great American market and the Boston Store, all three floors, and a florist's, an optometrist's, Carl's Drugs, Klein's Sporting Goods, a pizzeria, Carvel's, Endicott-Johnson shoes, the usual gift shop, the usual clothes stores, most of which would be closed a month after Christmas. Electrical cable threading through the shops swayed in the wind in glassless storefronts. Empty beer and soda cans stood on shelves where workmen had left them. He knew that in the half-basements, and under crawlways, and in the lots behind the stores, they'd left small mounds of excrement and all kinds of paper waste. It was part of a job in progress, and there wasn't any progress anymore, just empty cans and piles of shit and loose talk about black corpses—what people took for *because*.

He checked his watch and paced the site. He wore his high work shoes and wrinkled khakis, a gray work shirt, his lined autumn-weight parka that was the color of his pants. He wore his last clean clothes and sipped from a carton of coffee with what he imagined were fussy lips that pursed near the heat. He thought, in fact, that his gestures must look fussy overall—the stride through the site in shortened steps to keep from spilling the coffee, the measured sips, the stiff regard for caterpillar ruts and potholes. He guessed he'd be considered a fussy man, which, in light of his dark and horrible house, would be a joke if people thought about Carter and laughing in the same skull's walls. In fact, he had thought for a while that Catherine had liked his orderliness. Surely *her* system of life hadn't offered much actual order. He had always thought she'd needed him. And her need, what he'd thought of as her need, had been as exciting, he realized, as anything else about her. He checked his watch, then sipped at coffee as he stood above the markers he'd spiked in: four metal pipes with red plastic streamers tied around them, to keep his drivers from crushing the possible old black bones. He stood in the middle of thousands and thousands of cubic feet, looking at something not much more than forty by forty, maybe something less. They must have dug it deep, he thought again. And, like a little chunk of jagged metal in the tire of a long, fast car, it had brought things skidding and screaming, crashing, to a stop.

He was looking down through stone and earth in the direction of maybe the bodies of slaves or their children. He was sorry they'd been slaves. He was sorry there had been slavery. But he had not ordered people to start stealing and buying and selling other people, and he hadn't laid these people in the ground, or dug them up and transplanted them here. And—he checked his watch—he had five days before it wouldn't matter and if Olivia was right, maybe only one. He would go close to broke. HarJoe would survive, and, really, he would survive. But he was almost forty years old, and you're supposed to do more than survive at forty. He might not be able to afford the men and equipment in the spring, even if HarJoe paid the interest on their loans and kept their permits valid. He sipped his coffee and tried to think of parking stalls, Olivia, the Corps of Engineers. He thought of Catherine.

He figured she would eat marshmallow sundaes with Harry. She would drive the old van and Harry would tell her she was charming. He'd been close, Carter thought, to convincing her to trade in the van, with all its plumber's tape, for something new and entire. A woman like Catherine should wear good clothes and drive a sound car, he thought. If Harry stayed, she would drive the van until it exploded beneath her.

"So why did you *leave?*" he asked himself again. He heard his voice in the dusty wind and emptiness of the site. He wondered what the answer was, and when he felt he knew it—had always known it—he didn't want to hear himself saying the words.

But Carter knew, and he was cruel, his nature had to do with pain, he admitted, if only to himself. "Because you're scared of her," he heard himself say.

Dust devils blew on the pan and the tipping rigs, the dozers and the stone. He closed his eyes against them, and against himself. Catherine was the only person of whom he had stayed frightened for so long. He was frightened of earning her scorn, and frightened of losing her, frightened of her disapproval or even impatience. And yet, he knew, it was his nature to *give* fright. So he'd showed his fear through gentleness, a patience with which he wasn't always entirely comfortable. She made you better, he thought. And now she's sacking Harry for your trouble, and you're scared to lose her by fighting for her, so you lose her by leaving on your own. She asked you *not* to. She sort of did, he thought. He checked his watch.

Then he heard the slow crushing of gravel under fat tires, and he turned to watch a white Blazer with HARJOE in discreet lettering on the doors; the word was small enough for the lot at the

217

country club, but large enough to qualify the truck for a tax writeoff. Harvey Seymour blinked the lights. Carter nodded and made the shape of a smile, loosely defined, take over his mouth. You're spending half your life these days doing what you don't believe you should.

Harvey got out of the Blazer with difficulty, since it was a high truck and he was a short man. He wore highly polished cordovan loafers, dungarees with a crease ironed in, and a rich, thick bombardier's leather jacket that all the cocktail lounge pilots were wearing these days. "Carter," he said, waggling the cigarette in his lips and extending his very short arm. Carter held it silently as Harvey tried to squeeze his fingers hard.

"Hard times," Carter said, as low as he could. Harvey liked to keep his voice low, to radiate calmness and control. During the sixties, Harvey liked to tell anyone, he had run with crazies, had eaten of exotic mushrooms and smoked whatever was offered. And now, he always liked to say, he was in pursuit, a slow and casual, tranquil pursuit, of mellowness.

Harvey stood beside Carter, as if they surveyed the site together. Carter felt him nod, heard him sigh out cigarette smoke. "We're up against it," Seymour said. He asked, "You ever go to church?"

"No. I don't go, Harvey. I really never did."

"I get a feeling of peace from it. I fall asleep during the music, and I feel, I don't know, rested after services. I always feel rested."

"I wish I could feel rested."

"You're in a little trouble here, aren't you? Rented equipment, tough contract—I knew it was a tough contract for you when I had it drawn up. Remember? I told you that at the time. You were pretty confident, then. So was I, of course."

"How are the interest payments?"

He heard Harvey's aviator jacket creak as he rubbed his pointed, smooth-shaven little chin. He didn't want to look into

218

Harvey's eyes. They were very dark, they were like coal some-times, and didn't seem to reflect, so that even when Harvey wasn't wearing his tinted glasses he was threatening to look at, a minia-ture cop. And, since his boyhood, Carter had hated cops: they'd always brought him back when he'd run away from home—from the various homes.

"The payments are a bastard," Harvey said. "But we're well capitalized, and the other investments are working, the market's been good. Listen to this: chickens. We've been investing in chickens and turkeys, the new fad for healthy foods? Eat fish, chicken, whatever, but don't eat steaks and things that taste good? We put some money into poultry farming in the Midwest some-place, we're doing pretty good. Of course"—he waved a shaky spiral of smoke in front of Carter—"that's all Joey, he's got the brains for the books, he studies up on these things. They're about to fuck us on the nigger thing, Carter, you know that."

Carter nodded his head. He knew it wasn't necessary to Harvey that he hear a reply. Harvey didn't care what people replied. Harvey talked and you listened, and then he told you how per-ceptive you were.

"I hear from Judge Volusia that the order gets thrown out first thing in the morning. You could maybe call the blacktop guy at his house, have him go in early, get, you know, cooking. You could lay some down on Monday. The way'll be cleared. But after that, we're in the shit, I gotta tell you. Our next Democratic left-wing Communist-kisser candidate for president is, according to the judge's sources, and he's connected all the way to D.C., about to get on top of his white horse. When he finishes fucking the horse, he's riding it over to the Army Corps of Engineers. They send in the wetlands commando team, and we're out of business for a few months. A year? Just until the senator stops making speeches about his black friends and the sacred graveyard. I *know* this one'll be in the papers, the *mass grave* the bones were—listen to this—*unceremoniously dumped in*. Huh? He'll come up here, he'll send people into Syracuse and Binghamton to find some niggers in bars, they'll be standing around him saying, 'What in *fuck* the dude *talk*in about?' Except for ten seconds on the news on TV, it'll look like Abraham Lincoln and the slaves he just freed, you know? It'll fizzle. No liberal gets elected president anymore in America. That's over, thank God. But meanwhile, it doesn't matter, because it's wintertime, Christmas come and gone, the mall's dead, you're dead or anyway halfway dying, and Joe and me, we take it in the ass. You know? I can tell from your face: you know. You're a smart kid, you know that? I always liked it how smart you were."

Harvey flicked his cigarette away and shook out another one. The wind took the flame from his big, clicking Zippo, so he gestured Carter to him and in the shelter of Carter's hands he lit up.

"The senator's advance man's here," Carter said.

"I heard he was staying out there with Miss Hollander and you. He an old friend? How come a guy who's reaming you out is a houseguest? Unless you're not the only one he's reaming out."

Carter finished his cold coffee and crushed the cup in his hands, then stowed the wreckage in his coat pocket. Finally, looking directly at Seymour, he said, "The senator hasn't decided whether to call in the Corps yet."

"Oh, he will. The senator loves a heavy hit like that. He will. Are you friendly with the guy?"

"The senator's man? No."

"So Miss Hollander is."

Carter shrugged.

"You in trouble out there, buddy?"

"I'll be all right."

"Doesn't sound good for you."

"Doesn't sound good for any of us."

"Could we, you know, scare him away? Break some stuff in his body? I could send some muscular people to see him—not that

I do business that way. I work with paper. But everybody knows somebody who knows somebody, am I right?"

"You couldn't scare him away. You could *scare* him, but not away, I think," Carter said. He wished he didn't sound so bitter. He wished he didn't sound, too, as if he admired Harry Miller for needing so to stay in Catherine's house.

Harvey smoked contemplatively. "Then it wouldn't do any good to beat on him, and it's no use killing him since he's in touch, they know where he is, who's involved, all of that."

"Kill?"

Harvey shrugged, and the jacket creaked.

"Harvey: *kill?*"

"It was a passing thought, Carter. You know? That's all. A thought."

"Catherine lives out there, Harvey. Bobby's there. Randy's coming home from school on his, what's it, October break, they call it now. You couldn't—"

"Oh, good heavens, Carter. I'm sorry. Jesus. No. It would have happened away from the *house*. Oh, no, I never meant to worry you like that. I apologize."

Carter looked at his watch, still shaking his head, but looking as if he really needed to know the time that instant.

Harvey said, "You late?"

"I don't know, Harvey. I've been doing it all day."

"You feel like you're running out of time, that's what it is. I don't meant to pull a lot of heavy psychology on you, but that's symbolic action, Carter. You're in trouble, and you're starting to feel it."

"I'm in trouble all right," Carter said. "If we could—maybe you could talk to somebody. Listen to this idea. I could do it *now*, for chrissakes. I use the big backhoe, I dig the bodies up, I carry 'em up there in the front bucket"—he pointed up the ridge—"and I rebury them."

"The blacks wouldn't buy it."

"There *aren't* any blacks in this."

"I don't know. I always kind of thought Olivia had a little nigger in her. What's it called—touch of the tar brush? She wouldn't buy it, the senator's man wouldn't buy it, and the senator wouldn't buy it. You know why?"

Carter shook his head.

"Because you'd never get each person back into the original grave."

"But we didn't take them *out*!"

"Hey," Harvey said, stepping on his cigarette, "I'm not talking fair here, or smart, or logical, or what the fuck ever. I'm talking how these Soviets in Washington think, and little Miss Twat the banker's wife, those people. They want it done over. No. What am I saying?"

"Undone," Carter said.

"That's what I'm saying. A-plus. Undone. And we can't do that, can we?"

"No, we can't," Carter said.

"No, we can't. So what are we, Carter?"

"Dead."

"I'd have said fucked. But that's the answer anyway: fucked, dead—it's all the same."

"It's all the same," Carter said.

"So," Harvey said, gesturing Carter's hands up and lighting inside the cavern he made with them, "I'm going home. A little football action on the tube, a couple of beers, and a lot of sad thoughts about money down the toilet. You and me, buddy, we'll stay in touch, and tomorrow we'll see what's what. I gotta go with the contract. I know you understand that. Whoever writes the contract, whatever it is, we take the lumps and we go on. Am I right?"

Without waiting for Carter to ratify his conclusions, Seymour clambered up into his Blazer and started the engine. The carburetor needed adjustment and there was a whiff of raw fuel on the wind that overwhelmed what smoke lingered and made Carter's sinuses sting. Seymour honked, then waved without looking, and drove off, swaying on his soft springs. Carter checked his watch. He felt like a boy who was almost in tears. He hadn't wept since his divorce, and it had been for the same reason: the knowledge that he was trapped.

Standing beside Harvey Seymour, hearing his deep voice, he'd wanted just now what he'd wanted during his divorce: to reach out for somebody smaller than he, more vulnerable—he thought of Catherine in her bed, leaning over him; he thought of Olivia face down—and he pictured his arms tightening and a throat crushing, a skull cracking, a nose shattering, femur snapping, knee joints exploding backwards so that she flopped—so that Harvey flopped—like an old doll made of soft cloth and stuffed with paper. He was trembling, his face ran with sweat, and his chest felt congested, infected, the skin beneath his shirt prickly, his gums sore.

He thought of Catherine's house, and Drown, and Bobby, and the fishing rod in the pantry. He saw her house burning. He knew that when houses burn the heat is astonishing. It redefines catastrophe with new information on temperature and noise. Sometimes they burned buildings on jobs. It was efficient. They called in the local fire department, who enjoyed the opportunity of practicing techniques, and the wood frame buildings burned like hell, driving you back, always, farther than you thought you'd have to go. The noise came up and frightened you, always, and it was terrible, the roaring and the feeling that this was the sound of all your appetites out of control. "There are no reasons," he said to the silence of the empty site.

Then he drove to the 7-Eleven a half mile from the site and washed his car, using the high-pressure hot water to scour the red dust of the site from under the springs and in the wheel wells and tire rims. The heat of the hose made him think of burning build-ings, and he drove his car around to the side of the 7-Eleven and used the public phone. Harry, on the other end, said, "Hello?" He sounded as if he'd been waiting for the call. Carter couldn't speak.

Harry said, "Yes? Hello?"

Catherine murmured behind him. He thought of her as lying in bed. She would be wearing an old T-shirt and maybe nothing more. He held the phone, and he closed his eyes, and Carter saw the eighteen-wheelers, one after another, slow and heavy and steaming with asphalt, backing into the site and dropping the blacktop into his Barber-Greene. He saw the wearing course laid down on the binder course, and the little fleet of rollers pressing three inches of hot top down into one and a half. The seams knitted, the trucks rolled, the lot grew hard and smooth. Good blacktop made a chopped and pitted work site new. It was a way of cleansing, and you had to smile, seeing the white lines of the parking bays. But the best was when the asphalt adhered, and the lot was clean and even, like a blackboard no one had ever touched with chalk. You could always see her body press at the cloth.

He laid the receiver on the hook and let its weight hang up for him. He could carry the loss for a while. He would borrow to keep up the Barber-Greene payments and there would be other jobs. Businessmen in the area wouldn't care if Carter Kreuss was the man who had tried to bury the blacks under blacktop. He stood with his hand on the wall beside the telephone and he smiled. It might matter that he was the man who had been unable to get the burying done. Well, he'd see. He'd have to see. In spite of his coffee, in his own house, his eyes felt sandy, and his jaws stretched to yawn. He wanted to work, but there wasn't work to do. He would wait until Monday morning, when the judge would throw the order out. He would drive to the site. He would await delivery of the asphalt, and he'd try to lay it down. If they kept him from doing his job, he would look for other jobs. And Catherine and Harry would speak of him, and Harry would smile what he no doubt thought of as his big, winning grin. Yet she had been away from Harry so long. Could she possibly forget him again?

Carter went back to his car and he drove toward home. He remembered when they'd been making love, and he'd pumped and he'd pumped and he'd pumped, touching her tenderly, stroking as he'd read a woman wants to be stroked, not just for sex but caring for her soul. And after rolling her head back and forth on the pillow in what he'd been absolutely certain was a madness of pleasure, ecstasy, she'd whispered to him, "Stop! No more. You're hurting me." She'd pushed at his shoulders, and he'd moved. Though on his back, then, and separate from her, puzzled and embarrassed, he'd been hard as wood and desperate to come. The magazine advice had worked for him, if not for her. Catherine had sat up and looked at him and in the dark, little more than a melted silhouette against the white plaster wall, and with a kind of sad, resigned generosity, she had said, "Lie still." And she had curled, then bent to his penis, and, cupping his balls very gently, had taken the tip, and then more, in her mouth. As if she knew how to do it, she had done it, moving on him until he had cried out in what was pain as much as anything else, he thought. She had bent to him from a great distance in the dark. And still, in his car now, he grew excited and sad, wondering again how she'd known what to do, and how, if she had done that with anyone else, she could do it with him. For wasn't a profound and permanent love prerequisite? And how, he asked himself again, having done that with *him*, could she leave him, or permit him to leave? Could she do it with Harry? Would she?

In his station wagon, tall and strong, a man of the world and a temporary fiscal success, thirty-nine years old and with most of his hair, driving home to a house he feared, Carter Kreuss acknowledged how, in spite of the women he had known, including Catherine, he was virginal. His hand lay on his packed and desperate groin as he drove, and he grasped himself.

The Giants won a slow, slogging punchout, and Harry cheered by silently raising his fist in the air each time they made a first down or scored. He knew that he must look a parody of the Sixties—see what we've become, he said to the memory of those he'd been arrested with on Nixon's streets—but still he held his fist high, cheering, he knew, not only for the former team of Homer Jones and Spider Lockhart, but for Harry Miller, ex of New York and Washington, and now the man who sprawled on a doggy sofa *here*, where Catherine Hollander lived, and where she hid away and secretly bathed. He thought of the little splashes and deep small sighs from the bathroom outside of which he'd stood. He had wanted to press his ear to the door, in fact his forehead had rested against it, and whisper, "Cath? Catherine? You all right?" And of course what he'd really wanted to ask her was, "*Why?*" But he'd known it was not about him. It was exclusively hers. He was in the house, and Carter wasn't, and when he thought of the past twelve years, and of his life away from her, and of the hours with her that he'd been granted, like a wish for the power to fly becoming actual *flight*, then he raised his hand for distant, unimportant triumphs on the television screen, and in the roar of the exulting crowd he balled his fist and squeezed it hard and shook his arm.

The sky was darkening with roiled dirty clouds, and he could feel the increasing winds. He wondered if Catherine would want to go around the house closing storm windows, battening against what was perceptibly the arrival of autumn. He noted that his arms were folded now across his chest, as if to keep him warm. City slicker, he sneered. Then Catherine came in, to reinforce his sense of weather and change. She wore creamy socks, no shoes, and faded, tight jeans. A red-and-green flannel shirt was buttoned to the wrist and almost to the throat. She looked fearless about cold. Her helmet of chestnut hair would smell wonderful, he thought; it was fine and it glowed in the darkening air of the lightless room. She passed behind him with her smile, and then she stopped and bent, from behind him, and she kissed him on the ear and on his cheek. Whatever she wore was rich and dark, with cinnamon and vanilla in it. He breathed her in noisily. "Coco," she said.

"Cocoa?"

"The perfume. Coco Chanel? It's named after her."

"Carter gave it to you."

"How do you know?"

"I don't."

"And any other man—"

"You didn't mention other men who gave you perfume."

"And I didn't buy it for myself."

"You tend not to buy things like perfume and good jewelry for yourself."

She lay on his head and shoulders and then stood. He reached back to pull at her, but she stayed where she was. "You like the smell?" she asked.

"It's scrumptious. Yes."

"Then don't ask."

"No, ma'am. The Giants beat the Skins by ten."

"That makes you extremely happy."

"Extremely, yes."

"Happy enough to help me make tomato sauce with the last batch we picked?"

He thought of himself in the kitchen with Catherine, on a cold late afternoon. He thought again of lying on the air and feeling it receive your weight, and of that buoyancy becoming flight, and of the earth a hundred feet below. "What the hell," he said.

So, with Drown situating himself beneath their feet each time they settled to a single spot for one chore or another, lying like a great black flounder to receive what fell, in the kitchen lighted by wrought-iron lamps on the walls, which glowed yellow against the darkening day, Harry washed tomatoes in the sink, hundreds of them, muddy and still very cold, some blackened from frost and some from slugs, some puffy with rot beneath the tight skin.

Harry scrubbed at clay from the garden, plucked stems, and in a performance of vegetable triage, he sorted out the frost-killed and slug-ridden, which went into the large plastic compost bucket. Others were cleaned off, rotted parts excised with the serrated knife she had given him, dried in colanders. Harry worked slowly because they were doing it together and he wanted the work to last.

Catherine carried batches of tomatoes to her food processor, where she sliced them into chunks or dropped the little ones in whole and made a purple-red muck of them. This she brought to the four pots on the stove, which had olive oil and sliced onions and garlic in them. She poured the soupy stuff into each pot in turn, as Harry washed and plucked and sawed. When a pot began to simmer, Catherine threw in bay leaf and basil and oregano from her garden which she'd washed and chopped and frozen. She ground in pepper, brought more tomatoes to the processor, and turned them barely liquid, then added them to the simmering pots. Harry's hand grew icy, and he added a little hot water to the mixture in the tap. He thought, of course, of Catherine in her secret bath, upstairs. She had found, on a big old radio that sat on top of her refrigerator, a station that played traditional jazz. They were hearing Gerry Mulligan, she told him, playing "My Funny Valentine."

In the coarse green smell of raw tomatoes, and in the peppery fragrance of what cooked, under the whine of the processor and the rich, thick plopping noise from the pots on the stove, Harry listened to the sad brassiness of the Mulligan. "How do you know?" he asked.

"That it's Gerry Mulligan? I started listening to him," she said. "I started listening to music. Puccini, Rostropovich, Finzi, Count Basie—everyone, I guess. I got hungry for it. I buy recordings, lots of them."

"You never did that."

"No," she said. "Do you listen to music?"

He shrugged, wondering why he was so angry. "Yeah," he said. "I listen to the radio. Not a lot. On the job, I don't have a lot of time. I get home late, I'm tired, I've been *listening* all day. Late at night, on the radio, I listen to ball games in other states. I like to hear what's happening in the late innings in Seattle or some-place. Music, I listen to, I don't know—soothing stuff."

"Soothing," Catherine said. "Like elevator music? Shopping mall music?"

The pain from his blisters in the wash of acid tomatoes had become unbearable to him. He clenched his hands, again and again, in clear water, wondering how she had stood—he thought the word *manfully*—to soak her blisters in salt water. He won-dered if pus from his blisters was cooking on the stove. Catherine's arms were streaked with tomato and herbs. Her sleeves, rolled now to just below the elbow, were also coated. In a corner of her mouth, from a tasting, was a drop of tomato sauce.

She said, "*That* was uncalled for. Do I *look* like a social critic?"

"I sometimes, when it's very late, as I was saying, sometimes I listen to classical music, I guess you'd call it. Not wonderful stuff, nothing too smart. I like it to tootle along very gently, softly. My brain wouldn't handle much more. Baseball games, football games, college basketball—you hear the crazy deep-South guys hollering about Billy Bob driving into the lane. I'm not terribly clever when I get home. See what you've been doing with the tomatoes in that machine? That's what they do to my brain. Between Mrs. Tal-liaferro and the senator and the *idiots* on the Hill—"

She said nothing, which, he remembered, meant that she was preparing to say much. Mulligan bounced down, and down further, then rose softly to sigh metallically, metal imitating and shining up the sound of wood. Catherine said, "Harry. How come you do that job?"

He turned the water off and began to shovel scraps and slugs and rot around the sink with the edge of his stinging hand. "It struck me as a kind of grown-up work. Full of compromises and ugly stuff, and a little good stuff getting done. Pretty much money. The smell of very expensive sweat. The power of it, I'm talking about. The power's incredible. It's like your Coco, sometimes, and sometimes you can see them getting high on it. Their eyes get goggly. Mine too, I suppose." He sought a spatula in the pitcher of implements beside the sink, and he began to shovel debris and ferry it to the compost bucket. "Mostly, I think—I've been thinking about it, to tell you the truth. Mostly, it was because the job had so many *downs* mixed in with all the heady stuff you read about and see in the movies. And they're true. But I really think that was it. It said: Now you're a middle-aged man. This is what they do. They compromise. And you might as well be comfortable while you do."

She brought the food processor and colanders and utensils for him to wash. "Watch the blade," she said, leaning against his hip with hers, "it's really sharp. Don't hurt yourself." Then she asked, "Were you *trying* to be sad? Is that part of choosing this job? This kind of job?"

He shook his head. "Not consciously, I don't think. I don't know. You mean, did I elect a kind of secular high-tech monastery? Brother Harry of the Perpetual Sorrows? The Little Brothers of the Rich? I don't—no." He looked up to see her face close to his shoulder. He shook his head, but then he shrugged. "I didn't miss you every day," he said. "I never missed you all day every day."

"Good," she said in a small, taut voice.

"Yeah. When you were, ah. With other guys. And Carter. When whatever was happening and did happen and will happen and could happen and who in hell can imagine ten minutes from *now*. When any of that. Were you thinking of me, ever?"

He looked down into the sink. A slug was left in the drainer, and he turned the basket upside down, banged it at the drain hole, and flushed with hot water. He replaced the basket and he washed, waiting.

Her voice was even smaller. "Yes."

He nodded. "Good," he said. "I don't know what's going to happen, do you?"

She remained as she'd been, her hip leaning on his. She said, "No."

"No," he said. "I know what I *wish* could happen."

She said, "Yes."

"Do you wish it too, Cath?"

"Harry," she said.

"Okay. We don't need any rush. Fine."

"No," she said, "it isn't that."

"It *isn't?*" He despised his eagerness. It was as if the years in Washington had taught him nothing of control. You shouldn't need, he heard himself say beneath the music that was bothering his concentration. You should be able to look her in the eye and talk straight. And fly at will.

"That's Bob Brookmeyer on the trombone," she said.

"Great."

She said, "Harry, it is possible I've been in love with you one third of my life, counting time spent writing letters and talking on the phone and just thinking about you."

"Catherine," he said, as if warning someone.

"Isn't it true? Possibly true?"

He nodded, hard, as if to someone sitting at the far end of the kitchen table behind him, waiting for the sign.

"Carter means something, too," she said. "Not what you do. Did. Do. That's a fact I think I might have told *him*. I know I told me. But he was strong in my life. He was regular and even. He was kind. He was what I needed. Just the way being alone, when I needed it, was what—"

"—you needed."

"We were lovers for close to a year. We were friends a lot less. I don't know that we got to being any kind of basic friends, to tell you the truth. And I don't imagine you would think of us as fever-struck lovers."

"Oh, don't *tell* me anything, Cath."

"I'm sorry. I'm sorry." She was silent. Then she asked, "Did it ever strike you, about men in general—"

He said, "Yes. They can't cope with sex. That's right."

She laughed with real pleasure. "Well, it's a load, son," she said in some Western-movie-star voice.

"Is that Randolph Scott?"

"Who?"

"Never mind. What are we saying?"

"I liked him."

"Great."

"I guess I even liked Dell, once."

"That's got to be a mistake."

"I know you're right." She sighed. "Except look at the kids."

"Gorgeous boys," he said.

"So he did something right, then, didn't he?"

"Catherine," he said, "do we have to talk about people *screwing* you?"

She began to laugh, and he tried to join her, but while she was amused, Harry was bleeding, he thought, as surely as if the curved short blade of the food processor had been drawn across his body in deep long strokes.

Something slammed outside the kitchen, in the house, and they turned toward the doorway. Drown, sensing their urgency, but having missed the noise, was up a few seconds late, roaring and scrabbling for purchase on the wood floor. It was Bobby, delivered home from town. Catherine went to the radio and turned it off, while Harry dried his sore hands and, leaning against the sink, reminded himself of a father showing his son that he attends. I could do this, he thought.

Bobby dropped his jacket over a chair and went to the refrigerator, moving his mother with his hands on her arms. When he had a bottle of fruit juice and was sitting, he said, "Giants looked good. Skins need a secondary."

Harry agreed. Catherine was looking at them, and Harry assured himself he saw approval in her eyes.

"I'm doing a paper," Bobby said.

"That's *right*," Catherine said, clapping her hands. "He could *help*."

"Gosh, Mom. I wonder if that's why I'm asking him."

Harry wished he were Bobby's father so he could thunder, Don't you talk to your mother that way. Instead, he weaseled a grin and waited.

"It's about political science," Bobby said.

"It *is* political science," his mother said.

"*You* want to ask him, Mom?" She raised her brows and held her hand over her mouth, keeping it there long enough for Bobby to turn and see it. He turned back to Harry. "All right. All right?"

Catherine's voice, muffled by her hand, made *all right* noises.

Bobby asked, "How come this senator thinks he should be president? We're talking about branches of government, and my teacher—a real doof double-twee, this guy. His favorite song's 'The Star-Spangled Banner,' this guy." Bobby's sweet, long face writhed into masks of disgust that Harry supposed he wore at useful moments in school. "He hates welfare. He hates everything except the army. He says your guy's a liberal who throws money away or something."

Harry nodded. "I've heard words like that applied to him."

"*You* think he should be president?"

Harry said, "He's smart. He's one of the smartest men I know in Washington. But you don't need to be too smart to run the country. If you can qualify for a driver's license, you can handle it, I think. And he's tough. That would help. He knows a lot. Some people think knowledge is useful— God, Bobby, I sound so cynical. I'm sorry."

"But you do think this guy should be president, or you don't?"

Harry lifted his hands and dropped them. He wished that he felt more. "It couldn't hurt. It maybe could help, because of his feelings for poor people. I think he really wants to do something for them. I suspect he knows enough about foreign policy to find the men's room in downtown Delhi."

"India, right?"

"India, that's right. He doesn't like Asia. So he doesn't go there anymore. But he was in India once."

"Isn't most of the world Asia, these days?" Catherine asked.

Bobby said, "Wait a minute. Wait. Is he good or not good?"

"Bobby, compared to the bozos who work in Washington and want to be president, he's not too bad. He's all right. I'd probably vote for him."

"Probably," Catherine said.

Bobby said, "Who's good, then?"

"Wait," Catherine said. "Wait a minute. Harry. We were talking about this before, weren't we? How this senator could help stop the mall from going through? Because of his great compassion for the people who get buried under shopping centers?"

Harry nodded. Here it came.

"So if you don't believe all the way in this guy, and I can't see that you do, why would you be willing to come here and stop a nothing little mall in the countryside? Was it just to, you know, to *get* here?"

Harry said, "Well, God knows I wanted to get here, Cath. You wouldn't doubt that, would you?"

She looked at him. Her chin was up now, and her mouth was

gathered. She looked fifteen. She looked too far away for him to reach in time. In time for *what*?

"But what are you doing this to Carter for, Harry?"

"Carter? You're worrying about Carter?"

Her chin stayed up. "I think we call it loyalty," she said.

"To what?"

"Bobby, would you excuse us?"

"Wait a minute, Mom. It was *my* question."

"Now it's mine. Would you excuse us? We'll be done in a minute."

Bobby looked at Harry, who, as if he were his father, nodded. Bobby nodded back. He knew he was in for possible disembowelment, but Bobby's matter-of-factness cheered him. Glad but gutless, Harry thought. "Excuse me," Bobby said sullenly. He went upstairs. Drown stood at the foot of the stairs, gathering himself, rocking, and then, at last, springing in slow motion for the first step, following Bobby up.

"What are you trying to do, Harry? Just *hurt* Carter?"

"No. In the first place, no. In the second place, he was a man who you loved. I don't know, maybe you still love him. I wouldn't—"

"Don't fish! You want to know something, ask me. All right?"

"All right."

She said, "You're wondering what I'm angry at? It isn't on account of loving him. Okay? It's *you*!" She was unrolling her sleeves over her tomatoed arms and buttoning them. "You used to write poems," she said. "They weren't the greatest poems I ever saw. I mean, I don't know that much about them or anything. But they were poems that you wrote. You meant them, and you wrote them—you *worked* on them. And then you typed them up and mailed them out, and you brought them with you. You always brought poems."

"You were terrific about reading them," he said.

She stuffed her hands in her pockets. "That isn't what I'm talking about. You knew how to write good words. You put them in poems. Now you're putting them in God knows what for somebody you don't even think's that good! So what are you *doing*, Harry? What matters to you? That's what I want to know." All of a sudden her face was red at the forehead and the cheeks and nose, and her clear light eyes were wet. "You stopped writing poems after me. *I* know that. Whatever kind of cynic you became—"

"And sellout? You want to say that too, Cath?"

She dismissed it with a wave of her hand. "Whatever else happened to you," she said, almost crying, her voice very ragged, "you stopped writing poems because of *me*. I know it. I *worried* about it. But look what you started in to write! So"—she sighed with a kind of shudder—"not only did *you* do something bad, Harry. And I think you did. I think you really did, working for this man. But *I* did. *I* did."

She put her hands over her face, and then she turned away from him. Harry approached her. All of a sudden, her left hand sprang out and pointed up, parallel to the track of the stairs just outside the kitchen. "Bobby Hollander, you get your ass away from the steps and you wait in your room, please! I *mean* this!"

Harry was behind her, then. He touched her shoulders, he stroked down, hard, toward her waist—she felt hot beneath the flannel shirt—and then he put his hands on her hips and leaned on her. He slid his arms around her and held her, but not on her breasts, as he wanted to. His hands were above her belly, and he made them sit lightly. "You're tough," he said.

"So?"

"I can't figure out if I should apologize for leading my life the best way I knew how—I mean, what job's a blessing for *any*body, Cath? And I can't decide whether I'm supposed to tell you I quit poetry for some noble kind of reason, or what. Or say, yeah, you did it, but I'll take the blame. I mean, if you hurt me, is it *my* fault?

Assuming you hurt me, assuming that you made me stop."

"I did. I know it. And you went on and whored your ass, Harry."

"Is that what I'm doing?"

"I'm sorry," she said, whispering, dropping her hands and placing them on his, which were still atop her belly.

"And is any of this for Carter?"

She took her hands away, and then Harry had to as well, and neither spoke until Harry was tersely instructed to summon Bobby, who was given a soda with dinner. "Randy has sixteen a day. He told me on the phone," Bobby said.

"He hasn't talked to you on the phone," Catherine said. "Isn't that what you told me?"

Bobby said, "What? *I* don't know. Anyway, he does talk to me."

"He says, 'Hello, dude,' you told me."

"He's drinking them all the time," Bobby said.

Harry said, "Not beer?"

"He loves his body too much," Bobby said. "He wants to be lean, you know?"

Harry said something like "Mmm."

He was draining linguini while Catherine dolloped sauce into an ironstone bowl. She said, but didn't sing it, "Harvesttime." She set bottles of beer down, hard, for Harry and herself, and a second can of soft drink for Bobby, and Harry twirled his pasta neatly on a tablespoon until he noticed Bobby cutting his into chunks and Catherine twirling her pasta in air and sucking in strands, staring at him over spattering sauce and linguini. She said, "It can be fun, can't it?"

Harry sucked in a few pieces, then he told her, "You're right. You know you are."

Bobby managed to consume his sodas and spaghetti, eat a second helping, belch twice, hear himself berated by his mother, and then beg indulgence to leave the table early to study for a test. They

drank second bottles of beer. Catherine, sitting at right angles to
Harry, smiled. Her face was bright and taut. She looked as if
she'd done hard labor in the cold outdoors, and hadn't she?
Harry wondered about clearing the table with a sweep of his arm
and going for something violent and friendly in tomato sauce on
top of the table.

"Don't you look perverse," she said.

"Inspired."

"Well, forget it. I'm halfway into a body cast as it is." She lifted
his blistered right hand, which had been lying on the table like a
dog, belly-up, who waited for scratching, and she kissed it in the
sore center of his palm. He let his fingers close around her cheeks.
And then they cleared and started to ladle sauce into plastic freezer
containers that Catherine retrieved from a cupboard. He loved
how there were places and plans for sauce containers. You could
have the whole world in a house, he thought, and he remembered
what he'd heard in London, or read in a novel about the RAF—
how when everything was snug, and in place, and the usual menace
was somehow at bay, you were said to be as safe as houses. Harry
washed dishes while Catherine ladled, and then he wrote out labels
for the clear plastic covers: TOMATO SAUCE, he wrote on all the
labels.

He asked, "You want it dated?"

"Absolutely," she said.

"Today's the—is it the sixteenth?"

"It is," she said. "I want it on every label. October sixteenth."

"Okay," he said. And then he looked up, because her eyes were
on him as he wrote.

"I want to remember the date. I want to think of it when we eat
the sauce," she said.

He waited, but her face didn't move. He wanted to ask her:
Will I be at the table, then? He didn't. He smelled the harvest.
He felt her deepening watchfulness. He wrote the date.

238

Chapter Six

HARRY THOUGHT of it as dawn, though all he knew was that it was dark and cold, a few minutes past four in the morning, and he was rolling away from Catherine, the smell of her sleep, the reach in sleep of her neck, her vulnerable uncomposed mouth and disarranged hair and her eyes moving in secret beneath her lids to remind him that for all he knew of her or them or what his life might be if she were in it, he knew nothing. He moved and dressed and sneaked. Downstairs, Drown slinked from a sofa and wagged. Harry whispered good morning and he drank from a pitcher of orange juice at the open refrigerator, just as he'd drunk milk from the carton when a boy. Like that boy, he sneaked a handful of chocolate chip cookies. "Breakfast," he said softly by way of excuse, spraying crumbs, and slinking like Drown to leave the house. He had hoped to let the Mustang roll to the road, but it sat on its fat tires and wouldn't budge until, like a car thief or a chunky lover on the run, he shoved the car backward, grunting while chewing the last of his cookies. When it was moving he ran around to the open door and steered as he slid backward toward the road. Once there, he started up and took off for where he thought, working from Catherine's descriptions, Carter might live.

He drove for a while with the lights off, liking the danger of the darkness, and protected by two lanes of emptiness. But when a giant eighteen-wheeler whipped past him like a ship with its superstructure lit in three colors, he turned his own lights on and sang "Searchin' " to keep himself a better brand of company than he could find on the radio at half past four a.m. He thought he had won. That is, Carter didn't live with Catherine, now, and Harry thought that he wouldn't anymore. She was moving out, herself, away from what he wasn't sure. He was afraid that it might be Harry Miller, but he didn't know. You could say, he said to himself as if at a party or a seminar on modern love, you could say that we're lovers again. But we aren't lovers the way we were. There's too much uncertainty for that. Although *I* wasn't ever that certain about anything, the other times. I was always waiting for signs and signals from her. But you could say that we're lovers. Who knows, he thought. Catherine and I, we have to work from day to day, from hour to hour. We'll live our lives, and we'll see.

He discerned his hand on the horn of the Mustang, making it wail. He continued to lean on it, and then, since he didn't feel better, he replaced it on the wheel and summed up his declaration of love's condition in the country in mid-October: We do not know *shit*. We are waiting for Catherine to tell us.

He envisioned the senator flying in from Washington on a commuter jet, and landing in Binghamton. He saw him flying from the New York office by helicopter to the site itself. That's what he would do, Harry thought.

If she hadn't said, last night, as they lay in bed reading, fulfilling perhaps the final desire in the systematic erotic daydream Harry had dreamed for twelve years—that of lying next to Catherine, reading the Sunday *Times* in bed—"Carter isn't as tough as a lot of people think he is."

He'd put down Travel, in which he was reading questions and answers about sleeping in Irish castles and making reservations at a Maltese hotel. "He asked me to put my dukes up," Harry said. "I thought at the time he meant it."

"Oh, he did. He can be belligerent."

"Yes, he can," Harry said, reminding himself to be very careful of his tone.

"But he's frightened," she said. "He's frightened and confused. One of the things." She stopped, and Harry hated the fondness of her recollection. "One of the funny things about him, he was always very messy. His house is just horrible, although I think that's something else."

"Ah."

"But even though he was sloppy—at home, his office, every-place—he worked so hard here. He stacked things up, he was always washing things, dishes and laundry. It was only at *his* house."

"What was?" Harry said. "You mean, where he was really messy?"

"Where he was true. I think he was always on his best behavior here. Like a kid. Trying to impress somebody by showing how orderly he was. Dependable. He always wanted you, I mean me, I guess. Or everyone. To think he was a reliable man. And he was. He really was."

"But at his house he was, what did you say? True?"

"True. Despairing."

"Why?"

"I don't know. He bought the house after his divorce, he said. You feel horrible after a divorce."

"I recall."

"*You* weren't divorced, Harry."

"I wasn't even married. No, I was thinking of you. After Dell. You kept saying you were free, but you were guilty and sad, really down on yourself. That's what I was remembering."

"Yes," she said. "I should have known you'd remember my life. You always thought about me. I mean, I don't mean every minute, necessarily. But if anybody would ever say to me, Who can you count on to know you? I'd have to say you."

He said, "Yes," and even he heard how sad the word could sound.

"But Carter," she said.

"Carter."

"He bought the grungiest, ugliest, shabbiest old farmhouse I ever saw. It's on the edge of state lands, evergreen forest. He's all alone on this shady, dark, dirty road, it's always dark because of the trees, and it's always clammy there. I hated it. I went there twice, and then to hell with it. He never cleaned it. He pushed the dirt around for me when I was coming over, but he never really *cleaned*, you could tell. He wanted it like that, I think. He was all bleach and soap flakes and showers over here, but there . . ."

Harry was thinking of Carter and Catherine in a shower stall. He said, "Disheveled, eh?"

"Filthy. And I swear, that's where he was mostly him. That's where his secret was. I don't mean he had his ex-wife's body in the basement or anything."

"Cool basement in a damp climate, you'd maybe get a delay in the old whiff of corruption, but you'd know about it after a while."

She swatted him with the *Times* Magazine. "You know what I mean. The house was *Carter*, I think. You understand me?"

"Who can you count on to know you?" he reminded her.

She swatted him again, and then lay still, her knees up on top of the covers, several sections of the paper on her belly. "He's sad," Catherine said. "He and I—"

"I don't want to, Cath. Don't tell me you were sad, all right? I don't think I could cope with that in any commendable manner. Unless you were sad about me."

She lay silently.

242

He turned so violently, the bed rocked. She started to laugh, and he saw that she was pointing at what he could feel now: furrowed brow, bulging eyes, beseeching mouth. "Bitch," he said.

She kicked the papers and some slid off her and some sailed into the air, feathering. Asian princes and homegrown politicians, their evasions and their puffing speeches and their undeclared malfeasances floated about them and sank away, billions of dollars and tens of thousands of threatened lives, small cities and entire states rose and fell, and Catherine lay on her side, facing Harry. They were perhaps a finger's breadth apart, almost mouth to mouth, breathing each other's breaths. Harry thought that he could feel each inch of his spine, every hair on his body, every pulsing of blood beneath his skin as she brought him, by only proximity and her attention, to a state of the most exquisite alertness.

Driving on the narrow two-lane highway now, angling toward the state lands near where he might find Carter Kreuss, she was why he was here, and heading there. She had stolen his hatred of the man. Or she'd reminded him that the man—he detested this—had once been hers, and that she had been Carter's, in a way.

He went past the turnoff, realized it half a mile on, turned around with a squealing of tires that he enjoyed, and then made the turn on the second try. He went slower now, imagining the wheels feeling their way over ruts and giant pebbles, whole stones. The car wobbled on its tight springing and Harry rattled against the seat belt. Periodically, he saw POSTED signs that said that New York State forbade almost every activity he had ever heard of. At every stacking point, cleared verges on the road where loggers with state permission could cut firewood, he saw the sparkle of glass and the duller sheen of beer cans. The long drooping white things were condoms, he realized.

The house was low and narrow, sided in something that seemed to absorb the light, maybe old and moist asbestos, Harry thought. It was so close to the road that no driveway was necessary. Carter kept no mailbox, Harry saw, so he must use his office as his only address. He lived in a house to which no one could write. So he isn't where he is, Harry thought, disliking his cleverness at the expense of someone who was always in trouble. Just ask Catherine. Just let's don't anymore, he thought. Harry caught his secret brain humming "Bess, you is mah woman now."

He stopped the car. He was fewer than six or eight feet from the door to the house. He didn't know why he had come, except that she was part of the skewed life of this house, and Harry was somehow making the life in it worse. If he were to say to Carter, "Catherine sent me," he wouldn't be lying.

A light went on upstairs. It was dull and pale, a flashlight, Harry thought. He had to instruct himself not to start the car and peel out. The light went away, then reappeared downstairs, and soon enough the door opened in. When the light struck his face, Harry forced it to smile a little, the best he could do.

"Are they all right?" Carter said at once. "Is Catherine all right? And Bobby?"

"Yes. Yes. No problem, Carter. I'm sorry I woke you up. I was trying to be quiet."

"Yeah," Carter said, "I know. How come you were sitting outside my house at five in the morning trying to be quiet? That's what woke me up."

"That's right," Harry said. "Why would I drive out here and try and be quiet? I don't know. I couldn't sleep. I was worried about what in hell I'm involved in with this graveyard thing. I thought we needed to talk about it. I needed to, I guess."

"I guess so," Carter said, and he stepped back. The light receded. Carter's voice came through the open door: "Come on, then," and Harry left the car and walked inside in the dark.

From my kitchen to Catherine's and from hers to his, Harry thought, following Carter's flashlight beam that turned the walls brown when it fell on them. They paraded down a narrow hall and turned to what the light slowly showed, as if Carter were giving a tour, the room where a bachelor made meals. There were glasses on the counter and dishes on the table, and the table had looked, when the light swept it, as if someone's fingers, pressed lightly to its surface, would stick. Harry smelled cooking, stale and overheated oils, something darker and wetter, like mushrooms. A gas burner roared and then flared with a threatening small explosion, and the blue-red flame of a stove in need of adjustment lighted up the yellow surface of the stove and the dull wall behind it. "I'll make coffee," Carter said.

"I'm sorry I woke you."

"I can sleep any time," Carter said. "I can sleep for the rest of the year if I want."

Harry heard bottles and glasses. He said, "No, don't bother, Carter. Coffee'll be great. That's all I—"

"Listen," Carter said, "you ever drink *nature?*"

"I did France on the ten-day economy run," Harry said. "That's French you spoke, isn't it? I didn't get to see a hell of a lot, and the only French I talked was ordering up coffee in the morning or the house special for dinner."

"Well, this is a specialty of *mine*," Carter said. "This is the *specialité de la maison*. It's one of my favorite phony tricks along with hanging out with educated women. I actually learned it in night school at Mohawk Valley Community College. A rummy professor from Syracuse taught us. His nose glowed when he talked about French wines and brandies. You don't buy this around here, what I'm pouring you. This is really good Cognac. Nobody watered it, or otherwise messed it around. This is what it's supposed to taste like, and I'm inviting you to have a drink of it with me, along with some coffee, which I make lousy, and we can sit in here and talk to each other."

It was, by now, like sitting in a movie theater. The darkness had given way to defined shapes moving on a gray background, and Harry could see that Carter wore striped pajamas with snug white cuffs at the wrists and ankles. He wore old-fashioned high leather slippers, and his fine hair was tousled in a little pyramid. He slid a big brandy balloon along the kitchen table, which was indeed sticky, and Harry picked it up and sniffed the way he thought he was supposed to. "*Whoof,*" was the best he could do. "It's strong stuff, huh?"

"It's real stuff."

"Right. Here we go." He sniffed again, and the alcohol cut at his eyes, which watered. Carter was watching him. He sipped, and he tried to think of brandy casks and old wood, he forgot which country it was supposed to come from, and vineyards, a town they'd been in when they'd walked in the rain eating chopped olives in oil on chunks of fresh bread. Something in his gut, no, lower, near his balls in point of fact, gave a little kick after he swallowed. He wondered if that was the prostate, and if his middle years had just officially begun. It tasted like violets and berries and the rust from a can of nails left outside someone's garage, and maybe a very special kind of ink, with paint stripper added. "Man," he said.

Carter said, "You like it?"

Harry said, "Man!"

"Tastes like shit, doesn't it?"

"I guess you have to get used to it."

"*I* can't. You want some coffee?"

"Right away, please."

They sipped coffee out of narrow cylindrical mugs that had clever sayings on them, Harry was sure. He couldn't bring himself to read his. The coffee tasted boiled and it was thin. It burned his tongue and took the scar of the taste of the brandy away, and he sighed his gratitude. "I make bad coffee," Carter said.

"This is no lie, Carter: I'm enjoying the hell out of it."

Carter raised his mug, and Harry lifted his, and then they both drank. Carter put his mug down and said, "So Catherine's all right."

"Didn't you have lunch with her the other day? Didn't you see her out at the house?"

"She told you everything, right?"

"I don't know. She told me you talked."

"You're—what'd they used to say in the papers? You're an item," Carter said.

Harry leaned forward. "Yeah. An item. Listen: we knew each other *twelve years ago*. I used to pull Bobby in a little wagon through this tiny town they used to live in called Schuyler. He was *two*."

"I think it was a sled," Carter said.

"Really?"

"I think that's what Catherine used to say."

"She talked about it."

Carter nodded in the lightening darkness of the kitchen. "She talked about *you*."

Harry said, feeling foolish as he traded, "She was talking about you last night."

Carter nodded again, as if he weren't surprised. It was light enough now for Harry to see how pleased Carter was.

Harry said, "And she was hoping this thing with the construction site and the black people and the guy I work for—that you wouldn't get screwed over too badly. This has to feel like a lousy time for you. Catherine, and everything, and the job."

"Catherine and everything? You mean, Catherine and you."

Harry nodded. "I'm sorry."

"No, you're not."

"No. I'm not."

"As for the bones," Carter said, "I was talking to someone— Olivia Stoddard?"

"A very dedicated woman," Harry said.

"That's a word for it. Yes. And she was saying, it's out of hand. Out of control. Is that right? See, I was saying to her, what if I get those bones reburied, up on the ridge above the site? Where they really came from? Wouldn't that do it?"

"Has to, I'd think. I guess. I mean, it would take it all away from *my* man. There wouldn't be any occasion for righteous indignation on behalf of everyone and everything black in America and possibly the Free World."

"Yes. I was thinking along those lines. Except, Olivia says it's got away from all of that. Running on its own. I asked her if we could propose it to her and to you and the others. She said it was okay with her. And you—well, would you? Call it in to Washington as a compromise and tell him to stay home and not bring in the Wetlands Act?"

"Olivia said it wouldn't work?"

"She said it was in Washington, so now forget it."

"The Land That Brains Forgot," Harry said. "I don't know. I don't know. I have to tell you: before I call or don't call, do or don't do, I want to know what I really think about it. Really feel."

"Jesus, Harry, all of you intellectuals talk the same way. What's it *matter* what your true philosophy about it is? Do it, don't do it, screw me up, dig up the dead people—whichever! Just what's my goddam fate, you know? What's the story gonna be? Excuse me for yelling. I'm a violent man, sometimes. I'm sorry."

"No," Harry said. "I see how you feel. Look. I'll level with you. I think those people in the ground have some rights. More important, I think being a black person in this country is for shit. I think they are raped twice a day. I'm not talking about the guys with a houseful of suits, and the bronze yuppie puppies, or the dopes who get a job they can't do, don't deserve, barely care about, Affirmative Action and water, over and out. I'm talking about—well, *you* know. You're a grown-up in America. You *know*. They shouldn't see that this can happen, with those graves. I really think so. They don't need to be demeaned that way. It's—

fuck it, Carter, it's *embarrassing* to me. And if everything else was only everything else, I'd call in the senator on a preemptive strike and let 'er rip. But what I keep worrying about, you see, is Carter Kreuss. You know him. Strange guy, lives in a dark house, used to be the cellmate of the woman I've been chasing after in *very* slow motion for a lot of what's alleged to be my mature life. And he stands to lose his ass if I do what I should. I mean, I *really* mean, what a citizen should. A loyal American citizen *plus* a slightly ambitious person doing his job for extravagant pay. You understand me? I'd like to know if I'm trying to do you in or I'm striking a righteous blow."

They were silent, and they both drank the bad coffee. Carter, at last, said, "It's what I told you. You're a fuckin intellectual."

Harry lifted his brandy balloon and knocked back the drink. He groaned and sighed and seethed out loud. "Aren't we enjoying the *ass* off of our little talk together?"

Carter burped a kind of giggle, and he lifted his glass too, then drank it down. "Poom," he said. "You know what poom is?"

"The sound of a puma's headache."

Carter pointed his finger at Harry and said, "I knew you'd know that one."

"I used to be a poet," Harry said. And then he said, "So I really *don't* know."

In the darkness of the kitchen, like a watercolor wash now, as daylight fell through its air, Carter stared at him a long time, then looked at the table. One more kitchen table, Harry thought, as they sat with one another, and their empty glasses, empty cups, and nothing much to say. They said what was left, and then Harry stood, nodded, and walked outside, to shiver in the brightening air. He waved at the house in case Carter was watching, then he turned his car around.

He drifted, with the radio off, and then with the lights off as daylight came true, and with his mind clattering, like a teletype.

That wasn't a man to work at destroying, he thought. And that man had lived in Catherine's life, and still might, he thought, knowing that he didn't want to believe it possible. He offered the simulation of humbleness in case there *was* a God who might punish him for arrogance. And was Olivia right? Was it too late to make any decision at all? Had the question, issue, call it what you like, become the process? Were they all only part of it now? We are all officially black, in that case, he decided, noting that he did so with the generosity of a liberal white man who could, if it weren't for Catherine Hollander, live however he wanted as long as he had the dough.

He was on the strip of car washes and diners and fast food restaurants and video rental parlors near the job site, he realized almost an hour later when he stopped for gas. He found the place that looked most like a diner. Its large neon sign said DINER, and that was good enough for Harry. Inside, lean men in dark blue work clothes bent over coffee. Electricians and plumbers and carpenters on their way to work were loading in the cholesterol, and Harry got on board. The jukebox—a little set was on the counter every ten feet and on the wall of every booth—was silent; Harry wanted to bow to the fine judgment of everyone in the long room. A blocky woman with absolutely no expression on her powdered pale wide face framed by lavender hair in tight curls took his order for three eggs over hard and rye toast and a double side of sausages and fried potatoes with onions, juice and coffee now, please. Harry sighed inside his closed mouth. But, he warned himself sternly, there would be no prune Danish at the end of *this* little breakfast.

Carter's last words had been "Hi to Catherine." The words that had preceded them, and by a good three or four minutes, had been, "I'll probably go bust on this. I don't know why it should stop you. And if you wanted, I could tell you why I'm gonna take it in the ear. But it'll happen." They had sat there, then, and Harry had sought a syllable of consolation for Carter or excuse for himself. And then, finally, Carter had said, either dismissing him or helping him escape, "Hi to Catherine, all right?"

Harry cut the hard eggs with their solid yolk and browned edges into small squares that he loaded onto small squares of toast. He ate them happily as cooking grease ran through his teeth and the butter from the toast—why not?—gave flavor to the eggs. He added salt and cut some more and ate, and he suspected that a microphone nearby might pick up the sound of a podgy fellow humming to himself as he ate what he absolutely shouldn't. He cut a sausage in half and engulfed the portion, along with egg and toast. Hi to Catherine. Who would pick the table up and hurl it from the booth, tear the cushions off and send them through the air at the lavender-topped waitress, and then drive Harry into the parking lot—*parking* lots—and lecture him on hearts and health and middle age. Or would that be only if Harry were Bobby, her son? Mightn't she just sit, picking at her English muffin with margarine, sipping at her coffee, watching him from under her brows as he ate slower and slower, realizing with every bite that she was disapproving, that she refused to speak?

He put down the fork with its impaled piece of sausage. He set down the little slice of toast with its topping of fried egg. He drank at his coffee, then swallowed his juice. He left a five-dollar bill on the table, a kind of a bribe for the waitress, who clearly lived in a toy store at night. He paid his bill, and he left. "Killer dietitian," he said, thinking of the unfinished sausage.

He drove to the site and parked there. It was a little too early for the men to be showing up, though he thought he saw two work-booted legs sticking out the window of a distant piece of earth-moving equipment. In the litter of machines and torn earth and stone mounds, someone's decision would come by way of third parties. He wondered what the decision would be, and who would render it. He worked a piece of pork gristle loose from a gap between his teeth, and he nodded as if at someone watching, because he knew what his own decision would be, he thought.

Let this be a lesson to you all, he lectured the bulldozers and the trucks. Beware the woman who does not instruct you what to do.

Catherine was late and sad. She'd driven Bobby to school so he'd be calm for his weekly math quiz. She had been very careful to say nothing anyone might infer as having to do with numbers, examinations, keeping one's head, or checking one's answers. And Bobby, in turn, had said nothing. He'd looked out the passenger-side window, checking his hair in the van's right-side mirror, and he had made no sound. She'd chattered, hating herself for the bright and desperate need to make noise, and by the time he had left, pale and worried, she'd been furious at him, and probably had showed it, and doubtless would be responsible for his failing the quiz because his head was filled with his mother's problems. Moreover, she had forgotten the books she needed in the gallery, so had to drive back home instead of being able to take the short-cut over back hill roads to work. The books were the two volumes of *The Apples of New York*, which the despicable Mrs. Edith Hemstrought of Cooperstown had commissioned her to find. Once commonplace, the heavy, dark green two-volume set had cost her $90 from a dealer, and would be worth $125 if she resold it. Instead, she was going, on behalf of the awful Mrs. Hemstrought, to cut out half a dozen of the volumes' wonderful, detailed drawings of apples and mat and frame them, and sell them to Mrs. Hemstrought for $50 apiece. She might even manage to keep the damaged books, she thought, downshifting the van because the incline was nearly ten degrees and the compression at about the level of valve job. "Damn it, Bobby," she said as she managed fifteen miles an hour with her foot nearly all the way down.

When she pulled in beside his rental car, she thought of hot coffee with Harry, and then she remembered how early he'd been

gone, and that they were worrying about each other and their
long separate lives, and the transplanted graveyard at the site. She
decided to tiptoe into the house, seize the books, and scuttle off
to work. He was in the kitchen, sipping coffee, and leafing
through *The Apples of New York*. And when he looked up he
said, "What a wonderful outfit. Is that gabardine? You look
fantastic."

"I can be a little late," she said, taking down a clean cup.

When she was seated, he said, "I went to visit Carter Kreuss.
That's where I took off to this morning. This dawn. Last night.
Whenever it was. He's not in great shape, and I hate telling you.
I don't want you feeling sorry for him. Do you?"

"Do you?"

"Yeah. How can you not?"

"What kind of lousy shape, Harry?"

"He's sad. He's messy. I don't know: his place reminds me of
my place, before I took off to get here and be with you. It's—does
kindling point make any sense?"

She nodded, sipped, then nodded again. "He's needy. Need*ful*.
I know he's worried about money, his HarJoe contract, but I
don't mean that's all he needs. It's pure emotion, he's down to the
bone on emotion. That's why— You remember we went fishing
when you were here last summer?" Harry nodded. "I don't fish,"
she said. "I don't mind it. I didn't mind it then. But we went
because I thought he needed something slow and peaceful and
orderly and no strain. He's a stressy man."

"Stressy," Harry said. "Who isn't? It used to be brain fever,
and then it was nervous breakdowns. Remember them? All my
parents' friends had nervous breakdowns. My mother had them
weekly. Now it's burnout. Stress. Everything's in the head."

"It always was."

"Everything always was?"

"Of course. Pig. You're thinking about sex. Your balls are
where your brain should be. As I've said."

"Thank you, doctor. I have to call D.C. and get the verdict, speaking of Carter and stress."

"And your own," she said.

He nodded. "What would you like me to do, Cath?"

"Write poetry."

"And for a living?"

"Newspaper writing? Television? I don't know. Teach poetry someplace."

"God," he said. "To the young? I'm not strong, Catherine."

"It beats the hell out of writing lies for senators, Harry."

"You really think it does?"

"Yes. So do you."

"Don't be insightful."

"No. But you do."

"Isn't there something *noble*, to you, about being part of politics? Where the decisions get made?"

"Harry," she said, sliding her coffee cup along the table, "here we are, in where-the-decision-gets-made. He's going to save the bones of people nobody knows about so he can score a point with black people who don't live here where the bones are, so he can angle for the nomination. I missed the noble part. I hear a lot of high-sounding lies, some of which he wants you to write for more money than any lie could be worth."

"These are beautiful apples in this book," Harry said. "I was looking for the apple tree from your backyard in here. Where would I live?"

"Oh," she said, instructing herself that she would *not* color prettily and look away. She looked away. "God, Harry, I'm late. I really have to go."

"I'm calling Mrs. Talliaferro now."

"What are you saying?"

"You want to listen?"

"No," she said. "Yes. You remember being fourteen, Harry?"

He smiled, and she saw how tired he was, and under what

strain he was functioning. She saw, in the smile, the ghost of the boyish man she had known, and then the smile settled, and fell away, and the boy was entirely gone, and a man in some difficulty sat before her, drinking the last of coffee gone cold, and trying to reassure her. "He'll be all right," Harry said. "He's a nice boy. He's *your* boy. That really has to count for so much, Cath. He give you the silent treatment on the way in, today?"

She nodded. She wanted to yell at him to *please* be less sympathetic, and get on the phone and sell out his soul to Washington and stop being *generous*, dammit.

"He did it to me on Friday. Not a word. I figured—of course, I don't have a lot of experience in this." Whose fourteen-year-old were you being kind to in the recent past to get any, she thought of asking him. "I figure, he gets tense because he's going to be *seen*, you know? I remember, just being looked at used to hurt. Unless they didn't look at me, and that of course hurt more. He'll be okay. I really think so. He's a decent kid. Any tattoos, secret earrings, or unusual medications?"

She had to grin, both because of him, and because he knew that, for a parent, killer exotic drugs and authentic Tunisian body markings were about a breath away every morning. She shook her head.

"You see?" he said. "No problem."

He was moving toward the wall phone. "Did you tell me where you saw me living if I canned D.C.?" He dialed the numbers and gave the operator his credit card code. Then he sang out, "Mrs. T, it's me. No—*me*. And you knew it. Listen, on the graveyard matter. One of the parties, the man who contracted for the parking lot, as a matter of fact, has suggested a compromise. I think it'll work. Mrs. T, there are no black people in the community, at least who are involved, as far as I can see. The I guess you'd call it intellectual or professional community would like to hang certain parties, but that has to do with the usual cruelty toward anyone who makes money, I think. So, anyway: the guy's going to rebury the bones. There's an original burial site—suffice it to say, we can see that everyone'll be satisfied, no one will be dishonored, and the senator can concentrate on tariff realignments. All right? Not all right. Oh, he didn't. He *didn't*. Couldn't he have waited? Wasn't he supposed to *wait*? I thought he was going to wait for my fucking *report*, Mrs. T, excuse me. No. And I'm very sorry. I really am. But I thought—yeah. Things began to move. Yeah."

Harry's face was red and tight, and again she saw the ghost of the boy, but this time a sullen, enraged small boy, a kid who might pick a rock up and heave it through a window or into someone's face. She looked at Harry and she thought, poor Carter. She had no idea how many ways she might mean that. She knew there was more than one.

"When will the Corps make its appearance? I mean, do they telephone, or what? Now? They're announcing now? Jesus, Mrs. T, why're we in such a hurry? Because I do think we're making a mistake. Wouldn't we like to all of us meet and discuss it a little? We wouldn't. Wait a— I'm supposed to write remarks for *when*? Tomorrow? No way. No *way*. In fact—"

She saw him poise himself, as if he were going to make a running start, and then leap. And she heard herself calling to him: Jump. She heard herself calling: You *jump*.

"Mrs. T," he said, "I really respect your administrative skills and your ability to scare the living shit out of me in *spite* of your great-smelling shampoo and the way you look in those sleeveless silk blouses. And I'm going to probably need some kind of references one of these days. So I hope you can not take it personally when I tell you it is time to take the job, all of the job, the entire you know what I'm talking about job and, well, yeah. Yeah, Mrs. T. Jesus. Sure, I'll do it if you do it first. And my best regards to the senator. All my respects to the—ah." He looked at Catherine, and his grin was large and genuine, his voice a little shaky. "She told me to stick my speeches up my ass, and I couldn't write remarks for the man without splitting my infinitives and she would *not* give the senator my best. I'm no longer in the employ of anybody. They're giving me a month in light of services rendered, so long. Are you leaving for work right away?"

"No," she said. "I'm making a late breakfast. Tell me the part about the Corps—what was that?"

"You got any sausage, Cath?"

It was Catherine who sat at the table, nervously twisting her fingers, and it was Harry who roved through the kitchen, making food and making talk. He put eggs on to fry. After he broke the yolks he added salt and oregano and pepper. There weren't sausages, but he did find a package of frozen Smithfield ham, and he put that in another pan with a little oil, a little water, and a glass cover; when the water was boiled off, the ham was defrosted and cooked through, and it browned in the oil. He made another pot of coffee, all but drunk on unemployment, moving about too rapidly, talking disconnectedly, snapping a towel and telling bad Washington jokes—the congressman and the hooker, the Cotton Council lobbyist and the choir girl on her class trip, the attorney general and the Israeli Embassy women's bowling team. Catherine was annoyed with herself for wondering if she was going to have to take this one out fishing too, and in October, to get him calmed down. Did you hear the one about the former senatorial aide and the rural art dealer, she thought. He burned the eggs, as she'd thought he might, because she knew that the stove cooked hot, while all that Harry knew, dashing about with a dish towel through his belt, was that he needed to move. So Catherine clasped her own fingers and waited for him to wind down. He got through the preparation of what looked and smelled dreadful: lovely in the contemplation, flawed in the execution, hence your basic life's plan, she thought. Harry sat back in his chair, looking at the gray-green eggs, the mahogany ham, the fair-to-middling coffee, and he sagged. "Jesus," he said.

257

"How's tricks?"

"Jesus!"

"That's what I did when I made it official with Dell. I came home and I cooked. I made a seven-layer chocolate cake. You know how much work that is? I iced it, and I put candles on it, and I poured out a little drink, and I fell asleep. The sitter brought the kids over from where they were being sat, and she of course spread the word. I got a kind of a reputation. There I was, face down at the table with a drink in my hand and all these candles, I must have put fifty candles on the cake, dripping wax all over my butter-cream frosting. After a while, you just run out. Should we call Carter? Tell him about the Corps?"

"No," Harry said. The word stretched out, as though it were chewing gum he tugged so he could contemplate its color. "No, they're sending a telegram or calling or something. Then an official guy comes down, apparently, and serves some kind of papers. Some kind of notice. I think they go to HarJoe, but Carter'll hear, believe me. Later on, I want to tell him I didn't do it. No: I did do it, by coming here and staying in touch with the office. I'm part of it. But I'd like him to know what I decided, finally."

Catherine nodded. "I'll want him to know how I've chosen, too," she said. She looked at Harry, intending that they look each other in the eyes. Like a couple of dogs—like Drown, waiting under the table for his Smithfield ham and gray eggs over—they avoided each other's eyes. "You ever notice," she said, "how a dog will not stare into your eye? He'll always look away."

"Doggy, am I?" Harry asked.

She shook her head. "No more than I am. As *much* as I am. I was trying to gaze meaningfully at you."

Harry lifted his eyes and stared at her soulfully. She burst into laughter. "Thanks," he said. "For the respect and all."

"You looked constipated," she said, still laughing. "You really looked like someone in pain."

"Love," Harry said, "is a pain. Death is a pain. Slavery's a pain. Washington's a pain. So is love."

She laid her fork on her seaweed-colored eggs and said, "Do you know, I think that's the first time since you've been here, I *think* it's the first time you said 'love.' "

"And you?"

"Have I said it? I don't know," she said.

"How about feeling it," Harry suggested.

"How about that?"

"You're so damned hard to pin down."

"Where?" she asked. "In the garden? Upside down in bed? On the floor of my room?"

"Oh, that," he said. "No, everybody—" He stopped. His eyes *were* sad. "I was going to make a joke about what an easy piece of ass you were, and it's too stupid to say. I apologize. Every time I touched you, I wanted to say thank you. I've been—"

She held her hand, palm outward, in the air.

"You're always the boss," he complained, only partly joking, she thought. "Stop. Go. Well, *I* want a vote," he said.

Catherine nodded. "The American way," she said. "I'm sorry. I don't *always* mean to be bossy. I just wanted to say, you mustn't thank me. As if I've been doing you favors. Do you know what your coming here meant to me?"

They stared at each other. She was trying to find a way in, a path down which her words could go. My God, she thought. It's like some fairy tale. We'll be doomed to wander in the woods, we won't be able to get back home to each other. Harry stared back. For an instant, she was desperate to know what he thought. Maybe lovers stab each other, she heard herself think, so they can make a hole and get their *thoughts* in. Harry said, at last, "I don't, Catherine. No."

She heard herself laugh, as if she'd been holding her breath and now could let go. When Harry laughed too, at once, she was so relieved, so pleasured by his stony face's softening into wrinkles and folds—into countryside familiar as home ground—that she shut her eyes.

When I open them, she thought, I'll still see Harry.

"Cath," she heard him ask, "what is it?"

Harry fetched Bobby from school at dusk. Bobby threw himself at the seat and slammed the door. "Okay," he said.

"Yeah? Good day?"

"Yeah, it was okay," Bobby said.

He felt him shrug in the near-darkness as they pulled out. He gave it a little extra in second, for the sake of Bobby's friends, and he said nothing more. He thought that Bobby would talk if he wanted to, and it was his suspicion that silence was the sound of grace with this kid. Then Harry proved that he was ready to be a parent: he revoked his good intentions and ignored his sense of Bobby's needs. He asked, "Hey! How'd the teacher like that essay you did?"

And Bobby, of course, said, "Okay."

Harry nodded. "You passed, then."

He heard the sound of moving cloth, Bobby's nod.

"No"—Harry tried to laugh—"I mean, *did* you?"

Bobby gave him what gift he could. He turned to him, and he said, "I think I did, Harry. I think I wrote it pretty good. I passed, and maybe I really did good."

Harry slapped him on the leg. "Good man," he said, in the tricky maneuvering required while you compliment a kid and, simultaneously, call yourself a jerk.

The little wooden steps that led to trailers were bright with pumpkins, and in front of the shabbiest unpainted, wind-scoured sheds of house there were colored crepe-paper streamers and expensive cardboard and plastic faces you bought at Ames or Jamesway for nineteen dollars a pop.

260

"They really get into it," Harry said. "And this early."

"It's what they've got. It's all."

"You going out, Bobby? On Halloween?"

"I might. Some of my friends are going. I'd have gone with them."

"And?"

"My mom'll say no. She always does."

"She gets worried, huh?"

"She says I'm too old. *And* she gets worried. You'd think—if I was too old, what would she worry about?"

"Ever think of studying law, kid?"

"Mom calls me the lawyer."

"You'd be good at it."

"Harry—if you got a vote—"

"No, I don't," Harry said.

"Yeah. But if you did. Would *you* let me go?"

"Oh, man, Bobby. You putting me on the spot, or what?"

"You don't want to go against her, right?"

"I'd rather not. But I'd also hate like hell, keeping you home. But I gotta tell you. I would. I think I would, I'm afraid. Sorry, Bobby."

"No," Bobby said, "that's okay, Harry. You're straight."

Depending on who I have to lie to, Harry thought.

As they pulled in, they saw the lights in the barn beyond the lighted house. One outer light shone above the backboard outside, and there were naked bulbs glaring inside, Harry saw. When he stopped the engine, and they were outside the car, he heard and watched Bobby listening to the irregular, effortful, determined setting up and splitting of wood for the winter.

"Damn," Harry said.

Bobby said, "Oh, shit."

They both walked around the house and to the barn. Drown came to greet them, squealing and curving his rear toward his head, as if they had been separated over difficult months. Inside the barn, Catherine, in a down vest and a flannel shirt and jeans, was setting up logs and slamming her ax down into them. Harry saw her wince as her blistered hands took the shock. His own raw hands recoiled as the ax bit. Bobby crossed in front of Harry and stuck his very large hand up to stop the ax's descent. Harry detested the gratitude he felt, for he hated her insistence on arranging to be independent—*alone*—in the year ahead. He thought Bobby felt guilty for not having chopped, or maybe he took her nighttime work as rebuke. Harry hadn't seen him this set of jaw and enraged. Bobby yanked the ax from her hand.

"That's dangerous," Catherine said. "And don't you take the ax out of my hand like I'm your *child*. Give it to me."

Bobby moved to stand between his mother and the wood she'd been about to split. His broad back screened her away. Bobby was starting the ax above his head. From his angle, Harry could see Catherine's eyes: they were closed. She couldn't see, in her fury, where the ax was. She raised both fists and slammed them into Bobby's back as the ax was about to descend. Harry cried, "Cath!" Catherine made a wordless noise of anger. Bobby screamed from the heart of his throat as the ax slammed into his shin.

Catherine called, "Bobby!"

"Fuck you, bitching bastard," Bobby cried, falling to wrap his hands around his shinbone and roll on the floor.

Harry jumped forward and, gritting his teeth, pulled Bobby's hands from the bloody dungarees. "I don't see any bone," he said, panting already, soft pig. He pulled on the front of Bobby's shirt while puffing at Catherine, "You drive. Emergency room. I'll stay in the back with Bobby."

She turned and ran. Harry pulled harder on Bobby's shirt while ducking his head and shoulder to balance him, then lift. He hauled him, head down and legs on Harry's chest, across the darkness of the field that was Catherine's side yard. Drown ran about them, barking.

In the backseat of the van, as Bobby squealed and swore, as Catherine drove, saying, "Oh, Bobby, I didn't see it!" Harry used his belt on Bobby's thigh as a tourniquet. Instead of looping it taut, he buckled it loosely, then tightened it with a plastic snow scraper he found on the seat.

"It'll hurt a little," Harry said, between breaths, "but you won't lose too much blood. I don't know if you're bleeding that badly, understand? This is just in case. You feel shocky?"

Bobby said, "What in fuck does shocky feel like?"

Harry snorted. Catherine said, "Please don't talk like that!"

"Even if I cut my fucking *leg* off?"

"Oh, especially then," Harry said, urging Bobby to laugh. But he only lay and seethed. Catherine drove too quickly, and they spilled along the backseat, Harry bumping Bobby, Bobby moaning and swearing, Catherine saying again and again, "I'm sorry. I'm so sorry." Bobby breathed shallowly, loudly, raspingly, as if his lungs were filling. So Harry took the risk and said to him, "Bobby, it is only a cut. A cut. A lousy slice along the leg. That's all. You're *fine*."

Bobby said, "*You're* fine. *My* fucking leg's whacked open."

So naturally Catherine had to shout, "Can you stop *swearing*? Does it make it *feel* better to talk like that? Can't you show him any respect? *He* didn't cut you."

"You did," Bobby said. "You did."

Harry said, "Not exactly."

"That thing you put on hurts, Harry."

"I don't think you need it, kid, I just wound it around so in *case* it's bad, you won't, you know—"

"Bleed to fuckin *death*," Bobby said between his teeth.

"Along those lines," Harry said. Then he said, "Cath, you might want to slow down a little, all right? So we don't communicate quite so much overall urgency into the back here?"

Catherine said, "You slow down, Harry. When it's your baby, you slow down."

In the darkness of the back of the car, as Bobby turned and rolled and winced beneath his weightless hands, Harry nodded.

She made her wheels squeal pulling into the pavilion of the county hospital's emergency room, and then she left the motor on, and the lights, and the van rocking in park, and Catherine ran through the wide swinging doors as she called, "Hello? Is— we've got a boy *bleeding* here!"

So then there were the nurse and orderly with a gurney, and Bobby was strapped on and wheeled in, his face white and sweaty, set in pain or rage. And there was the one nurse forcing Catherine to sit, and breathe, and then talk about medical insurance, while the other loosened Harry's tourniquet and laughed at it, and permitted Harry to stand with a gauze compress on top of Bobby's leg until she returned with a basin of something that looked like blood. She was thin and pale, she coughed a lot and her knuckles looked swollen, her sallow face febrile. Harry moved his hand away as she gestured at him, and she finished cutting at Bobby's trousers so she could work on the wound.

Harry said, "Here we go, kid."

Catherine called, "What?" Her eyes were huge. Harry indicated that nothing was happening, and she returned to the forms over which she'd been laboring. Meanwhile, the nurse next to Harry was wiping at the wound with some of the thick, dark liquid from the bowl. Bobby howled, Harry squeezed his arm, and Catherine jumped away from her chair, dropping a clipboard that held a form. "Betadyne," the nurse said, "and hot water. It'll sting, but we have to clean it so we can look at it." Harry rubbed Bobby's head, which felt as warm as Catherine's wood stove on the morning after the frost. Catherine held Harry's forearm, but then let go. She stood, touching no one, and she looked at her wincing son, at the furrowed gash on the side of his hairy shin, and she looked sadder than anyone he'd ever known, Harry thought.

The nurse told Bobby that they'd wait for X rays, since the

hard purple bulge beside the wound might signify a break. Then, she said, a doctor would stitch up the cut. So Bobby was wheeled to the small adjacent surgery, where a technician prepared to shoot the X rays, and Harry leaned against a wall of tan, large, shiny tiles and watched Catherine finish the paperwork and look for something to do.

She looked at gray folding chairs. She picked up a booklet on heart disease—he could see the pulpy organ on its cover from across the room—and then she threw it down. She held her hands against her lower jaw, she shook her head as if to grind it into her fingers, and then, looking purposelessly up, and at the opposite wall, she saw—he saw her remember him—that Harry was there. Her eyes closed, then they opened, and she took a step toward Harry. He held his hand up, as if he said to her, No, that's all right. And what she did was helplessly shrug. And where he stayed was where he stood. And what she did, then, was sit.

Two hours later, Harry drove them back in the big, drifting van. Bobby lay in the backseat, with his head on Catherine's lap, and she pulled at his hair, plucked at it, rubbed at it, as if she were carding wool. Harry tilted the rearview mirror to watch them. Bobby didn't protest, and Catherine, looking up to see his intruding eyes, simply met them an instant, blankly, then looked down. Bobby had swallowed two painkillers, he'd received fourteen stitches and a tetanus shot, had been told that his leg wasn't broken by his mother's ax and their mutual stubbornness, and had been given a pair of crutches. The crutches leaned on the passenger's seat near Harry, and they shifted as he yanked the wheel to force the rattling van back onto course.

"So this is being a mom and a dad," Harry heard himself say.

Before Catherine could answer, Bobby said, "I can still do my chores."

"On crutches?" she said.

"I don't need them. I mean, it's a *cut*."

Catherine said, "You mean it's a fuckin cut."

"Yeah," Bobby said, "I'm sorry about that. Sorry, Harry," he called. "I was panicking."

Catherine said, "So was I. I kept thinking: what if he loses his leg? What if he *dies*? Because of *me*!"

"I shouldn't have grabbed the ax," Bobby said.

"I shouldn't have, either," she said.

"No," Harry said, "you shouldn't have been splitting wood in the first place today."

After a couple of seconds, Catherine said, coldly, "Do you think so?"

The first of the tip-bed trucks, its steaming asphalt covered with canvas from the back of the cab to the gate on the tail, was backing up to the Barber-Greene at the far end of the lot. The second truck, in reverse, was already coming slowly in, and the rollers were idling. Carter was waiting for something to stop the happiness of this moment, its hot, dark smell, the sounds of gravel being crushed under giant tires and the high-traction shoving under the lowest of gears as the Barber-Greene moved the dump truck, which was in neutral, while taking in its blacktop. It was like watching a creature feed, he thought. He was pleased, as a mother must be pleased when something ill starts eating again. He saw, several hundred yards back, another dump truck, the third, swinging off the two-lane and backing slowly in to wait its turn. It was like listening to one of the operas Catherine tuned in on Saturdays: he never knew what in hell they were singing about, but when the soprano began, he unfailingly wanted to cry.

But he understood the odds. He stood in his hard hat and held the little transceiver that would put him in touch with his crew, and he waited for signs. He might see Harry Miller, in a Superman costume, come flashing across the Chenango valley sky to put a halt to unfair treatment of the Negro dead. Perhaps they would send Mignonette's husband, who had torn a man's nose off with his teeth and fingers. He gave new meaning to *deface*, Carter thought, resisting the urge to laugh loudly. There was time, still, for them to stop this pleasure. It was the pleasure of completion, he thought. It was watching the inevitable finish of something that, when it began, you knew was supposed to end this way.

He watched the white Blazer come off the two-lane in a low gear, slowly. He saw it cut in front of the first and then the second tip-bed truck. He noticed a small delta of Canada geese, flying low, taking off, and he realized that for all the noise of grinding gears and chugging engines, and for all the gasoline exhaust and diesel fumes and smoky steam of asphalt, the trees they had left at the edge of the site were filled with crows and blue jays and smaller black or brown birds. They were the audience, he thought, looking at three children and a very pale old man who walked together across the highway. The white Blazer with its discreet HARJOE, INC. came across the job site. Well, it sure ain't Superman, Carter thought. Harvey Seymour didn't get out of his truck. He lifted his arms, he shrugged, he nodded. Carter made the sign of his throat being cut, and Harvey nodded again. Then he backed, circled, and drove away. Carter looked down at the little patch of earth, ringed by spikes connected by fluorescent tape, under which the bodies were. He kicked at the chopped, beaten surface of the red clay. "Okay," he said. "Okay."

He squeezed the handset switch and said, "It's me. Okay? Over."

After about fifteen seconds, he heard, "Yeah. Over."

"Cut it. Over. Send 'em back. I think we just got drafted. Over."

"The wetlands thing? Over?"

"I believe. Over."

"Yeah. Fuckers. Over."

Carter watched his foreman in an orange vest jump out of the cab of his long-bed four-by-four and walk to the Barber-Greene. He saw him draw his hand across his throat, and then repeat the

gesture for the driver in the dump truck. The drivers in the waiting trucks got the same sign. Those in the rollers by then had
stopped their engines too. What Carter wished, and what his
younger foreman might have expected, he thought, was that the
dump trucks turn around and drive the eight miles to the asphalt
factory. But the drivers knew what they were doing. They huddled on a stretch of clean stone, and then they climbed back into
their trucks. The one at the back of the Barber-Greene disen-
gaged, drove to roughly where the drivers had huddled, and
tipped out the rest of his load. He drove away, and the other two
trucks, as if demonstrating precision unison driving, backed,
straightened, backed again, parallel to one another, and dumped
their giant loads side by side. Now the drivers could report that
they'd delivered their asphalt to the site, as originally ordered by
Carter Kreuss Engineering, Inc. As the trucks drove off, air horns
wailing regrets, the foreman was talking to the last of the roller
operators. Then the foreman told him, in crackling, static-charged
tinny tones, that he and the others were leaving. Should they, he
wondered, report to the company garage? Carter told them no,
they were to come to this site in the morning, and start moving
the equipment back. Over. Okay. Over.

Dusk deepened, and traffic began to light up. The Army Corps
of Engineers would investigate now. They would see whether
some form of plant or animal life made this parking lot and its
run-off areas qualify as wetlands. The famous wetlands parking
bays of the high Chenango, he thought. HarJoe would pay the
interest and take out loans for some new job. Maybe he would
get their parking contract. But it was autumn, and then winter,
and in winter here they didn't even bury the dead. They kept
them in special lockers in the funeral homes because the backhoes
couldn't get into the ground to dig out graves once the ground-
frost set in. In April, the winter's dead were buried, and it had
always struck Carter as unfair that families had to mourn a second
time, whether they wanted to or not, whether they were able to

or not. So Carter Kreuss, sure as shit, would not be digging parking lots. And while there was usually enough work in the winter
to help him make his payments, there wouldn't be what he'd
need. He might be driving fuel oil for Agway or Blue Ox, and
maybe he could make the early morning and late afternoon runs
for the district school buses. He might be driving Bobby, he
thought. Now you be sure and say hello to your mom, he heard
himself say as he opened the yellow door to let him off. Or would
she drive him to and fro, now that he'd be fourteen, too big for
school buses? He'd be playing sports all winter, Carter thought,
if the coaches worked smoothly. She'd have to pick him up after
work. Unless Harry was there to drive him. He wondered if
Harry would stay and, if he did, whether he would keep the
rented car.

Of course he would stay. Who would not stay for her?

You. You left.

That was the same as staying, Carter thought. It was the same
in that you did it for her. Right? I don't believe I'm making sense,
he thought. Well, it's all right, son, you've taken a blow. You've
taken a blow. As if someone were comforting him, he slowly
nodded his head: as if someone with rough affection rubbed it
back and forth.

"Okay!" He said it to the emptied, darkening site. He said it to
himself. "You're sounding nuts. And you know he couldn't drive
that little front-heavy wobbler of a car on ice in dead winter on
that road."

He nodded his head, slowly, as if it were being rubbed. He
stared at the fenced-in grave he stood on. "If you die," he said,
"you ought to do it in the fall."

He climbed out of the rectangle of fluorescent orange he'd
been standing in, and he walked across the site to the Perkins,
parked near the trailer, its bucket and hoe leaning on the ground
as if it were exhausted. It wasn't. He knew. He choked it a little,
and it started at once. He was sitting so that he faced the hoe end.

He leaned back to bring the bucket up, and then he faced the right direction and he brought up the hoe. He threw the engine into first, and, swaying across the site, passed the mounds of useless cooling asphalt. "Pure shit," he called them as he drove to work.

At the taped-in rectangle, he stopped and let his stabilizers down. He saw his white ghost's hands in the darkness of the cab. They knew what they were doing, so he just looked out, ahead, down, into the tunnel of headlamp light. When he was leveled, he turned to drop the front bucket onto the ground. And then he turned his seat to face the gravesite, and with the touch he was proud of, as proud as every backhoe operator he had ever known, he delicately peeled the earth from the grave. So as not to do damage, he worked the soil as if it were an onion, feeling, through the hydraulic boom and then the dipper, then its toothy bucket on the end, each level of clay and shale. Every now and again he stood, looking hard, and then he'd sit and let the boom drop flatter, let the dipper slide, and make the bucket scrape.

He had forgotten how brown-and-yellow the bones were. He had seen them once, had ordered them covered, had supervised their excavation again for Olivia and her friends and the judge's clerk, and now, a third time, he was exposing the cheese-soft, streaked, and blurry-looking bones. Each time, he'd expected the sharp white definition that he'd seen in cartoons or horror films, or what he remembered from biology class in school. These were almost turning into earth themselves. He was certain that for all their age there must be shreds of ligament, whole cages of rib still intact, a spine with its little bony rings on it, hands.

He heard himself making a desperate sound, and he said, as if he were a parent, "Now. Now." He carefully laid the bones, in their envelopes of clay, on the gravel to his right. He brought up four bucketsful, and when he went down for a fifth he had to lean forward, peering into a darkness that resisted his lights. The fifth load came up with a small skull impaled on a tooth of the bucket, and he gagged. Water dripped from the clay, which had turned a little lighter, and small brown-yellow particles fell from the bucket, and he said, "Now."

He brought the dipper back into the boom, telling himself how skilled his hands were, still, and then he retracted the stabilizers and turned his chair, standing to scoop its reversed seat beneath him. He engaged the front bucket and drove into a dozing position. With the big bucket, he dropped, pushed, and slowly pushed again, until he had lifted the whole load in one bucketful, and had brought it up, above the level of his eyes and then of his head. He half-turned, bringing the hoe in close, like a curled claw, and then he turned to look out again, from under the front bucket of bones and shale and earth. They were cradled above him, so that the backhoe would look, from the front, as if a wide strong man were in the process of lifting great weight.

Then, slowly, in first, and then in second to the edge of the site, and then gearing up once he'd reached the blacktop of the highway, with his headlights on high and his work lights blinking, he continued with what he knew he wanted to do.

When they came down the curve above the house, Catherine heard herself say, "I think I'll make a fire in the stove tonight." It was only after she'd said it that she realized how wood, fires, all of her long-winter's-nap apparatus had got them to a rural emergency room at seventy-five miles an hour. "Damn," she said. Harry looked into the mirror for her and, seeing his face, she shut hers like a gate. "God*dam*," she said.

Bobby said, softly, "I'm really sorry I cursed at you, Mom."

"I didn't understand you were cursing at *me*."

"No," he said, "I guess maybe I wasn't."

"No."

"Just at getting hurt like that."

"That's right," she said. And then she said, for she had just seen the front of her house, "Dear me. Dear *Lord*."

The bright yellow backhoe glowed in its own lights in their drive. Against the softer lights of the house she could see Carter in the cab. He had a large, round, boy's head, softened in silhouette by his wispy hair.

"Why don't you let me—Cath? Why don't I stop here and I go down and talk to him?"

Catherine said, and she sounded so waspish and annoyed that she wanted to bite her tongue, "Oh, nonsense. Carter wouldn't hurt me. He wouldn't hurt anyone."

Harry said, as he slowed in defiance of her words and her tone, "You said he might hurt *me*."

"Yes," she said. "So why should I let you walk down there alone?"

"Alan Ladd would, in *Shane*."

"What's *Shane*?" Bobby asked.

"A dirty movie for boys," Catherine answered. "A porno-bravery flick for little warriors. You two wait here, I'll be right back."

Bobby said, "What?" as she got out of the car.

"Amazon porno-fantasy," Harry said, opening his own door. "Your mother thinks she has to prove she has balls."

Catherine turned to rebuke him. She heard Bobby murmur, and Harry whisper back, and she turned from them—some masculine back-and-forth about *cojones*, she'd no doubt—and she went toward Carter. Harry was behind her, stumbling in the dark. She grinned because he would always trip like that, and always manage to get himself into an ambiguous situation like this one. So why not wait for him? she wondered, not waiting.

Catherine walked into the light of the backhoe as if she were walking into Carter's field of vision. The backhoe responded; the diesel whistled, as if he'd revved his engine; then Carter lowered the wide front bucket. Catherine saw it come down. She felt her

eyes widen, her mouth open and drop. Then the bucket stopped.
Carter was studying her face, she knew, and she tried to compose
it. But the rich, sweet smell had struck her—it wasn't unlike the
sick and flowery invisible fog that came when the cesspool was
pumped: luring and corrupted and finally too dense in its power.
She had to place her hand over her nose and mouth when she
stared into the bucket. She saw the several skull bones, including
one that was splintered. She wondered if they'd found a clue to
murder. She thought she saw a leg bone, but she couldn't tell one
from an arm. She knew about ribs, and she saw some—they looked
like dead whales, or the hulls of rotted-out boats. For an instant,
she had thought she'd seen a piece of the ship that had brought
these people here.

Harry, behind her, reached for her shoulder and held it. Then
he put his hand around the back of her neck, and she leaned back
into it. His grip didn't give, and she stood in it, and in what was
before her, but then she had to move. She turned, she pulled, and
his hand went away. She leaned forward, and Harry walked
around her, up to the edge of the bottom of the backhoe door.
She watched him knock, politely, as if outside a house. The door
opened out and Catherine went up to where Harry stood.

Harry waved to Carter, who, his hands on the control levers,
nodded back. Carter said, loudly, over the chugging engine, "Hi,
Catherine."

Harry said, "What'd you bring, Carter?"

"Can't you tell?" he called.

Harry said, "What are you going to do with them?"

"What?"

"I said, what should we do with them?"

In the sound of the van's engine and the harsh, coarser noise of
the backhoe's, in the spill of Carter's lights and the full glare of
the van's, they waited, all three of them, she thought, for someone
to reply.

Catherine was surprised to hear herself, much less the words she spoke. "Let's bury them. Once and for all, and to hell with Washington and Olivia and HarJoe and all of it, let's just— They're people. They're dead. Let's bury them."

Harry turned to her, and his smile, the discovery she saw in his eyes, the glad lift of his arms, were his answer. She looked up at Carter, who was looking past her, she saw. She turned, and there was Bobby, wobbling slowly toward them, wincing, pale. He said, "Ma? What? You all right?"

"You should lie down, honey."

"I'll come. What's happening? I'll come with you."

"Yeah," Harry said, "he should if he can, Cath."

Carter turned his engine off, and the silence fell on them. Catherine thought of a sudden hard snow. "Your ground doesn't slope right," Carter said. "I'd be worried about the water table. Let's see. Your well's out front, right? Over there? And the cesspool, dry well, and leachfield are out back? I always meant to say, you want a hundred yards or so between the well and the leachfield. I don't think you've got that, Catherine. But, you know. Anyway. I was—oh. Right. How about across the road? Isn't that yours?"

She said, "Almost a quarter of a mile in, Carter."

"I'd feel better about it. I mean, these are clean bones and all, but I know they all died off on account of *some* damned disease or other. You never know. I don't know how long sicknesses hang on."

"Forever," Harry said.

Bobby said, "Really?"

Carter said, "*I* don't know. Let's do it that way anyhow, on account of safety and everything, Catherine. All right?"

She was crying. Her eyes felt sore already, and she realized that tears must have been running on her face since she'd seen the bulldozer. Surely, she thought, since she had looked into the bucket, and breathed the air that rode it. She nodded because she didn't think she could speak.

Carter replied by leaning toward the door and extending his

arm. Harry looked up, then looked behind him, at Bobby. Bobby looked at the pale hand that beckoned, and then at his mother. Catherine felt herself nod permission—mostly, she thought, because he'd thought to ask it, not because she thought it safe that he ride with poor Carter and his load of corpses, or skeletons, or whatever you called what he'd hauled here.

Black people, she finally told herself. Bobby propelled himself one-footed while pulling on Carter's arm. His arms were always strong, she remembered crazily. Then Bobby disappeared behind the cab's closed door. Harry stepped back and took her arm, as if they were about to cross the street. She didn't know why she stepped back. She smiled guiltily at him. He smiled uncomprehendingly back. The engine revved and rumbled, went into gear and, with its lights blinking, the backhoe led them up the little drive, and to the edge of the state road, and then across it, through a tilted, rusty barbed-wire fence and over high grassy weeds and the bright fall flowers, around the exploded hulls of milkweed, past trapping roots and dangerous holes, holding onto each other and following the lights of her former lover, her injured son, a cargo of the victimized dead to what, it seemed, they really ought to do.

Carter went farther and farther ahead, and over a small hummock and out of sight. They heard him grinding away, and by the time they had staggered and tripped—Harry whispering, "It's a mighty morbid field trip, Scouts"—to where Carter had stopped, out of sight of her house, his stabilizers were down, and he was cutting into the earth with his hoe. The bones were in the bucket that sat on the ground behind him, ballast in the darkness as he worked. The engine grumbled, and its noise swelled and subsided, and he'd taken only a few bites before he stopped, turned in the cab, ignited more lights, and spun the machine to gently lower its load. They walked around the backhoe to the lips of the jagged, semicircular trench. Carter lowered the bucket. She could see Bobby in the cab behind him. She wondered if they spoke.

Carter looked out at them. She could see his eyes. He blinked his lights, off and then on, off and then on, and the bucket came lower still, and then began to tip. The back of her left knee was shoved, and she almost went down. Harry said, "Yeah. How could you miss *this*, huh?" It was Drown, of course, nuzzling and shoving because he was with them on an adventure.

The bucket lowered a last few inches, and then it tipped all the way. Wet red clay, slimy shale, the bones of men and women, babies, older children—"*Kids!*" she said, as if she had proved anything, she thought—came spilling into the hole.

Then Carter made the bucket shake, loosening the last fragments. He banged the bucket against the edge of the hole, and then, letting the stabilizers up, and going into gear, he circled the ditch, using the bucket to start backfilling. While he was using the hoe in tight against the boom, like a crippled hand, to smooth the dirt—the mechanical gentleness moved her—Catherine was still trying to think of something that someone ought to say.

"Are we just hiding them again?" Harry said.

"Not like that," Catherine said.

"What?"

"Let's not say political things right now, all right? Nothing political, sociological, historical, analytical, legal—anything to do with anything like that."

"Then *what*, Cath?"

In the darkness, she nodded. He would know, she thought, because his hands were on her hair, above her ears. He was standing that close to her, and holding her head, as if he tried to read her mind or touch her thoughts. She was tempted to let her head come down and rest on his mouth or chin or chest, whatever it could reach, for some support right now. But she held it erect. She nodded again.

He said, and she could feel his regret, "*I* don't know."

She shook her head, now, to tell him that she didn't know, either. The noise of the engine stopped, and she thought again of snow. She was leaning forward, and her forehead was on his face. She felt his lips. She heard the cab door open to lie against the cab. There was a scuffling sound, an intake of breath, and then a canine grunt, and she knew that Bobby had climbed down, that Drown had gone to greet him.

In the long silence, there was only the squeaking of quail, crying alarms and trying to decoy danger from their nests. She was shivering, then, in the rising winds. Bobby said, "He told me they were people we kept burying."

She said, "I would imagine that might do it."

Carter started the engine, and she gasped at its noise. He laid the dipper and boom in close, raised the front bucket, and then he slowly drove away, winking, bright, loud, soon gone, although the wind took the sound of his engine over the hummock, from the highway to where they slowly walked, tripping, holding onto Bobby, who was in a lot of pain and trying, she thought with surprise, not to show it. For a while, Drown panted behind them, but soon he was gone. They pitched from patch of brush to hilly hole. Her head ached from the cold and from crying, from what it worked to encompass tonight.

When they were finally across the highway, and when Harry had shut down the still-rumbling motor of the van and turned off its lights, and when they had come at last to the front door and Harry was turning the knob, Catherine heard Bobby call, "Good boy!"

Harry said, "Please, no."

She knew it. She had known it since he'd left them. She knew she couldn't cry any more, and she didn't have a laugh left. There was nothing to do but stand with Harry and Bobby, watching her busy dog return, triumphant head high, to display the damp and crumbling yellow-brown bone he worked in his teeth as he delivered his prize.

🏵 *Chapter* Seven

ON THE FLOOR near the stove was a wide pale basket with a high handle in which Catherine had put her last batch of vegetables from the garden. Small white and large red onions with their long green stalks lay in it. The moist onion bulbs gleamed, and there were clots of mud among the root hairs of some of them. Cucumbers, long and thick and dark, lay on the heavy leaves of the onions, and over and among them all were the damp lacy leaves of parsley, thick green brushes of fennel, their dense bulbous bases streaked with mud. All of them dried in the heat of the stove, and all of them gave off sharp, living aromas that hung in the air of the kitchen along with the turpentine smell of creosote. They were what in this house seemed to Harry most possible; everything else, both inside and out, was exhausted, he thought.

The icy night that lay around them was squeezing hard and Harry could feel it. There wasn't much air left. He heard himself sigh, but no sigh bit deep enough to press the air he needed into his lungs. In the wood stove, resin popped, but the chimney wouldn't draw with any energy either, and a heaviness made them stupid. Bobby slept upstairs in a sprawl, if not collapse, while they pretended to alertness.

Catherine blinked a lot, and Harry wondered if the wood stove were poisoning them. He hoped that if it did they could die while burning wood that Catherine had split this week. I'd like to laugh dying, he thought. He poured whiskey into mugs and added sugar and almost-boiling water. Stirring with the end of a wooden spoon, he sipped, shivered at the heat and alcohol, then brought a mug to Catherine where she sat, at the far end of the table. "I learned this from a friend," Harry said. She didn't ask who.

She raised her brows to signify appreciation, but she didn't sip.

He said, "Are you all right?"

"Don't you hate it when people ask you that? When you're sitting there, inside. And—"

"Inside of what?"

"*Inside,*" she said. "You know. You must. You value privacy."

"You're saying you hated it when I asked if you were all right, Cath?"

"It's proprietary."

He said, "And invasive."

Catherine shrugged. She said, "It's needful."

"And need is bad?"

"Need's need," she said. "Who doesn't have a few trillion?"

"But certain needs," Harry said.

"Yes?"

"Tell me about certain needs, Cath. The ones you don't approve of."

"Wait a minute. Wait a minute. Are we picking fights? Did we travel all the way here—"

"Excuse me," Harry said. "Pardon me. *I* traveled all the way here. That's my rented car outside, those are my cash receipts for gas in the glove compartment. Those are my bags upstairs, Cath. *I* traveled here. To get to you. On account of goddam need.

You're right. So now tell me, please, which ethics I've rubbed the nap of in the wrong direction." He fired a bolus of very hot toddy down his throat, and it burned going in and when it hit. He sat as if pain were unimportant.

Catherine laughed as if she might choke. She pointed at him. In the dead tired kitchen, as wood hissed and popped in the stove, and as Drown behind the wood stove grunted in the heat, Harry worked at his dignity, and Catherine laughed so hard, so high and hard and long, that he knew it wasn't fun.

"Are you all right?" she finally said.

"That's what I asked *you*. I got a lecture on need. How come you can ask *me*?"

Sipping, she said, "Hot stuff," and started to giggle again. She bit her lip. She shook her head. "I know," she said. "I'm being disloyal. Laughing like that is disloyal."

"Who said anything about loyalty?"

"You did. You used to. You'd get all pissed if I didn't hang around with you at parties, remember?"

"We never went to parties, I think."

"Oh, yes. Remember the thing, the benefit in Schuyler for the volunteer firemen? The lasagna night, when we got dressed up in blue jeans and boots and flannel shirts and we went to the fire hall and they were all wearing the saddest cheap coats and ties and dresses and their good shoes? And I went over to talk to a couple of women I knew, and you didn't know anybody. And you'd have thought I'd been snogging out behind the barn with farm boys."

"Snogging?" Harry said. "We're in the middle of—Jesus, I can't imagine what we're in the middle of, or what you'd call it, anyway. And you're talking about *snogging*? Loyalty oaths? Twelve fucking *years* ago, Catherine?"

"Not loyalty oaths," she said. "Loyalty *tests*. And you know damned well that for twelve years we've been remembering everything. That's how we got into this trouble in the first place. I wonder if you're not supposed to, after a while, like a sickness, or giving birth—just let it go, and *forget*, Harry."

"No," he said, turning the mug around and around. "It isn't that simple if you want to forget it."

"No," she said, "I don't *want* to forget it. I'm saying, I was wondering if, you know, forgetting isn't easier than remembering. That's all."

Harry observed that he was nodding his head, as if they conducted a conversation, and as if he were a rational man, and as if there were little more than language at stake. He noted too that he was capable, at that instant, of saying nothing more than "It's impossible," and in a remarkably young, sullen voice.

Catherine smiled, as if she knew he required forgiveness, he thought.

"I'm not your son, Cath."

"Shall I say something smoky like 'I've noticed,' or do you think we ought to let it pass?"

"I mean, you're sitting there, you're talking about this stuff, Cath, and it's like I'm the one who wins or loses here, and all you're going to do is decide."

Catherine looked up, hard. She squinted. She was studying him. "One of the wonderful things about you, Harry, is how smart you are. You always were. You often knew *exactly* what in hell was going on. Everybody runs around, clucking and quacking, and you cut through it like the big, bad wolf after a roaster."

Harry said, "Thank you. What are we talking about?"

"Exactly what it is we've been talking about," she said. "And you know it."

Harry tried to stare back, but he couldn't match her gaze. He'd never been able to. And as he looked and as she looked in return, she lifted her chin slightly, and then slightly more, and she broke his heart in a quarter of an inch.

"Your heart can't break," Harry said.

"I've always hoped that was true," she said, in a soft, injured voice.

He had to move, so he went to the sink and studied it. He shook in scouring powder. He ran the water a little, and scrubbed at the stainless steel with a dishrag. Little pieces of dried tomato came up, and various dark, hardened shreds. He flushed them down the drain and wrung the rag out, draping it over the spigot. He said, "There."

"You scratch the sink with that stuff," Catherine said.

"How come you keep it there, then? On the sink it's going to scratch?"

"I wanted the sink to look, I don't know, complete, I guess. It's good for cleaning the stove, anyway."

He nodded, keeping his back to her, leaning on his palms, and looking at the dark kitchen window as if he stared outside. But outside was only the dark. Inside, behind him, at the other end of the table, she sat and stared at his back. He watched her reflection as she looked at him as he'd wished to see her looking for a dozen years. He watched himself as he captured in reverse and like a thief the wide eyes and speculative mouth framed in her palms and long fingers. She seemed so tired as she sat and held her head in her hands and looked perhaps at him, or maybe also through him and out the window and into something more than a cold and moonlit night. He stood and watched himself see Catherine watching Harry and whatever else she saw.

"Carter's broke now," she said. "He'll survive, but he's in trouble."

Harry said, "I'm sorry. You know I tried for him."

"With that phone call?"

"Well, for me too. Admittedly. But also him. I did try and do what was right, Cath. I'm out of work too."

She sighed. "Have I filleted you both? Carter will find work. He'll get back on his feet. Will you?"

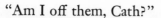

"Am I off them, Cath?"

"You know," she said, "he never knew his father's name. He found his mother, I think he saw her a couple of times. He said there wasn't anything. She was a cow, he was a calf, and that was that. She gave him a cup of coffee, she told him her story, but she wouldn't tell him the name of the boy who sired him."

"I didn't know that about him. And you know I wish him well. I probably really do. I can write for a paper. I can write for magazines. Maybe I can write a book about Washington, please don't yawn. Of course, we *were* thinking about me in an office in the town of Chenango, or someplace. Weren't we? Once upon a time this weekend?"

He turned around, as if to surprise her, and he found her partly out of her chair. "I need a blanket, or a sweater," she said. "I'll be right back."

"No!" he heard himself say. "I'll stoke the fire up, Cath. Sit here a while. Don't go away."

She sat back down at once, folding her arms across her chest and leaning into them and at the table. "Sure," she said. "Harry."

"I'll do the fire," he said.

He went to the stove, opened it, and laid two quarters of log inside. They were cold, they felt dense and alien, unmanageable. The smoke rose against his face, and he winced, saying, "It's not drawing very well. Probably all the ectoplasm is clogging the chimney."

Catherine nodded, but she was thinking that tomorrow or the next day, Olivia Stoddard would follow Carter's backhoe tracks. Butt in the air, nose to the ground, both twitching, she will appear here with a posse of goodhearted citizens to *demand* the bones so someone else can use those people a little bit more. Maybe Carter will tell her, Catherine thought. Maybe he'll barter his late-night resurrection-and-deposit for a little comfort, an itsy-bitsy whimper and an itsy-bitsy moan. I couldn't blame him. I couldn't blame *her*. Small-town girl gets away to someplace cheek-bony and

New York, wasn't it Vassar? And she comes home. And instead of marrying the minor English-speaking Oriental despot she had planned to, she ends up with the biggest-banker-in-the-smallest-city-in-the-state-in-training. And there's Carter, with his forearms and his boy's face and all that *need*. A little nursing goes a long way, she thought, but it goes for a while. He'd work so hard in bed for her, she'd need to install a punch clock. And he'd watch her to make sure he wasn't asking too much, which of course is the way you ask too much. So, yes, she will be here. She'll say: Stand and deliver those bones. And I will tell her: Let those people be. I'll tell her: Let my people be. Or is it that you're supposed to let them *go*? We could at least have given them a discount for dying.

When she focused, instead of leaning on the table and not seeing whatever it was she saw, Harry was seating himself at the other end of the table. Dear Harry, didn't we? Really: didn't we? This has been the longest courtship. Or a long, terrible divorce.

She sighed, and she expected to see her breath steam in the kitchen's cold air. She thought of Carter's awful house, and his child's face pressed to a windowpane, like someone in a fairy tale about kids and being eaten and the dark woods. She thought of Harry in Washington, and women in expensive shoes, and subtle lighting, unspoken threats, the many words for *get*: that was being eaten and the darkness, too.

Randy would choose between the woods and the world, she thought, and pretty soon. And he would pick the world. He'd have to. And Bobby, when he was small, had told her that when he was grown he was going to live in a trailer by himself with a dog and eat steak and watch TV. She would have to talk about cholesterol, she thought, shaking her head, at least in her thoughts. She would have to warn them about everything, and then get lost in gardening and the house.

Didn't we?

He sat sideways to her, so that he might face either her or the stove. She said, "In the summer, in August, when it's very hot, the garden catches the heat. Holds it. There's usually a pretty good wind down there, and it keeps the flies off. The aspens rattle, and the heat just—comes up. Everything smells like basil. You know that smell? It's very rich and very oily and green. It smells like Italy. I was never there, but it's the way I think that Italy must smell, in the summer here."

"I missed that," Harry said. "I'm a season late."

Her chin was resting on her hand again, and she nodded her head so that her arm moved. "Sometimes I go down there for beans for dinner, or an early tomato. As you well know, tomatoes here come late. I pick parsley and basil to wash and chop up and, you know, freeze it for winter. Or I make some pesto, except pine nuts are expensive, so I sneak in walnuts. Nobody knows the difference. And Bobby hates it. He wants tomato sauce, just like at the pizzeria downtown. It was Randy who liked it the way I like it. I won't make it much, now, I guess, unless I'm ready for a fight. In fact, now that I think of it, I'll make it when I'm especially in the mood to *have* the fight. I don't think a kid should grow up getting special meals made for him, or with his mother too scared of him to make what *she* wants for dinner, come to think of it. And a mother who works all day. This is delicious," she said, sipping more toddy, "and of course some woman showed you how to make it."

Harry waited for her to ask about the woman. He was bothered that she accepted the fact of another woman in a way that he, thinking of her with other men, could never emulate. "Men, I think, stay boys," he said.

"How nice for them," she said.

"I interrupted," he said, "I'm sorry. Yes. A woman in D.C. showed me how to make toddies. A medicine against the cold, she told me. But they don't really work. Go ahead."

"No, they're good. It's good medicine," she said, smiling as you smile at people who bring you drinks to drink. "I was done. I don't know. I was talking about what I tried to say before, when I totally failed at it. I was saying sometimes I go down to the garden in the summer, when it smells like that and gives that feeling off, and I don't do anything useful at all. I sit near the beans or peppers and I think about work, whatever the project is I'm doing at the gallery, or here. It's more often something interesting than boring. Or I don't think about anything. I just feel the sun on me, and I stay by myself."

How do you measure a season *too* late, Harry wondered.

"It's funny," he said, "with all that—before—about remembering and forgetting. I remember you used to have a little garden in Schuyler, out back, but nothing like this. Nothing so busy and big, that you cared so much about."

"No," she said. "I think it's being middle-aged. Getting old. Losing the kids—you know, the way you're supposed to. To their own lives. The calendar. The clock. It's—you look the seasons in the eye, this way." She gathered her legs with her hands so that she could place them in an Indian squat on the chair, partly sitting on them, and she leaned forward in her eagerness. Her smile was innocent, absorbed. "Sometimes, if I have trouble sleeping," she said. "Do you have that?"

"You think, and you're over twenty-five, you have it," Harry said.

"I'm so glad to hear that. I thought I was really neurotic," she said.

"Well, you are. But everybody has it."

She smiled again and said, "So I'm in bed, and I just can't sleep, say. I tuck my legs up under me—"

"You just did."

She looked down, then up. "I guess so," she said. "Anyway, I tuck up, I wrap myself in the comforter, and I plant the garden."

"You say to yourself, 'Here's where the cabbage goes, here's where the marijuana goes'?"

"Harry, I get very serious about it. I *am* very serious about it.

I see the whole garden. I divide it into rows, and then I divide the rows. Then I plant it. I see the spading fork and the trowel and the weeding rake, and I see my hands. I see my fingers in the dirt, pushing seeds down. And I do that until I get tired, seed after seed, row after row. And then I fall asleep."

They sat a little while, each drinking, each looking down the kitchen table at the other. He instructed himself not to ask. He acknowledged the instruction. Then, because he had to, he said, "Excuse me. I apologize. I didn't intend to ask you this no matter how much I wanted to, because I wanted to be low-key, unde-manding. But I'm, well, I'm scared as hell, Cath. Let's say you've planted your garden, in your bed and out of it. You know, in fact. It's a real garden, and it's hot. It's August, next year, say, and it's hot and the winds are blowing, and it smells like Italy. You're sitting down there, smelling it and lying back with your eyes closed, thinking about your life. All right? So of course I'm won-dering. What would I be doing? Picking, I don't know, lima beans and stuff with you? For you? Or turning things into a crowd? Cath, would I *be* there?"

"I don't grow lima beans," she said. "Or wax beans. Or any-thing that isn't fun." She knew her smile had appeared instantly, and that it was large and that she felt relieved. She said, "Harry, you're the one person who would ask that question that way. You know? The one person *I* know who would."

It seemed to Catherine that Harry's face was rigid—that, if she were to touch its surface, she would find it hard, like wood. She understood from him what it meant to compose oneself: you build your face out of hard materials so that the wrong words from people couldn't shatter it.

She said—deceitful bitch, she thought—"Bobby wanted to call Randy before he went to sleep. He wanted to tell him about his leg. And poor Carter, I suppose. That sad, crazy burial."

"That's what you get for digging things up," the hard face said.

She looked at him, and she could only shrug. She tried to smile with all her teeth. "Oh, Harry," she said. Then: "Anyway, I probably should call him. Randy. And tell him about Bobby and everything. He'd want to know."

Harry nodded. She waited for him to say something direct and powerful, galvanic, persuasive. But what do you say, she asked herself, or told herself, after you drive all that distance to lay your entire *life* down on the floor at someone's feet? What good are words after that? They pick it up, or they don't pick it up, or they return it and go wash their hands. Oh, Harry.

Catherine said, "Do you think you'd mind making one more toddy? Or two, if you'll join me?"

"I'd be happy to," he said. "Was that enough whiskey, or should I add some more?"

"I'll tell you what," she said. "Why don't you pour in the whiskey, and not add water, and don't add the sugar, and we'll rough it?"

Harry smiled. "That's my kind of cooking," he said.

And she told him, "You're my kind of cook."

She watched him let his face turn hopeful before he composed it again. She felt as if she might be ill, physically sick, here, in the kitchen. She wanted to comfort him as much as she wanted to sleep, dreamless, by herself.

Harry poured slugs of whiskey into their mugs. He set hers down on the counter near the telephone, where she stood, dialing. He went back to the chair near the stove. Drown, as if wakened to his condition by Harry's scraping chair, slowly rose and wobbled toward him from behind the stove. He was stupid with heat, and his head, when Harry slowly rubbed it, was as hot as a pan off the flames. "You have to go and cook your brains, don't you?" he whispered, and Drown waved his tail in thanks.

Catherine, behind him at the wall phone, murmured as Randy reported and she, judging from her noises, approved. Harry was thinking of the puckered flap of skin on Bobby's leg, the dark glistening meat beneath it. He saw Catherine again, in the cold barn, providing for herself. His shoulders grew heavy and drooped forward. His spine felt limp. He wondered how he would stand, and where. "No," she said, "just us."

He turned in his chair, needing to force his torso around, steadily growing heavier and weaker, as if gravity crushed him down. He heard her say, "Bye, baby. Take good care." She continued to face the telephone, though, on the wall.

No, just us.

"How's Randy?"

"Great," she told the wall. "He's forsworn sleeping and animal fats, he's in love with a French instructor from Senegal, admires Broadway and 114th at dawn, and when he comes home for his Thanksgiving break, he was wondering, would you be here? I mean, that's what he *really* asked. He asked," she told the wall on which she now leaned her forehead, "would there be company for dinner."

"Maybe he meant Carter," Harry said.

"No," Catherine said, wondering why she had to tell him, reviling the impulse not to, "he was talking about you."

"I'm grateful," Harry said. "I always really got a kick out of him." Do pule for us, Harry thought.

I feel like I'm divorcing again, she thought.

He thought: This is one son of a bitch long trip.

She thought: Thank God I'm home.

"You said—what was it," Harry asked, " 'just us'?"

"Yes."

"And doesn't that go back to my question about the garden," he said. "Which us?"

"It does," Catherine said. "You're right. You're usually right."

"I don't *want* to be right!" Drown shifted when he bellowed, and he said, "I'm sorry. I'm—this is the only important thing to me, Cath."

"I know," she said. "Thank you, Harry."

"Oh, you're welcome," he said.

She said, "You do understand this. Haven't you been thinking it too?"

The gathered onions and fennel and the smell of burning wood seasoned the air of Catherine's house. They were her smells, now. Harry and Catherine stood and stared, from his end of the kitchen all the way to hers. He thought of dicing the onion, frying it in sweet butter until it was golden green, then slicing country sausage in.

"Harry?" she asked him gently.

Sure.

A NOTE ABOUT THE AUTHOR

Frederick Busch was born in Brooklyn, New York, in 1941, and educated at Muhlenberg College and Columbia University. He is Fairchild Professor of Literature at Colgate University, where he has taught since 1966. He has held a National Endowment for the Arts Fellowship, a Guggenheim Fellowship, and an Ingram Merrill Fellowship. He was awarded the National Jewish Book Award for *Invisible Mending*, and in 1986 he was given an award in literature by the American Academy and Institute of Arts and Letters. He and his wife, Judy, live with their two sons in Sherburne, New York.

A NOTE ON THE TYPE

This book was set on the Linotype in Janson, a recutting made direct from type cast from matrices long thought to have been made by the Dutchman Anton Janson, who was a practicing type founder in Leipzig during the years 1668–1687. However, it has been conclusively demonstrated that these types are actually the work of Nicholas Kis (1650–1702), a Hungarian, who most probably learned his trade from the master Dutch type founder Dirk Voskens. The type is an excellent example of the influential and sturdy Dutch types that prevailed in England up to the time William Caslon developed his own incomparable designs from them.

Composition by Heritage Printers, Inc.,
Charlotte, North Carolina
Printed and bound by Fairfield Graphics,
Fairfield, Pennsylvania
Designed by Harry Ford